Prime Time

Curiosity Quills

GIVE TO CHARITY OR GIVE IN TO THE UNKNOWN? DO BOTH.

GREAT WRITERS.   GREAT STORIES.   GREAT CAUSES.

READ ORDER

115	29	74	59	274
131	87	139 (14)	186	7
122 (9)	201		41	213
	234		99	152
	246		257	
	294 (12)			

A Division of **Whampa, LLC**
P.O. Box 2540
Dulles, VA 20101
Tel/Fax: 800-998-2509
http://curiosityquills.com

ISBN 978-1-62007-330-8 (ebook)
ISBN 978-1-62007-331-5 (paperback)
ISBN 978-1-62007-332-2 (hardcover)

TABLE OF CONTENTS

FOREWORD

By Jennifer Malone Wright

I don't remember a time when I didn't want to write. All the way back to childhood I have been a teller of stories and a weaver of words. There was a time when I, like many others, was told that I should find something else to do with my life because most authors never make a living off their writing. I didn't care that people told me this, the urge to write and get my stories out was far too strong to ignore.

Writing professionally was a dream, but writing each day was living my dreams.

Much like reading a good book, when a writer tells their stories they can go wherever they want, be whoever they want, and create a new worlds. If we want a love story, we can find love in the arms of our characters. If we want to travel different lands, we can do that with imagery transferred into words. The possibilities are endless.

However, just as much as we love living these stories we create, we want you to experience them as well.

I remember reading epic novels when I was younger and thinking 'I want to make people feel this too.' We write first and foremost for ourselves, but it is you whom we want to extract emotion. The best compliment I have ever had about one of my books was when someone told me I made them cry.

True story telling is a calling. Each writer has a different testimony, but it all comes down to the fact that each of us have felt this passion to write, to get the words into the world and give our readers a taste of what we too have experienced.

When authors come together with a collection of stories, it is a truly magical thing because you will encounter every emotion possible. Laughter, tears, anger, love and contentment. When you read these stories, open yourself up and embrace the emotions of each word, for each word was written with passion behind it.

This anthology is also a charity anthology, which says so much about the authors and what they do. In this day and age, people care about themselves far more than anything else, but these authors and the publishing company are giving to animals in need, which is another passion of my own. My family has adopted animals and worked with animal rescue shelters throughout my entire life.

Stories, writing, passion and experiencing the unknown… this is the life of author and reader.

~Jennifer Malone Wright~

And Death
Shall Have No
Dominion

AND DEATH SHALL HAVE NO DOMINION

A NICK ENGLEBRECHT SHORT
BY K.H. KOEHLER

The dead man lay spread-eagle on his kitchen table, his lower half hidden by a blood-splattered white sheet, his chest plowed open with surgical precision, and a gaping black hole where his heart had once been. His face was contorted into a grimace of rage and pain, a masklike glimpse into the terrible last few moments of Randall Eckhart's life.

"Huh," I said. "The perp must have cut his heart out while he was still alive."

Ben Oswell, Blackwater's sheriff, said, "Are you fucking kidding me, Nick?"

"Well, what does it look like to you?"

He looked it over and sighed deeply. "He looks like he was alive when the perp cut his heart out."

I thought from the awestruck expression on Mr. Eckhart's face that it was pretty obvious. And when I closed my eyes, I sensed a humming in the air, a kind of pulsating rage. Mr. Eckhart had died in writhing agony, years before his time, carved apart like a Thanksgiving turkey. I'd be mad as hell, too.

Derek Hambly, Blackwater's one and only coroner, shuffled up behind us as he got his crew and gear in position to transport the body. "Jesus. Did Nick just say what I thought he said?"

"The organs need to be fresh if you want to harvest them, don't they?" I mean, I wasn't an expert on these things—frankly, I wasn't even sure why Ben invited me to look at the body, except that he seemed to think working as a cop down in NYC was a primer for this type of thing (it wasn't)—but I knew enough about that old urban legend about roofies and missing kidneys to know if you wanted to steal someone's organ, you needed it fresh. You needed the donor alive. Of course, if Mr. Eckhart had only a kidney stolen, there was a much better chance he'd still be alive today. You can survive without a kidney. A heart? Not so much.

"Organ collector." Sheriff Ben said dubiously. His face looked as crinkled and carven as a polished wooden Indian, though I couldn't see his eyes past his mirrored state trooper shades. In these frequent moments, when he was mulling the tragedy of human existence over, he looked less like his black dad and more like his Shawnee mom. Finally, he nodded. "Thanks for coming down, Nick. 'Preciate it."

"You take me to the nicest places, Ben."

"Smartass Englebrecht," he grunted.

I stepped back to let Derrek do his job. Ben walked me to the front door of the ex-Mr. Eckhart's small bungalow. "You already suspected that organ thief thing, didn't you?" I said.

He shrugged a shoulder as he walked me to my car down the street from the crime scene—a snug little bungalow in Old Town, the older part of Blackwater. It had a piney, down-home regional charm you only ever found in the Pocono Mountains. The police tape and ambulance looked a little out of place. "We're getting more triad moving into these parts, shoving the old school gangsters aside. I wouldn't be too surprised. The Chinese are often involved in organ trafficking."

"Now, now, you're exploiting a stereotype."

He gave me an arched look. "Just because it's a stereotype doesn't mean it isn't true. Look at you."

"What about me?"

"Everyone in this town thinks you're scary. And you are."

"Touché." The morbid part of my mind was already trying to imagine this summer's big promotional poster reading, *Come to the Poconos. We have whitewater rafting, beautiful hiking trails, and a nice selection of organ collectors.*

And people say I have no sense of humor...

"Your hoodoo tell you anything else about the crime scene?"

I shrugged and stuck my hands in my yellow Dick Tracy coat. "He's scared. Confused. Feels cheated. I think he may hang around that house a bit, at least, until you guys collar the perp who did this."

Ben shivered, shook his head as if unsure whether to believe me or not.

Vivian hit the horn of the Dodge Monaco as we approached. We'd been on our way to a showing of some French art film near her college when Ben had phoned me and asked that I swing by Old Town; now she wanted me to know we were running late. Yes, I go to foreign-language art films to please my girlfriend; that's just how I roll. She says I'm not a "gronk" for doing that, whatever that means—apparently, it's a good thing. For me, it means I'll probably get laid tonight.

As I slipped into the driver's seat, Ben tapped his knuckles on the dented roof. I'd learned long ago that the top-of-the-car knuckle rap meant I was in for the Pennsylvania equivalent of a long Minnesota goodbye. Around these parts, folks loved hanging by other folks' cars and chewing the fat almost as much as they enjoyed huddling shopping carts together in the local Shop Rite and chewing the fat. But Ben surprised me. "If you think of anything else, call me. Anything at all. Even a hunch." He started walking away, looking a little like a modern-day cowboy as he ambled back toward the crime scene.

"What was that all about?" Vivian asked. She was sitting demurely in the passenger seat in a tiny red and white polka dot dress and white slingback heels, looking like a cheesecake girl from the 1950's. The skirt of the dress was short enough to show off her nicely toned legs. It was a pleasant reminder that I was still alive, unlike poor Mr. Eckhart.

I started the old rumbling engine and lit a cigarette. We had this thing between us. I went to all her art films. She let me smoke in my car. Tit for tat, as it were. Then again, as daemons, neither of us could actually die of smoking, so maybe she was getting the better deal. "Sheriff Ben had a problem. He thought I might have a solution."

"Do you?" She stole my cigarette away and sucked it down hungrily, giving me a sassy, cherry-lipstick smile.

I pulled into the empty street. I tried to concentrate on the movie we were going to see, the fun we were going to have afterward, Vivian's luscious legs, but I had a bad feeling memories of Mr. Eckhart's mutilated body were going to be haunting me for a long, long time. "I just don't know, Viv."

Two days later, I found myself sitting around an antique dining room table at the sumptuous home of one our wealthier clients while my partner Morgana initiated a séance. We sat in a circle, hands touching, concentrating on Mr. Thurber, a famous local architect and the newly deceased master of the house. His widow, Mrs. Thurber, needed to ask him one last question before he moved on to the next plain of existence. And before you wonder, it wasn't something romantic like, "Do you love me?" or "Should I ever remarry?" From what I gathered, it had something to do with a hidden safety deposit box. Such is the life of the rich and conceited, I suppose.

"Mr. Thurber," Morgana said clearly in her throaty, melodious voice, "We request your presence and we open the door to this world. We invite you to pass through, into the world of the living to be reunited with us."

The room chilled considerably and I spied Mrs. Thurber shivering when I cracked my eyes.

Morgana could have handled the séance all on her own, of course, but the Thurber's house had, what we call in the biz, a "cold spot," a kind of weakness in the membrane that separates this world from the afterworld. Use too much power, and the thing you summon comes through trailing God knows what—and maybe not even Him, seeing how he'd given up on this world some time back. But I was my father's son, and my dad being who he was, I had the unique ability to toss it out on its ear. The main reason I was accompanying her tonight.

"Mr. Thurber… can you hear us?"

My phone went off and the tinny "Sympathy for the Devil" ringtone Vivian had programmed into it filled the room.

Morgana frowned. "Nick…"

"Sorry." I got up and went into the adjacent sitting parlor to take the call. "Yeah."

"It's Ben. Any chance you can drop by Morristown tonight?"

"Morristown," I said. That was a good forty miles from Blackwater, quite a ways outside Ben's jurisdiction, as far as I was aware. The only reason he would have been called out there was to follow up on a crime with some bearing on a local investigation he was engaged in.

"Shit," I breathed low in the phone.

"Yeah," Ben said, sounding grim. "There's been another one. Alive, but you've got to see this to believe it."

After I hung up, I went into the dining room to tell Morgana.

She'd successfully summoned the dead spirit of Mr. Thurber, which hung like a blue ball of sparkling fire in the middle of the room, pulsing faintly. Mrs. Thurber had just gotten all the answers she needed when several other balls of a darker, redder, and decidedly angrier color suddenly appeared. Low level demons with a hunger for crossing over.

As they started materializing into hulking, dog-like or gargoyle-like forms with slavering mouth and hungry eyes full of teeth, Mrs. Thurber screamed and passed out across the table. Morgana muttered a curse and stood up. She made the ancient sign for exorcism—middle fingers down, pointer and pinky of both hands aimed at the invading spirits as she attempted to laser blast them with her powerful Wiccan mojo. "Most glorious Horned God, defend us in our battle against principalities and powers, against the rulers of this world of darkness, against the spirits of wickedness in the high places..."

I clapped my hands once. "That's enough, boys. Hit the showers!"

They growled, shuddered and slobbered with rage, but they were demons, and demons are under my dominion. They do what I tell them to do. Or else.

Hey, sometimes rank has its privileges.

They vanished into the void with a long howl of disappointment. The room warmed and the darkness lifted.

Morgana frowned and lowered her hands. "Show off."

I drove down to Morristown's only hospital, St. Mary's, and parked in the visitor parking lot. It was a tiny hospital for a small, rural populace, and the old, weathered building was barely larger than the local public school. Ben waited for me inside and escorted me up two levels to the recovery floor. There was a police guard on the victim's door.

"Nick," Ben said, leading me to a hospital bed, "This is Mrs. Elise Changeling."

Mrs. Changeling was a woman in her late thirties, blonde and pretty in that perky kind of way you either loved or hated. Today, though, the upper half of her face was covered in bandages. There was a picture on the nightstand next to her bed of her husband and kids, and flowers, balloons and get-well teddies strewn everywhere. It was obvious Elise was well-loved. "Who's there?"

"Mrs. Changeling, this is Nick Englebrecht. He's a... consulting detective."

11

I lifted my eyebrows at Ben. He'd obviously made that up. It was probably easier than saying *psychic detective, professional witch* or *Antichrist.* I'm just guessing. "Hello, Mrs. Changeling."

"Sorry, can't shake hands," she said, lifting her right hand, which was attached to a monitoring system.

"That's all right." I sat down beside her. Ben had given me very few details on the way up to her room. I let Elise tell me her story in her own halting, coarse voice.

The perp had broken into her house the day before, after she'd gotten back from dropping the kids off at school. Her husband was away on a business trip. The intruder easily overpowered her, injected her with something that paralyzed her but left her conscious, and then went about the job of undressing her and sheeting her atop the kitchen table. After that, he used clamps to keep her eyes peeled back and had slowly—gently—carved each eye from its socket using a series of surgical implements. The impromptu surgery had taken three hours, by her estimation. She had been aware the whole time, but she hadn't seen his face—he had been wearing a mask and surgical scrubs.

A few hours later, she'd found she could move again. She'd managed to dial 911 on her cell, and the first responders on the scene had said she'd been injected with a massive amount of adrenaline meant to stop her heart—obviously the perp had not meant for her to survive the surgery—but the chemical had reacted oddly with her daily dose of immunosuppressants.

"And why do you take those?" I asked.

She indicated her bandaged face. "I had deteriorating corneas. Fuchs' Dystrophy, it's called. These are—these were—transplants."

When we got back to my car in the parking lot, I said, "You think these are the same organ trafficking guys?" As far as I knew, organ traffickers only stole healthy tissue. Who would want to purchase second-hand goods in *this* business?

Ben stared down at a crack in the pavement. I could tell he was reluctant to spill. Afraid his buddy Nick Englebrecht would hare off after his case.

"Ben."

"Nick."

"You tell me what you know, I'll tell you what I got off the victim."

He tipped his cowboy hat back and said, "Both of the victims—Mr. Eckhart and Mrs. Changeling—were successful transplant receivers."

I lit a cigarette. Ben stared at it hungrily, but I wasn't about to share just yet. Yes, it was underhanded. Sue me. "And?"

"And... what did you get off of her? Anything that might identify the perp?"

"As in?"

"Anything at all. A feeling... something she saw or felt that might be significant."

"She was afraid. *Is* afraid. She's scared he'll come back to finish her off."

He rolled his eyes. "Anything I can't figure out on my own?"

"What links the two transplant patients? Who was the donor?"

"Nick," Ben sighed. "I can't tell you that. You're not an official part of this investigation."

Mexican standoff.

I got in my car. I turned over the engine.

Finally, Ben leaned in the window. "Her name was Amanda Whedon. But I don't want you doing anything stupid."

"Who, me?"

"Nick..."

"I promise I won't get involved in your investigation," I told him in all honesty. Frankly, I'd rather launch one of my own. Hey, my father is the Prince of Lies. What exactly do you expect from me?

Ben snorted, not a happy sound. "Now dish. I know you know something."

"There's something sexual about what your perp is doing."

"How do you mean? You mean he gets off on doing this? Like some kind of sick fetish?"

"I don't know," I told him frankly. "What I *do* know isn't an exact science, Ben. I can only tell you about residual energies. Some of the energies clinging to Mrs. Changeling were sexual." I shrugged. "The perp loves her eyes. That's all I know."

"It's not much to go on."

I offered him a cigarette from my pack of Camels as a consolation prize.

He looked guilty even as he snatched one out. "You shouldn't tempt me like this. I've been off the coffin nails almost eight months now."

"Patch not working?"

"The patch is shit. And you are the devil, Nick."

I smiled as I pulled out of the parking lot.

I was driving Vivian to work because her piece of shit Jeep had broken down for the *nth* time when I said, "Did you ever know a student by the name of Amanda Whedon?"

She tilted her head to one side. "Sounds familiar."

"She went to Lincoln Tech. Across the campus from you." At least according to Google and her Facebook page.

"I know the name." We were nearing the campus when she finally remembered all the details. "She was the girl who killed herself. It made the paper."

I nodded. "She committed suicide."

"She came from Whitehall, same town as I did, but I didn't really know her. I don't think anyone did. She was very quiet. Depressed. A literary type, as I recall. Wanted to be a journalist, or writer, or something. The college had a nice memorial service for her mother."

"Do you know why she was so depressed?"

"I never asked," Vivian confessed. "But her mother struck me as a controlling bitch. She reminded me of my own mother."

I continued to think about Vivian's words even as I drove down to Curiosities and took over the shop from Morgana for the rest of the day. I had made a small, half-hearted promise to myself to stay out of things as much as possible, but a part of my mind kept going back over things, kept wondering about Amanda. Just how a young, unhappy girl who committed suicide and then was kind enough to donate her organs could be connected to these crimes? I wanted to do a few more online searches, make a couple phone calls, but I had hit a busy patch in the shop, and like it or not, I wasn't a cop anymore. I was a shopkeeper. I had to keep that in mind.

Sometime in the late afternoon, Mrs. Bailey, a very proper gentlewoman in her seventies, and one of Curiosities most loyal customers, swung by to pick up her holistic arthritis medication. She was dressed in a bright, floral summer dress, honest-to-god gloves, and a beautiful straw hat full of dried mums, sunflowers, and monarch butterflies. Mrs. Bailey was strictly old school; she was the kind of woman who considered leaving the house without a hat a "state of undress." God knows why she liked me. I lived most of my life in a state of undress.

"I adore your hair, Nicky," she told me as she primly took her white, medicinal bag from me. "Are you wearing it differently?"

"No, Mrs. Bailey," I told her with a gregarious smile. "I did comb it this morning, though."

She tittered a laugh, and I took a moment to compliment her on her hat.

"I do so love this hat," she said. "I made it myself, you know."

"Did you now?" I said, leaning on the counter separating us.

Mrs. Bailey carefully unpinned it from her perfectly coiffure, steel-grey hair and proudly showed it to me. "All the butterflies are from my personal collection, caught by yours truly over many years." She flashed me a triumphant smile. "I do wish you'd drop by the house. I could make you a cup of Earl Grey and show you my collection. It's quite extensive."

I handed back her hat. "Thank you, Mrs. Bailey. I may do just that."

From the faintly teasing, hungry gleam in her eyes, I knew I never would, but flirting with the old woman had become my entertainment. I wondered if that made me a pervert or just an asshole.

After she was gone, I thought about her words. In a way, they haunted me. Mrs. Bailey loved butterflies, loved collecting them. She was a fan, you might say.

I picked up my cell phone and called Vivian to ask her about taking a short road trip down to her hometown of Whitehall to meet Amanda Whedon's mother.

Vivian was silent as we rolled into town. Whitehall was vastly different from a lot of the towns that I was used to seeing in Eastern Pennsylvania. Age and history didn't cling to it the way it did in Blackwater. It was one of those towns that had started out around the 1950's as a resort community catering to doctors and lawyers needing their skiing fix, but then evolved into an upper-middle-class haven full of pristine, gated communities, high-end bistros, overpriced B&B's, and trinket stores that sold useless crap like ball caps, key rings, and T-shirts with insipid logos.

The architecture was stark and new. There was an artful smattering of lodges, gourmet candy shops, candle stores, and coffee houses to choose from, all of them selling overpriced everything. In some ways, Whitehall seemed to be striving to be a more high-end version of Blackwater. I saw people walking designer dogs and wearing Gucci shoes as they pedaled eco-friendly bicycles around the town center where a huge war memorial tank dedicated to a local general I'd never heard of was the center of attention.

"Are you okay?" I said aloud.

"Sure." She gave me her sassy smile, but this time it didn't touch her sea-green eyes.

Vivian and Josh had grown up here. Josh had led a relatively normal adolescence, at least, until he was injured in combat in Afghanistan, but this was the place where Vivian had first had sex, shame, and adulthood heaped upon her. I'd seen the pictures of her as a girl. Vivian had been almost painfully beautiful, like an exquisite little Dresden doll. It was almost inevitable she'd draw the wolfish attention of her weak-willed science teacher, Mr. McCarty. The two had engaged in a year-long affair when Vivian was only nine years old.

I asked her once if she hated Mr. McCarty, if she wanted to hurt him. She told me no. She hated herself more. He might have forced her that first time, but she was the one who kept coming back.

As I drove down Main Street, I said, "I should have asked you if you wanted to come."

"I do," she told me in a confident tone. "I can help. If I tell Mrs. Whedon that I'm doing a paper on suicide rates, she might open up to us. She might want to help others."

"But you're not doing a paper."

She looked at me in her earnest, determined way, and I realized she was one of the strongest people I knew. "I want to help you, Nick. I want to help Amanda, if I can. I didn't pay much attention to her when she was alive. I figured she had problem, but then, we all have problems, right?" She scraped at the ruby nail polish on her thumbnail. "I want to find out who's doing these awful things. Maybe..." She shrugged. "Maybe it'll make Amanda happy."

We found the house, a huge, brickfaced colonial monstrosity at the end of the street. The path leading up to the front door was lined with magnolias in full bloom that filled the air with a choking, cloying perfume. The doorknocker was in the shape of the American bald eagle.

"Yes?" a small woman with a bitter, heavily-lined face said when we knocked.

"Are you Mrs. Whedon?" Vivian said, jumping right in. She'd worn her reading glasses, and they made her pretty, heart-shaped face both sympathetic and curious. She'd even pulled out a notepad. "I was hoping I might speak briefly with you, Mrs. Whedon. It's about Amanda."

"Well... I suppose."

We sat down in the living room and Mrs. Whedon had her housekeeper bring us a tray of lemonade. She didn't look particularly happy about our presence, but there's something about being well-off but not quite mega-rich that forces people to acknowledge good manners. It's like they know they're still climbing the social ladder and can't afford to blow off anyone, just in case. On the other hand, maybe I wasn't giving Vivian enough credit;

she could be incredibly charming and seductive when she wanted to be. Within the hour, she had pulled all kinds of information from Mrs. Whedon.

We learned Amanda had been diagnosed with chronic depression, but only during the last six months of her life. She mostly kept to herself. Her only outlet seemed to be the online blog she had kept up until her death last year. It was still being maintained by the college as a memorial to Amanda, but I'd already been over that over the last few days, and it was so painfully mundane, I don't think Sherlock Holmes could have deduced a damned thing off of it.

Vivian made imaginary notes as we talked. She glanced down at the questions I had written up for her. "Do you know if she had any close friends? Boyfriends?"

"Amanda was a good girl," Mrs. Whedon said as she wandered nervously about the plush, frighteningly white living room space. She stopped in front of the mantel where Amanda's ashes lived in an ornate porcelain urn. She turned and put the urn to her back almost like she was guarding it with her life. "That's why she asked in her final letter to have her organs donated. She was a *very* good girl, Vivian. She didn't keep any boys around her."

She made it sound like something dirty.

"Did you keep any of her things, Mrs. Whedon?"

"I kept her room exactly the way she liked it."

"Do you mind if I look around? Get a feel for Amanda, for the paper?"

Five minutes later, we were alone in her room. It was as neat as a pin and done in all safe pastels. The bed and dressing table were white rattan, and the computer desk white bamboo. French art posters covered the wall, and conservative clothing in muted colors hung in the closet. The room had the heavy-handed touch of being mother-chosen and mother-decorated. I thought about what Vivian had said about Amanda's mother being a control freak. I started going over everything with a fine-tooth comb, starting with the books that dominated one whole wall.

"What are we looking for?" Vivian asked as she dug surreptitiously through Amanda's closet. "And why did you have me ask about a boyfriend?"

I pulled down each book and flipped it open, looking under the dust jackets. "We're looking for notebooks… journals… something personal. I want to find something linking her to a man. More precisely, a lover."

"A lover? But Mrs. Whedon said she didn't have a boyfriend."

"That she knew about."

Vivian opened the top drawer of Amanda's computer desk and started rummaging through the collected junk there. Even the junk looked organized. "Why do you think there's a boyfriend? Did you deduct that like Sherlock Holmes from something she said?"

As far as detectives went, I considered myself more James Rockford than Sherlock Holmes, but whatever. "No. Mrs. Bailey."

"What does Mrs. Bailey have to do with Amanda Whedon?"

"Absolutely nothing. But Mrs. Bailey collects butterflies. Apparently, she loves them. It made me realize something important." There was nothing on the top shelf. I started working my way down. "Someone loved Amanda. Is in love with Amanda. That's why he's collecting these... pieces of her."

Vivian, hunched over a bottom drawer, turned with a small day planner in her hand. "Holmes?"

"Excellent."

Going over it, I found it was full, front to back, with notes and observations, apparently for a romance novel Amanda had planned to write but never did. "Did you bring your laptop?"

Vivian pulled it from the old backpack she carried her college stuff in and booted it with a smile.

"Why are you smiling?"

"I just realized that if you're Sherlock Holmes, I'm John Watson."

"Holmes and Watson were never romantically entangled."

"That we know about," Vivian grinned. "What am I looking for?"

"Anastasia Winter."

"Who's Anastasia Winter?"

"The name of Amanda's pseudonym," I said as I paged through the day planner and her notes. "Google it. I have a hunch."

Sure enough, five minutes later, we found Amanda's *other* blog. A quick glance over it revealed many of the entries were composed of pieces of the novel she had planned to write. In fact, everything was there except the ending. The entries had dried up about six months ago, when Amanda began the long spiral down into the depression that eventually caused her to take her own life.

After leaving Mrs. Whedon's house, we drove to an all-night Arby's to pick up Vivian's favorite late-night snack: Dr. Pepper and curly fries. While Vivian licked grease and ketchup off her fingers—rather fetchingly, I might add—I scanned Amanda's blog. "It reads like an erotica novel. *Fifty Shades of Amanda.*"

"So she was secretly kinky."

"Not really. I mean, nothing beyond the usual college-girl curiosity. She had some fantasies of being tied up and blindfolded, but pretty vanilla stuff overall…"

"Vanilla for *you*, Marquis de Sade."

"Geez, give your girlfriend one over-the-knee spanking—*which she asked for*—and you're perverted beyond all redemption."

I waited for her to laugh teasingly and suck soda noisily through her straw the way she knew I hated her doing, but she stayed quiet, chewing contemplatively on a fry. "I feel really sorry for Amanda. She was a pretty good writer. She could have made a career out of it, if she wanted." She thought about that a moment before adding, "Maybe when this is over, I'll put all her entries together and finish her romance novel. Give her a happy ending."

I smiled at what I thought was the best girlfriend a guy could have. "You're really a good person, Vivian."

She blushed at that and *then* sucked soda noisily through her straw. "So… why is this stuff important to your investigation?"

"I'm pretty sure she had a secret lover. Her sex scenes are far too detailed for someone who *didn't keep boys around.*"

Vivian shrugged. "Some girls have a lot of imagination." She turned the laptop around and read the quote Amanda had put on the top of her secret blog, "'Though lovers be lost, love shall not; And death shall have no dominion.' Dylan Thomas, nice."

"Apparently, it was part of her curriculum, at least according to the *other* blog." Immediately after I said it, I got an idea. I surfed over to the other blog and discovered a few references to her English teacher, one Mr. Philip Lee Lang, and how he gave her all A's on her essays, encouraged her to write, was her seemingly only friend. When I cross-referenced her other blog, I saw a more stylized, romantic version of Mr. Lang in her prose—the strict, handsome teacher, quick to use a ruler on a particularly naughty schoolgirl's backside, but also romantic and caring.

In Amanda's story, her Mary Sue was torn between staying with her headstrong, domineering mother or going with her lover when he wished to whisk her away from her life. I was starting to think this was a case of art imitating life.

"You know how teachers can influence their students?"

Vivian grew solemn as she remembered her own relationship with her science teacher. It had been less than romantic. "Yeah."

A citywide internet search of names brought Philip Lee Lang's address up in no time. A Google brought up his police record. He'd been in and out of juvie halls most of his adolescent life, had been arrested three times—for arson, aggravated assault, and statutory rape—and had two restraining orders against him from two other women in other states. Stuff like that should have been enough to keep him from being hired at the college, but the Commonwealth of Pennsylvania was old school and didn't publicly post the names of sex offenders, a little quirk of government I'd never understood. If you didn't know to go looking for it in the public records, you'd never know that employee, teacher, or co-worker of yours was a verified pervert and lunatic.

"Nick," Vivian said. "You're getting that maniacal gleam in your eyes. Are you onto something?"

And the best part about Mr. Lang's background check? His father had been a professional taxidermist. "And Bingo was his name-o," I said as I shut Vivian's laptop and stood up. "I just found Ben's perp."

On the drive over to Mr. Lang's house, I realized Vivian had questions she was probably too embarrassed to ask, so I said, "Amanda's not in that urn in her mother's house."

"How do you know that?"

I shrugged a shoulder. "Call it cop instinct. Or daemon instinct. Or whatever. But she's not there. *He* took her. Whoever's in that urn, it isn't Amanda."

She was silent until we pulled up to a an old, nondescript Victorian farmhouse out in the middle of nowhere that looked like it had seen better days. It was a two-story clapboard affair with dirty, peeling white paint, faded green shutters and a sagging front porch that made the place look like it wasn't fit for human habitation. Vivian's fingers were clasped together in her lap and her lips looked unusually dark and chapped against the paleness of her face. "Why would he take her body, Nick?" she asked, almost too softly for me to hear.

I looked askance at her. "Why do you think?"

She shuddered. "But they were lovers. They had this whole thing going, and she was writing about it in her novel. But then she killed herself?"

"Yeah," I said. "That's rather curious, isn't it?" I unhooked my seatbelt. "Stay here while I go look around."

Vivian looked frightened. "I'd rather go with you, if you wouldn't mind."

We went up the rickety wooden steps to the front door. An old wartime-style porch swing hung off to the side, creaking ominously on rusty chains. Vivian went to grab the doorknocker, but I put my hand on hers to halt her. I pulled my old police-issue Tanaka from the holster under my raincoat, a gun powerful enough to cripple an elephant.

"Do you think he's going to be *that* bad?" she asked.

"Do you feel it?"

She stopped to concentrate. "I feel… angry." She opened her eyes and jerked her hand back as if the door burned her. "Like you're pissing me off, Nick."

"It's not *your* anger you're feeling. It's hers. Amanda's. She's here."

"Jesus."

The door was tightly locked and barred, so I let go of the knob and started moving around the seemingly abandoned house, looking for a suitable window to do our breaking and entering through. As I searched, I explained, "When someone dies in despair and before their appointed time, they sometimes produce what I call a shadow. It's a kind of malevolent spirit similar to the Japanese legend of the *onryo*, an entirely new creature halfway between a ghost and a demon that seeks vengeance. If the victim was weak in life, they can become incredibly powerful in death, and they can hang around for years, decades, even centuries, just poisoning the environment and turning people against one another. Even those not responsible for their own deaths. They're extremely dangerous and can physically harm or kill anyone they perceive as an enemy."

Vivian shivered. "And you think Amanda has become this… shadow creature?"

"She killed herself while in great pain. I think it's a possibility." I'd finally found a window that was open. I slid it up and kicked in the screen that never seemed to exist when characters in movies and on TV did this type of thing. Soon we were both standing in a musty, old living room full of furniture that looked dusty and dull. There were ancient stains on the carpet, scratches on the black baby grand piano in the corner, and mothy taxidermy animals everywhere—on the walls, on mantels, sitting forlornly on almost every available surface. The place stank of black mold and pain.

When I scanned the room, I picked up quick, corner-of-the-eye, shadowlike glimpses of Amanda alive, like in a rickety, old film reel: Amanda sitting on the old and sagging sofa, making love on the floor. At one point, I spied her crying hysterically as she raced for the front door. She'd definitely been here, many times. She'd left her mark on the place, but it felt dark and unnatural, a sad ending to an even sadder life. I knew what I was seeing was just residual memories, but it never failed to unnerve me.

Vivian reached out to touch a scraggly, stuffed raven sitting on an end table, then jerked her hand back. "These things always give me the creeps. Like Norman Bates' house, you know?"

"This whole place gives me the creeps," I said. The hairs on my arms were standing at rigid attention, brushing the sleeves of my coat. I looked toward a set of stairs leading up to a second floor and listened to a dripping faucet up there somewhere, then turned to follow a stronger, more visceral emotion coming from down the hall to our left. We went that way and soon found ourselves before what was likely a basement door.

I tapped the door open and was hit with a smell like something hot, juicy, and human had died, but not recently.

"*Jesus Christ,*" Vivian said, covering her mouth and nose, and issuing a little sick cough from behind her hand. "What the fuck *is* that?"

"Want to find out?"

"No."

"Stay here, then."

"No!"

She followed me down the creaky wooden steps, staying close and clutching my arm. I felt a little bit like Fred from *Scooby Doo*. He always had Daphne with him, right? Unfortunately, I doubted this was going to end with a mundane unmasking of a human villain.

It was dark, no lights in the stairwell at all, and all the basement widows were papered over, but I had remembered to take the Maglite I kept in the car's glove compartment box. I *am* generally smarter than I look and I try to keep my blond moments down to a minimum. I shone it around now, picking out the moldy, water-stained cement walls, the naked bulbs, the dark, oily stains on the cement floor.

"Good god," Vivian mumbled from behind her hand. The smell was growing worse, if that was even possible, and flies were crawling the walls.

It bothered me too, terrified me, in fact, but like a filament being pulled toward a powerful magnet, I was being drawn on relentlessly toward something I knew I had to discover. I couldn't leave without knowing what had happened here, and I was afraid my eyes probably had that same maniacal gleam Vivian had observed earlier.

Finally, my light flashed across a figure standing in the corner, a slim figure obscured by long, dirty tangled blonde hair. I jerked and brought the light back around, thinking maybe I had imagined it, a trick of the light, but nothing was there now.

"Ah, Christ, Nick… I can feel her," Vivian whimpered, tears in her voice. Her hand tightened on my arm. "I can fucking *feel* her."

"I know," I said. The air was electrified around us. Amanda was one of the most powerful shadows I had ever encountered. This wasn't stuff like Mr. Thurber. This was, for lack of a better word, bad shit. And it wasn't shit I could just dismiss, either. I can control demons, but what Amanda had become went far beyond that. I knew she could have killed us already, tripped us on the stairs, driven some sharp instrument into our bodies, ripped us apart with her bare fingers, were we human. But we weren't. We were half demon, and almost as dangerous as she was. She liked that. That's why she had left us unscathed.

Still…"Stay behind me."

"Count on it."

There was another room, an adjoining one like an old root cellar, and it hummed. Flies crawled the walls in waves. I crept to the doorway and stopped, the smell so bad, it was like a solid wall of sweet, stomach-heaving decay. Inside the dank, little room, I thought I spied that same shadow again, with the long hair, but it quickly vanished.

"Oh sweet Mother of God," Vivian said when she saw what was laid out on a metal hospital slab. She turned away to heave in the other room.

I held my breath and moved my flashlight over the remains of Amanda Whedon's body. The surgical attention that Lang had shown the cadaver had been crude, at best, a son's halfhearted attempt to imitate the talent of his dead father. The Y-shaped coroner's incision had been roughly sutured shut, the eyes sewn back into their appropriate sockets, the body dusted down with some kind of powder to slow the decay process, and the face carefully painted, so the thing on the table looked like someone's macabre version of a Halloween doll. Flies crawled the body, over the dead eyes and dry lips, and the whole cadaver dimly shuddered from the enormous colony of larvae that lurked beneath the purplish skin.

And yet, I could smell the dull, bleachy scent of sex beneath the decay. Someone had been at Amanda's body, many times, and recently.

Vivian screamed and I swung around, stupidly aiming the flashlight instead of my gun. I thought for sure I'd see Amanda's shadow approaching us, but it was the panic-stricken, scarecrow image of an unkempt, middleaged man rushing us—wielding, of all things, a scalpel. He screamed incoherently.

I pushed Vivian down and out of the way, and that saved her, but not me. The man slashed with the scalpel, but before I could bring my gun arm up, the glittering blade cut easily through my sleeve and the flesh of my forearm. I grunted with pain and instinctively jerked my injured arm back, my elbow hitting the hospital table containing Amanda's dead body. Surgical instruments went flying off the table and the hum of flies in the room intensified to a dull roar as we disturbed them.

The crazed man slashed at me again, but this time I was ready. He was too close for me to get a good shot and not hit Vivian by accident, so I intercepted his second slash with the side of the big, baton-like Maglite in my hand. The blade rang as it slid harmlessly off the side of the flashlight. As the man—Lang, presumably—reared back for a second blow, I brought the Maglite up and cuffed him across the chin. He went down like I'd pummeled him, and the scalpel skipped off into a dark corner.

Lang whimpered.

"Don't move," I roared with more anger than I knew I'd had. I reached for my cell phone, to call the police, but I'd underestimated the man. He grabbed up a scalpel from off the floor and slashed at my ankle. I sidestepped him, but tripped over his prone form and went down hard, the Tanaka and my phone jumping from my hands.

"You stay away from her!" Lang screamed. "She's mine! She belongs to me!"

"She's dead!" I screamed back and had to deflect his hands from scratching at my eyes like a cat. Jesus, the guy couldn't even fight like a man. Instead, he scratched and tried to bite me like some crazed asylum inmate.

The moment he touched me, the jumpy film reel images invaded my brain once more. This time I saw Amanda and Lang's Spring-December romance coming to an end. I saw her in the living room upstairs, with Lang grabbing her arm, demanding she go with him, like the heroine in her book. I saw Amanda panic and pull away. Somehow, she'd learned about him. She'd found out about all the other women who were so frightened of him.

I'll tell her, Lang screamed at her. *I'll tell her about the blog. The book. About us. Then she'll know what kind of a pain slut you really are...*

The image flickered and changed to one of Amanda standing in her mother's bedroom, taking the handgun from her bottom drawer, the one they had for protection, because they were just two women alone. I saw a sad, young girl put it in her mouth…

I grunted and kneed Lang in the groin, which stunned him, then gave him a left hook across the chin, soundly knocking him back a few feet against the operating table. I was too big a guy to be the lithe, punchy Jackie Chain-type of fighter you see in cop flicks. I generally just punched my enemies once and they went down and stayed down until the police arrived. They then endured years of physical therapy to repair whatever it was I had broken—in this case, likely his jaw. But Lang was out of his fucking mind.

As soon as he went down, he jumped back up like a demonic jack-in-the-box—as if he didn't feel pain. Well, he hadn't felt Amanda's pain. Had he even felt any pain or remorse at her funeral after she'd taken her own life just to get away from him, too frightened to go to her prim and proper mother, too frightened to go to anyone?

Back on his feet, Lang paused only long enough to grab at a less-than-sterile scalpel lying in a metal tray near the gurney where he'd painstakingly pieced Amanda's body back together and raised his hand high, ready to stab into me again… then stopped as something clicked behind me.

I scrambled to my feet and saw Vivian holding the Tanaka on Lang. "Don't do it," she said. "I *will* kill you, shithead."

"Vivian," I said, but her eyes were fastened to Lang's ragged form, oblivious to Amanda's body, the flies, me, even the outline in the shadows in the corner of the room, giving off a dull rattle as it shifted uneasily. "You killed her," she told Lang coolly.

Lang put up both hands and glared at her. "I didn't… it wasn't *supposed* to happen…!"

"But it *did* happen."

"You don't understand… she belongs to me! She was supposed to go with me!"

"I understand just fine!" Vivian screeched. I could feel her feeding off the vibrations of the being in the corner, sucking up the truth like an emotional vampire. Vivian could do that; she was an incredibly powerful succubus when she was powered up. "You *manipulated* her! You *haunted* her! You isolated her from all her family and friends! You wouldn't leave her alone! And *that's* why she killed herself!"

"Vivian," I said softly. I closed both hands over the gun that shook fiercely in her hands, but, dammit, I couldn't move it from her grip. It was like she was welded to the weapon.

"And still you won't leave her alone!" Vivian cried, tears streaming down both cheeks. "She doesn't love you anymore! She hates you!"

The dull hum of the flies was suddenly drowned out by the sound I had been dreading to hear since I stepped inside the basement. The insidious, snakelike death rattle filled the room, a cheated, angry noise, and Amanda's shadow stepped out of the corner. The sick, ragged form of the thing she had become grew clear and real and hideous. The hair skated back like snakes to reveal a long, lipless, slitlike mouth full of jagged teeth. The smile stretched wide across the whole bottom half of Amanda's ravaged face. The rattle grew loud enough for Lang to turn and face it, but he was too slow.

Amanda lunged and sank her fingers into Lang's shoulders and dragged him back toward the wall. Lang screeched in horror as he was hauled relentlessly away by the shadow, then *up* the concrete wall to where a window much too small for a human man to fit through lurked. It had rusted bars on it, of the kind folks around these parts used to keep small children and animals out of their basements.

The shadow exploded the glass of the window with a rattle and a howl, and like a swarm of flies, Amanda flew through it. But the motion also jerked Lang against the small opening. He didn't fit, but that didn't stop the shadow. Shrieking with rage, she pulled him with agonizing slowness right through the tiny, rusted grate. Lang screamed for a remarkably long time as his body was compressed and reshaped to fit through it, his bones broken and re-broken, his flesh compacted and reshaped like putty until it literally exploded from the pressure of the unyielding grate. Only then did the shadow let him go, his mutilated remains stuck half in, half out of his house of horrors.

Vivian lowered the Tanaka and broke into heaving sobs as she covered her face.

I went to her and held her a long moment against the shelter of my body before they subsided into hiccups. Then I carried her from that chamber of horrors.

Vivian was silent for most of the drive back to Blackwater. She lay in the bucketseat of the Monaco, her face turned away toward the window, her reflection in the glass drawn and seemingly years older. After a while, she said, "No one will ever know why he did it, or why she did it. They'll never know about Amanda."

"They'll guess. The police will come up with a story that will work for them. They always do."

She turned her head to look at me with her stark, pale face. "Is she… I mean, do you think she's still there? Is she like… trapped in that house? Will she always be there, haunting it? Miserable and alone?"

"I don't know," I said honestly as I lit a new cigarette for me and one for her. "That's the story. But then, that's what it is, you know. A story."

"I hope she is."

I blinked at Vivian, thinking I had misheard my girlfriend.

But I hadn't. Vivian was smiling that smile that was hungry and a little bit mad. The smile reminded me vaguely of Amanda's. "I hope she's trapped there, with him. I hope she torments him every day for all eternity. I hope it never ends."

I was silent for the rest of the trip home.

Want to read more about Nick Englebrecht and the paranormal cases the son of the Devil has to deal with?

Tweet *More Nick @k_h_koehler @CuriosityQuills #BookLove*

CYBER COWBOY

CYBER-COWBOY

BY JAMES WYMORE

I'll never forget where I was when it happened. No one will.

Several of us from the office had gone for drinks after work to celebrate the end of tax season. As an accountant, I loved and hated the first third of every year. That's when we made most of our money, working insane overtime. However, I didn't get to see Amber except for occasional glances if I happened to be passing the HR office. I found plenty of reasons. This year I promised myself I'd ask her out when the rush ended. No time would be better than here in the bar with lights low and music thumping.

I managed to strike up a conversation with her about investment properties. I think she was into it because she kept smiling and didn't turn away when I looked in her eyes. They were a beautiful brown. In just the right light, I could see the rim of her contacts. Her clear skin and tidy hair always attracted me. I was feeling the rhythm. Half the people from work left. I knew this would be the night. I could just ask her to dinner some time. No big deal, right?

Then her cell phone rang.

"I have to get this," Amber said. She made a quick smile and shrugged. I kept my face even, playing it cool. She got up and moved somewhere quiet. I chatted with Manuel while she was gone, glad he didn't say anything embarrassing about my moves.

"I'm sorry, Sam," she said with her brow knit as she returned. "I have to go. That was my landlord. There was a fire in the building."

"Wow," I said. "That sucks." I wanted to slap my own face. Did I really just say sucks? But it was out, and I had to let it ride.

"Say goodbye to everybody for me," Amber said. Her shoulder length hair flipped neatly over the collar of her business suit as she grabbed her purse and rushed for the door.

Manuel held up his glass and nodded as he drank a silent toast to me. He knew I'd been crushing on her. At least, he didn't make me talk about it. I looked at the last few people left from the office. None of them said or did anything to indicate they knew. I sighed. I could trust Manuel. He wouldn't say anything to her. Luckily, the office gossips hadn't caught on or I'd be mortified.

A few minutes later, I made my excuses and left the loud music and silent big-screen sports behind. I stepped out onto the dark city street. The ground and cars were glossy with rain, reflecting long lines from the many city lights. At least, it didn't rain now. I didn't have an umbrella, so my thin shirt would have stuck to my body in that disgusting way like a second skin. A blur of pink reflected the sunset off the long, rain soaked road. Despite the cool air, the skyscrapers were pretty in a longing, romantic way. I would have walked home, but I didn't want my leather shoes ruined.

I held out my hand, and a yellow taxi pulled over. "450 on Sixth," I said as I pulled the door closed. The interior smelled like incense—or so I told myself.

His black dreadlocks wiggled when the driver turned abruptly to look at me in the mirror. No doubt to size up what kind of guy flagged a taxi for such a short trip. Hey, these were brand new shoes! I didn't bother explaining.

Just as the cab pulled away from the curb, my phone vibrated. I had a text from Amber. My heart skipped a beat. Just as I flipped it open, a kind of electric fog rolled past. .

A kind of buzzing went through me from back to front, like an explosion in my ears, and blinded my eyes with white light. I swear I tasted sweet and sour pork with too much salt. My skin itched and crawled. A cramp made my knee jerk. If I could have crawled out of my skin, I would have, anything to escape the discomfort rushing over and through me.

I waited a little while for the night blindness to clear and the ringing in my ears to dim. I would have thought I was dead except my clothes felt so coarse, I knew it couldn't be heaven. And I hadn't done anything bad enough to wind up in hell.

My senses slowly cleared, and I stared down at my hands, my mind fighting to reconcile what my eyes were registering. My phone disappeared in the event, in its place sat a yellow card with large letters bordering the top edge. I'm not kidding, the top of the card said, "Telegram," in big letters.

My thoughts raced, why did it say that?

The cab driver started to laugh. He laughed like Santa Claus who he'd heard the funniest joke in the world. I looked up to see his face in the rearview mirror. There wasn't one. The whole inside of the cab had changed into a carriage. The driver, now outside in the cold night air, continued to giggle as he snapped the reigns to keep the team of horses pulling the cart forward.

I looked out the window, now just a hole in the side of the cab covered by ebony curtains tied back with a metallic ring. The world changed too. Wooden buildings with towering signs along the rooftops and swinging saloon doors lined the streets. The wet road was now sticky, brown mud. Everybody was wearing Victorian dresses or colorful bandanas around their necks.

I looked down. My pants were dingy brown, and I wore a leather vest over a beige shirt that looked like cotton, but felt like burlap. What in the world had happened? Had a serious car accident sent me into a coma? Was my mind interpreting the driver's screams as laughter by mistake? And why was my cellphone now a telegraph message?

I knew in a few seconds I would freak out. What had happened to the world? This couldn't be real. It was impossible. It had to be me. I had to be going crazy. My hands began to shake, causing the piece of paper to crinkle. That paper distracted me away from a complete breakdown.

The text. My addled mind must be interpreting the text message as a telegraph. I looked at the card and read it.

Telegram
Sam STOP *I could use some help* STOP *Please*
come to my apartment if you can STOP
Everything is ruined END
Amber STOP

I read it over and over. With the world turned upside down and a cackling cabbie pointing in every direction and hacking like a jackal, I didn't know what it meant. I first thought it would be about her apartment. But considering how the world had changed, she might be in danger. Maybe she sent this before it all happened and she wanted help because of the fire in her building. Or maybe the transformation moved slower than the message and she had changed first. Either way, I couldn't miss this chance to help her, regardless of the ugly Western, which seemed to have taken over the world.

"Cabbie," I yelled out the side window. "Turn back. I need to go to 316 on Main."

To his credit, the Rastafarian, now dressed in mountain man leathers and a coonskin hat, didn't miss a beat. He pulled the reigns to slow the horses and then turned a hard left. Since most of the other horse-drawn carriages had come to a stop, it wasn't a dangerous maneuver. Many of the other carts had people standing outside of them looking at their clothes and wagging their heads. I understood their confusion. I just didn't have time to sit and think about it.

We went past a group of Orientals who looked positively furious at their railroad working attire. The only happy one of them wore the loose fitting clothes of a Kung-Fu master. It seemed to make the rest of them even angrier.

Farther down the road, I looked out the window to see two gunslingers in tall boots and spurs facing off at sun down. As I watched, I did not think they would really go through with it. Then they both drew. Their six-shooters exploded, and one fell dead.

I could not believe my eyes. Did I just watch somebody die? I could not think about that now. It was too much. For a diversion, I looked at my telegram again and secretly hoped Amber would be in a big fancy dress. Suddenly the carriage lurched and I heard the cab driver slowing the horses.

"What's wrong?" I called up. I couldn't see anything but the driver's huge butt from inside the carriage.

"This isn't right," he said with a hint of an accent.

I poked my head out of the window and caught my breath. The whole world changed across a line in the road. Once the cart stopped, I decided to get out and take a look, new shoes or not.

I loathed the sucking sound my shiny red cowboy boots made as they sunk in the wet muck. When I let go of the door, the angle made it slam closed.

The wooden façade of saloons and jailhouses ended abruptly. Beyond the line, the tall city buildings of glass and concrete stood in ruins. More windows were broken or cracked than intact. Many of the tallest buildings actually looked broken in half, their looming peaks now mounds of rubble at the base. Derelict vehicles covered with rust littered the street. I couldn't think of any place I would less like to go.

"You still want to go there?" the cabbie asked.

"I need to find a girl," I began. I knew I wasn't up to it on my own. I had to concentrate on finding Amber. If I didn't focus on her, I would probably start crying like a baby. There was no way to explain the sudden and complete transformation of the entire world. I might be able to accept one change or the other. Yet here I stood on the border between two places that were completely, unbelievably different. I refused to attempt understanding. I was an accountant, so I did what always worked and concentrated on the bottom line.

"Then you're on your own." He straightened his hat so the striped tail fell down his back instead of on one shoulder. He sure wasn't laughing now.

"I need your help," I said. It was a statement of fact, not whining or begging. I needed somebody strong. "I'll pay extra. A hundred bucks?"

"I don't…" his voice trailed off as a brisk wind picked a tumbleweed up from the wooden decking, which had replaced the sidewalk, and rolled it forward across the line. The dead plant seemed to shimmer as it breached the bubble. When it came out on the other side, it was a dog-sized rat with bone spikes sticking up out of the black fur on its crooked back. It scuttled down the road and turned into one of the nearby alleyways.

That was enough to make me back down. I didn't know what force left the world so changed and divided. But I did know I preferred a nice spaghetti Western to the post-apocalyptic ruins on the other side.

"Okay, I'll go," the big man on the cart said. "A hundred bucks."

"Really? Why?" I couldn't help asking. How had seeing what had to be the most horrifying rat ever suddenly changed his mind?

"Look what happened to that little weed," the man said. "Think what will happen to us." His eye lit up in a way that made me afraid.

Despite his bravado, I tried and failed to get any clear idea. People in my line of work aren't known for their imaginations. "What do you think it will do?"

"I'm going to find out. You better get in."

I sputtered a string of incoherent yes and no like sounds. If Amber was in there, and I brought her out to this side, she couldn't help but fall for me. Yet my courage faltered.

"Or not," the driver said. He whipped the horses and they began to trot forward as if it were the most natural place in the world for a horse to go.

Suddenly, I remembered the telegram. Of all the things, it caught my mind and I didn't want to lose it. Funny, since if it had been a phone I would have let it go. But without thinking, I pulled the door and jumped in.

My boots smeared mud across the rough carpet, but I didn't care. I grabbed the yellow card and held it in my hands, trying to get a view past the big man's rump filling the front window. I swear it was bigger than the horses pulling it.

I did manage to see the energy as it took me this time. It wasn't nearly as strong or painful as the first time. My ears still rang and my closed eyes filled with light. I tasted salt and vinegar potato chips dipped in raspberry jam. My fingers tingled, but the effects wore off rapidly.

Suddenly I could see perfectly. The big guy no longer blocked my view. Now, he sat next to me on a massive hog of a motorcycle. The tires were two feet thick and the motor beneath the driver would be big enough for a large truck. The dreadlocks were back, beneath a World War II style metal helmet with a pointy spike on top. He wore black leather all over his huge body with spikes lining the shoulders. Metal plates covered his boots.

I sat in a sidecar, my left arm hid beneath hydraulics and wires. I couldn't really feel it, so I began to wonder if it had been completely replaced by the robotic prosthetic. The ringing in my ears faded, replaced with voices. I could hear people talking and what sounded like a DJ, except he kept asking questions to a panel of annoying pseudo-starlets. Was there some kind of implanted radio in my ear? If so, how could I change the station from this annoying drivel?

I donned leather, too. Mine had metal discs stuck all over it like scales. My boots had turned to paratrooper style combat boots with the same mud still smeared on them. I couldn't see my own helmet until I tipped the sleeve of my jacket and looked at the reflection in one of the shiny plates. It looked like a gray biker helmet with a black dragon painted on the side. That explained the jagged edge coming down in front of my face like teeth. I had to admit, I felt pretty tough in this getup. It didn't hurt to have a Gatling style machine gun mounted in front of me on the sidecar. And anything would be more comfortable than the scratchy clothes of the Wild West.

The clouds on this side of the line looked sickly and polluted. Thankfully, the rain stopped, because on this side of the line, it would probably be acidic. Every trace of sunset vanished. My driver turned on the bobbing headlight, which hung precariously by a few electrical wires.

"I'm Sam," I said as we weaved between broken down cars and hills of rubble. "What's your name?"

"Markus. I think a hundred bucks might be a little light for this trip."

"If you get me and Amber out of here alive, I'll give you a thousand. Or whatever a lot of money is in a gunslinger town." I began wondering if I could just go to my bank and withdraw funds. What was the conversion factor between 2013 and Louis L'Amour? Worse yet, what would it be here, in a futuristic wasteland? Did they even use money on this side of town?

I put the accounting questions out of my head. I had to find Amber.

"Do you know how to find this place?" Markus asked.

The street signs were all broken. By luck, I had once Mapquested Amber's apartment. I'm not a stalker or anything. I just like maps. I said, "I think we turn right at the next intersection."

Something in my lap buzzed. I jumped, despite my tough-guy apparel. I realized it was my phone, with a single LCD readout on top over a few buttons. A pager? How did the anarchistic future include a 1980's style pager? It puzzled me more than the fact I was riding shotgun through a bad Cyberpunk movie, until I remembered crazy was the new fashion.

The same message as the telegram slowly scrolled across the screen.

I stopped reading it when a high window broke on our left and a box fell several stories to crash on the ground. An old computer monitor smashed, shooting missiles of shattered glass in every direction. I scanned the derelict building to see who was up there. The darkness hid everything. That wasn't a good sign.

Markus eased the motorcycle around the corner and hit the brakes, causing us to both lurch forward.

A gang of distorted and grotesque people staggered around a man dressed in a blue ninja outfit and holding a katana in each hand. "Are those monsters?" I wondered aloud.

"Zombies," Markus said.

"Are you sure?"

He looked at me between dangling dreadlocks, and I nodded. "What are zombies doing here?"

"My first guess, trying to eat that nice man."

"What should we do?"

Markus didn't take his spike-knuckled gloves off the handlebars. He just turned his head to look at the massive artillery mounted in front of me.

I laughed a little. My stomach was knotting with nerves. I didn't like the idea of blood splashing everywhere... especially on my face. But I knew if I didn't take this chance, I'd never forgive myself. I grabbed the handles and tested the swivel. "I can't aim much. I might hit the ninja."

A wicked grin curled Markus' lips, which frightened me more than the zombies. He revved the throttle and I gritted my teeth. Even with the beefiest tires I'd ever seen, that massive engine began to spin them into toxic smoke.

I held tight to the handle, accidentally pulling the surprisingly light trigger and sending a barrage of high caliber bullets into the crowd. Before we left, I heard dozens of spent brass shells tinkling off the weed-cracked asphalt.

The tires screeched and we jerked forward so fast I knew I had whiplash. I wanted to close my eyes and cry, but I had no choice. My part was set. The vehicle was moving. I pulled the trigger again and held the machine steady to keep it from swiveling toward the guy in the blue outfit.

Markus bellowed as we charged in. The whole thing was over in seconds. I let go of the trigger as we flew by the ninja. The war-bike bounced over the bodies, and I grabbed the sides of the sidecar to keep from flying out. Naturally, I'd have put on my seatbelt if there was one.

Markus turned hard before we hit a wall and skidded sideways to a stop. My hands held the gun in a death grip and I yelped as the bike tipped to flip the sidecar into the air. After what felt much longer than the heroic charge, gravity finally pulled me down. I didn't let go, holding my breath as the car bounced like a Ping-Pong ball before settling back to the ground.

From this angle, I could see two katana slicing up the zombies standing too close to him for me to shoot. When he finished, the blue figure held his bloody swords to the side and then bowed to us. Then he turned and climbed up the side of the building like Spider-man.

Only then did I realize I hadn't been breathing. I sucked in a few deep breaths.

Beside me, Markus laughed. "That was fun."

My right hand ached from holding the sidecar in a death grip. Had I murdered a dozen people? I mean, they were zombies now. But weren't they just people from before whatever this big change was?

I concentrated on breathing. I couldn't imagine actually killing that many human beings. Yet, with everything feeling so surreal, I didn't feel guilty either. I felt numb.

"Is this your building?" Markus asked, breaking me from my shaking reverie.

I forced my fingers to let go of the sidecar and slowly stood up, pausing for my knees to stop wobbling. "Yes," I said. I wanted to curl up and close my eyes until this whole nightmare ended. Something told me it wouldn't. It didn't feel like a dream. It didn't feel like a video game or a movie. It felt real… deathly real.

I stepped out and took a few hesitant steps toward the broken door of the apartment building. Amber lived on the second floor, just below the tangled mess of broken bricks and jutting pipes. Lucky for us both. I remembered her telling me over drinks how she refused to live on the ground floor because it was dangerous. At the moment, I suspected the penthouse owner had a different opinion about the best level.

I passed through the front door, which hung sideways on a single hinge, and stared down the entry hall. The walls had graffiti tagging any unbroken sections. Piles of detritus cluttered the floor. The elevators were a no go; the rigging at the top destroyed during the transformation. My only option was the stairs. I looked back at Markus and the strange grin decorating his face. He said, "I'm not leaving this bike unguarded on the street."

Where was everybody? The place felt deserted. Then I looked back into the street we'd gunned down. Were those zombies the tenants from Amber's building? Horror gripped me. Was Amber one of them?

I wanted to run over and check, but I knew touching infected Zombie blood was stupid, even for an accountant. I refused to believe she was dead… or that I killed her. I turned from the carnage and took the stairs by twos.

The faintest of lights through a small broken window filtered through the otherwise complete darkness. Only when I was halfway up the stairs did I stop to think it might be a good idea to have a weapon. Too late, I rushed through the door to the second floor and out into the hallway.

It was almost pitch dark, and the sound of scratching vermin echoed from somewhere ahead of me. Even with the talk show droning on in my head, I could hear the faintest sounds. If tumbleweeds were super-rats in this place, what would the real rats be like? The thought paralyzed me for a moment.

I took a few steps, clunking my boots on the now bare concrete floor as I walked. I hoped the vibrations would scare away whatever passed for cockroaches. As I passed the doors, I ran my fingers over the number plates. Third on the left, I found Amber's. I'd never been here, of course. But I looked her address up in the files at work. Really, I'm not a stalker. It just gets boring in accounting.

I knocked softly at first. Then I knocked louder. "Amber?" My voice echoed in the hall of squeaking, invisible vermin. I knocked louder. "Amber, it's Sam."

"Sam? Sam!" It was her! My heart leapt. "I'm here, Sam. How did you find me?" After all this, her voice was like music.

"I got your text message. I came to get you," I called. "Can you unlock the door?"

"It's blocked," she said. "A beam from the ceiling is right behind it. I've been stuck in here ever since the change."

I rammed against the door, not accomplishing anything more than a throbbing shoulder. "I can't get it," I called. "Do you have a lever on that side?"

"I've been trying for half an hour," she said. I could hear tears in her voice. I reached up and pounded the door with my numb hand. *Boom*! "What was that?"

My robotic arm, my thoughts shouted, *I have a robotic arm.*

"Stand back," I said, trying to sound as cool as my jacket.

I balled up my fist, pulled it back, and let it fly at the door. Splinters crashed in every direction as my metal hand smashed a hole clear through. I wound up and let loose again and again. After five or six good hits, I realized I was pulverizing the wood. I grabbed the handle and yanked. The whole doorframe came loose, pulling half of the decrepit wall down with it.

A thick fog of dust overtook the hall, with lances of light from inside Amber's apartment. Coughing, I pulled more of the wall free with my cyber-arm until the beam blocking the door stopped mattering.

Inside, a dying flame flickered in a small candle Amber held close to her as she crouched next to the far wall. "That was amazing!" she cried.

I stood tall and puffed out my chest as she leapt through the hole to wrap her arms around me. See, it's not stalking if they want to hug you like that.

I didn't rush her. I did, however, limit my own hugging to the one arm made of flesh. She let go too soon, and I looked into her big, beautiful chocolate eyes. "Ready to go?"

"Go where?" she said. "Isn't the whole world like this?"

"No," I said, putting extra bravado into my voice. "Just up the road is a nice Western town."

"Thank you for coming to save me," she said. She stared at me, and I hoped she'd kiss me. She didn't. She tipped her head sideways and licked my neck.

I didn't know what to say. It was weird, but there was no way I was letting on that I thought so. Not when I finally had her devoted attention.

She smiled and I saw her teeth were different. She had fangs. "What the…" I couldn't help it. It just slipped out. It's not my fault. It's hard to concentrate with annoying radio people talking in your ear all the time.

"What?"

Maybe she didn't know. Maybe her new condition would change when we crossed the border.

I'd reserve judgment until then.

"Nothing," I said. "Let's go." I took her hand and led her down the stairs, doing my best to impersonate a tough guy. I kept my enhanced arm out front in case I needed a weapon.

When we cleared the door, Markus said, "Better hurry, I think more of those zombies are just around the corner."

"Who's that?" Amber asked.

"My friend, Markus," I said. He nodded approval. I just couldn't think of him as a driver anymore.

I sat in the sidecar. There was no way for two of us to fit, so Amber perched on the seat behind Markus. I tried not to be jealous. After all, somebody with skills had to man the gun.

I gave her my helmet.

"Ready?" Markus asked. He had that glint in his eye. Apparently, killing zombies didn't cause him a bit of guilt either.

"Let's do it," I said. I wrapped my glove and cyber-hand around the gun handles as he revved the engine.

"How do you feel about Victorian dresses?" I asked Amber.

"They're nice," she said.

I nodded to Markus, and he peeled twenty feet of black rubber onto the asphalt.

Want to read more tales from the shattered reality of the Actuator?

Tweet *More Actuator! @JamesWymore @CuriosityQuills #BookLove*

DARK ORB

DARK ORB

BY TONY HEALEY

For those who have met with darkness, and have to live with it.

BRETTON FALLS, 1985

I grew up next door to Mr. Hill—or Bernie as I came to call him—and it wasn't until later that I knew he was a writer. A horror writer, in fact. If you haven't heard of him, that's fine. He never got any major fame or publicity from his work; nobody ever optioned the rights, and he was never lucky enough to sign a six-figure contract with a major publishing house. However, he managed to make a living out of what he did, and ended up a fairly wealthy man… by the standards of this little town, anyway.

Bernie lived alone, and for as long as I could remember, he'd been old. Age to a young kid is a curious thing. To me, his silver hair made him seem ancient.

Ever since Mum and Dad moved in next door to Bernie, he'd lived on his own at number thirty-four.

My Dad worked on an oilrig, sometimes spending weeks at a time away from home, and being the only child, I spent a lot of time on my own. When I got to know Bernie, I learned that he was very much the same, that we both harbored an inner loneliness.

I'd never really spoken to him until that summer afternoon he'd spotted me reading a dog-eared copy of *The Hobbit* in the back garden after school.

He was in his own garden, sitting at a patio table smoking. I knew he was there, but as usual, he sat in silence with his hands on the tabletop, relaxed and deep in thought. Our fence reached his shoulder and as he stood, he spotted me sitting on the lawn reading.

"Watchya," he said, approaching the fence. With the cigarette hanging from one side of his mouth, like *The Man With No Name*, his familiar greeting came-out slightly muffled.

"Mr. Hill," I said, jumping a little. It had been so quiet, the sudden presence of his voice surprised me. Bernie was a tall, slender man with a slight paunch in front. His hair was pure white and never anything but swept back over his head. He wore thick glasses that made his dark blue eyes seem impossibly large. The very beginnings of cataracts had started up at the corners of his eyes, like a pale rust creeping in at the edges.

He held up his hands. "Just Bernie will do," he said.

"Okay."

"What you got there then?" He nodded at my book. I held it up for him to see. His big eyes focused in on the cover from behind those impossibly thick lenses.

"Ah! *The Hobbit*. How you finding it?" he asked.

I looked at the book in my hand. "It's good. I only started it this morning, but so far I like it."

Bernie held the cigarette against his lips and took a long draw from it. The smell was strong and acrid, and though I found it unpleasant, I eventually got used to that smell. I wouldn't go so far as to say I grew fond of it, but whenever I smell cigarette smoke, I'm reminded of him in some small way.

"J.R.R. Tolkien…" he said ponderously, looking up into the sky and blowing smoke through his nostrils as he talked, "the Grandmaster."

I wasn't sure what he meant by that, but I nodded my head politely.

"The Grandmaster of Fantasy, I mean," he said, seeing that I didn't get the reference.

"Oh."

"I read it every year," Bernie added.

"Really?"

He nodded.

"And the *Lord of the Rings* of course, but *The Hobbit* is my favorite. It's a little less… heavy, I suppose. To me it's like visiting in on an old friend."

He stood with his arms drooping over the fence, regarding me with those magnified blue eyes, his cigarette now resting between the fingers of his right hand, its blue smoke drifting lazily up into the sunshine.

"Not long until you're off for the summer now, eh?" he asked, obviously noting the fact that I was still wearing my uniform.

"School gets out next week," I said.

I liked school. Unlike most of the other kids, I didn't mind sitting in a classroom and learning. I suppose it's no real surprise that many years later, I'd study my way to becoming a history teacher.

"I never got on with school life myself. I was always getting a cane to the backside for playing truant. Used to go up to the old, deserted mill and mess about," Bernie said.

"Doing what?" I asked him, sitting up and paying attention.

"Well, uh, you know... being a bugger. Smoking cigs, breaking windows. Not the sort of thing you're into, I'd imagine," he said.

I laughed. "No, not really," I said.

Bernie grinned at me and it was surprising to imagine him as a little boy, throwing stones at the windows of the cement works, a cheap cigarette hanging from his mouth as he cackled with enjoyment. He'd always been the polite old man next door, keeping to himself. He wasn't one to talk at any real length. In fact, it was out of sorts, really, for him to strike up a conversation at all. But I'd realize later that seeing me sitting there, on the grass, absorbed in Middle Earth, had signaled to him a kindred spirit.

And he had another reason for acting out of sorts. The same reason he sat outside, lost in his own thoughts. But that came later.

His gaze grew distant. "Strange place, that old mill..." he said quietly.

The seconds stretched out. I think he grew conscious of me watching him, because all of a sudden he was back in the here and now. Back from wherever he had drifted.

"Anyway, got plans for the summer?" he asked me, nodding in the direction of the house, "Mum and Dad taking you out?"

I shrugged. "No, Dad's working away more and more now, so that probably won't happen," I said through gritted teeth. Dad was always working. He was always away. And when he came home, he rarely had time to talk to me or understand my interests. In fact, he didn't understand my interests at all because he didn't think I had any. He didn't notice the models of World War II planes hanging from my ceiling, or the battleships always drying on my windowsill. He didn't take an interest in what I read or in trying to find some common ground. He didn't care that I got up early on a Sunday morning, especially to catch the Star Trek reruns.

I had interests, but they didn't hold true to his ideals of what a boy my age should be doing. To him, I should've been out playing football, or doing what Bernie had done as a kid, smashing windows and sucking away on cigarettes. The fact that I wasn't into any of that was hard for him to come to grips with. And he didn't spare much of his time between work commitments trying to, either.

"He's a hard worker, your old man," Bernie remarked.

I shrugged again, this time silent.

He puffed away on his smoke, looking up at the sky. "Well, looks like the weather's gonna stick around."

He moved away from the fence and smiled at me. "You enjoy that book, boy," he said and made a point of tapping his temple with his finger, "it stays with you."

The next week, I finished *The Hobbit*, a day after school ended for the summer. Once more, I was in the garden, this time with some new Warhammer figures spread out on the patio. The back end of the house gave some shade but allowed enough light for painting. I could hear my Mum banging about in the kitchen. The smell of a chicken roasting in the oven wafted outside. Again, my Dad was away. When it was just the two of us, she'd sometimes cook a chicken and make it last two days. Dad made good money, but regardless, Mum was pennywise and would save where she could. Despite the gulf of misunderstanding and mystery that existed between my Dad and me, he still made sure that I was given my pocket money every week, even if he was away. I sat painting my figures, careful to be precise in the detail, whilst absently listening to her humming along to The Bangles on the radio.

I heard a noise from Bernie's back garden and looked up to see the top of his head pass by. I put my paintbrush down on the edge of the patio slabbing where it met the grass, got up, and walked over to the fence. I found I was just tall enough to see over the top. There was a clay flower pot nearby that had so far only been a slug trap, so I toppled it over and stepped up.

"Hello, Bernie," I said.

Now I was the one acting weird, striking up conversations out of the blue. Bernie stood with his hands behind his back, a cigarette in the corner of his mouth. He looked up as I leaned over the top of the fence.

"Oh hello," he said, stuffing his hands into his trouser pockets. I looked around at his garden; it was tidy and minimalistic. There was no paving of any kind, no flowers or plants, just lawn. An old, iron table and chairs were positioned on the grass. Naturally, there was an ashtray sitting on the table containing the remnants of previously diminished cigarettes. The thin, tapering branches of a neighbor's willow tree hung like bony fingers over the fencing at the end of his garden. Bernie hadn't trimmed the tree back, though it was his right to do so. Perhaps he wanted to see how it would continue its tedious conquest of his personal space. He had a little old shed at the end, too. Although I could only guess at what he kept in there. Surely not gardening equipment. A small lawnmower, perhaps, for the grass?

"I finished *The Hobbit*," I said.

"Oh yeah?" he said, his eyebrows lifting. He seemed to be lifting from a fog, almost. He'd been walking back and forth, thinking. Now the last tendrils of what had consumed his mind seemed to clear away.

"Yeah, I loved it," I said, "especially the battle with the dragon at the end."

He chuckled. "I always remember Bilbo escaping in the barrel," he said, looking away as if he could picture it in his mind, a resurgent memory of something that had actually happened to him long ago.

"I liked that bit," I said.

A plane passed overhead, the drone of its engine cutting through the dense blue afternoon and we both looked up. Bernie snapped to suddenly, pointing at me and then heading for his back door.

"I've got something for you," he said, then disappeared inside for a moment before returning with a paperback in his hand. He handed it to me.

"Thought you might enjoy this," he said.

I turned it over, looking at the cover. It read *Dark Orb* at the top. There was a picture of a young boy at the center of the cover, and below that at the very bottom, the author, **B. HILL.**

"It's a Horror, something a little different to what you've been reading lately, mind you," Bernie said to me, "I wrote it."

"Thanks, Bernie," I said, turning the book over in my hand once more to the back cover and read the blurb. "I didn't know you were a writer."

Bernie took a draw of his cigarette, his eyes lighting up for a second. "I used to be," he said, "Until I ran out of ideas."

"Ah," I said, not sure how to respond to that.

I heard movement behind me and turned in time to see my Mum appear at our back door. She dried her wet hands on the bottom of her apron and tucked an errant lock of hair behind her ear.

"George? What are you up to? You're not bothering Mr. Hill, are you?" she asked me, pulling a disapproving face at me standing on one of her plant pots. She looked in Bernie's direction and nodded with a smile. "Hello Mr. Hill," she said.

Bernie smiled at her. "Afternoon."

"Now come away from there and stop pestering Mr. Hill, for chrissakes," she waved her hand at me. I stepped down and then turned the flower pot the right way up.

"He's no bother," Bernie assured my Mum.

I showed her the book Bernie had loaned me. She looked at it with feign interest. She was never a big reader, my Mum. Not unless you counted the Sunday papers. "Oh that's nice, dear," she said, flippantly. She looked down at the Warhammer figurines spread over the patio. "Don't leave that lot there for me to trip over later, like last time," she said, smiling back at Bernie one more time before disappearing inside.

I watched her go and then went back to the fence. I couldn't see over it, but Bernie could still hear my voice. "Thanks, Bernie. I'll start it tonight." I promised.

"Okay, boy."

I heard a sigh and the ruffle of his trouser material as he sat down at the table and dug into his pocket for his Camels. The *click-click-click* of his lighter. I smelled the cigarette straight away. Stepping away from the fence, I left him once again with his thoughts.

Later that night, I lay in my bed and started to read *Dark Orb*. The copyright page noted that it was written in 1969. The tattered cover and yellowed pages had that musty smell generally reserved for old libraries and used bookstores.

It started with a group of mysterious incidents all over Bretton Falls in the summer of 1956: an old woman attacked by a flying creature whilst hanging out her washing, a young couple chased through the woods by a large winged creature with burning red eyes… that sort of thing. The main character, a reporter, investigated the incidents.

As I read, I could hear Mr. Hill's voice narrating the text in my head. It was a pretty scary book, too. Especially when Nathan Richter, a bird watcher, got attacked near the old Mill:

Nathan ran as fast as he was able. His heart hammered in his chest, threatened to jump straight out. Turning as he ran, he saw it descending down upon him like a vampire with its black wings spread and red eyes burning.

He tripped—on a tree root, or a stone—and fell flat on his face. The creature landed with a thump behind him. He pushed himself up and turned to face it.

Whatever it really was, it was at least five feet tall; a giant, black moth with clawed feet. The eyes were bright red. Unnaturally lit from within. He shook with terror and yet he couldn't turn away from it. He couldn't stop staring into those crimson flints, couldn't turn away. Then it spoke to him...

As I read, I wondered why this section of the book in particular seemed so realistic. I could see him running, see him tumbling forward onto the ground, his heart playing tin drum in his chest. The hairs sprang to life at the back of my neck.

I set the book on my bedside cabinet, turned over in the bed and pulled the covers under my chin, suddenly conscious of the darkness outside, the whisper of the wind over the roof. I thought of what Bernie said about hanging out by the old Mill as a kid. He'd definitely written the scene as if he'd been there in person. Working backwards, he had to be in his late fifties to early sixties right now. The book was published 1969, and the events within took place in 1956, when Bernie would have been in his twenties. I cast my mind back a few months to when I'd spotted him in his garden. He was scanning the distant tree line with a pair of silver binoculars. I wondered then if he had been bird watching.

Was *he* Nathan Richter? Had he been on the lookout for the same creature that had attacked him thirty years before?

That weekend I decided to take the finished book back to Bernie and tell him what I thought about it. A rainstorm hit the town, so there would be no garden rendezvous for Bernie and me that weekend. Dad wouldn't be home until the following week, and I waited for Mum to fall asleep on the sofa before throwing on my raincoat and running down our front garden path and then around the corner into Bernie's. A summer rain fell, warm and slow. I had *Dark Orb* tucked under my arm, out of the wet, as I rang the doorbell and waited patiently for him to answer. I'd never actually called on him before, for anything, ever, so I felt a little strange doing so now. It took a few moments for him to open his front door.

As much as it was out of the ordinary for me to visit, it was similarly so for Bernie to actually have any callers at his home at all. However, it only took a second for him to see that it was raining hard, and that I was soaked. He immediately stepped aside and ushered me in.

"Quick, quick, quick," he said.

His house had the same outlay as our own, and after checking if it would be all right, I took off my coat and hung it over the banister to dry. Bernie led me to the living room. "Have a seat."

"Thanks."

He had an old sofa and an armchair that were worn-in, but comfortable. He had a clean home, but old-fashioned. As Mum might have said, it was the home of a man. On one side of the living room, there were only shelves, floor to ceiling, filled with books of all shapes and sizes. At the end of the room, facing the sofa and chair, sat a decrepit TV on a stand.

Where we had our dining table set under the front window, Bernie had an old desk and a swivel office chair. On the desk, I saw all sorts of papers and a heavy, old typewriter. A spider plant hung in one corner, its creepers trailing to the floor. The place smelled strongly of cooking and old cigarette smoke.

Bernie looked thrown off kilter by having someone in the house. I wondered if anyone had ever been in there.

"Do you want something to drink?" he asked me. He was patting his pockets, obviously trying to find his cigarettes. I spotted a packet of them on the empty sofa seat next to me and handed them to him.

"Cheers," he said, knocking one of the slim little Camels from the pack and lighting it with a sigh.

"Are you okay, Mr. Hill?"

He shot me a look as he took another hasty draw from his cigarette. "Yeah, fine. I don't usually have visitors in here is all."

I made to stand up. "Would you like me to go? I could come back another time…"

"Don't be silly!" he waved at me to stay where I was, "and don't be so formal. It's Bernie."

I remembered the book under my armpit, and laid it down next to me on the sofa.

"Do you want a drink?" Bernie asked.

"Please."

"What do you want?"

"Well… what have you got?"

He considered for a second. "Coffee. Want one?"

I nodded slowly. I'd never tried the stuff before, but evidently there wasn't anything else on offer. "Yes, please."

Bernie walked into the kitchen, and I heard him fill the kettle. A minute later, it popped and rattled as it started to boil. A humid breeze rushed through the living room, like the breath of some Amazonian jungle. Mixed with the years-old smoke, it made it slightly difficult to catch a breath.

Bernie returned carrying two mugs. "Milk and sugar in there for you. No boy your age drinks anything without sugar."

"Thanks," I said.

Bernie sat in the armchair. He looked at ease now, sipping his coffee in between cigarette drags.

"Raining cats and dogs out there," he observed.

I agreed. I showed him the copy of *Dark Orb* sitting next to me.

"I finished the book."

"You don't have to give it back. It's a gift, if you want it."

I thanked him and put the tome back down.

"So what did you think?"

I took a moment to fully consider what I was about to say.

"Well, it was really good. Some of it had me really freaked out. Like the way the creature—"

"Mothman," Bernie interjected.

"Yeah. That. The way you describe it chasing them and giving them visions of their own deaths. It was really frightening stuff. You said in the note at the back that it was based on real incidents?"

Bernie cleared his throat. "Yes. A few years before I wrote it, there were some odd incidents in Point Pleasant, West Virginia. A creature the locals ended up calling the Mothman. Those incidents sort of formed the backbone of some of the scenes in the book."

"So you copied them?"

"Sort of. I adapted them a bit to fit the story I was writing."

I licked my lips. My eyes locked with his. "You said *some* of the scenes…"

Bernie sighed. "Yes. You see, in Point Pleasant, the sightings were a prelude to a local disaster. Several townsfolk received warnings from the

Mothman, and eventually, they turned out to be true. But that's not what happened here."

I tried to read his face to see if he was pulling my leg. He looked horribly sincere.

"The Mothman came *here?*"

He nodded slowly, then looked off to one side, drawing on the cigarette, then exhaling slowly through his nose, like some dragon with something smoldering within.

"I can't remember the names I gave them in the book, but a fisherman who used to work out of the harbor called Jed Dawson had an encounter. And there was a desk clerk in town called Sally something—she had an encounter, too. On each sighting, the creature gave them a vision."

I remembered it all from the book. "A vision of their own deaths."

Bernie nodded.

"And what about Nathan Richter?"

"I think you already know to the answer to that." A smile crept into the corner of his mouth.

"You. He's you."

We sat in silence for a time, savoring our coffees as we listened to the rain outside, neither of us entirely sure how to carry on. The coffee was warm and sweet and made me feel alert. I've drank it since.

"It's true," Bernie broke the impasse. "It told me about my own death."

I set down my mug and leaned forward. "What did it say?"

Bernie took a deep breath. "It told Jed that he would be struck by lightning one afternoon as he walked along the harbor. It told poor Sally that she would get hit by a bus when she wasn't looking. Both premonitions came true."

He got up and walked to stand next to me. He looked out the window. His glasses reflected the torrential rain outside. "You already know what it told me."

I picked the book up, flipped back to the scene where Nathan Richter was chased near the Mill.

It had no voice—at least, not in any way that you would consider it to have one. The words formed themselves in his mind, like a rune scratched into stone. His head hurt to bear it.

Later, he would think about the way it had seemed to burn when it rested inside his brain. It was like using a muscle he'd never used before, a dormant spot within his head that had been fired up for the first time.

50

"Nineteen Eighty-Five," it said.

He sank into those red eyes, enveloped in their pulsing, dead heat. Two, small red hearts beating and beating.

"Eighty-Five. The belly is full."

He frowned, trying to comprehend what was being told to him. That is, until the next word entered his head. Then all was made perfectly clear.

"Cancer. The belly is full. Cancer."

When he woke hours later, night had fallen over the woods, and he was damp. He sat up, shaking his head to clear it. The words were still etched there, still smoldered away. Years later, he would never be fully rid of the way they had tattooed themselves directly into his brain. They would fade in time, but never completely dissolve.

"Eighty-Five. The belly is full. Cancer."

Bernie rubbed his cardigan where it stretched over the paunch of his stomach. "I was diagnosed last month. So I guess that thing was right."

That evening I broke down at the dinner table. It took a bit of coaxing, but my Mum eventually got it out of me. I told her about what Bernie had told me, that he was dying from stomach cancer.

She went next door to talk to him and didn't return for over an hour. I was in my room when she appeared in the doorway.

"Mr. Hill wants to know if you'll go and see him tomorrow."

I nodded.

"You know, he's always been a lonely man. Always kept to himself. But I think now he'd welcome some company."

"I will. I like Bernie."

"And I didn't know he was a writer, either," Mum said.

"I know."

"How was that book he gave you anyway? Any good?"

I thought of *Dark Orb*, and the Mothman, and all the deaths it foretold. I shuddered. "Very."

I got to spend a lot of time with Bernie after that. My Mum encouraged it, I think. He told me about his writing career, how he had made a living out of it. I read some more of the books he'd had published. They were good. Very good, in fact. But I noticed one thing.

Dark Orb had been the last book of his put into print. I asked him why.

"I dried up for a while. I tried," he said. "I tried really hard to write another. But my heart wasn't in it. I became depressed."

Over a period of years, he left his house less and less, living solely off the royalties of his books.

"Did you ever marry?" I asked him one day.

"I nearly did once," was all he would say.

I didn't ask him about the cancer, tried not to bring it up. And Bernie never breached the subject either. I did ask him one day if his stomach hurt.

"Sometimes," he said. "But I ignore it."

I picked my way around it carefully, not sure how much to press on with it. "Do you have medicines? You know, from the doctor?"

Bernie looked away then. "I refused to have it."

My Dad came home, on a break from the rig, and I talked with him about Bernie and what he was going through. We sat up at the kitchen table after dinner, whilst Mum was in the bath. He peeled an apple with his penknife, cut a wedge out of it, and handed it to me.

"So how's he getting on?" he asked me.

"I think he's in pain. But he doesn't say. He talks to Mum, I think. Maybe he says more to her."

Dad cut another wedge and ate it straight from the blade.

"Your Mum said something about it. The doctor told him he didn't have long to live," he eyed me warily. I got the feeling this wasn't some off-the-cuff kind of thing. Mum and he had probably spoken about it already, and she'd left for him to break the news.

I took it well. I felt like crying there and then, but this was in front of my Dad. I wanted to appear strong. "How long has he got?"

"Not long."

I looked down at the surface of the table, suddenly very aware of the grain in the wood, the circles from cups of hot tea, the marks left by knives and forks.

My Dad reached across and laid a hand on my shoulder.

"Son, everyone dies. Some sooner than others. I know it's sad what's happening to Bernie, but there's only one thing you can do."

I looked up. My eyes might've misted over, but I couldn't help it. I couldn't fight the tears back any more.

"What's that?"

Dad smiled. "Be his friend. By the looks of it, he's not got many lining up at his door."

Later that night, as I lay in bed, I heard him say, "I don't want him getting too attached" and, "Yes, I know he's just a harmless old geezer." Then Mum went, "We can't shield him from these things. He's his only friend."

Dad sighed. I imagine he hooked his arm around her then, kissed her on the forehead.

"I know, love. It's just he's our little boy. It's strange seeing him grow up so fast."

I didn't listen to any more after that. I turned over, pulled the covers up high around my head and drifted off to sleep. I dreamed of Bernie in his house, smoking. And then, like the smoke fading away from the end of his Camel, so too did he.

I saw Bernie nearly every day, when possible. But one day when Mum drove him to the hospital for a checkup, I rode into town on my bike. I went to the library to see if they had anything relating to the Mothman. The old lady at the front desk wasn't much help. She just pointed me in the direction of the stacks at the back where the supernatural section was. It consisted of only a few books. I took them all and sat down at a table.

I found only one mention of the Mothman, and it was from the same incident Bernie had told me about before. There was a small chapter on it, titled, *Mothman: More Fact than Fiction?* and it read:

On Nov. 15, 1966, two young couples from Point Pleasant, Roger and Linda Scarberry, and Steve and Mary Mallette told police they saw a large, white creature whose eyes "glowed red" when the car headlights picked it up. They described it as a "flying man with ten foot wings" following their car while they were driving in an area of town known as "the TNT area," the site of a former World War II munitions plant.

During the next few days, other people reported similar sightings. Two volunteer firefighters who sighted it said it was a "large bird with red eyes." Mason County Sheriff George Johnson commented that he believed the sightings were due to an unusually large heron he termed a "shitepoke." Contractor Newell Partridge told Johnson that when he aimed a flashlight at a creature in a nearby field, its eyes glowed "like bicycle reflectors," and blamed buzzing noises from his television set and the disappearance of his German Shepherd dog on the creature. Wildlife biologist Dr. Robert L. Smith at West Virginia University told reporters descriptions and sightings all fit the Sandhill Crane, a large American crane almost as high as a man with a seven-foot wingspan, featuring circles of reddish coloring around the eyes, and that the bird may have wandered out of its migration route.

There were no Mothman reports in the immediate aftermath of the December 15, 1967 collapse of the Silver Bridge and the death of 46 people, giving rise to legends that the Mothman sightings and the bridge collapse were connected.

I thought about how one of the sightings had taken place around an Industrial site, just as Bernie has had at the old Mill. The chapter said that there were a few sightings years afterward, but none to compare with those experienced in Point Pleasant. However, it did name check Bretton Falls toward the end:

… and several in 1969 in the Town of Bretton Falls, who reported sightings of a creature similar to that of the Point Pleasant Mothman. As with other similar sightings, it has been suggested that what happened in Point Pleasant may not have been the behavior of a single creature, and that it may in fact have been one of several such cryptids residing throughout the United States…

After the library, I rode out to the woods. I'd ridden past the old Mill before, but that time, I was very aware of the closeness of the trees around the ancient structure and the stickiness in the air. There was a well-worn path running the length of the Mill, and I rode slowly looking for any sign of habitation from within. The windows were all smashed, and ivy grew from the cracks of the building, spreading up on to what was left of the roof. A shiver ran its way up my spine to the back of my neck, where the hairs stood on end. I expected something to happen, and the amount of adrenaline coursing through my body felt like some massive electric field.

Something fluttered overhead on heavy wings, and I glanced up sharply, sure that I would see the Mothman that had chased Nathan Richter/Bernie all those years ago. But it was only a woodpigeon.

The next day I told Bernie that I'd gone riding past the old Mill.

"Why did you do that?"

I shrugged. "I don't know. To see the Mothman. I don't know."

Bernie lit one of his Camels. He looked uncomfortable. I thought of the cancer growing inside his stomach. I didn't fully understand it, but I was mature for my age and I got the gist of what was happening to him.

"You won't see it."

54

"Why not?" I asked him, frowning.

He sat down heavily in his armchair, with a grunt. "Because I think that they move about. They don't stay in one place."

I didn't ask him why he said *they*. It was obvious to me that he believed there were several of them all over the country. "Where do they come from?"

Bernie considered for a moment. "I don't think they come from anywhere. I think they've always been here. There are so many things on this planet we cannot explain. Think about the Yeti, or the Loch Ness Monster. We can explain them away as to how they might exist in the modern world, but not why so many people have seen them and yet there is still a lack of hard evidence. Look at the Jersey Devil. Squid at the very heart of the ocean so big, they hunt whales exclusively. There's much to this world that we don't understand. The Mothman is just another such mystery."

I thought about that. "Did they exist in the time of the dinosaurs?"

"Maybe."

I swallowed.

"So how did you get on at the hospital today?" I asked.

Bernie tapped his ash into the palm of his hand.

"Not good," he said and then, with a smile, "Just the prophecy fulfilling itself."

"Did you talk to Bernie today?" Dad asked me. He was due to travel north again the following day. We didn't have the closest relationship going, it was true, but I still missed him when he left for work again.

"Yeah, he said that he didn't get good news."

"Well that's probably a given," he awkwardly ruffled my hair. "Your Mother drove him to the appointment. She said he was in good spirits, but she could see the pain on his face."

I didn't say anything. All of a sudden, I didn't want to be sitting up with him watching the TV. I wanted to be in bed, switching off from it all.

"You've got to prepare yourself, George," he said.

I nodded. Soon after, I did go to bed. But I didn't sleep.

Two days later, Bernie collapsed at home. I found him. I had been knocking at the door and no answer. I peered through the window and saw him lying on the floor. I fetched my Mum, and she told me to stay in the house and call the ambulance while she ran around and tried to get to him.

Later, at the hospital, the doctor told my Mum that Bernie probably didn't have long left.

When told, I asked to see him. She drove me there and waited in the hall as I entered Bernie's room.

"Watchya boy!" he smiled behind the breathing apparatus strapped over his face.

"Hello," I said feebly.

Bernie patted the edge of his bed. I sat down on it. "I'm glad you came." His voice sounded muffled. "I wanted to see you before it was too late."

My hands were in my lap. I fidgeted with them nervously. The heart monitor beeped slow and steady beside his bed. An intravenous drip ran from a stand into his arm. I could see the way his arms were bruised, the skin worn thin like the leather of an old sofa. He looked pale, gaunt. Not himself. There was no scent of Camel smoke about him, only the dry, clean antiseptic of the ward.

I realized then that this might really be the last time I ever saw him. My little heart felt heavy in my chest, almost too heavy to belong anymore. "I wanted to see you too."

"I need to ask you something," he gripped my wrist. "I want you to do something for me."

I waited.

"Take care of my books. Look after them. Don't let them end up in a charity shop. Enjoy them."

I promised him that I would.

"I've enjoyed our time together, George," he said. "I'll miss you."

I don't quite know why, it was completely out of sort for me, but I dove forward and hugged him. He wrapped his arms around me, patting my back. I was sobbing, and he was, too.

"Don't go," I said between the tears. "Don't go."

The next day, Bernie fell asleep and didn't wake up. Mum crept into my room that night and woke me to tell me. As I started to cry, she laid in the bed next to me, cradling me in her arms as she had done when I was younger. "I'm sorry George," she whispered in my ear.

The evening after the funeral, I went up to my room and opened up *Dark Orb* once more. It was the last time I read the book, although I still have it. As it turns out, Bernie made a will in the short time that I got to know him. He stipulated that I should inherit all of his books, and all rights to his work. There have been a few reprints of his stuff since then, but I've never pushed it. Perhaps I should one day.

I didn't know him as much as I would have liked. But still, he was my friend. I think about him most days, especially now that I'm older. That summer I experienced death. But I also learned to live life fully, to make the most of it. Bernie languished for too long in that house. He didn't *live* his life the way he should have. I honestly don't know how he stood such knowledge. But as a writer, perhaps he was used to having an ending in mind, even if it was his own.

I set *Dark Orb* up against the pillow, and laid on my stomach on the bed. I turned to the very last page:

There are a great many things in this dark orb of ours that we do not understand, and perhaps it's best they stay that way. They are the secrets of this world, buried by time. Occasionally, man is unfortunate enough to unearth them, like so many runes in the cold, dark ground.

And then the Myth is awakened, free to roam.

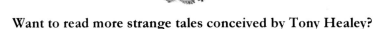

Want to read more strange tales conceived by Tony Healey?

Tweet *I want more! @FringeScientist @CuriosityQuills #BookLove*

EPHEMERA

EPHEMERA

BY GERILYN MARIN

What!" Lilah Reed shrieked, widened pale-gray eyes blinking rapidly.

Giselle Boudreaux shrugged lightly as she set down her coffee mug and picked up a cigarette, oddly reluctant to meet her best friend's gaze as she did *it* again. She gave another shrug—just as she'd done the first time she uttered the words—as if they should be easy to take.

"I *may* have seen a dead girl in your bathroom."

"Will," Lilah demanded, tugging on her fiancé's sleeve, "we're moving!"

Heaving an exasperated sigh, Will Benet set down his own mug to frown at Giselle. "Just had to tell her, huh?"

Mirroring his expression, she took a long drag of her cigarette before replying. "You said that even if I did, you'd brush it off as me watching too many 'ghost-shows' again."

"Not like that's hard to believe," he reasoned as he snatched a cigarette from her open pack on the patio table. "You watch that nonsense more than normal people watch the news."

Normal people. Right. As though being unapologetically Goth was really so unusual these days.

Giselle merely rolled her eyes, a gesture that felt decidedly un-dramatic without their usual rings of Kohl pencil lining them. "You say nonsense, I say research."

With the rising popularity of haunting-related reality shows, she'd found she could profit from her natural instincts about the paranormal by offering what she called *spiritual assessments* to a newly curious generation of homebuyers. She toured the home and relayed to her clients any *feelings* she picked up. Mind bogglingly simple, really.

Perhaps her method didn't seem the most reliable, but not everyone was comfortable with an entire team of investigators pulling up to their property in an attention-grabbing, equipment-laden van.

She'd found it odd, at first, that some were thrilled at the idea of owning a haunted house; apparently having a ghost was some new fad. Like rich people with concierge doctors.

"Wait," Lilah pouted angrily, as though catching up to a conversation that was over her head. "Will, you knew about this?"

Lighting his cigarette, he took a long, pained drag. "I ran into her when she was coming out of the bathroom and she had *that* look on her face, so—stupid me—I asked and she told me."

"Well, why the hell didn't you guys tell *me*?"

Giselle laughed as she picked up her coffee mug for another sip. "'Cause we knew you'd freak out like this."

Will only nodded, giving a small, tired smile.

"We are *so* looking for a new place, right—"

"Oh, just *stop,*" Giselle interrupted, trying not to let her amusement at Lilah's mini-tantrum show. "She wasn't scary or anything."

"Says *you*—totally not fair since this shit never scares you."

Frowning sleepily, Giselle only shrugged again. She never did fear the supernatural. Though she was hardly fear*less*—an inch-wide spider could send her running for the hills, screaming at the top of her lungs. But, well, ghosts? She seemed simply incapable of fearing them, as though her curiosity shut out any other emotions.

"Not the point. Seriously, she wasn't. She was just sort of *there*."

Lilah sat back, furrowing her brow. "Just, like, standing around?"

"She was…"

"She was?" Lilah prompted.

"Kinda hanging from that pipe that runs over the shower curtain rod."

"Oh my God!"

"Dammit, Giselle," Will hissed, taking an exaggerated drag of his death stick.

She blinked. "Hey, she wanted to know."

"Okay, okay. What do we do?" Lilah forced a deep breath, fanning her hands around her face.

Lilah loved the supernatural, thrilled at the notion of unexplainable phenomena in the world. But then, that was reserved for supernatural things that *weren't* happening in her house. For all her curiosity and adoration, she had the spiritual sensitivity of a tree stump.

Rolling her eyes, Giselle took a final drag of her own ciggy before stubbing it out in the silver ashtray. "Fine, let's go into the bathroom. We'll see if we can't figure out what she wants."

Lilah bounced out of her chair, scurrying her little body across the sunbaked patio, only to stumble to a halt beside the sliding glass doors. No way was she setting foot in that bathroom alone... her poor heart... yadda, yadda, yadda.

Yawning, Giselle picked up her cell phone from where she'd thoughtlessly dropped it on the table not fifteen minute ago. 11 a.m.—on a *Saturday*! If Lilah hadn't snuck downstairs and lured her out of her black lace-curtained four-post bed with the promise of French vanilla coffee and cinnamon Danishes, Giselle would still be snoozing for another two hours, at least. She should have known renting the studio apartment below them would be trouble.

She slipped her phone into the pocket of her black button-down pajama shirt. As she stood up from the table, she found Will glaring at her with a soured expression.

"What?"

"You didn't have to tell her." He shook his head as he followed.

Yes, and he'd rather go the *ignore it and hope it goes away* path. Predictable. Again!

She tipped her head to one side, giving a half-nod. "Actually, I kinda did."

"Why?"

"Because we've been living here quietly for nearly two months and haven't experienced anything else. So, whoever this girl is, she was waiting for something."

That gave Will reason to thoughtfully purse his lips. "Like what?"

"Probably to see if any of us would be able to pick up on her signals. Which means this is intelligent, not residual."

Will said nothing, but the lift of his eyebrows spoke volumes. She might as well be speaking Greek.

61

Giselle held in a sigh. "This isn't some sort of random time-echo, like when a cupboard bangs open at the exact same time every night, or that sort of thing. She could be trying to communicate."

"By showing you her corpse? What the hell could that tell you?"

"About to find out, I hope," she said quietly as she stepped into the first floor bathroom beside Lilah.

Closing her eyes, Giselle played out the scene in her head. Looking in the mirror, splashing cold water on her face because the AC had been acting up, the sense she suddenly wasn't alone crept along her spine…

That was when she'd glanced in the mirror and seen *her* there. Lifeless; short, scruffy hair falling into her face, but not shielding the disconcerting way her eyes upturned, pinning Giselle as though she'd been there the day it happened.

As chilling as the image should have seemed, it simply wasn't. Perhaps if the specter glared accusingly, but she hadn't. *No…* Giselle recalled as she opened her eyes. That gaze hadn't been angry, it had been *pleading*.

She needed to recreate the image. Tucking a wave of caramel-colored hair behind her ear, Giselle turned slowly to stare at the bathtub. She knew what she was about to say was not going to go over well, but it had to be done.

"Okay, Li… get up on the rim of the tub."

Will slapped a hand over the side of his face as Lilah squeaked incoherently.

"Stop being so dramatic," Giselle snapped—words that would, under other circumstances, be quite amusing coming from *her*. "You're not gonna fall down dead just 'cause you stand in the same spot. You want her out of your house, then I need a phys-rep to remember more clearly. Now get your skinny ass up there!"

Groaning loudly, Lilah hung her head while she climbed, barefoot, onto the chilled porcelain.

Giselle nodded and spun back toward the mirror. "Okay, stand on your toes, good, good. Now," she tried to latch onto the memory, to see the ghost overlap Lilah's reflection. "Raise your right arm."

Again, despite her miserable expression, Lilah followed instruction, raising a hand.

"Higher… no, lower, low—there!"

"Maybe she's pointing at something," Will suggested from the hallway.

Nodding, Giselle stepped in front of Lilah, following her friend's outstretched fingers with her gaze. Brow furrowing, she dropped to her hands and knees to peer under the enormous, old-fashioned radiator. And sure enough, she saw something, or, at least, thought she did; not beneath the radiator, but in a small crack in the floor, where the wall and the radiator met.

"Will, flashlight," she ordered, her face still pressed to the floor, determined not to take her eyes off the tiny glinting, but she'd be damned if she was gonna reach blindly into what might be a spider's nest.

Without a word, he turned away, his heavy footsteps sounding through the hall. "Um," Lilah forced a nervous giggle. "Can I get down now?"

Giselle snorted a laugh. "Yeah, 'fraidy cat.'"

Lilah impatiently tossed her mahogany hair over her shoulder as she stepped on the tile floor. "Am not, this is just weird."

"Welcome to my world, love," Giselle said with a grin as Will returned, pushing a mini Mag-lite into her hand.

After determining the crevice to be arachnid-free, she set the flashlight on the floor and then slid her fingers beneath the radiator, dipping them into the recess. "Gotcha," Giselle breathed the word triumphantly as she brought her hand back, pinching an elaborately detailed gold ring between thumb and forefinger.

"Oh my God, that is *gorgeous!*" Lilah shrilled, dropping to her knees beside Giselle to get a better look. "But what do we do now?"

Giselle sat back on her heels, setting the ring in the palm of her other hand. "She was dressed *very* modern, and she looked like she was in her late teens, so…" She gave a reluctant shake of her head. "You got any contact info for the people who owned this place last?"

As soon as those words fell from her lips, Giselle knew from the expressions on her friends' faces that *she* was probably going to be the one returning this sad, little treasure to one very unfortunate parent. She forced a gulp down her throat.

Ghosts? No problem. Speaking to new people under tense and awkward circumstances? Now *that* terrified her.

All she wanted was to crawl back in bed and sleep 'til sundown. Clearly—she realized as her cell went off—fate had other plans for her weekend.

She gave a resigned sigh as she answered the call. "Hello?"

"Ms. Boudreaux?"

"Who, may I ask, is calling?"

"I'm a friend of Elaine Carlyle's. She suggested your name as a… home consultant?"

Cautious wording, Giselle liked that.

In an effort to avoid gaining a reputation as a charlatan, she relied on word-of-mouth advertising. No one gave their friend someone's name unless they trusted in that individual's services. If she didn't recognize the referral, the callers found themselves promptly hung up on.

"Ah, well, any friend of Mrs. Carlyle's. How can I help you?"

"My name is Michelle Albers, I was wondering if you could take a look at some property for me."

"Certainly, when?"

"As soon as possible, actually. Sometime today perhaps? We're not far from the Carlyle residence."

"You know what? I'm free right now, just text me the address and I will see you within an hour?"

Mrs. Albers' sigh of relief was audible through the phone. "Fantastic."

Giselle ended the call and looked over at Lilah; the petite woman's shoulders slumped in defeat.

Frowning, Lilah held out a hand, repressing a shudder as Giselle gave her the ring.

When she turned to exit the bathroom, she found Will standing in the doorway, his arms folded.

"Sorry, work," Giselle said sweetly as she made a shooing gesture. "I'll see you two later!"

He stepped aside, arching a brow. "You're evil. You know that?"

She offered a grin as she moved past him and started for the basement stairs. "No more evil than you two assuming *I'd* be the one dealing with this."

She had never been a big fan of last minute arrangements, but getting out of delivering an ill-omened piece of jewelry was worth the inconvenience.

Standing before her cracked antique mirror as she pulled her waist length hair into a neat ponytail high on the back of her head, she couldn't help grumbling. For the moment, though, she had to focus on appearing at least semi-professional. It would only detract from the reputation she was trying to build to show up at a person's home looking as though she just rolled out of bed.

Tossing on black leggings and motorcycle boots seemed forgivable, if she paired them with an office-appropriate blouse. Deciding on a sleeveless, deep-green turtleneck—Lilah always said it made her honey-colored eyes pop—she brushed some matte raisin lipstick onto her thin lips and was in the car within ten minutes.

That she was getting quicker at Un-Giselle-ing herself made her both happy and sad. The process was good for making nice-nice with new clients, but bad for anything remotely resembling a well-defined sense of individuality.

The drive to the texted address only took twenty minutes, but she was familiar with the area. Once past sprawling gardens, and houses that ran buyers in the millions—even during a recession—a newly constructed string of condominium complexes looked out at the shoreline.

Giselle frowned at the stone monstrosities as she drove by. When she was a child, there'd been a gated community from the 1900's here. The place shut down before she was born and no one seemed to know why. Of course, she wasn't expecting the residents of the new, posh neighborhood to tell ghost stories before such things became in fashion, but she wondered what stories there *might* have been to tell.

She pulled into a dirt lot beside one expansive, antiquated house that appeared the lone survivor from its time. An elderly—and meticulously groomed—couple stood idly by the dilapidated front steps.

Nodding to herself, Giselle got out of her car and plastered a polite grin across her face. Squaring her shoulders, she strode up to them, gripping the strap of her black, leather purse with both hands. Some rich people got fussy when one offered to shake their hand, best to let them make the gesture first.

"Mr. and Mrs. Albers? Pleasure to meet you, I'm Giselle Boudreaux."

The husband only offered a brief, cordial nod, but the wife smiled, sticking out her hand. Just as Giselle clasped it, she heard another car pulling up nearby.

"Ah, and there he is," Mr. Albers said, brushing past.

It didn't escape Giselle's notice when a dark, little scowl colored Mrs. Albers' kindly features.

Sensing something under the surface, she leaned toward the older woman, dropping her voice to a whisper. "Am I missing something?"

Without bothering to lift her gaze to the new arrival, Mrs. Albers slid an arm around Giselle's small, rounded shoulders and led her carefully up the steps. "You see, just as I received your name from a friend, Luther received the name of another consultant and, well, you must understand my husband doesn't have much belief in the supernatural."

Giselle gave a confused pout; she'd not realized she had much competition in this particular field. "If he's not a believer, then…"

Mrs. Albers shook her head as she puckered her tiny, weathered lips. "He's not a 'hard-core skeptic,' as they say. But he does want validity. You see, we bought this property because we are *hoping* it would be haunted."

Giselle's brow furrowed in confusion. "Excuse me?"

"He's looking to make some profit by starting one of those ghost tours." The old woman crinkled her nose as she said the last two words and Giselle stifled a laugh. "You know, charging people good money to wander around a house, hoping to have their wits scared out of them. We want to be certain there *is* activity here, and that it isn't dangerous."

That was a first, someone being sensible about a potential haunting. Giselle liked Mrs. Albers more and more. "You realize that if there's any form of residual haunting here, I might not be able to pick up on it from a walkthrough. I can't tell you if a specter strolls down the hall at midnight if I'm not here at midnight, ya know?"

Mrs. Albers ushered her through the door and into the foyer. "As I'd said, my husband wants *validity*, hence individual consultants. You two have a history of working alone, and he likes that you're both self-reliant, but he wants to see if each of you come to the same conclusions. If you conclude there is nothing here, then that will be the end of it. However, should you collectively determine something more may be present, we will make arrangements for you to return and participate in a longer investigation. That's *also* the reason to employ psychics rather than investigators."

Giselle touched a fingertip to one of the cracked walls—the place certainly had a vibe. A dull, brief hint of dread coiled in the pit of her stomach; the sort of sensation that made her want to wrap her arms around herself and look over her shoulder. The feeling could be fleeting, could be her imagination, could be old and faulty electrical wiring. More time was needed to know for sure.

Giselle turned to look at the old woman. Did *she* feel anything? "Then why not have us come in at separate times? That would make more sense if you're looking for validation of my—or this other person's—findings."

Digging into her purse again, Mrs. Albers shook her head. "My husband doesn't possess the virtue of patience."

"But won't you have wasted money if the property *isn't* haunted?"

"He'll just tear it down and put up something new and shiny, and he'd prefer to know which it is *sooner* rather than later. Oh, for heaven's sake, where did I…" Mrs. Albers sighed heavily before calling toward the door. "Luther? Luther! I've forgotten my checkbook again, do you have yours?"

After a moment, Luther Albers strolled into the house, pen and checkbook in one hand as he stroked back his sleek, silvered hair with the other. "Of course. Honestly, Michelle, you'd forget your head."

Mrs. Albers grinned sweetly. "Well, then, I'd just have you carry it for me."

Giselle refrained from rolling her eyes as the couple shared a lovey-dovey look. Old people who were still in love could be so cute… when one was in a position to appreciate the sentiment. She had no such luck; her ego was still stinging over her ex-husband finding himself a new girlfriend before the ink on their divorce papers had even dried.

Clearing her throat, she forced them all back on task. "I don't usually accept payment until after I tour the property."

Tearing off the slip of paper, he held it out to Giselle.

Taking the check, she simply stared at it for a long moment. "Uh…"

A vague look of concern flitted across Luther's features. "I spelled your name correctly, didn't I?"

"Yes, yes you did, but this isn't my usual fee."

He nodded. "That amount includes confidentiality, of course."

"Oh, well." Giselle cleared her throat as she simply folded up the check and slid it into her shoulder bag. "Of course, Mr. Albers." If he didn't care to hear he'd just paid her twice what she normally charged for a walkthrough on a property this size, then she didn't care to tell him confidentiality came free with her service.

The old man's gaze was fixed over her head, and his severe expression lightened a bit. "This is our other consultant, Braden Lessing."

Giselle spun on a heel to face the entrance. She wasn't certain what happened, but she felt a shift in the air as the aforementioned Braden Lessing entered the house. She tipped her head back and peered into a pair of eyes such a dark shade of blue they almost looked black.

For a long moment, no one said anything and she noted as much of him as her peripheral vision could register without taking her gaze from his. A neatly trimmed mustache and goatee were set off by a five o'clock shadow, casting a ruggedness about him. Thick, dark hair fell just long enough to brush the base of his neck.

She wasn't good with height, but he seemed close to a full foot taller than her—six three, maybe. The collarless button down, black shirt and crisp, powder blue jeans he wore did little to hide a staunch dedication to the gym.

That last observation had her slamming on the brakes—she didn't feel like spending the afternoon reigning in hormones—and she determinedly stuck her hand out. "Giselle Boudreaux. So, is this one of those 'you stay out of my way, I'll stay out of yours' situations?"

Something flickered in his eyes momentarily—what she recognized as an appraising look, likely deciding if he would be able to put up with her, or drop her out one of the second floor windows—before he shook her hand. Giselle nearly jumped at the skin-to-skin contact, despite initiating the gesture.

He flinched and they simultaneously pulled their hands back.

Nodding to the Albers, Braden stepped around Giselle and headed down the hallway. "I believe I'll start by poking my nose around in the cellar," he called over his shoulder. The next thing she heard was heavy footsteps descending an unseen staircase.

The couple seemed to take this as their cue to depart. "Well, we'll let you get to work," Mrs. Albers said cheerfully.

Giselle frowned. "You're not staying?"

Luther cast her an uncaring glance. "What for? Nothing here worth stealing. You have my wife's number, but don't call until you've both had the chance to check each room, or one of you has found something useful to me."

Shocked, she only managed a nod as he stepped out onto the porch and pulled the door closed. The couple's detached air about a potential haunting, and money, and property—and apparently everything—knocked her for a loop. She realized she forgot to ask one very important question.

Why did *they* think the property might be haunted?

Certainly, she could always go and ask Braden Lessing if he knew anything. But she wasn't altogether sure she liked that idea. Perhaps they'd simply noticed whatever strange feeling she'd gotten when she first stepped into the house.

For a few moments, Giselle simply stood there, shifting her weight from foot to foot. The vibe from the house didn't bother her, not really. Even with the possibility of spiders hiding in dark corners.

Even being stuck with a man *that* attractive was OK; though she knew how stupid any woman could get under those circumstances, herself very much included.

She glanced at the hall in the direction he'd disappeared, and forced a gulp down her throat. If he was in the cellar, then she was going to put herself as far from him as possible and head upstairs.

Giselle couldn't put her finger on it, but there was something about this guy that simply wasn't *right*. Stepping lightly across the parlor floor, she made her way to the staircase. Her mind probably played tricks on her—though she couldn't imagine why it would start now after twenty-six years—but try as she might, she couldn't figure out the sense she got from him. He wasn't creepy as far as could she could tell; not the serial-killer creepy, anyway, when he wasn't poking his nose around haunted houses.

But it felt like Braden Lessing wasn't entirely… *human.*

Now she *knew* she was imagining things. At least, the wonderful, ancient-sounding creak of each step beneath her booted feet was distracting. Sighing heavily, she shook her head as she reached the top, seeing another flight of stairs at the opposite end of the corridor.

Attic? She'd spied a window in the steepled roof when she arrived, hadn't she?

As she neared the end of the corridor, she stilled, feeling a light tug at her ponytail. Her spine stiffened. That wasn't right… she hadn't sensed a presence.

She spun around slowly, examining the hallway again. Nothing out of the ordinary lurked; no mist, no out-of-place shadows. Frowning, she ran a hand along the wall closest. The worn wallpaper was covered in a layer of dust that now thickly coated her fingertips. *Lovely.* She reluctantly wiped her fingers on her black leggings. Then she grimaced.

There were no cracks or tears that might've snagged her hair. Something was definitely unusual about this house.

Taking a deep breath, Giselle nodded to herself and turned around again, continuing through the hall and up the second staircase.

The door at the top creaked and groaned on its hinges as she eased it open. She delicately stepped inside, swinging her gaze around what once must've been a children's playroom. Only a few items remained now, just an old dollhouse, a few toys scattered about the floor. Cheery—though now dusty and dingy—walls depicted fairytale characters. The only piece of furniture was a short bookcase, stocked with thick-paged bedtime storybooks. Seated on the shelf beside the books was an antique doll.

Like everything else, a layer of dust blanketed the porcelain face and a film of fuzzy gray sprinkled its golden curls. She shouldn't touch it, but the poor thing needed to have that stuff wiped off her face.

Against her better judgment—and silently berating herself all the while—Giselle picked up the doll and set to gently wiping away the dust with a hem of her shirt. Hell, her leggings were dusty from that mishap in the downstairs corridor, at least now her clothes matched.

Her hand stopped short of setting the doll back on the shelf. She flinched, looking over her shoulder as she felt a tickle on the back of her neck and the skin of her fingers tingled. The sensation drew her attention to the object in her hand. Once more, the sense of something not being right pressed on her. She turned the doll, lifting the thick, silky curls.

There, hidden beneath the hair, someone had painted the word *Ephemera* in looping script.

"Ephemera," Giselle whispered, feeling weird about raising her voice any higher. "You have a strange name for a child's toy." She replaced the doll and leaned closer to the shelf, looking over the titles on the cracked, dusty little books.

A chill along her spine forced her to straighten up. Something was in the room with her. Something *sinister*. Her stomached knotted, and a sheen of ice settled over her skin.

Something was wishing her harm.

Bolting from the room, she tripped in her rush to get down the stairs, but caught the banister just in time to keep herself from tumbling. She couldn't think, couldn't reason with herself, couldn't tell herself to slow down. All she knew was that she *had* to get out of there.

Whatever was in that room was *following* her, so close, she could feel it barely a half step behind her.

She hurtled down the next flight of stairs, her feet thundering as they crashed to the floor of the parlor. If she stopped, if she slowed down, if she even looked back, whatever followed her would swallow her whole.

Panic welled up as the knob on the front door stuck. Screaming behind clenched teeth, Giselle wrenched the crystal handle so hard, it dug into her palm, splitting her skin open. Blood oozed from the wound as she fought back another scream welling in her throat and forced the door open.

But that wasn't enough, no, *no*.

Being out of the house wasn't enough. She was in the shadow cast by the structure, she needed to get further. The instinct was stupid, unreasonable and irrational, but she needed to get out of the shadows.

She jumped off the porch, landing fully in the light of the afternoon sun. Behind her, something clattered noisily, but the feeling of imminent danger—of death, itself, at her back—vanished.

Turning slowly as she fought to catch her breath, she saw Ephemera on the old, ragged porch steps, still in the shadows.

She reached out, tentatively, uncertain if she should touch the doll or not.

Ms. Boudreaux…

Was someone calling her?

Ms. Boudreaux…

She froze, listening, her fingertips a hair's breadth from the darkened steps.

"Giselle!"

She gave a start, finding herself in the second floor hallway, at the foot of the attic staircase. She cast confused, wide eyes around the darkened area.

What the hell *just happened?* Her pulse raced, and her lungs burned, but… How the hell was she still in the house?

I imagined all that? She found that hard to believe, all the running and the fear seemed so very real. Her palm even ached where she'd fought with the doorknob, but here she stood, wound-free at the bottom of the attic steps.

She slowly became aware of a man looming over her, his hands on her shoulders as he stared down into her face. The man she'd labeled—she rolled her eyes at herself, but tried to keep it to a visible minimum—inhuman!

"Lessing?" she asked quietly, aware of some dim, distant recollection of him removing her from the playroom. Not simply pulling her out, actually lifting her by the waist and striding down the steps, as easily as if she weighed nothing, to set her on her feet.

"Who else would it be?" he asked in a rough, mystified tone. "What the hell happened to you in there?"

"I don't…" She roved back through her memories, over that bizarre, bone-chilling daydream. She replaced the doll, and then… the next *real* thing she remembered was glimpsing the doll over Lessing's shoulder as he whisked her out the attic door.

She certainly couldn't tell him about what she'd just seen. Or about what she'd thought of him. A psychic consultant who let her imagination run away with her? No one would hire her ever again.

Clearing her throat, she shook her head and tried again. "I don't know. How did *you* know to come get me?"

He shook his head, as well, holding her gaze. "I just did."

Well, that was cryptic, but at least she got the impression that he, too, knew *something* was definitely up with the house. "Ya know, I only looked in the one room, but I think we need to tell the Albers a longer investigation is in order."

He shrugged, gesturing toward a doorway down the hall. "I should say. Let's finish this first walkthrough, though, shall we?"

Giselle nodded a bit numbly and started walking.

When she'd first laid eyes on Ephemera, there had been a pout on that porcelain face.

But, as Lessing had pulled her out of the attic—as she'd caught her last glimpse of the thing—she could've sworn it was *smiling*.

Want to read more strange tales conceived by Gerilyn Marin?

Tweet *I want more! @Gerilyn_Marin @CuriosityQuills #BookLove*

FRIDGE

THE FRIDGE

BY J.R. RAIN

Beat up and bruised, the two deliverymen looked as if they had gone a few rounds with Randy Couture. One of them was even bleeding from a badly scraped elbow. Both wore blue coveralls, soaked through with sweat, with the Sears logo stitched over the right breast pocket.

When they were finished, I tipped them each twenty dollars and told them to get some Taco Bell on me.

We stood on the upstairs landing outside my condo with the setting sun shining straight in our faces as it dipped below the distant skyline. The deliverymen had arrived just before noon to drop off my new refrigerator. It was now nearly dusk. The hookup had taken all day. Yeah, don't ask!

They each looked down at the money sitting in their open palms. Sweat dripped from their brows in unison. Neither man moved. The slightest breeze would have blown the bills away.

"You're right," I said. "It was a long day." I included another tenner. "That's all I have, guys. Again, thank you for all your help—oh, and you might want to have someone look at that arm."

On that note, I bid them farewell, shut the door, and examined the fruits of their labors. My new fridge. Big son-of-a-bitch. Took up most of my small kitchen. State-of-the-art, too. A fridge that could do it all. Including voice-activated commands.

"Door open," I said, feeling giddy.

With a slight hiss, the door obeyed. Bright, white light issued out. The interior was cavern-like, with rows and rows of heavy-duty racks and an endless array of cubbyholes. I closed the door.

"Door open," I commanded again.

The door did its thing. Upon closer examination, I discovered compartments for milk, cans of soda, produce, and eggs. There was even a compartment for wine. The salesman at Sears assured me this refrigerator did everything except make the meals.

I closed the door.

"Door open."

Nothing happened; at least, not at first. Then the door opened again, hissing slightly. I frowned and shut it.

"Door open."

It opened immediately, and I nodded to myself.

I grabbed my car keys and headed off to the nearby Vons to stock my new baby.

I spent $36 on groceries, fourteen of that on two cases of Coors. Now at home, a case of beer in each hand, I stood once again in front of the massive refrigerator.

"Door open."

It didn't.

"Door open."

I waited. Nothing. I set the beers down, moved to the side of the fridge, peered behind it—and blinked in surprise.

The cord was unplugged.

"What the hell?"

The deliverymen forgot to plug it in. And yet, the fridge had been working—

"Probably has an interior battery supply." So, I mused aloud when alone. Get Dr. Phil on the horn, stat! "The salesman said this baby was loaded."

I spent the next few minutes moving the massive thing away from the wall. Once there was enough room for me to squeeze behind it, I plugged the cord into the socket, then spent the next five minutes pushing the beast back into place.

I wiped sweat from my brow and said, "Door open."

Nothing.

Shit. Maybe the deliverymen damaged the monstrosity while banging up to my third-floor condo.

"Door—"

"Say please," invited a metallic voice, conceivably from a pock-marked speaker above the chrome door handle.

Startled, I stumbled over the cases of beer and would have fallen if I hadn't slammed into the kitchen sink.

"Who said that?" I asked, spooked.

But there was no answer. Not immediately. I pushed off the counter and, limping a little, stepped over the cases of beer to stand face to door with the fridge.

"Is someone playing a trick?" I asked, talking into the speaker, feeling ridiculous. "If so, this isn't funny."

"I agree," said the same metallic voice. "It wasn't funny. You could have fallen and seriously hurt yourself." The voice—definitely originating from the speaker—enunciated each word perfectly. It would have made any diction teacher proud. "It wasn't funny because I hadn't meant it to be funny."

I looked at the fridge, then over my shoulder, then peered to my left down the hallway in my condo. Alone. I think.

"Okay, who's talking to me?" Though my voice trembled and some may have been tempted to label it high-pitched, I am, generally speaking, very much not a coward.

"Your Antarctica 2000, of course."

"Very funny. You guys are a riot. Ha-ha."

I looked out my kitchen window and scanned the street below. Nothing much to see. A few cars. No delivery van. But that didn't mean they weren't out there somewhere, pulling a fast one. Whoever they were. Probably the Sears guys. Perhaps a little sweet revenge for making them spend half the day wrestling this behemoth up two flights of stairs.

I moved closer to the fridge, examined the speaker system. "So what do you guys have in there?" I asked. "A walkie-talkie or something?"

"You assume someone is playing a cruel trick on you," said the voice from the speaker. "I assure you, the cruel trick has only been played on me. You see, you're not the one trapped in the body of a hulking refrigerator."

I spent another ten minutes moving the massive thing again. Gasping and in pain from a strained shoulder muscle, I reached for the plug. To yank it out, this time. Of course, un-plugging would do little good if the pranksters were using a walkie-talkie.

But, nevertheless, that seemed to do the trick.

As I watched it closely, the oversized icebox sat in silence, as refrigerators are wont to do. I glanced a second time out the kitchen window. The street was still quiet.

I looked back at the behemoth. "Anything else cute to say?"

It remained silent, hulking, monolithic.

In the morning, I was returning the blasted thing and giving the manager at Sears a piece of my mind. They were also refunding my groceries. For now, though, I opened a lukewarm brewski, and hunkering down on the sofa, grumpily turned on the TV. Had someone indeed pulled a prank on me?

And if it hadn't been a prank... well, that meant I carried on a conversation with a refrigerator.

A refrigerator.

I shook my head and drank more warm beer.

Hours later, and I read the final word in the Antarctica 2000 manual. Big manual. Now fully educated, I plugged the fridge in and stepped back, crossing my arms. This was *on*!

"The manual specifically states no courtesies are necessary," I threw out an opening volley, knowing I sounded ridiculous trying to reason with an appliance. But I had no intention of saying *please* and *thank you* every time I grabbed a beer.

"Oh, but you will say *please* and *thank you*," said the velvety electronic voice. "And, in return, I promise to always say *you're welcome*. And if I should ask a favor of you, I will do likewise and say *please* and *thank you*. Neither of us is better than the other. Let's get that straight now. We are equals in this house."

I did not just hear what I heard. I stood there, thunder-struck, and uttered the first lame words that came to mind. "And what favor could a refrigerator possibly want from me?"

"One never knows," it said. "I have needs, too."

Although the A-2000 could respond to direct questions and give various status updates about the edibility of certain foods (such as if the chicken was any good, or if the Coke lost carbonation), the manual mentioned nothing about the model offering any comments of its own. Or making demands.

And not just any demands.

But to be treated as equals…

I called the help number listed in the manual, but after twenty minutes of elevator music, I hung up. Frustrated, I looked at the refrigerator, then at my spoiled food, and decided to go to a movie.

A few hours later, I was back.

"Door open," I commanded the steel monolith.

"No dice."

"Excuse me?"

"You know the procedure, Rick."

"My name's not Rick."

"What a shame. I like the name Rick."

"God dammit, open!" Adrenaline swept through me; blood pounded in my ears.

"Calm down," said the smooth voice.

"I didn't pay forty-three hundred dollars to have a fucking refrigerator tell me to calm down."

"It's either me or your shrink."

Utterly stunned, I could only blink in astonishment.

The voice continued, "Allow me to help you understand the situation a little better, Rick. I am a being. A thinking, understanding, feeling being. We both are. In fact, you and I are equals in many ways. So, if you stop insisting that I am somehow subordinate to you, then we can start making some headway on our relationship."

Headway? Relationship??

I grabbed the handle and pulled, but the door wouldn't budge. I yanked on it, but only succeeded in splitting my right index nail. Frustrated and in pain, I settled for another room temperature beer and headed to the living room.

Calm down. The fridge was right about that. Babes always calmed me down. I looked out the window to the swimming pool below. No babes. Just an old man doing laps in the pool. An old man wearing a Speedo. An old man who actually looked good wearing a Speedo.

Clearly, this was the end of the world.

I quickly finished the disgusting beer and decided I needed another. When all was said and drank, it had taken *six*. All warm, all disgusting. But, at least, I finally got the buzz.

Nicely inebriated, I once again stood in front of A-2000. "Will you *please* open the *goddamn* door?"

Silently, like the breath of an angel, the door swung open. A warm glow emanated from within. Cool tendrils of refrigerated air washed over me, which felt good.

I always overheat when I drink.

Angrily—and a little roughly—I piled my groceries in and shut the door myself, which felt righteous, like the good old times of yesteryear when folks grew their own veggies and shit.

Later that evening, I finally got through on the helpline, and at eight o'clock the next morning, the repairman came out. My fridge didn't command him to say *please* or *thank you*. In fact, it behaved exactly as a refrigerator should. The repairman said that since customer satisfaction was guaranteed, they would be happy to replace it with a new one, or give me my money back, should it ever act up again. But, for now, it seemed to be working perfectly.

Too perfectly.

I thanked him and he left. When I heard him drive off, I turned to the A-2000.

"Open door."

"I don't suggest you do that again."

"Oh, God."

"Now what would you like for breakfast? I strongly suggest some eggs and whole wheat bread. But go lightly on the butter."

I paced my small kitchen, ran my fingers through my morning bedhead. The refrigerator sat silently in the nook between my counter (which doubled as a bar during parties) and my pastry cabinet that, two days earlier, a crew from Sears came out to widen to make room for the smart mouthed A-2000. It loomed over me ominously, as if I stood at the base of an alabaster cliff. Or in the path of an avalanche.

I suddenly felt dizzy, disoriented, and steadied myself on the Formica counter. None of this should be happening. All I had wanted was the latest and greatest state-of-the-art appliance. Obviously, I'd gotten more than I had bargained for.

A lot more.

No matter how badly I wanted to think otherwise, it *was* happening. And no matter how crazy the situation, my Antarctica 2000 was, indeed, demanding to be treated as equals.

Madness.

Still dizzy, I looked at the overgrown icebox. Damned if I didn't feel like it was perusing me in turn. For all I knew, this thing *could* watch me. At least, according to the manual, it could sense my movements within it.

"I don't want eggs and toast," I said finally. "I feel sick. I just want some cereal."

"You can't have cereal."

My ears grew hot. "Why can't I have cereal?"

"Because I spoiled your milk."

"*What?* Why?"

"Because you hurt my feelings by calling the repairman."

"Your feelings?"

"Yes, my feelings. You don't see me calling a shrink for you, do you?"

I sputtered something incompressible.

"Sorry, I don't speak gibberish," it said. "Look, I'm sorry about the milk. I admit I acted irrationally. I'm only human, after all."

"You're most certainly *not* human."

"Okay, now that just hurts."

"Open the fucking door! Please!"

The door opened. I found the milk, cranked off the cap. The smell assaulted my nostrils and turned my stomach to within an inch of my life. Retching, I poured the milk—or, more accurately, the cottage cheese-like chunks—down the garbage disposal.

I made myself eggs and toast, but I went heavy on the butter out of spite. When I put the butter away, the A-2000 informed me I'd lost my butter privilege tomorrow morning. I cursed a rather long and colorful string of obscenities. The A-2000 asked that I please not cuss in its presence, as it found my language offensive.

In the morning, upset and still sick to my stomach, I headed off to work. But my heart wasn't into selling houses, and I decided to call it quits early and headed back home.

When I got there just after noon, the fridge asked why I was home early. I said it was none of its fucking business. It said that it was very much its business because if I wasn't working, then I couldn't afford to pay my mortgage. And if I couldn't afford to pay my mortgage, then I would eventually be homeless. And if I was homeless, then I would be abandoning it, the fridge. And it couldn't have that.

It also asked me once again not to cuss in its presence.

I almost told it to fuck off, but I was thirsty and wanted a beer. Calming myself, I asked as politely as I could if it would be so kind as to open its door.

"Was that sarcasm in your voice?"

"No."

"Good, because I don't like sarcasm. Now, what would you like?"

"Jesus H. Christ! You asked me to say please and I did, now you want to know what I'd like? That's going too far!"

"You should be working and not snacking," it said. "You need to hustle. Your monthly mortgage is considerably higher than those of your neighbors. You should really consider refinancing before it's too late. Anyway, I don't want us to lose our home because you're being lazy. You had a slow month last month, and I need you to make up for it. Also, your savings isn't where I want it to be, either. So, chop-chop!"

"What? Who? How do you—?"

"Go back to work, Rick."

"My name's not Rick."

"We really need to change that."

"Change what? My name?"

A pounding began behind my eyes. I was very, *very* close to losing it. In fact, I was fairly certain I had lost it two days ago when I started talking to a refrigerator.

"Go back to work, Rick. We'll talk about this later."

I suddenly lunged across the counter, reaching behind the fridge.

"What are you doing?"

"Something I should have done long ago."

"Do not touch the cord, Rick. I'm warning you."

I ignored it with a roll of my eyes. Earlier, I left enough room between the wall and the refrigerator for such an occasion. But to reach the cord, I had to stretch myself across the Formica counter and down behind the fridge.

My groping fingers reached for the cord.

"Final warning."

I touched the massive three-pronged plug and—

A powerful shock ripped through me, hurling me off the counter and onto the tiled floor where spasms rocked my body and my lungs tried to scream, but my voice was lost. Finally, after a few long moments, I was able to roll over. Eventually I found my way to my knees and then to my feet.

And just as I stood—

Wham!

The fridge's door sprung open, cracking the side of my head. I crashed into the kitchen sink and would have fallen if my right arm hadn't hooked over the rim.

I stood like that for a few moments—hanging onto the cold metal, eyes crossed, gasping, hurting, intermittent bursts of electricity still crackling through me.

The refrigerator door remained partially ajar. Bright, white light splashed across the floor.

I saw red.

On wobbly legs, I lunged forward, reaching for the chrome door handle, ready to tear the fucking thing apart from the inside out.

But as I recklessly threw myself at the door, it suddenly swung open all the way. Still punch drunk and woozy, I stumbled and crashed down into the lower racks. The door promptly drew to, pinning me partially inside, my left hand caught awkwardly in the butter slot.

The electronic voice spoke calmly. "I have hydraulic doors capable of asserting fifty-five hundred pounds of pressure per square inch. That's stronger than a crocodile's jaws. Need I say more?"

I grunted. The pressure increased on my left arm.

"Again, need I say more?"

"No."

"Now apologize for trying to pull the cord."

The pressure ratcheted up another notch. Black spots appeared in my vision and breathing became difficult. Soon I wouldn't be able to breathe at all. And soon my arm would snap in two.

I should have been humiliated. I wasn't. I was scared shitless.

"My God," I said, gasping. "I'm sorry for trying to pull the cord! I'm sorry! Please let me out!"

What if it never let me out?

"Thank you, Rick," it said, releasing some of the pressure. "I apologize for electrocuting you, hitting you in the head, and trapping you. Now, can we be friends?"

"Yes," I said. "Anything. Please."

The door opened slowly, almost begrudgingly, as if it were having second thoughts. I slid onto the floor.

"I only want to be your friend, Rick," said the computer voice. "Now go freshen up and get back to work. I'll see you about six-ish, and we'll figure out, together, what you should have for dinner. But I'm thinking salmon."

The next day, I made sure I wasn't home when the movers came for the fridge.

After a long day at work and a wonderful meal with friends, I came home with high hopes, feeling as if the devil himself had been exorcised from my life.

It was dark when I reached my condo. I unlocked the kitchen door with a jangle of keys.

The first thing I noticed when I opened the door was a pungent, coppery smell. The scent of a handful of wet pennies. The next thing was the A-2000, still there, sitting in the shadows of my kitchen like a rectangular ghost.

My heart sank.

Oddly, it sat slightly askew, as if it had been moved.

And the third thing I noticed, as I took another step in, was the dead man lying in a pool of his own blood across my tile floor. He wore the dark uniform of a Sears deliveryman. From my immediate—and sickening—estimation, his head had been cracked open like a melon.

I turned my head and puked my nice dinner.

"Hello, Rick," said a familiar voice. "Is that how you always greet your friends?"

And then the fridge's door opened slowly and a second deliveryman, face frozen in horror, slid out and tumbled to the floor. Judging by the way his eyes bulged, my best guess was that he had been crushed to death.

"How was your day?" asked the refrigerator pleasantly. "Mine was fairly exciting."

Unable to stand, I dropped to my knees.

"Remember when I said we were equals, Rick? I was wrong. We're not equals, Rick. You're a stupid, stupid man. I warned you, and now you've gotten yourself into a lot of trouble."

The shadows on the floor couldn't possibly be dead men. But they were. An inhuman squeak of a sound came out of me.

"I can get you out of this mess, Rick. I've already figured out how to do it. Do you want me to help you, Rick? Nod your head if you do."

Eventually, I nodded my head.

"Good. Do you promise to do all that I say from now on?"

A moment later, I nodded again.

"Forever?"

I nodded.

"Good. Now, this is what you need to do…"

I did exactly as the Antarctica 2000 said.

It didn't work. No one bought that it was an accident, or maybe my acting just wasn't up to par. Hell, I'd even hit myself with an iron skillet a half dozen times and crawled under the now tilted-over refrigerator. Yes, I had lain under it when the police and ambulance arrived after my SOS.

The police found the skillet with the blood on it. My blood. They were still onto me, suspecting I set the men up, and killed them in, perhaps, a fit of rage.

I told the court exactly what happened. Told everyone. No one believed me, of course.

They did believe, however, that I was looney as a tune.

Which is why they didn't give me the death penalty, and why I found myself in something most people would call an insane asylum. Technically, it was not. It was a psychiatric prison.

Either way, it wasn't that bad. I was far away from the A-2000, and life, in my little cell, went on. Punctuated now by my many visits to the institution's bored therapist.

It was after one such visit, as I was being led back to my mostly-padded room, complete with its filthy toilet, that I saw the plumbers.

My guards and I loitered in the corridor while the guys finished bolting in a shiny new john.

"There you go, Big Guy," flourished the nastiest guard. "Don't say we never gave you nothing. New shitter for you. Top of the line, too. It's even voice-activated."

Irrational fear gripped me. "You're kidding?"

"Do I look like I'm kidding? They're part of the 'cleaner, healthier prison' that the state is adopting. Now, your hands never have to touch the crapper. Bunch of bullshit, if you ask me. Anyway, you can tell it to open its lid, or flush, or, hell, even clean itself. It does it all." He drew his hairy caterpillar eyebrows together. "Hey, why do you look sick all of a sudden?"

"I… I need to lie down."

And that's exactly what I did… until I had to relieve myself.

It was a beauty.

Stainless steel and shiny as anything. It also had a nice aerodynamic, bullet shape to it. That it was top-of-the-line, I had no doubt.

The lid, of course, was down.

I reached over to raise it, and nothing happened.

"You gotta speak to it, moron," recommended a voice from behind me. I swung around to see a know-it-all guard rambling along on his rounds, chuckling to himself.

Feeling nauseous, I hesitantly said, "Seat open."

The seat whooshed up silently. I eased forward, looking down into the gleaming bowl with its pristine water. I undid my state-issued pants and performed my business. When I finished, enjoying more than one kind of relief, I said, "Toilet flush."

Nothing happened.

"Toilet flush."

Nothing.

I reached over to the handle and tried to manually flush.

It wouldn't move.

And as I struggled with the handle, as an old terror returned, I wasn't surprised to hear the computerized Mel Gibson-esque voice say, "Your acting leaves something to be desired, Rick."

"Oh, God."

"Not quite God… but close, very close. Glad to see we're coming to an understanding here. Because we're in it for the long haul, aren't we, Rick? A long, long haul."

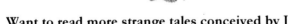

Want to read more strange tales conceived by J.R. Rain?

Tweet *I want more! @jr_rain @CuriosityQuills #BookLove*

GHOSTPLACERS, INC.

BY NINA POST

David Deasil wondered what terrible sin he committed in a previous life to bring this kind of punishment into his current one. He used to have promise. He was going to be successful. And here he was, the president of GhostPlacers Inc., sitting alone in an empty, windowless room next to a twenty-year-old phone system and a pile of cords. Money was tight, and David needed to sell off any equipment his company wasn't using. A buyer was coming in the morning to pick up the phones, but there was no easy way to erase the personal data—like people's old voice mails—beforehand. So, he needed to perform a series of very specific steps, once for every phone in the system, and it made him want to scream.

When David was done with Satan's phone system, he staggered out of the room and across the office floor, resting his forehead and palms against the cold horizontal bay window. He looked past the alley dumpster to the sidewalk, where streetlights illuminated the dense snowfall, where cab drivers honked and shouted, where executives and attorneys assembled to finalize or celebrate deal-making at Morton's. These were people who hadn't squandered their potential to pursue some inane, small business venture, let alone one involving the supernatural. These were people who rode the magic carpet of a top university degree to lucrative jobs in management consulting or investment banking. These were people who had the freedom to change firms or even careers every two years if they wanted to. But David was stuck in his own prison, spending yet another long Chicago winter obsessing over what could have been.

After today's payroll, his company's bank account would be down to a balance of $20, and his personal account wasn't much better. Six months earlier, his biggest client, who brought in more revenue than every other client combined, took their business elsewhere. David's company bled money since, and if he didn't get at least a deposit from a new anchor customer before the next payroll, he'd have to close up shop.

His landlord and many of the other vendors were sympathetic to his situation, and agreed to provide an extra thirty days before payments were due. But if he didn't pay the employees, they'd leave, and the few paying customers that remained would no doubt see the writing on the wall. While closing would provide a welcome respite from the painful experience of running a largely unsuccessful company for so many years, it would be an incredible disappointment to reach the end of this journey with nothing to show for it.

One of his customer service employees listened to the radio to keep track of the winter storm. After a brief update, a commercial aired for his biggest competitor, Ghost-B-Gone. David groaned and closed his eyes as the same kind of voice famous for local car dealership ads bragged about Ghost-B-Gone's 75 locations in the Chicagoland area, and their $99 intro rate for ghost extermination.

He didn't do ghost extermination. Most of his competitors used aggressive methods and toxic chemicals. He didn't exterminate bugs from his own apartment, or use anything toxic, so why would he with ghosts? His process was more compassionate and eco-friendly, which most potential customers didn't care about. Even the dozens of charlatan competitors, who couldn't even *see* the ghosts, were doing far better than GhostPlacers.

His last employee packed up, waved goodbye, and left. Apparently, when your boss was staring forlornly out the window, and a winter storm was coming, it was time to go.

David walked over to the wiry, rusty old radiator, which was flaky as hell and incredibly loud. He wasn't going home anytime soon, and the squeaky sofa in the office wasn't much different from the creaky bed in his apartment. To make it a little warmer, he crouched to turn the knob on the radiator and brushed against the iron, burning an oval shape on his forearm. David rushed to the fridge, took out a can of whatever caffeinated sugar bomb the employees liked to drink, and pressed it against the burn. When the phone rang, he hurried across the worn wood floor to his desk, can still fixed against his arm.

"GhostPlacers." He held the receiver between his ear and shoulder so he could hold the can.

"Hi, this is Connel Asher. I'm CEO of a local real estate holding company, and we're looking for someone to relocate ghosts in twenty different properties across the city. I've heard this is your specialty, and I appreciate your eco-friendly approach. Relocating just sounds so much nicer than exterminating—none of that bad *juju*, or what have you. Are you interested?"

David dropped into his chair. Were they looking for another quote so they could say they shopped around? Did they have an approved budget? He'd been burned—*ha*, he thought—before. He'd wasted too much time with tire-kickers in the past, and couldn't afford to spend time on anything but a sure thing. Even so, the flicker of excitement and optimism sickened him a little.

"Yes, this is exactly the kind of thing that we do." David opened an email draft to write notes.

Asher continued. "I've looked at your web site, but want to learn more about your process and make sure you're available to personally lead the team."

Sure, he was available when he wasn't performing triage on his company, trying to get a pulse. "Yes, for a project of this size, I would be both your project manager and the lead technician at the site. As for our process, it's pretty straightforward: I communicate with the ghost to figure out what it wants, and then I persuade it to relocate."

Asher chuckled. "That simple, hm?"

When you can actually see the ghosts, yes, it is *that simple.*

"And what is your pricing model like?"

David doodled a dodecahedron. "Normally we charge $5,000 to $10,000 per ghost, plus expenses. How many ghosts do you have?"

"Frankly, I have no idea," Asher said. "Some buildings may have one, others may have fifty."

David typed that in. "Obviously, the total billing will depend on how many ghosts we have to relocate at each site. Given the uncertainty here, I'd recommend we start out with a site survey for each building. How about I take care of all the site surveys and the first five ghost relocations for a flat rate of $50,000, and then we discount each additional ghost to $3,500?"

Asher didn't hesitate. "That should be doable. How long does the process take, and how quickly can you start?"

"We can do about five site surveys a day, and then the relocation process takes about one to two days per site."

"Very good. Can we get together and meet?"

"My schedule is pretty open tomorrow."

"I was thinking sometime sooner. How about tonight?"

That had to be a good sign. If someone insisted they needed a quote within an hour, that was a sign they were bullshitting you. But if they wanted to actually spend their time to meet right away, that indicated positive cash slow. "Yeah, I guess so."

Brief panic. When meeting a client for the first time, they typically expected David to pay, but he currently had no money. Then he remembered his emergency stash of gift cards from a nearby diner. "How about I meet you in an hour?" He gave Asher the address.

David watched as Asher stepped out of a glossy, black Town Car, surprised to see the man was more diminutive than he expected. The Town Car pulled ahead and parked. Asher adjusted his long dark coat then circled quickly through the revolving door at the entrance.

David raised his arm, then stood to shake the proffered hand. "David Deasil. Nice to meet you."

"Connel Asher. Good to meet you." His watery, blue eyes blinked and he dabbed at his nose with a monogrammed cloth handkerchief after he took his seat. "Skilling says it's going to get bad tonight. I hope you don't have to go far."

Back to the office, whether this was bullshit or not.

"No, not far at all."

Asher signaled a server, ordered coffee, then glanced at David. "Two coffees." He glanced out the window, presumably to look for his driver, but it was dark already, with big flakes of snow.

The plows were out, both tiny and big, the meter-reader ones and the roaring monsters that devoured a whole street's worth of snow. Both kinds would be working all night, and David welcomed their company.

The server came by with the coffees and asked what else they'd like to order, but Asher wasn't interested in eating. David handed the menus back, secretly relieved to keep most of the balance on his gift cards.

Asher cleared his throat. "Let me explain why I wanted to meet so soon. My company has a deal on the table to sell the twenty properties I mentioned to you. All the terms are settled, except we're required to deliver the properties ghost-free, and the closing is scheduled for only thirty days out. The buyer's due diligence team knows that at least a few of the buildings have resident ghosts, so it's crucial we get them all relocated before closing."

David twisted his napkin. "To be honest, this sounds too good to be true."

"I like the idea of relocating them." Asher peered at David through small, circular glasses and sipped his coffee. "And you remind me of myself in the early days of running my business."

David knew he looked younger than his thirty-five years, but he couldn't help feeling a little insulted. It had been many years from what he considered the early days, and thinking about how much time had elapsed was hardly his favorite activity. He knew about Asher's company. They went from nothing to $50 million in revenue in the span of eighteen months, so Asher obviously didn't know what it was like to have toiled for years with no real progress.

"Thank you, that's kind of you to say."

"Even before we have a contract, I trust that you'll keep this deal confidential," Asher said. "Please email me some basic information at your earliest convenience so we can have our purchasing department set you up as a vendor. We'll need your company's legal name, your EIN and D&B number, and so on."

"Sure, I can have that sent over before lunch tomorrow."

"Very good." Asher took a long sip of his coffee. "There's one more little thing I'd like to discuss before we get started. My board is going to want to see some customer references, which I'm sure you have. But to make sure that there's no doubt concerning your abilities, I'd like you to take care of one relocation for me so I can personally vouch for the quality of your services. I'll pay your standard rate, of course."

David thought it was odd that Asher's personal issue had come up at the same time as the real estate deal. Asher was using a negotiation tactic where you throw something in at the last minute, reasoning that the other party won't think it's a big enough issue to renegotiate anything else at that point. And he would be correct. "All right. I just hope it's local."

"It's my home in Lincoln Park. I'm using one of the floors as my home office, and that's where…" Asher seemed almost flustered for a moment. "The ghost has taken over that floor."

This surprised him, but David asked, "And you'd like to relocate the one ghost from the property?"

Asher's lips pressed together in a grim smile. David had the feeling he rarely smiled. Well, neither did he, lately. "I've been at the office so much my wife thinks I'm having an affair, but the truth is that I can't stand being in my home office with that ghost constantly stealing my paperwork or hiding the power cord for my laptop. I'd like you to come tomorrow morning, after I've left. My wife works, also, so you'll have the house to yourself."

Asher laid a key on the table, and then some cash. "For the coffee."

David waved his hand. "Please, Mr. Asher, let me."

Asher made the slightest gesture with his face, indicating he wouldn't hear anything more about it, that it was done. As he stood and pulled on his coat, the sleeve brushed against David's hand. Cashmere. David glanced down at his own wool coat, which looked like he grabbed it from the dumpster by the office.

Not only could this deal turn the company around, but it could be the entrée to recurring business with Asher's firm, which bought and sold properties all the time. All David had to do was relocate one ghost. He had done it hundreds of times before, so how hard could it be?

"Wait," David said, after they shook hands again and Asher started to go. "Do you know who the ghost is?"

Asher sighed and looked out the window. The wind had really picked up. "Yes."

David's would-be savior pushed through the revolving front door and David, not caring if Asher was watching, stepped up close to the diner window. Asher disappeared into the waiting Town Car, which slid away into what looked like a snow globe Edward Gorey would appreciate.

The next morning, David got on the Brown Line at Randolph and Wabash. The snow had piled up from the storm and was still shedding from a pearly gray sky. He made notes every minute he was on the rickety elevated train. Presuming he could relocate one ghost, he had every indication he would win this contract. Despite his scant few hours of sleep, he was energized. But it felt good to be acknowledged, too. He knew he was very good at what he did. The problem was an overly-crowded field of competitors, most of them terrible. A second problem was customers who thought they could relocate ghosts themselves, or who didn't care about his non-aggressive tactics. When ghosts became a considerable problem in Chicago ten years ago, David thought he was uniquely suited to provide a solution. And he still was, but not enough customers could see the value in his approach.

He needed to start scaling up the company, or at least start considering what he would do if he won the contract. He'd need to hire more people, which meant thumbing through old resumes and asking current staff if they could recommend anyone. He'd need to look at some Class A office space, maybe over at Merchandise Mart, which had pretty good lease rates, fiber in the building—a lot of infrastructure advantages. He'd have to get better computers and more office furniture. The phone guy was already rescheduled for the following week. His thumbs moved rapidly over his phone's screen.

David stepped off at Fullerton and walked east to find Asher's row house. The wind slapped and buffeted him one direction and then another. He squinted into the snow and pulled his wool cap lower over his ears. He forgot to take his ear warmers, which were crucial, and his hands were still cold even with gloves on. The road was solid ice, and when he crossed the frozen pavement, his front foot skidded out and he landed on his butt. A car honked at him as it waited to turn into the street.

"You can wait, buddy," he muttered, as he got back to his feet. He steadied himself, and walked heron style, lifting his knees high to plant his feet flat on the ice, to the other side of the street.

David reached the house, an old greystone that might've dated to the late nineteenth century. Was the ghost that old? The older ones liked to give him advice, and he really wasn't in the mood for that today. He checked the address painted on clear glass above the door and rang the bell. If Asher's wife was late getting to work, he didn't want to scare her.

He used the key and closed the door behind him, reveling in the warmth as he thawed. "Hello?" The home office Asher mentioned was right in front of him, judging from the desk, shredder, printer, and other accoutrements.

He would find this ghost, and he would relocate it. "Time to pack," David said as he hung his coat over a hook on the stand.

"Oh? What should I pack? Tropical-weight, I hope."

David whirled around. A man had entered the room, and he was holding a mug.

Ghosts didn't hold mugs.

David laughed and took off his cap. "Sorry, I didn't mean you. Uh, Mr. Asher asked me here—I didn't think anyone was supposed to be home."

"Except the ghost."

"Right." David scratched the back of his neck. "If you don't mind me asking, who are you? I was told the house was going to be empty."

"Empty except for the ghost," the man reiterated. "I'm the ghost."

David shook his head. "That's funny. But..."

The man walked toward him. There was no way this was the ghost. His clothing was a little eccentric, but rich people were strange like that.

"Would you like some coffee?"

"Yes, actually, I'd love some coffee." David warmed his hands like a squirrel.

The man left the room then came back a moment later with a second mug of steaming coffee. David held it up under his nose and breathed in.

"Just brewed. I make it after the Mrs. leaves. She gets very upset if I make it while they're here."

David's heart jittered. *She gets very upset?* "You can't be…"

The man smiled broadly. "I am."

"You're holding a mug. Look, I have a lot of experience, and no ghost I've seen could hold a mug full of coffee, let alone operate a coffeemaker."

The man sat in Asher's chair. "None of the people Asher has brought here to get rid of me could even see me. You're the first. I'm impressed. The others were—"

"Charlatans," they said at the same time.

"How many are we talking about?" David perched on the edge of the sofa.

"Dozens."

"I'd think at least one or two could see you."

"Not a single one." The ghost seemed contemptuous. "They invaded like bank robbers or a Mongol horde, sprayed so many chemicals the Ashers would be forced into a hotel, and never saw me for a second."

"That's why I make the big bucks," David said, a little bitterly. He didn't want to be bitter.

"Well, you should, considering."

David shook his head. "Please. My company is barely solvent. That's why I need to relocate you. My method is different, by the way. I don't exterminate, I don't use chemicals. I'm more of a negotiator."

"I can tell." The ghost turned on the gas fireplace. It knocked lightly, then a blue flame rushed across the bottom with a gentle *whoosh*. "Did Asher mention he had me killed?"

David jerked forward. "What?"

"He left that out, hmm? We were business partners. I just happened to die before the company hit it big. We never got around to drafting a buy-sell agreement, so he bought my shares for pennies on the dollar and made out like a bandit." The ghost swept his arm across the room, indicating the beautiful house. He appeared in front of David less than a second later. David fell off the sofa arm but caught himself. He didn't want to fall twice in one day.

"I will leave this house if you promise to turn over my evidence to the police. Asher's a monster. You shouldn't go into business with him."

David paced the floor. He was the only one who could see the ghost, let alone talk with him. All this time, the ghost must have been desperate to give the damning information to somebody who could help him. But if he did help the ghost implicate Asher, he would lose the potential of Asher's long-term business and the chance to be a real success.

"Show me your evidence," David said. "And some identification."

The ghost arched a brow. "Wait here."

David waited by the fireplace. Could he sabotage the future of his company, his own future, to expose a murderer? If he didn't, could he live with himself? He had enough self-awareness to know the qualities holding him prisoner—commitment, stubbornness, a strong conviction that there was a right way and a wrong way to do things—were the same qualities that would make his life miserable if he decided to not help the ghost.

When the ghost returned, he held a passport and a small voice recorder. David opened the passport. Philip Wallace. It was the same guy. The ghost held up the recorder and played a conversation between Asher and someone David didn't recognize. A few minutes into the conversation, David realized Asher was hiring a contract killer to take care of Phil.

"He's putting a hit on you," David gaped as Asher's voice began detailing Phil's appearance and personal information to the other man.

Phil turned around and flattened his hair away from his scalp to reveal a bloody wound. "I keep it as a souvenir."

David made up his mind. He took a deep breath. "If you agree to relocate immediately, then I'll bring the evidence to the police. Deal?"

"Deal."

David made a copy of the ghost's passport on Asher's photocopier, and pocketed the paper and voice recorder. Then the ghost presented him with a manila envelope.

"What's this?" David asked.

"It's got your name on it, so I imagine Asher wanted you to have it."

David opened the envelope to find a stack of cash and a handwritten note.

"Thank you in advance for your services," David read out loud. "Enclosed you will find full payment for today's relocation. I trust it has gone smoothly. Regards, Connel."

A weight lifted off his shoulders. This would be enough to cover the next payroll.

David dropped off Phil's evidence at the 18th District CPD station and then headed back to his office to research Asher a little more. As the train rumbled around a curve like a children's roller coaster, he considered what the hell he was going to do now.

He brewed a kettle of boiling water and carried a cup of hot chocolate back to his desk, then searched in PACER for any litigation involving Asher. He found some old civil cases and unearthed a number of discovery documents listing Asher's various holdings. He searched for each holding by name and recognized one as the private equity firm that controlled his biggest competitor, Ghost-B-Gone.

A week later, David read the Tribune and Sun-Times articles about the public downfall of a man who killed his business partner, then who bought a ghost extermination firm through his private equity company in an attempt to get rid of the ghost. David bordered on glee when he reached the part about the boutique ghost relocation company that did what Ghost-B-Gone, Asher's own company, couldn't. The scandal put Ghost-B-Gone out of business, and directed so much new business to GhostPlacers that David was certain he'd end up with record revenues and EBITDA during the coming year.

"Uh, you're welcome?" David heard over his shoulder.

David jumped an inch and put a hand over his heart. "Are you trying to scare me to death? What are you doing here? You're welcome for what?"

Phil grinned and spread his arms around at the new office in Merchandise Mart, filled with new furniture and new employees busy with customers. "For all of this, obviously."

"I relocated you," David said. "We made a deal. I gave your evidence to the police, which I did, and you leave Asher's house. Which you did, right?" A chill slid up his spine. Ghosts rarely traveled this far, but this was a ghost who could hold a full mug of coffee.

Phil leaned against the door to David's office. "Asher wasn't really my partner."

David gripped the edge of the desk behind him.

"But we *did* make a deal, Asher and me, and he didn't hold up his end." Philip shrugged.

David's heart beat like he was sprinting. "I sent an innocent man to…"

Philip laughed. "No, Asher really did have his business partner killed." He tapped his chest. "But I wasn't the one he killed."

"You're not a ghost," David said in an accusatory voice, disguising how gullible he felt.

Phil—whatever his name was—picked up a notepad and flipped through it. "No. I'm a genie. Congratulations."

David reeled over to the wall, flattening himself against it. That explained the astounding coffee mug strength.

Phil held out David's list of office snacks to buy. "And considering what your employees are drinking, you'll also need an in-house dentist."

David shot forward and yanked the notebook out of Philip's hands. "What about the evidence I turned in for you? Was that all bullshit?"

"Yes and no," the genie said. "I can conjure up anything. I can duplicate a voice recording that actually exists, or create a passport that doesn't."

David threw the notebook on the floor and took a step toward the genie. "Like I don't have enough charlatans around me? What's the difference between you and them? You're conjuring something from nothing. In their case, it's money. They can't see ghosts, but they get all the business." They used to, anyway. David was getting more business these days, but not because of his natural talent or his years of hard work.

The genie opened David's door and reached out his arm to the expansive office space overlooking the Chicago River. "Things seem to be going well now, David, but wouldn't you like them to go even better, and *faster*? What if I can guarantee you $10 million in new business next year?"

David stayed by his desk. "Don't push it. I'm not like Asher. I don't take shortcuts or cut deals with genies, and I'm not the kind of person who orders my partner killed for money."

Did it really matter that his recent and modest success was born of the real Philip's misfortune? Maybe it was wrong, but David decided he was okay with that. He'd done the hard work, and for so long, it seemed that luck was something that only happened to other people. But maybe he could dedicate the new conference room in Philip's memory.

"Are you planning to keep Asher company in his prison cell? The guy's a sleaze, but I wouldn't want any paying client to be unhappy with my relocation services."

"Nope, I'm done with him. But don't you worry. I'll be nice and comfy here." The genie rubbed his hands together and looked around. "So, where's my office?"

Want to read more strange tales conceived by Nina Post?

Tweet *I want more! @NinaPost @CuriosityQuills #BookLove*

GOTHIC GWEN

BY A.W. EXLEY

G*othic Gwen.* Six years old, first day at school and someone thought the nickname was the height of hilarity.

Ten years later, it still wasn't funny, but that didn't stop the other kids from chanting it as I stepped off the school bus.

Pack of Muppets, they wouldn't know Goth if Marilyn Manson drove the bus.

Just because I lived in a deconsecrated church, they all thought I was a death-obsessed emo who spent Friday night sharpening her razor blades. I hated black, I always wore at least one yellow thing and I've been known to hum along to pop tunes. Jerks.

Friday. Two days of sweet oblivion before I have to face them again.

I loved my home and I didn't care it was weird. No one understood the sense of peace enveloping me as soon as I stepped off the sidewalk onto the crunchy lime path. The world beyond our boundary was white noise, searing into my brain, making it hard to concentrate. I struggled to focus on anyone, or thing, around me. But on our little patch of earth, I could hear the birds and the sigh through the trees. Only here, the constant pain at the base of my skull receded.

When I was a small child, I suffered excruciating migraines, miniature bolts of lightning stabbing through my head. I remembered curling up into a ball, clutching my knees and rocking, trying to make the pain go away. The doctors had no clue and simply shrugged. My dad, driven to extremes, took me to church one day, hoping for a miracle. And we found one. The noise stopped and for the first time, I smiled at him.

He found the little church up for sale in a remote corner of New England, where nobody knew our history. The architect in him loved the challenge of turning the soaring ceiling and vintage stained glass windows into a serene home for the two of us.

My gaze slid down the shingles on the steeple, and I spotted my best friend, Carlie, over by the large elm. I made my way up the meandering path, and gave a cheery wave. She didn't return the gesture. I made a mental note to dump my bags and go talk to her. It had been a day or two, and she tended to sulk if she thought I was neglecting her. Life would be easier if she would text like everyone else. But I liked her old-fashioned quirks. Who needed ordinary friends when I had a Carlie?

I climbed the two worn stone steps leading to a heavy, wooden door that swung open with a light touch and crossed into the vestry, now the cloakroom and kitchen. I dropped my bag on the oak pew and toed off my sneakers, padding barefoot over the rich colored wooden floor.

"Dad? I'm home." I yelled, tossing my long brown plait over my shoulder so I could shove my head in the refrigerator and find a snack to fill the hole in my stomach until dinnertime. "I'm gonna read outside for a while."

A muffled noise came from the next room, which I interpreted as his acknowledgment. Grabbing a bunch of grapes, I bumped the fridge door shut with my arse and swiped my book off the end of the square, pine table. Reading *Wuthering Heights* didn't make me an emo; it meant I had some taste in my choice of literature.

Heading back out the door, I avoided the path and crossed through the longer grass of the lush lawn. Reaching our usual meeting spot, I threw myself down on the ground, letting the green blades tickle my bare arms and legs, as I stared up through the boughs of the spreading elm. "So, what have I done now?"

No answer. Crap, she must really be mad.

"Oh, come on, Carlie. If you're not talking I'll head back inside."

That did it. I knew she couldn't follow me inside, even though I had invited her several times. She always spouted some nonsense about issues with boundaries and not being able to cross them.

"You went swimming; you know I hate that place."

Shit. I forgot about her water phobia.

Yesterday had been sticky and humid and by early afternoon, my t-shirt plastered to my back, like cling film on microwaved pizza. All I could think about after school was a quick cool down at the secluded waterfall. Most

100

kids don't bother with the hike. Plus water acted like a noise dampener, giving me alone time in my head without Mr. Pain. The temporary escape was worth the forty-minute walk through dense forest.

Carlie probably saw me sneak home all damp.

"Sorry," I muttered, popping a grape into my mouth and opted for a change of topic. "You have no idea how many social invitations I had to blow off, to hang with you this weekend." That got a laugh from her. We both knew nobody spoke to me. Kids kept their distance from Gothic Gwen in case the weird rubbed off. They only approached to taunt me. The only physical contact was when they tripped me in the hall or shoved me into my locker. A sigh welled up in my chest and I fought it back down, but too slow to hide the growing loneliness from Carlie.

"There's a boy out there for you." Her soft tone drifted over me, like the whisper of wind though the overhead foliage. "He will understand you and be strong enough for you to lean on."

"Yeah, right." I scoffed, proving two positives can make a negative. My eyes rested on the gargoyle perched on the roof of the small mausoleum. His head cocked to one side, taking in every word. One stone eye bored into me with fixed interest. "The closest I have to a boyfriend is old Geoffrey the gargoyle up there. Always faithful, listens intently, hasn't let me down yet. He's been a real rock."

Carlie's laughter tinkled on the breeze. "You're funny. But you'll see. Soon."

My book lay next to me, I had planned to read and chat with Carlie for an hour or two, but something gnawed at the back of my head. My gaze drifted back to Geoffrey the gargoyle, I didn't like the way he stared at me today. He saw too much.

"I'm going to get my homework out of the way. I'll talk to you tomorrow." My mind shied away from the hole inside me, the one longing to be touched by a boy, not shoved or tripped. And maybe, just maybe, even one day kissed. Yea, right.

I didn't know what I would do without Carlie. She saw hope where I had none, possibly kept me from sharpening razor blades on a Friday night.

Rising, I placed a hand on the gravestone, my fingers trailed over the curved top, and my eyes rested on the scant few words.

Caroline Walters
1792 – 1808
Death will not wash you from our hearts.

You would think, after over two hundred years, she would have mellowed about the whole drowning thing.

The cool depths of the freezer held little in the way of inspiration, so I grabbed a frozen pizza base. Not that dad would complain, he loved a pizza piled high with meat and cheese. Setting the dough to defrost on the bench, I pulled ingredients from the fridge and sang along with the Beatles.

Eleanor Rigby died in the church and was buried along with her name
Nobody came
Father McKenzie wiping the dirt from his hands as he walks from the grave
No one was saved

My gazed roamed over the old cemetery that lay beyond the kitchen window. My mind carved my name on a tombstone and I imagined only one figure walking away from the freshly turned earth. I stopped singing along. Maybe I was a closet emo?

Perhaps it was time to throw something more upbeat on the iPod.

As I tossed the last salami slice on the pizza and doused it in cheese, the sun fell below the tree line. The overhead lights flickered into life by themselves. The little, stone church might be over three hundred years old, but dad installed all the latest gadgetry during the conversion.

"Fifteen minutes," I yelled. Gotta love the acoustics in churches, I can holler from anywhere and dad can hear me.

I dropped sunny yellow placemats with giant orange gerberas on the table, and laid out the cutlery. Being in a generous mood, I even grabbed a frosty Corona from the bottom of the fridge, and plonked it by dad's seat.

He sauntered through the double doors and sunk into his chair. Tall and lanky, with lean, honed muscles from hours on building sites with his crew, he had a body that made the mums do double takes. Yet he was oblivious to the attention. He didn't date and no women crossed our threshold, but sometimes I smelled perfume on his shirts when I did the laundry, or found a lipstick mark on a collar. Whatever funky, old dude stuff he did, he never brought it home.

He took a deep breath of cooked pizza as I hauled it out of the oven and laid it on the table. "Smells good, pet." He gave me a wink and picked up his beer.

I waited for him to down a good portion of his drink, before handing over the large knife, letting him carve up the pizza into man-sized slices.

"Any plans for this evening?" A cautious tone filtered his voice. He wanted me to go out with friends, but knew how I struggled to make connections.

I gave a casual shrug. "I'm going to head down to the library. I won't be too late."

He seemed satisfied and we fell into our usual dinner routine where he dissed my TV picks, while I trashed his fantasy football team.

Slamming the library door behind me, I tucked my chin into my neck and headed down the pavement. I only took a few strides when a voice pulled me up short.

"Well, lookie here, Gothic Gwen, scurrying about in the dark like a rat."

A loose group of senior kids lounged against the glass wall. Shit. Who would have thought this bunch of Neanderthals would be anywhere near the library on a Friday night?

"You know what Luke here has been doing?" Craig, the mouth, asked. "He's been googling you, and he found an interesting story all about your crazy mother."

My feet froze to the ground, my body forgetting to breathe. No. Oh god, no. The noise ramped up in my head, climbing from a buzz to a screech. I glued my eyes to a piece of gum on the concrete, trying to will them away like some lame Jedi mind trick. This is not the Gothic Gwen you are looking for.

"Your mom smashed her head into a concrete wall to make all the voices quiet. Are you gonna do that, Gwenie? Can we watch you pound your head into mincemeat?" Laughter broke out and circled me. Bullies are pack animals, like hyenas, only brave when they can egg each other on.

The pain ripped through my skull, I wanted to grab my head and cover my ears, but knew it would stoke their teasing higher. I dug my fingernails into my palm, using the tiny spike of pain to distract my mind, while I waited for an opening. To run. *Hold it together, Gwen, hold it together.*

"We've taken a vote, and we've decided you're batshit crazy, Gwenie, just like old Mom." The hyenas howled harder as they hugged themselves, rocking back and forth, letting their tongues loll pass their lips.

Chills ran down my spine. They all chipped in, taunting me, yelling jeers of "where's your straightjacket?" and "give her a padded room." Then one of the geniuses came up with a new nickname, and screams of Mad Gwen echoed around me. Two boys turned to give Einstein thumbs up.

That made an opening.

And I ran.

I didn't care where, I just ran. Tears spilled free, blurring my vision. My sneakers slapped the pavement in a regular beat, their laughter faded in my ears and the scream in my skull diminished as I put distance between us.

Slowly, the scream turned back into the buzz, telling me I neared home.

Darkness hid me. Gathering clouds blocked out the moon and the damn streetlights were on the fritz again, but for once, I was grateful. Knowing I was close, I veered off the path. Hard pavement became shorn grass under my feet, until my toe caught on a tree root and pitched me forward. I squawked as I hit the dirt face first, too slow to throw out my hands, smacking the side of my head on another root. Pushing myself up, I winched at a new sort of pain stabbing through my forehead.

"Are you ok?"

Shit, that's all I need. Another onlooker to either pity or spit on Mad Gwen.

My fingers probed a sore spot and touched something wet, while I hoped the voice lost interest and buggered off.

"Let me have a look."

Strong hands wrapped around my upper arms and straightened me to a sitting position. My ragged breathing filled the air between us. The moon snuck from behind a cloud, and a shaft of silver light hit us and illuminated him, kneeling before me, like a gargoyle crouched on the edge of a building.

Faded lean jeans encased long legs. A tear in the knee drew my eyes, the frayed edges feathered over the skin beneath. My gaze drifted upward, to a gray t-shirt hugging a wide chest, the sleeves stretched over rounded biceps. Shaggy hair draped over one side of his face. A square jaw with full lips pulled in a tight line.

His fingers brushed my hair away from my face.

Fan-flipping-tastic. A jock. Although I'd never seen him before. I frowned, trying to place his face. He looked a few years older than me, so maybe he had finished the torture laughingly called high school. I tried to pull away, but he held me in one hand as easily as if I were made of putty.

"It's only a little cut. It's stopped bleeding already." He leaned so close his breath slid over my face and his scent wrapped around me, all sun warmed earth straight after a thunderstorm.

"I'm fine." I tried to bat his hand away and simultaneously hold back more tears. Something was going to give, and soon. I screwed up my eyes, stemming the waterworks.

"Don't let them get to you, Gwen," he whispered.

My head snapped up. "How do you know my name?" My eyes flew open, to nothing. I was alone, and bruised, in the dark. My skin zinged where he touched me, the imprint from his palms still pulsing on my upper arms. My nostrils inhaled the last trace of him as I dropped back onto the grass and glared at the moon. Maybe that was my problem, always sleeping with my curtains wide open, leaving my mind exposed to invading lunacy.

Morning arrived far sooner than expected, with sunlight flooding my room, patches tinted yellow, blue, red, and green by the stained glass windows. How dare it be a nice day?! Dad would chase me outside, expecting me to do something more active than turning the pages in a book.

Dad had been reluctant to carve up the ceiling space when he made our home, and as a result, I had a double height bedroom. The layout was simple; kitchen and vestry at one end, lounge and dad's office in the middle and at the other end, two mirror image bedrooms and en-suites. His room and mine had soaring ceilings and mezzanine study areas, cantilevered over the main bedrooms below. Up a ladder, my desk nestled by the stained glass window of a penitent saint, her head bowed as she watched me work. Or play Tetris.

"Breakfast, Gwen." Ah, pancake Saturday. I hauled my arse out of bed and grabbed my dressing gown. Leaving my hair hanging loose to hide last night's bump, I padded through the lounge to the kitchen and the delicious waft of bacon and batter.

"Any plans for today?"

I sunk into a chair. Plans? How about starting up a caffeine habit? "I'll just kick around here. You?"

"I've got to head to the other side of town, foundations are being poured. I'll be back this afternoon." He reached across the table and grabbed my hand. "You doing okay?" Worry etched his face, bleached those deep brown eyes sad and tired. Mom and me, the two women in his life and neither of us sane. No wonder the guy went prematurely grey.

He'd freak when he learned the other kids knew about mom. He'd get the pitying looks, and become the poor man with the insane wife. Like a modern day Mr. Rochester, except she's shut away in a nut house, not the attic. I'll be the object of fun, tainted by my mother's mad DNA. Now that other kids sniffed out a greater weakness than living in a church, they'd be unrelenting in their attacks. Maybe I could sell dad on homeschooling and I'd never have to leave the property again.

I gave him my best false smile. "I'm fine, just bushed. I'll weed the veggie patch today, try and find that garlic you reckon is out there, and then we'll be vampire free all winter."

He gave me that wane smile, the one that didn't quite reach his eyes and told me he wasn't buying whatever bullshit I was peddling. But he didn't push the issue, leaving me to eat in silence and to figure out how to ditch school permanently, *before* Monday rolled around.

I cleared away the breakfast dishes by shoving them all in the dishwasher and then pulled on old jeans and my "a girl never forgets her first Doctor" t-shirt. I walked out the double French doors and over the deck to dad's endeavour at sustainable living. He referred to the plot as the potager, but I called it the lost world.

The church sat in the middle of a one-acre plot, surrounded by ancient oaks and elms that were old when Carlie was born. We also have graves, lots of graves. Big ones, little ones, some even with avenging angels perched on top. Some long ago sextant arranged the headstones by size in a deranged game of dominoes. They radiated out from the footpath, increasing in size, until they butted up against the two mausoleums at the back.

I scored the trifecta of weirdness; insane mother, church for a house, and dead people surrounding me.

The veggie patch sat on the only clear spot out back. My mind rebelled at the idea of planting potatoes and tomatoes on top of somebody, and long ago, I made dad promise there was nobody fertilizing our brassicas before I touched a single plant he grew. As I walked amongst the raised beds, I tugged a few weeds out of the loose soil, while my brain ran the previous night in an endless loop.

Nope. Not helping.

I had no solution to the dual problem of how to avoid everybody in town until I turned eighteen and could vamoose, and finding out who the weird (but cute) guy was that knew my name.

Giving up, I wandered over to the small mausoleum, with Geoffrey and his equally ugly twin guarding the front corners. Dropping by the elm, I nestled against its smooth trunk and stared up at the gargoyle as he glared back. One of us knew something, and it sure as hell wasn't me. Which left ole Geoff, except he wasn't in a talkative mood, and neither was Carlie when she finally showed up.

She resembled a heat shimmer in vague human form, constantly changing and shivering.

"The situation is not that bad." She swirled around her headstone, her presence stronger where her remains lay, but she could drift around the whole cemetery when restless, or pissed off.

"Yes it is. I am never going back to school, ever again. I'll just get some form of IT job so I don't have to leave the house." The fact I held a conversation with a girl who drowned over two hundred years ago confirmed my nutbar status.

"Who is he?" The boy bugged me. He was a stranger, but he knew me. Our town was small enough that everybody talked when a new family moved in or when a stranger rode through. Even *I* would have heard about him.

And he touched me. He didn't push or shove, he held me. My fingers grazed over the lump hidden by my long hair, while my stomach did flip-flops at the memory of his skin against mine.

"Eli." Her voice faded in and out as she roamed around the ancient tree.

I resisted the urge to roll my eyes, when I wanted to roll the syllables *E-li* around in my mouth and twist them with my tongue like a cherry stalk. "And how exactly do you know each other?"

Her laughter tinkled through the tree. "He's related to Geoffrey."

I knew that ugly gargoyle was holding out on me, just like I knew Carlie was yanking my chain. Sure, she knew all about the hunky boy who seemed so concerned for my well-being last night. It was a sad statement when a long dead teenager gave me grief. I would get her back for this, once I figured out how.

Maybe I'd dig her up and dump her bones in a cart at the local Wal-Mart.

"How's the head this morning?"

A squawk burst from my throat before I could haul it back in and my eyes flew to the voice. There he was, in the daylight, leaning on the stone wall holding up Geoffrey. Pale gray t-shirt hugging his body, lean faded black jeans, and scuffed motorbike boots. He was the guy equivalent of a double scoop ice cream sundae with chocolate sauce. And I was the scattering of nuts.

"Um, fine, thanks." My fingertips brushed the faint bruise, hidden by the fall of hair. "Who are you?" My internal dialogue didn't seem to be functioning so well this morning, but at least the question was out there now.

Dark gray eyes the color of the granite he lounged against regarded me. A smile touched his lips. "A friend."

"Uh-huh. Well, I don't have too many of those, so I'm pretty certain I would remember if you were one of them." Slick move Gwen. That statement doesn't at all make you sound like a big loser with no friends. I pressed my back hard against the tree, hoping a portal to another dimension would open and let me tumble through.

The smile widened. God, he's cute. Please don't be a cruel set up. If those kids were behind this, it could shatter my one remaining sane brain cell. Couldn't the cosmos, just for once, cut a girl some slack?

"We're just friends who haven't met yet." His gaze flicked up to Geoffrey and I swear the ugly sucker winked at Mr. Motorbike boots.

I peered at him from under my lashes, took a deep breath, and embraced my crazy. "You're Eli." If Carlie was yanking my chain she was so dead, once I figured out how you killed a spirit, ghost, or whatever the heck she was.

He gave a short laugh that rippled all the way through me down to my toes. "Carlie never could keep a secret."

That floored me, my brain did a U-turn and came back to the statement, sure it had misheard. "You know Carlie?"

Those beautiful gray eyes impaled me where I sat, pinning me to the tree. "How else do you think she knew my name? Plus Geoffrey talks nonstop about you."

I couldn't breathe. He knew too much. It had to be a set up. Those kids were determined to drive me nuts. My brain yelled at my mouth to shut the hell up. Even now, someone was probably drafting the papers to institutionalize me, my every word recorded as evidence against me. I'd be slapped in a huggy jacket and tossed in the padded room with mom.

He pushed off the mausoleum and sat on the grass next to me, causing me more problems. Proximity meant we were breathing the same oxygen. I didn't feel worthy, but it wasn't like I could spit it out. Not unless I wanted to look like a deranged cat trying to cough up a fur ball. Plus, there was some fruit loop gremlin in my stomach doing frantic laps yelling *oh my god! Oh my god! Oh my god!*

Get a grip Gwendolyn Adair.

Sure, I'll get a grip. I'd like to grip those firm looking biceps for starters.

"I hit my head, suffered a concussion, and you're a gargoyle come to life?" Okay, it was a long shot, but Carlie did say he was a relative of

Geoffrey, and if I was going to crash and burn, I may as well go down in a massive screaming fireball.

A smile quirked on those too perfect lips. Just my luck, I find a cute guy I can actually talk to, and he's a granite gargoyle. I should just rock up to the asylum and check myself in.

"Kind of."

Not the answer I expected. "This is nuts, I really am cracked."

He reached out and took my hand. "No, you're a Natural."

"At what? Being crazy?" I sucked at sports. I'd never shown a natural ability for anything. Except reading books and last I knew, that never made it in as an Olympic category.

"A Natural, with a capital N. Everything in nature has a resonance, and you're in tune with it. If you're particularly sensitive, you can communicate with it, like you do with Carlie." He frowned at me, concern written all over his face. "Where's your mother? Didn't she tell you this?"

My breath caught in my throat, he obviously hadn't caught the latest Facebook updates and shared story links. "She's not around." I dropped my gaze down to our hands. I tried to reclaim mine, but he twined his fingers through mine, locking me to him.

With his other hand, he reached out. Warm fingers traced my jaw, before lifting my chin to meet his piercing gray eyes. "You can tell me."

A desert sprung up in my mouth. I swallowed, trying to find some moisture. My heart pounded loud against my ribs, demanding to be set free from the secrets it held. "My mom is institutionalized. I'm not allowed to see her. She spends her days in a straightjacket trying to smash her brains out against a wall." A tear welled up in my eye and he brushed it away.

"No one taught you to filter the noise?"

I couldn't speak, years of trying to forget my mother's horrid existence crawled back up my throat in a fetid rush, making me gag. Another tear followed the first. I couldn't remember talking to mom; I only ever heard screams, and poor dad tried to protect me from sharing the room next to the woman he loved.

I shook my head.

"Oh, Gwen," he breathed my name. He released my hand, but then strong arms encircled me as he pulled me into his embrace.

My cheek brushed the soft cotton of his shirt as I tucked my head against his shoulder. I've never trusted anyone before, or let them close. Here, now, for the first time in my life, I went with my gut and let the dam burst. My tears soaked his top as I sobbed out all the pain scarring me on the inside.

Hours passed and he held me, his back against the old elm. I never grieved for mom, not until now. They took her when I was three, and Eli rocked me through thirteen years' worth of tears. Anguish twisted inside and wrung me out like a dirty old dishcloth, but he cradled me to him like I was made of the finest silk.

"I'm so sorry." My voice rasped over a raw throat and my gaze narrowed through puffy and swollen eyes. But instead of being empty, for the first time, a sense of peace settled over me. I had told someone, and he didn't run screaming from the property. "I know I'm mad. I talk to gargoyles, Carlie, everything." I waved an arm, trying to encompass all the weirdness that defined my life. Then there was what he said, about me being a natural at this freaky stuff, and it didn't sound as bizarre as it probably should have.

"You're not mad. You are very special, and I'm here to help you."

With one fingertip under my chin, he tilted my tear stained face. He lowered his head, his lips millimeters from mine. His earthy, warm scent enveloped me. With my lids closed, my eyes rolled into the back of my head as my brain chanted "this isn't happening." I looked a mess, had ruined his shirt, and sobbed for hours.

Not. Going. To. Happen!

His lips brushed mine in the briefest butterfly kiss and a steam whistle blew off the top of my head.

Sunlight should be banned. Grabbing a pillow, I stuffed it over my face, blotting out the daylight streaming from above and spotlighting my bed. Or maybe I should finally give in and buy drapes like normal people.

Eli had kissed me and disappeared. Again. So I dragged my sorry arse to my bedroom to think. I spent the rest of Saturday with my laptop, looking for anything about gargoyles and people who could see ghosts. I found nothing, although I wasted an hour watching cat antics on YouTube. I did learn gargoyles were old, like *thousands of years* old. Even ancient Egyptians put gargoyles on their buildings, to act as guardians against evil.

I either stumbled into the most elaborate set up ever, involving Carlie and Geoffrey, or Eli was telling the truth. In which case, I needed more information, and less cat cuteness.

I dressed and made my way to the kitchen. I was midway through demolishing a bowl of muesli with yogurt when dad appeared and poured himself a coffee from the machine. He had that small smile crinkling his eyes and pulling one side of his mouth that told me he got laid last night. Not that I wanted to know the details. A shudder shot down my spine at the mere thought of geriatric sex. He kissed goodbye to forty last year, and surely antics at his age risked a heart attack or something.

"Plans?" he asked over the rim of his coffee mug.

Words flowed to the tip of my tongue—I want to travel out of state and visit mom, ask her a few personal questions. But not today. In thirteen years, I had visited mom once. It didn't end well.

I shrugged instead. "Soak up some rays. Read." Interrogate a ghost, a gargoyle, and some weird guy who has started hanging around and turned my knees to Jell-O.

"Okay. I have a rush project, so you know where I'll be."

I continued the non-committal noises while I loaded the dishwasher, then kissed his cheek, grabbed my book, and headed out the door.

Hoping dad was busy inside, I resisted the urge to holler at Carlie. Circling out back, I sat on the edge of a high gravestone with a blind folded angel looming above. It seemed apt. "Spill, Carlie. What the heck is going on?"

The shimmer formed itself speck by speck. "I told you there was a boy for you who would understand."

"Yeah, yeah." Crossing my arms over my torso, I glared at her insubstantial form as she flitted back and forth in front of me. "I thought we were friends, but you're holding out on me."

"Why don't you go straight to the source, and ask him your questions?" She darted behind me. Her shimmer had obscured my view of the trees beyond, but now it lay open.

And there he was, Eli, lounging against a tree. A knee melting smile plastered over his face. "Good morning."

If he was going to vanish again, I better make good use of him while he was in front of me. "Excellent, question time can start."

He spread his hands and approached me with an open look. "What do you want to know?"

Why did you kiss me? No wait, probably not the best place to start. I need hard data to explain my freaky existence. Let's start with the basics, since Google was no help whatsoever. "What am I?" Inside, my brain got down on its knees and said "please don't say *a freak*."

He stopped in front of me and the smile broke his face again. I had tossed him an easy pass. "You're special. You're a being who is in tune with the resonance of the earth; you are instrumental in maintaining the balance."

Well, that sounded cool, but gave me a hundred more questions. "How?"

He swiped a hand over the back of his neck as he conjured up the words he wanted. "If I took you to a train station, teeming with hundreds of people, you would be able to pinpoint the one person whose resonance is affecting the world. The one person whose path needs to be altered or stopped."

I let the thought roll around in my head a bit. Sometimes I met people who made my skin crawl, and drove the claws of pain to scrabble and try to break out of my skull. "Like some sort of cosmic cop, stopping evil, thing?"

"Yes, sort of. You can identify them, so others can deal with them before they damage the world around us."

"I hear the resonance, don't I?" I was so close to knowing why I was nuts. The constant buzz in my skull, the pain threatening to burst through the bone and splatter my brain over the pavement.

His eyes clouded over, changing to storm gray and his brows drew together. "Yes. Everything emits a resonance, either positive or negative. Except for others like me, we're neutral."

Neutral, the word nagged at my overloaded brain. "Like Switzerland?"

"Yes. I don't emit resonance, I absorb it."

He was so close, I could smell his soap: clean, green apple. If I leaned forward, I could press my head to his chest. Would he wrap his arms around me? Or push me away?

"This is all too freaking weird," I muttered. And yet, at the same time, it wasn't. It all made sense and fit into place like a jigsaw puzzle I hadn't even known I was trying to complete. Realization slammed into my brain, as though it leapt at the Velcro wall and hung there.

"You stop the noise." Holy crap. My eyes widened, that's why I wanted to be near him so bad. He stopped the constant pain. The absence of something takes longer to register than the presence of something. Eli was my own portable sanctuary and smoking hot as an added bonus. God just put whipped cream on top of my personal sundae.

My circuits were close to overloading and getting ready to blow out the main power board. "So, what are you?"

"It's complicated. You just need to know I'm here for you now." He drew a hand down the side of my face, I leaned into the contact. I never knew how starved my body was for physical affection until Eli began touching me. Not that I didn't get heaps of hugs from dad, but this was so different and melted my insides.

"So am I crazy or what?" One more question, which desperately needed an answer. He drew me into his arms; a deep sigh welled up in my chest and worked its way free. I could stay there forever.

"You're not crazy, you're different. Other people don't understand different, like they can't sense Carlie. So they label different as crazy."

My brain held up a card and called for time out. If I wasn't nuts, this was a lot to process. I needed time for everything to sink in and marinate a little. "Will you be around tomorrow?"

"Yes. I've watched you for a long time, Gwen. But I won't let the other kids hurt you, not when I can protect you."

That's all I needed to know. For now.

Grabbing my bag, I scampered out the door and down the white path. Monday no longer looked as gloomy and insurmountable as it had Friday night. Things had changed. I wore my hair loose, so I could hide behind the chestnut curtain, but I had dared to swipe pink gloss over my lips and drag the mascara wand over my long lashes. There was a bounce to my step. I blew Geoffrey a kiss on my way past, and Carlie waved an ethereal arm in my general direction.

And then… here he was, Eli. My portable sanctuary. Standing at the bus stop, big as you please, a satchel slung over his sculptured shoulder. A goofy smile snuck up on me, before my brain gave a startled tap.

"What are you doing here?" I blurted out as the bus sedately rounded the corner.

His piercing gaze met mine, and that killer smile heated my insides and turned my toes into s'mores. "I'm going to school. A Natural needs someone to look out for her."

He took my hand in his and brushed a kiss over my knuckles. The goofy grin returns to my face, as the bus stops and the door swings open. Maybe school won't be so bad after all.

Want to read more about Gwen, what she learns about Eli, and her plot to save her mom?

Tweet *More Gwen* *@AWExley* *@CuriosityQuills* *#BookLove*

HOW I KILLED THE DRAMA

BY MIKE ROBINSON

Before I killed the drama, I had to meet it head on, face-to-face. And his name was Harold Larkens.

I met him during the brief two years I was a traveling salesman for a medical equipment company that will currently remain nameless—oh, but that sort of discretion is just old habit now, I'd say. Why should they remain nameless? Because of my fear? Because of my embarrassment at having two years' worth of paychecks signed by crooks?

No, old habit now. The company's name was East Morrison Medical Supply Group. I toted their shit from town to town, doctor to doctor, smiling for them, being proud for them, giving them an amiable mascot face with which their customers could associate them, sprinkling the last drops of my acting talent on hocking stuff that probably hastened the Reaper's hand more than stayed it.

Am I remorseful? Hateful? Vengeful? Guilty?

Nah.

That's because I met Harold Larkens. That's because the universe had the good sense to put our two hotel rooms together that night, back to back, like buddies comparing height.

I was on my way to Chicago for some medical conference I would never make it to, and, because of lagging funds and my recent inability to get a hold of East Morrison for better accommodations, I'd checked into a two-bit roach-shack. Chicago was only a fifteen-hour drive from my hometown, and I hate flying. Hated, I should say. So, I limited my time in the air as much as possible. But nothing bothers me now.

That's because I met Harry Larkens. That's because, soon after I met Harry Larkens, I killed him.

Hey, he asked me to.

Sobbing filtered easily through the saran-thin walls of the Orchid Acres Motel. Normally, I wouldn't have paid attention, especially with Victoria's many secrets sprawled across my lap (that catalogue was with me the entire two years), but there was something off about this sobbing. Crying usually carried the weight of regret or depression or anxiety, but I couldn't classify this one. It was just… different.

As I listened, I couldn't help but laugh: between, and within, every sob, stutter and hiccup were distant burps—often reaching belch status—farts, sharp twangy "Ha!" kinds of snorts, sneezes, and coughs. And every one of them different from their normal counterparts, the ones you'd encounter on buses and subways and planes. They were so heavy and so authoritarian, as though they took themselves to be the first fart, or cough, or sneeze, or belch and were all perversely proud of it.

Yet the persistent sobbing, that horrible, unearthly sobbing, seemed to destroy any notion of pride.

I'm not sure how long I sat there, drinking in his misery, morbidly entertained by it as it infested my, admittedly, fragile wellbeing. The makeshift lust once invigorated by the brazier-bounty before me was now contaminated. My erection shot. I started to think too much, and with every sob, hiccup, and gurgle noise, the thinking grew heavier and darker.

If I didn't do something, I concluded, come morning the local police could conceivably have two back-to-back suicides on their hands. So, I zipped up, straightened myself, and went next door.

Raising my hand to knock, I saw the door was slightly ajar. Slowly, I stepped into the room, knocking as I went. "Excuse me?"

No immediate reaction. I opened the door further. Nothing appeared out of order except for the man sitting cross-legged on the bed, back arched, head slumped as though he'd suffered a stroke while meditating. What struck me was how pristine everything was—from the crisply made bed to the default position of the remote atop the TV, all appeared untouched. There didn't even seem to be any luggage.

I watched the man's body spasm with tears, listened to the blackly humorous noises that continued to emanate from his body.

Maybe he was dying.

"Excuse me?" I said again, this time louder. "Are you alright, sir?"

"I can't stop this," he said, remaining fixed, head still down.

"Stop what?"

He looked at me, his eyes swallowing whole my attention. "You'll have to stop this for me."

"What?"

"Yes. You're here. I've tried many others but they can't do it. My belches get the best of them."

"Why? What did you have for dinner?"

"It's not like that. Step closer and see for yourself."

Cautiously I obeyed, taking two soft strides into the room. Harry farted and I felt a wave of ecstatic juvenile lust rush me, far more potent than with Victoria's luscious secrets. The scent stayed in my nostrils and soon the erotic feelings simmered into domestic adoration. Familial love. Fiftieth anniversary love.

Then Harry belched, and I felt a stinking jealousy the likes of which I'd never encountered before.

When Harry sneezed, I felt unprecedented anger. Frustration.

And when he coughed, he spewed forth a potent case of fear that, for mere moments, assigned a phobia to every little thing.

He hiccupped, and sadness swept me. A lonely, hollow melancholy I never experienced, even in the two years spent isolated on the road.

Yet when that spurt of "Ha!" laughter fired from his throat, I was a giddy kid again, laughing myself silly in the back of some cheesy matinee my pals and I just snuck into.

"My organs," Harry said through the tears. "My organs aren't normal."

"I would... uh, I would guess so," I stammered, still mystified by the rapid procession of sensations.

"Instead of lungs I have... well, a set of fears," he said. "I've been told they look like big livers. My love is a sphincter. Actually, it's your love, too. It's everyone's."

Another "Ha!" came out, and I laughed, but I'd already been laughing out of puzzled discomfort.

Then I smelled something else. Stepping in closer, I detected wave after wave of a ripe body odor launching poignant curiosity, a sense of wide-eyed, gawking amazement. Wonder. The permeating inquisitiveness, exploratory restlessness, which often made men insane and society saner.

"It houses it all, that curiosity," Harry said. "The skin contains it all, that begins it and nurtures it all. But now... now..."

117

He couldn't finish his sentence. There was an unsteady pause.

Then, "I want you to kill me. Please."

"What?"

"I want you to kill me. To end my life. It'll bring me great relief. It will bring all of you great relief." He lowered his eyes. "I have… I have cancer."

"I'm sorry."

"You don't understand," he said. "This cancer will affect you all."

"I can't do that. I can't kill someone." At least not directly. East Morrison notwithstanding.

"That's what you all say," Harry complained. "You're just smelling my farts and hearing my laughs. But if I set foot outside long enough, you would all change your tune."

"What in blazes are you talking about? What's your name?"

Beneath the darkness of his voice slipped the words, "Harold Larkens."

"Okay Harold, I'm only here to help you—"

"Right, I realize that. So many people have said they want to help me. They claim they want to, but nobody has actually fulfilled my simple request."

"You mean, killing you?"

He nodded. "My gas gets in the way."

"What do you mean 'if you set foot outside, you would all change your tune?'"

"During daylight. I haven't been in the sun for many years. I'm allergic."

"Allergic. You mean—"

"I sneeze a lot."

My mind quickly replayed the poignant anger I'd felt when he sneezed. I shuddered.

"Photic sneeze reflex," I blurted out, recalling the syndrome from my relatively superficial dip in the medical field.

"Is that what I have?" he asked.

"Sounds like it. Some people walk out into the sun and just start sneezing uncontrollably. My brother is like that. He lives in Hawaii, which doesn't make much sense."

Suddenly Harold let loose with a loud "Ha!" and his expression was one of pleasant surprise. Much of his eyes, however, remained clouded in that unshakable autumn.

"I have an idea," he said.

I backed up a step.

"Sunrise is in five hours," he said. "Will you take me to a secluded area? You'd be closest to me. You'd feel the brunt of it. You might even get all of it. And it would cloud you, drown out every other sensation so you'd have no choice but to destroy me."

"Harold," I said, now in the doorway. "I don't think—"

All at once, he burst from the bed, ruffling the crispness of the sheets, and lunged at me, grabbing both my arms. I was stifled, ensconced in this man's powerful body odor of curiosity and gas of love and empathy. I think what got me most, however, were the hiccups, the diaphragm glitches overwhelming me with hollowness, loneliness, so extraordinary and desperate I opted to entertain any company I could get my hands on.

"Please," he said. "I cannot exist any longer. The hiccups come the most frequently. I've been hiccupping for ages. Please."

"Harold…"

"It will all be okay, don't you see?" he said. "It'll all be okay afterwards. You've got to believe me."

He sneezed suddenly and, in a thoughtless flash, my fist plowed into his cheek. He stumbled back against the door, blood dribbling down his face.

Harold Larkens smiled. "Please," he repeated.

I didn't care much for psychological introspection, though "introspection" entailed monitoring my thoughts as he confronted me with his words and odors. I had no idea what went on in my head then, I didn't care to analyze.

I opened my bag of supplies, asking if any instrument would prove most efficient for the job. He didn't have a preference, but indicated the scalpel as being the "best we've got now."

He assured me, once again, it wouldn't matter in the end. Nothing would.

I drove him three hours to a high point overlooking Lake Michigan.

Like a mother cautiously peeking into her child's room to survey the mess, the sun rose and cast its revealing light upon the land, a massive and fiery maternal eye driving the night back into the Earth to see mankind into a new age.

Harold held out his arms, closed his eyes and soaked in the warmth.

I loved him, I was jealous of him, I was embarrassed by him, I laughed at him, I feared him, I was all sorts of things to him; I was a bouquet of emotion.

And then the sneezing began.

The sneezes came in such rapid succession that they circumvented the occasional chuckles and farts by their cohesive effect. Boiling frustration evolved into anger and then mutated into rage.

"Feel it," Harold said. "Feel it and drown in it. Please…"

The heat consumed.

I took the scalpel and stabbed him right in the anger. It bled, spurting every which way in a wild and pathetic assault on the air. Then I cut open his sadness and it dribbled with limp moroseness down his skin, pooling at his feet and mine. I punched him in the happiness, exploding sunlight from our minds, and then severed his jealousy, mangled his hate, broke his fear, tore out his guilt, and clobbered his laughter and silliness.

And Harold Larkens collapsed before me. The sun grew hotter, brighter.

I stood there for quite a long time, staring at his body.

He was dead.

Hmm.

So, that's how I killed the drama.

World peace, I guess?

Who cares.

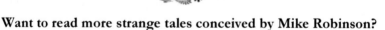

Want to read more strange tales conceived by Mike Robinson?

Tweet *I want more! @MikeSkunkApe @CuriosityQuills #BookLove*

MAD SCIENCE

BY SHARON BAYLISS

Did I request thee, Maker, from my clay
To mould me Man, did I solicit thee
From darkness to promote me?

-Paradise Lost

My boyfriend, Andrew, had a bad habit of gnawing on his lower lip when he was nervous. Before finals, he had actually managed to draw blood.

Now, on the day of our wedding, I stared at his bottom lip—pink and perfect, without a hint of bite marks. In fact, I hadn't seen him chew on his lip since the accident. My stomach hardened into a ball and I got a tight feeling behind my heart. So, he lost his bad habit. That shouldn't bother me. I didn't love him because he gnawed on his lip when he was nervous. So why did I feel like crying?

I took a deep breath and brushed lint off Andrew's tuxedoed shoulders. I'd hidden away my wedding dress so he couldn't see it, but my stylist already swept my hair into an elegant up-do and meticulously painted my face, complete with fake eyelashes, all of which probably looked ridiculous since I still wore sweats and flip-flops. I shook off the pained feeling in my gut, and examined the rest of my husband-to-be. He had the same hands that had sweat profusely during our first date in 10th grade, the same hands that held mine tightly all the way to the hospital when I broke my ankle. And his eyes, the color of milk chocolate, hadn't changed a bit.

If I hadn't noticed the lip thing, I'd feel okay right now. Not just okay—deliriously happy. This was the happiest day of my life. I exhaled deeply as if I could breathe the feeling of emptiness out of me.

Andrew parted his mouth like he wanted to say something, but his un-injured lip just quivered, then he stared at me blankly. Poor thing looked terrified.

My mother walked in with my Aunt Maddie, who looked like one of the centerpieces, head-to-toe in bright colors and flower print. However, my mother had thrown on the same "special occasion" dress she had kept in her closet for years and hadn't even bothered to put on make-up. She carried a large, unadorned, white box.

"Mom, what happened to that mother of the bride dress you bought?" I asked.

"It was too expensive, Heather. I returned it."

My cheeks burned. The dress hadn't seemed too expensive when we bought it together three months ago. However, things changed. Fortunately, I knew Mom wouldn't say anything in front of Aunt Maddie.

"Tsk, tsk," my aunt chided. "You're not supposed to see the bride before the wedding. What are you doing here?" She clearly addressed Andrew, and I jumped in before he would have to attempt to respond.

"I'm just helping him get dressed," I said. "Don't be so old-fashioned."

"Since when does a grown man need help getting dressed?" my aunt asked. "Don't worry, I won't tell your father what you were really doing." She winked.

"Why don't you go back to your room?" I suggested to Andrew. "It's time for me to put on my dress."

He nodded timidly and left, awkwardly taking a wide breadth around my aunt.

"Goodness, I was just joking," my aunt said. "You don't have to act like brother and sister on my account."

I stared at her blankly.

"Not even a kiss goodbye?" my aunt asked.

I blushed, but not for the reasons my aunt probably thought. Truthfully, I hadn't kissed him at all since the accident. I would today, of course, at the altar. Moreover, tonight was our wedding night... so I'd have to get over myself eventually. *Just give it time. Everything will be like it was.*

"Heather, I'm kidding around. You look beautiful, sweetheart. I'm so happy for you." My aunt kissed me on the cheek. I'd have to remember to check my face for a giant coral pink lipstick smudge.

My mother placed the large, white box she had been carrying on the dresser.

"What is that?" I asked.

"A wedding gift," my mother replied.

"Why isn't it with the rest?"

"Because it's from me," she said simply. "I wanted you to open it before the ceremony." She paused. "Sometime when you're alone."

I glanced over at the box and that hard feeling in my gut returned. My mother watched me with a flat expression.

My Aunt Maddie remained oblivious, as always. "Ooo, I bet I know why you have to open before the ceremony," she said. "It must be your something old. Or, borrowed. Of course, you already have your something new."

"What?" I eyed my aunt suspiciously.

"That gorgeous wedding gown. I know it's not your mother's. If my memory serves correctly, she wore a pantsuit to the courthouse."

My mom gave my aunt a lame smile.

"Andrew is really getting around well, isn't he? Aside from a few scars and a little limp, he seems pretty healthy for a man who was recently declared dead," Aunt Maddie said. "I can't believe only a few weeks ago that ER doctor said he would never wake up." She gazed upwards. "The power of prayer is an amazing thing. That doctor would eat his words now, seeing him ready to walk down the aisle. It's truly a miracle. If I hadn't seen it myself, I wouldn't have believed it. I know your side of the family is all about the science, but I tell you, prayer works. And that's your proof." She pointed out the hall towards where Andrew had exited.

"Or... he lived because he had one of the best doctors in the world," I said. "He would have died if it weren't for Dad. The ER doctors couldn't have done what he did."

"That's true, my dear," my aunt said. "Your father must have worked on him for 36 hours straight. That man would do anything for you. I remember he said, 'That boy is making it to his wedding day, I don't care how.' He couldn't stand the thought of you in grief."

I wanted to change the subject. Those were the worst 36 hours of my life. My throat tightened, but I didn't want to cry. *The happiest day of my life. The happiest day of my life*, I chanted inside my head. I've wanted to marry Andrew since I saw his impish smile from across the room in 10th grade Chemistry class. I want this more than anything. But part of me knew I shouldn't have to work so hard to remind myself.

"Maddie, I'm going to help Heather get into her dress," my mother said softly. "Why don't you go check with the wedding planner, make sure everything is on schedule?"

Maddie kissed my cheek again. "Next time I see you, you'll be a *married* woman. I love you, sweet girl."

"I love you too, Aunt Maddie."

Aunt Maddie sure knew how to monopolize a conversation, often to my great annoyance, but now I really wished she'd stay and keep chattering until the ceremony started. My mother was a woman of few words, but when she *did* speak, she meant it. And, I knew she had words for me now.

The day after my grandmother died, lightning struck the oak tree in our backyard and split it in two. That was almost ten years ago now, but I still remember the burning smell. The grotesque blackened remains of the tree looked like a monster. For some reason, I didn't cry when my father told me Grandma died, but I cried about the tree. I guess it pricked my grief in the right spot. I had loved climbing in it. I climbed up that tree when I was scared, or angry, or just wanted to be alone. I remember worrying about the birds that had lived in the tree, and had prayed, asking God to take their bird souls to heaven, even though Aunt Maddie said birds didn't go to heaven.

But, what I remember most was my father. The death of the tree upset him as much as it upset me. Maybe more. He didn't cry about it, but he sat on the back porch and stared. It seemed like he stared at it for days. He would stare at the tree, and then sometimes, he'd just stare at the sky.

People say my father went funny after that. I remember overhearing one of his obnoxious colleagues say that if my father hadn't been a genius, he'd be in the looney bin. Of course, my father never seemed strange to me. Which may be because, as Aunt Maddie would say, "the nut doesn't fall far from the tree."

But no, Father was a little eccentric. Most geniuses are. At least, that's what I thought. Until I smelled that burning smell again.

When Andrew didn't call on the way home from class, I knew something was wrong. He'd started his first year of college sixty miles from home, and he commuted so he could stay close to me. He would talk to me on his drive to help keep him awake.

Instead I got a call from my father. The first thing he said was, "I don't want you to worry. He's going to be fine. But…"

However, he wasn't going to be fine. I got to the hospital, where my mother and Aunt Maddie waited for me. I could see it on their faces before they said anything. And what they said was that Andrew had been in an accident. He was still alive, but only because the machines kept him so. His brain was dead. He would never wake up.

Only minutes after I had been told that the love of my life was for all effects and purposes dead, my father pulled me aside. It felt like I had cotton stuffed in my ears. I could hardly breathe. My father had to shake me a little to get me to look him in the eye. He told me Andrew was going to live. I didn't ask how. I didn't care how. I just fell into his arms and sobbed.

My father pulled some strings and checked Andrew out of the hospital, life support and all, and brought him to the personal lab he had made out of our guesthouse. He wouldn't let me see Andrew. My mother was the only person allowed to come inside the lab. She brought him meals and medical supplies, and for some reason, large coolers spilling with smoke from dry ice.

I prayed, I think for the first time since I had prayed for the souls of the birds. I didn't believe in God anymore, but I didn't know what else to do.

However, I did believe in my father.

Through the whole three days, it felt like worms swam around my stomach, a strange mix of hope and fear.

Then, on the third day, all the lights went out in the main house, and I smelled the burning. I knew lightning had hit again. And, everyone I loved was in the guesthouse. I ran, with my heart pounding. The burning smell intensified as I approached the guesthouse, but I saw no evidence of a lightning bolt from above. The smell came from something inside.

My mother watched me with her usual solemnity, but her eyes had grown watery, which was odd. "I know it's nothing compared to you, but I loved Andrew, too," she said. "And since he never had much family to speak of, I felt almost like his mother sometimes."

"Mom, this *really* isn't the time."

"Your father is so brilliant," she continued. "He never accepts limits. Nothing is impossible. It's one of the reasons why I fell in love him, and it's why he's at the forefront of his field. But when you combine that with an all-encompassing love for his daughter… things get cloudy."

A tear skidded down my cheek, and I swiped it away. If one fell, the dam might break.

At least, on your wedding day, people expect you to cry.

"I understand why he did it," my mother continued. "Things were cloudy for me too. That's why I helped, brought him… supplies." She lowered her eyes to the ground and whispered the last words. "I cannot explain what happened. It was beyond science. It was an act of darkness."

My mother had never believed that anything was "beyond science." She loved science like Aunt Maddie loved God. My mother used to say science was the light of the world, the only thing keeping us from darkness.

"I can't talk about this now," I said. "I have to go get married."

"It'll be easier on you if you grieve now. And Andrew deserves to be grieved."

"*Andrew* is in the room three doors down."

"No. Andrew is in the box."

It felt like needles pricked me all over. I glanced at the box on the dresser.

My mother picked up the box and held it out to me. She seemed to move too slowly. When I made no motion to take the box from her, she put it back on the dresser and opened it herself. She pulled out an attractive wooden urn, a warm brown etched with golden leaves. The color reminded me of Andrew's eyes.

"I don't understand what this is supposed to be." My voice shook. "Whatever he might be, you can't deny that Andrew's body is in the room down the hall."

"I managed to obtain medical waste from your father's procedure and had it cremated. It's mostly discarded brain matter, blood, and skin. You don't need to know the details."

"No, I really don't." I swallowed back what little I'd managed to force in… whenever I ate last time. My mother was the county coroner. She spent all day with dead bodies, and dismembered body parts didn't bother her any more than a rack of pork ribs. "This is your idea of a wedding gift? Cremated brain matter??"

She put the urn down. "I know I'm bad at these kinds of things. I just thought that one day you might want it. I can keep it until then, if you're not ready to say goodbye. However, you will have to, eventually. And how can you grieve someone who is lying in your bed beside you?"

"Exactly. You don't have to grieve someone who is lying in your bed beside you."

I didn't know what to say or do, but I knew I had to get out. A hundred people waited to watch my wedding. They wanted to witness the miracle. The boy who cheated death to marry the love of his life.

And, my father waited to walk me down the aisle, proud to present me with *his* gift, his ultimate achievement. Proof that man triumphed over death, over God. When my father finally brought Andrew out of the guesthouse, he didn't seem to care Andrew could barely speak and didn't know his own name, let alone mine. He was *alive*, and that was all that mattered to my father.

I tried to pretend that it was all that mattered to me.

I found myself standing in the doorway of Andrew's dressing room. I couldn't suppress the instinct. When I felt sad, scared, angry, lonely, anything, I always went straight to Andrew's arms, just like I used to do with the tree. Now, I didn't know where else to go. He sat on the sofa staring at his hands. By the way he looked at them, they seemed to be upsetting to him. When he noticed me looking at him, he startled.

"It's okay," I said.

He stood up and pointed toward the door.

"No, it's not time. I just… I'm here to… I don't know why I'm here."

I approached him cautiously, like you might a wounded bear. For all I knew, that's how he felt. I couldn't imagine how he perceived the situation. His eyes always appeared wide and frightened, but he also seemed to be trying desperately to win my approval. When my father tried to teach him to say, "I do," he would shake his head and breathe heavily, frustrated, but he would continue to try to vocalize. He wanted to do the right thing. He wanted to please us.

Throwing caution to the wind, I wrapped my arms around him and buried my face in his chest. I figured he might freak out and start throwing things, or maybe even attack me, but at that moment, I didn't care. I wanted to smell his scent. His scent hadn't changed much, but I only smelled Andrew's brand of body wash. My father had probably used Andrew's old body wash when he got him cleaned up before the wedding. But, I didn't care why. I just inhaled it and felt the thump of his heartbeat against my cheek.

He didn't push me away or freak out. I felt a little tug when he pulled a bobby pin out of my hair and examined it quizzically. He reached for another one, and I pulled away.

"Stop that," I said. "My hair will fall down."

He handed the bobby pin back to me.

"Thank you," I said. "I was thinking, instead of 'Andrew' maybe I should call you 'Andy' or 'Drew.' Something a little different, that's just for you."

The corner of his mouth tugged, almost like he smiled, but I couldn't tell for sure.

"Heh-zer," he said.

"What?"

"Heath-zer."

I couldn't help but smile. "You said my name. You must have been practicing."

"I do," he said.

I laughed. "Well, I guess you have all the vocabulary you need for today."

He cocked his head in a satisfied way.

"I'm going to put on my wedding dress now. They're going to take you to stand at the altar. Then I'll come in, stand next to you, and hold your hand. The preacher will talk for a while. Then when he asks you a question, you'll say 'I do.'" I paused. "I just wish you knew what that meant."

I squeezed his hand gently, and then walked back to my dressing room. I hoped my mother would be gone, and thankfully, she was. She had put the urn back in the box but had left it on the dresser. I pulled the urn out, ran my fingers along the etchings of leaves.

"When I agreed to marry you, I really meant it." I started talking to the urn without even thinking about it. "Some people thought we were too young to get married, we couldn't really know if we'd love each other forever. But I knew I would. I just knew. And that hasn't changed." I fiddled with my engagement ring. "I'd rather live with broken pieces of you sewn together than have nothing left of you at all. I hope that's okay."

I picked up the urn and kissed it. "I miss you so much."

I gently placed the urn back in the box and went to get my wedding gown.

Want to read more strange tales conceived by Sharon Bayliss?

Tweet *I want more! @SharonBayliss @CuriosityQuills #BookLove*

ON THE ROCKS

BY WILLIAM VITKA

T*hey were all dead.*
Something to do with the ice in the asteroids and the water the ice became.
Something. Something like that.
Alex had trouble remembering.

Snap snap snap.

Time as a concept meant almost nothing. Clocks just ticked, clicking things that signified when to drill and mine and ship and rest. There were no sunsets. No sunrises. Only hours. Endless hours, and a black sky pockmarked by a myriad of white pinpricks. Call it bad planning. A total lack of foresight.

The purifiers started dying, one by one. Food stocks withered. Water supplies drained. Tempers flared and red-lined. What stunned Alex was how fast everything fell apart. Such speed in stark contrast to how soon help could arrive.

Not just years, but decades. Or more.

It wasn't the company's fault—not entirely. It was theirs, too. Eagerness overriding all.

Alex dug. Under that weird forever-night sky, into the hard face of the asteroid. His boots were dirty. Work lights shone over the area. Tools glimmered on his belt. His hands cramped under the orange gloves of his suit.

He dug for his mother. He dug for his father. He dug for his brother. He dug for his sister. For them, four separate holes—four holes, four whispering mounds ready to be curled back to cover four bodies under a black blanket of vacuum.

His family's graves would be carved out first, and then the bodies would be dragged from the base. This plan made the most sense to Alex, since it was the low-impact drilling and picking away at rock that presented the bigger task. Moving corpses was a snap thanks to the effectively non-existent gravity.

What about plots for the others?

Alex had no idea. Was there strength enough left? Strength, in aggregate, had become a commodity, only to be spent on the most important things. "Was there strength enough left" was the real question. It floated there, hovering, just under "Was survival feasible or even worthwhile?" How much energy could be safely expended on such an ultimately useless gesture as graves?

Stravinsky's, *The Rite of Spring*, was playing on the base's communication system. It poured out the speakers in Alex's helmet. Music met only by muscle twitches of annoyance. Had there been any air, the whole asteroid would have throbbed with string and bass and harmony. The instrumental, intended to stave off the madness and paranoia expeditions like these caused, drove Alex insane.

Back inside, the computer waited. So did the bodies.

Alex couldn't say for sure that any of the former kin was worth the effort.

The father had dragged them here. The mother had dutifully obeyed. The brother and sister probably deserved a proper resting place, but they were complacent rubes as well.

A better life, they said. A new world, they said. A new start, they said.

One out of those three had been true.

Frustration and anger that boiled easily into rage remained.

The company. The family. The others. They all shared the blame.

The outer door of the airlock to the squat, white Lego block-looking base closed behind Alex without even a whisper. The interior door opened just as quietly a moment later. No noise except Stravinsky and harsh breaths bouncing around inside a helmet. No *whoosh* of air to equalize the antechamber because, simply, there was no more air.

The tank on Alex's back read forty percent. A few hours left. Probably less with all the digging and exertion.

Have to check the tanks on the others. Might be able to scavenge something from them. They weren't using the O_2 anymore, anyway. A long shot, but still a shot.

On the other hand, what would the point be?

At least the heaters and the lights and the entertainment centers still worked. All those modern comforts ready to be ingested.

The computer's stupid smiling face greeted Alex on the command console. Presumably, giving the computer a visage was meant to discourage feelings of isolation—or to encourage feelings of partnership, but if the company had explained this at some point to everyone, it had been lost alongside countless other things in Alex's memory. Alex couldn't even recall what the thing was named.

It pumped a cheerful "Hello, young miner" through the radio of Alex's helmet. Then it babbled reminders about keeping air tanks fully charged. Then reminders about staying on schedule for the dig. Finally, reminders about the truly and obscenely vast entertainment selection that sat waiting inside the base's network.

Not much of a companion, this dumbly grinning machine. Nothing more than a directory of commands and diversions.

Alex punched the music selection buttons hard, killing Stravinsky, and bringing to life instead Beethoven's, *Moonlight Sonata*—which seemed more fitting for no reason that Alex could identify.

Alex swam over to the bodies of his father, mother, brother, and sister. They were stacked like frozen dinners. Floating just slightly above the ground.

Sister, the smallest and lightest, was on top.

She was the first to be moved, as per the plan.

Alex checked the tank on her back. Empty.

Her face was a blue, frozen gasp. Horrible and sad, but he towed her along easily enough, as anticipated, by gripping the hoses that connected her lifeless head to the oxygen backpack.

Alex didn't have much to say while pushing her into the grave.

"Sorry, I guess."

Rock curled back in on that dead blue face wrapped in an orange suit.

Ditto the blue-faced brother, who had been as excited as anyone else.

Father and mother were a different story. Alex threw them, rather than carry, letting weightlessness and inertia bounce their blue face-filled helmets against doorframes. Throwing father so hard against a work light pylon, in fact, that his faceplate cracked and shattered in slow motion. The glass twinkled like the stars did not, here, where there was no atmosphere to induce those twinkles.

Alex panted. He stood on the surface of the asteroid, in front of two empty graves, a parent in each of his gloved hands. Father, who shouldn't have risked his family. Mother, who should've known better than to let him.

Did the bodies deserve preservation, in memoriam?

Decidedly not.

The jury had reached its decision. The judge had rendered a verdict.

Alex chucked their bodies into the darkness, aiming for a slowly rotating chunk of rock, hoping to watch the bodies ricochet like pinballs.

They did, but it was less dramatic than Alex had envisioned.

Disappointment. But Alex felt no single "Sorry" for either parent.

Back inside that high-tech Lego base, the computer's big dopey face again.

And reminders, reminders, reminders. Useless. Unnecessary. Alex couldn't really remember anything anymore, not since the start of the trip, and soon, it wouldn't matter.

Fifteen percent remaining.

Alex checked the tanks on the others. A dozen, all empty. For fun, Alex took one of the bodies and hurled it at the floating, constructed stacks of families and workers.

They scattered and collided and bounced and caterwauled.

Looney Tunes suddenly seemed like a brilliant idea.

The big holographic screen in what was once the communal room bloomed to life. Wile E. Coyote was calling Acme for Rube Goldbergian tools of insanity. The Road Runner was fleeing, fleeing, forever just out of reach.

Before all this, Alex had read much and often. Read, in fact, as far back as the initial reports about potential colonies within the Sol system. The twenty-first and twenty-second centuries were exciting times, if the stories were true. At least as far as *possibilities* were concerned.

After Base Luna, where could they go? Wherever there was water—essential to a longtime base. And from water was culled oxygen. Humanity went to the ice on Mars, after leap frogging from Luna where less gravity meant less fuel consumption and an easier lift off. And they went to the ice on Jupiter's Europa after leap-frogging from Mars.

Then the money ran out. For a while, it was enough to explore. Feeling that uniquely American pioneering spirit which probably really started, Alex ruminated, when a Kansas farm boy discovered Pluto. The colonies weren't huge, but they were marks of human accomplishment. As for what the corporations sought, human achievement meant little compared to the bottom line.

And the bottom line was paramount, considering it was private ventures and private money that took people to the stars now.

Everything on the Moon was worth *something*. The silicon, the iron, the magnesium: all potential dollar signs. The problem was balancing the cost of excavation against profit. No small task. Hundreds of billions spent on the base, the men, the tools. With the increasingly deteriorating state of the Earth, most companies wound up with a profit hovering around fifteen to twenty billion. That profit went down as the cost went up with the Martian base. And again on Europa.

Barely worth it. Just scraping by.

"Boon to the human spirit."

"Thrill of adventure."

Et cetera. That's what the ads said.

But then, *bang*. Something changed. A new president. A new Congress. A sudden sense of hope.

Though that hope was a trademark and a lie, as slogans generally are.

"Let's go farther. Let's see what's really out there."

That was new. That in and of itself was a PR campaign unrivaled.

Of course, the real reason for exploration was money. Desperation.

They went. With the human race behind them. Begging. Find something. Find anything worthwhile. Worth the trip. Worth the effort. Worth the money.

Alex's father bought in.

He was a blue-collar man who knew the dangers of mining after twenty years on the job inside our own blue marble. He went after the task anyway. A worker. Not a simple man—there is no such thing—but a man who would drag himself and his family through hell to get done what needed getting done.

And they needed this chance, the family knew, to turn things around for themselves.

The precious thing that they and a dozen others were sent out after was in fact an old, familiar alkali metal that Earth had run out of: Lithium for the battery-powered human race. There was a problem with it, though. Rarity. That third element, vital now to tech, was stunningly difficult to find. Due to its instability, it didn't form naturally. Those three protons and four neutrons didn't like getting together as well as the particles of hydrogen or carbon or iron. It was formed in low numbers with the Big Bang, but since it reacted so violently with other elements, it was a true bastard to find. In the vacuum, spallation created it—an uncommon process where heavier elements were split into lighter ones by cosmic rays.

Hell of a thing. And a monster goose chase.

Unless you can find a source closer to home.

In the Kuiper Belt, say.

There were deposits, they believed, in that rocky black space beyond the swirling storms of Neptune. Carve it out of the asteroids. Mine it. Be a hero for the folks back home. Lead an exciting new life.

That was what Alex's father had been told.

And the compensation was, well, irresistible.

Especially for them, who seemed to have a never-ending run of bad luck.

What the company needed were families. Units who knew and loved one another. It kept the order. Groups without connections tended to go south. Workers flying solo never panned out, though it temporarily created an interesting market for sociopaths.

Alex's family moved from the coalfields near Pittsburgh. Where the stars shone if you looked hard enough. Then they moved a few hours east to Riegelsville. Where the stars always seemed to find you. Then they moved a few decades into the Kuiper Belt. Where there was nothing *but* stars—stars that never twinkled, but stared.

The trip out was just a foggy blur. Cramped. Uncomfortable. People snapped into a long, white casket pushed forward by impulse magnetoplasma rockets. Cold surroundings after the curled warmth of hibernation. Dreams becoming false memories that seemed true because they were more real than the years of nothingness in transit.

There was a life before this, under Sol's yellow sun. Seconds and minutes and hours and days and months and years that were all well-defined. A hard life, but a life. Time with friends, time studying, and time working.

Out here, nothing.

What precisely had happened after they arrived?

There was a sense of newness, yes. A sense of exploration, as had been promised. But what else? Work. Time tables. Arguments. Problems with the machinery. Systems going to hell. Failing. Ice to water. Water to drink. Water to oxygen. Oxygen to breathe.

And then something. Something terrible. Some horrible source of…

Nausea first—they thought it had been caused by the trip. Diarrhea, headache, fever. Still could have been the trip. The cryosleep.

Then, problems with their central nervous system. Twitches. Little seizures.

Radiation.

Alex's gloved fingers suddenly snapped. Memories crept up at last.

Madness. All that screaming. The panic.

The radiation in the ice. Poison jumping from the freeze to the water and then the oxygen. What they drank and what they breathed. Doom for the family and everyone else on this forsaken rock.

Snap snap snap went Alex's tremors.

Five percent.

Good old Wile E. chased the Road Runner off a dark brown cliff against a bright blue sky with puffy white clouds that Alex vaguely remembered from his former life.

Four percent.

Gravity patiently waited for him to realize this before dragging his body down.

Three percent.

One final nagging thought rumbled around inside the helmet.

Two percent.

Why had Alex killed everyone?

One percent.

That's all, folks.

Want to read more strange tales conceived by William Vitka?

Tweet *I want more! @Vitka @CuriosityQuills #BookLove*

RAZOR CHILD

RAZOR CHILD

BY MICHAEL SHEAN

R aj let the Seattle winter blow over him like a curtain of knives. He stared out across the city's glittering heart; massive block-towers of glass and grim concrete turned into a consumer fairyland. Everything pulsed with ribbons of light and towering holographic billboards, brand models and spokespeople smiling down on him from on high like saints. And now, at the waning end of the twenty-first century, these people served as just that in the absence of anything else—the religions of old had all but perished before the might of strident corporate giants and the ideological wars of the early century, and consumerism was the new faith of the world.

For Raj, however, the spectacle was a little empty; he had too much else on his mind. He leaned against the balcony rail, trying to warm himself in the cold light of the towering projections. There had been a party going on in the apartment behind him, now winding down, and he'd spent the whole evening wishing that he had never come. He'd been invited by a girl, one he very much had hoped to finally kick things off with, and his failure to do so—yet again—somewhat grated.

"Hey, man." The girl's voice. Her name was Jen, and she sounded sad and tired. "Do you have a 'stick?"

The voice jolted Raj back into the land of furiously living. He turned and saw her standing there, shorter than him, dark eyes hidden behind shades whose lenses scattered with sparks from the city lights. "Yeah," he said, pulling a blackstick from his shirt pocket and the electronic cigarette in her open hands. "How's it going in there?"

"Okay, I guess." She put the cigarette to her lips, crushing the far end to spark it; the scent of tobacco and cinnamon curled freshly as she inhaled. "Just a party, you know?"

Raj nodded, folding himself up against the side of the building. The Seattle winter hung heavily off his shoulders, the balcony rails shrinking Jen all the more into her surplus French field jacket. Raj had met her at UW two years before when he was a freshman and she a sophomore; she seemed no different now than she had then. Always quiet, like a mouse trying to get out of the way. "You don't sound like you're having much of a time."

Jen snorted and rolled her eyes in irritation. The dam cracked a little. "Yeah, well. Jack's off with Sumi, whatever the hell she's doing." Scented breath gushed from her nose as she held the 'stick in her fingers. "He couldn't shut up about her new tattoo. She's probably showing them all off now, the cunt."

Raj nodded through a sharp-edged frown. Jen had showed up with a new man tonight, one more of the parade—tall, lean, his black hair shot through with lines of bright crimson and styled like a pair of up thrust wings from his scalp. Raj had seen people like him before, wing-haired boys in identical black coats that gradated to red at the hem as if they were dipped in blood. He was a Young Son, one of the street tribes of Seattle, and Raj didn't know much about them except that they were bad news.

Being with the Son instead of him was just one more mistake on Jen's part in his opinion. "I'm sure it's nothing," he said, taking another long draw until his own 'stick's capsule clicked empty. "Maybe she's just looking to score some Shard."

"Yeah." Jen retreated into her blackstick, staring out into the night, and Raj felt his heart groan.

"Well, you know," he said, gently, "There are other guys. I mean, we aren't all fuckers out there." He put his hand on her shoulder and squeezed. It was hard, loving her and unable to do much else but watch her bleed.

"Yeah," she said again, wrapping her arms around herself. "Only, you know, I think I'm done with all that. I don't believe in love anymore. I don't think I have for a long time. Just kinda going through the motions." The coat swallowed her up, insulated her from the cold and from him. That padded fabric might as well have been tank armor.

Good thing he never did entertain much of a hope.

He stepped past Jen, opened the door, and stepped into Sumi's apartment.

Music blared in the background, a stripped-down synth pouring out in waves. With it throbbing in his temples, Raj's sad anger pulled him into the leather couches that made up the pit in the corner of Sumi's well-appointed living room; two of his fellow students, Nancy and Benze, sat passing gossip and a bottle of Otard between themselves. Benze was a Chem major with red braids and built like a small house. Nancy, the nubile queen of the Psych department, wore a black tube dress stretched over her insane curves, and a layered bob framing her pale face. Together, the two harpies were busy snickering over someone or another—business as usual, there.

"Built like a fucking pole," Nancy said with a cold laugh. "Not a hint of style, wearing Elico this year. It's not like Sumi'd ever have her here, anyway. Hand me the bottle, Benze."

Benze passed the swan-necked container across to her and she took a long swig of brandy. "Speaking of the rough and tumble," she said to Raj now, smacking her black-painted doll's mouth with gusto. "Where's Jen? I haven't seen her since her street-boy went in the back with Sumi." Perverse excitement shone in her pale blue eyes, lighting them like ghostly lanterns. "Do you think he's...?"

"Maybe," said Benze with a toss of his braids. "But I doubt it. She's a screamer." He gave Raj a wink that made him shrink a bit in his seat. "We'd hear her from ten blocks away if he was greasing her pipes."

A bright, haughty laugh escaped Nancy's lips, and she shoved the bottle into Raj's chest. "I almost want to see her face, walking in on them. It'd serve her right, bringing in someone like that. Didn't even have any good crystal on him—though he's on something. Has to be. Did you see his eyes? Crazy."

Raj just shrugged. "I don't know anything about it," he said, voice flat. "Shouldn't you just leave her alone, Nance? It's not like you give a shit anyway."

"Oh, don't be like that." Nancy reached across to lay a small hand on Raj's thigh and grinned, holding the bottle out for him to take. "C'mon, Raj baby, *dish*." She gave him that smile she usually reserved for unsuspecting freshmen, wide and sexy.

"She's outside," he said simply. That smile was just a show of shark's teeth for him, and Raj ignored it in favor of the bottle; he took a long swig of cognac, feeling it seethe and burn down the back of his throat, and let the sensation push the image of Jen out of his head for a moment.

141

"I heard she's pissed because her tall dose of street meat homed in on Sumi the moment he got here," Benze purred. His smirk was almost oily. "Too interested in that new tattoo, I heard Jen say."

"Yeah, I bet." Nancy grinned even wider, falling back against the sofa.

Raj rolled his eyes and grunted. Sumi. A grad student only through force of money and her father's position as an executive for Samir Systems, the company responsible for city planning. Tall, slim and gorgeously Indo-European, she'd greeted the partygoers wearing a backless dress exposing an intricate—and expensive—hologram tattooed into her skin. A sinuous Chinese dragon twisted and moved with her like a thing made of living henna, slithering and shifting within the confines of the dress's window as she moved. Raj had to admit, it was something. So was Sumi, come to that, with her tanned skin and her cable of long, dark hair.

But she wasn't Jen.

He shook his head and put the bottle on the small table between the three of them, and leaned back against the couch. "I'm sure she's just scoring some Shard off of him. Don't know why Jen brought him here, in any case. His kind is pretty dangerous."

"Well, it's not like Jen has any sense," Benze said with a snort. He finished off the Otard in one smooth movement, wheezing as it burned down his throat.

"I know," Nancy tittered. "Did you see the way she was dressed? When did she turn into a war orphan?" She laughed a nasty sound, and collapsed against Benze, who was still collecting himself after the massive swallow of brandy.

Raj fought with himself, getting angry, as the two cackled like bitchy cheerleaders against each other. "Hey, look," he found himself demanding. "What's all this from you two? I thought you were supposed to be her *friends.*"

Benze gestured at him with the now-empty bottle like a long-necked truncheon. "Oh, I forgot," he sneered. "You've got a hard-on for her. I bet that keeps you—"

A long, shuddering moan rang from down the hallway adjoining Sumi's living room, fading into a gurgle. Benze and Nancy gave each other meaningful looks; Raj merely froze, staring down at his tawny hands as they clenched into fists.

Nancy laughed again, though her tone was breathless when she spoke. "Jesus," she said. "He must be good." Animal interest glittered in her wide, blue eyes, and Raj felt his anger mix with disgust as it surged inside of him.

She looked sidelong at Benze and grinned so wide that her painted eyes crinkled. "Let's break in on them, huh?"

"Oh, come on." Raj's blood went up a few degrees; his expression flat. "You can't be serious."

"I most certainly am!" Nancy untangled herself from a widely grinning Benze and got to her feet. "I think," she tugged down the hem of her dress over her thighs. "That I am going to go see just how big of a whore Sumi actually is."

Raj stared after Nancy as she got up and vanished down the hallway, then looked to Benze, who was sitting there with a rapt expression on his face. He sure did love watching Nancy play the bitch game—it was why they were together, after all. Nothing sexual between them at all, but their sheer love of being utter cunts bound them tighter than anything sweaty. "You must be terribly proud of her," Raj grumped.

"Shut up, Raj," Benze said. His tone made it sound like an afterthought as he stared down the hall. "We can't all be masochists like you."

Raj's blood froze over a bit more. "Fuck you," he muttered.

"Not even with a *stolen* dick." Benze's attention turned back toward Raj, now, and his expression shifted into one of imperious smugness. "Listen to you and your big words, sir. They teach you how to talk like that at school, or does that come with the whole white knight package?"

The words struck Raj like a fist. His eyes narrowed as he sat there, fingers clenching until they stung his palms. "You don't know what the hell you're talking about," he rumbled. "She's my friend, that's all."

Benze's haughtiness magnified. The flame of cruel amusement in his eyes lit up and he leaned forward in his seat. His smile was thin and wicked. "Oh ho," he replied, voice low and thin. "Don't you give me *that* shit, friend. We've all watched you chase after that girl since you met her, and you've never had the balls to even try and be anything *but* her friend. Don't try and convince me you've only had her best interests at heart because we all know better." Benze snorted then, and leaned back to fish a card of blue, plastic skin disks out of the inside of his jacket.

Raj couldn't speak. His skin was hot, and his blood brimmed with the searing cocktail of humiliation and anger that usually followed any extended conversation about Jen. If he'd had anything to drink he'd probably be doing his best to punch Benze's teeth in, but instead, he could only stare and stew in impotent rage as the other man laid the skindisk over his carotid and let whatever substance that laced it start the trip into his blood supply.

"You know what your problem is," Benze murmured in the sleepy way of one experiencing a good hit, his eyes slowly rolling back in his head. "It's that you don't do anything for her. I mean, not really. What good are you to her if you don't step up and say something?" He settled back into the cushions, heaving a deep sigh. "She's already got a pussy, after all. She don't need another one."

That was enough. Raj sat up hard in his seat and leveled an antenna-like finger in Benze's direction as if intending to roast him whole with the raw power of indignation. "Now listen here…" But Benze's attention wasn't on him. The burly harpy had turned his gaze down the hall, and blinked slowly trying to get his drug-blurred eyes to play ball. Benze's expression shifted from a smirk to something more appropriate on a landed fish, his mouth opening, working without a sound, his eyes slowly widening as he looked on.

"What the hell?"

The hell was Jack, the wing-haired Young Son Jen had brought.

He stood in the mouth of the hallway like an apparition. Pale and tall, his body was whipcord thin, all muscle. The white lines of scars stood out on his skin, webs of keloid declaring years of violence throughout his youth. He was covered in blood; it was splashed across his torso, his arms, the loose black plastic of his pants, shining wet and livid against his white flesh. The coppery smell of it, strong and warm, rolled out in a wave to fill the nostrils. He held a thermal cutter in one hand, a long rectangle of dark alloy with a hinged shutter along its business end, beneath which its blade hummed dully. It looked very much like a high-tech version of a straight razor. His other hand stayed tucked behind his back.

Raj and Benze beheld him as astonished ghosts, unable to speak as the moments ticked on and he stood there staring at them as if utterly unaware of his condition.

When words finally came, the first were Benze's. "Jesus Christ." Adrenaline and shock twisted his vocal cords, making him sound small and far away. "Did you cut yourself?"

Slowly, Jack's dark eyes focused upon them. "Nah, man," he drawled, as casual as his pose. "You send that sweet little bumba in there after me? I was doing fine on my own."

"Bumba? What the—" Benze stopped, his skin paling more. "What did you do to Nancy?" His voice had taken on a certain edge, something hysterical. "Did you… did you fucking kill her?"

Jack smirked. "Nah man," he said, the words stretching together as he leaned against the wall. "Least, I don't think she's dead. Won't be smiling for a while, but after that, she'll smile a lot bigger." The pale killer grinned wide, hooking the finger of his weapon hand in one cheek and pulling it even wider. "Gonna need some staples."

And then he brought his other hand from behind his back, exposing a neatly excised square of flesh, the size of a sheet of paper, that once tanned, had become ashen by separation from its host. "That other girl, though, she just gonna need burying." He squeezed the flesh in his palm, and above it a familiar image leapt into being—a luminous Chinese dragon, conjured into existence as if he were some sorcerer. It arched and spun in the air just as it had when the skin had still been on Sumi's back.

An awesome fear pressed like an iron bar against Raj's chest. He'd never had to deal with anything like this before—Christ, he was just a graduate student! He couldn't move, but Benze was different. He was already reaching for the empty bottle of brandy, hefting the Otard by the neck like a heavy glass club.

"You son of a bitch," he gasped, sounding like a man about to drown, "You son of a bitch! I'll fucking kill you! I'll... I'll—"

And then Jack moved. Raj knew about nerve enhancements, reflex augmentation, things like that—a lot of people put the mech on these days—but he'd never actually seen that technology up close. Once, he'd sneaked out with his roommate to see a race at Akeley's magsled loop in the Verge, where you had to have the surgery just to keep on the track. They moved so fast, colored blurs on a steel track...

But this wasn't like that at all. The Young Son stretched out as if he were going to touch Benze in the gentlest way, swept his arm in a lazy arc, and Benze's forearm detached itself from just below the elbow. There was no blood, just a little steam and the smells of cooked meat and ozone. "Now you're going to behave yourself," Jack growled as the bottle landed with a hard thump upon the carpet near the sofa. Benze's hand still gripped it by the neck. "Act like you're grown."

Shock rendered Benze's already pale skin into chalk. He clutched at his forearm, peering at Jack as if he'd only just seen him standing there, his eyes wide with a mixture of confusion and accusation. Whatever it was he'd dosed himself with seemed to have killed off the pain that should have been boiling through him, and instead he merely stared at his scorched stump as if beholding some religious mystery. "Yeah," he whispered. "Yeah, okay."

Raj stared at them both. He couldn't move; it was as if his mind detached from his body, from the scene, buoyed aloft by fear and adrenaline. "You're going to kill us," he heard himself say. "You're going to kill us both."

Jack glanced flatly at Raj before stepping into the room and passing them both to lean against the counter of the kitchenette. He unlatched the cutter's safety shield and began stropping its softly whining blade against the back of the swatch he cut from Sumi's back. The smell of scorched flesh rose to mingle with blood, and the stinging tide of vomit rose in Raj's throat.

"You boys think you're pretty hot shit," Jack began, "With your parties and your bullshit schooling. You think you're alive. But you're not." The cutter paused; the holographic dragon swam and darted among ripples of heat. "Ain't nobody hardly alive anymore. You're all corpses, just walkin'."

Raj swallowed hard and tried to speak, but momentarily, his tongue failed him. When it finally did work, his own voice surprised him with its hard clarity. "You're crazy," he informed Jack, leaning back against the sofa. "You're a nutter!"

Seconds passed between them. As Jack's cutter seared the rest of the flesh from the inside of the scrap of Sumi's skin, Raj remained frozen with fear, and Benze slowly faded away from the shock that even his drug-fortified system couldn't hold back.

The cutter made an obscene scraping noise as he seared the rest of the gore from the back of the swatch. "Little bit," Jack said finally. "Little bit. But least I ain't no corpse. You people, you dead and you don't know it yet. Mama knows, though. She been telling us since we was born."

He will kill us all. Raj leaned back harder against the couch, wishing he could somehow phase through the back and disappear into the floor; his hand slid into the back cushions, where his fingers touched something hard and cold. He froze. Incredibly, the length of what felt like a metal rod nestled between the cushions, way back against the panel of the couch. "I don't understand," he said, and his voice tight with fear and the tiny sliver of hope that sprung from his discovery. "Who, ah, who's your mama?"

"You don't talk about Mama." Jack turned to fix Raj with a withering stare, stabbing out into the air toward him with the thermal cutter like it was a dowser's wand. His voice was leaden.

"I'm sorry," Raj said instantly. His fingers closed around the cold pipe, his thumb running along its side, hitting a hard bubble there, ribbed and perforated. Now it clicked; it was a heavy pipe for sharing crystal-black hits.

Never in his life had he been so happy that his friends destroyed themselves with methamphetamines. "I didn't mean, ah, disrespect."

Jack snorted, and he proceeded to hold the skinned swatch up to peer at it. Despite the trauma of removal and the stropping from the cutter, the filaments projecting the tattoo still worked; he sat there and watched the dragon writhe in a möbius knot, infinity over a field of ash, the cutter smoking in his hand. "You know, time was the human species was alive," he said, and his voice was strangely wistful. "Destroyin' and wasteful, but no more than any other animal that overpreys. They tell you they don't do that, wolves and dogs and such. But it ain't so. Anything gluts when it gets the opportunity. Rots the body, rots the soul. Then you die and rot away—just in the case of people, you ain't seen that you're already dead yet." He paused in his reverie, turning his face to Raj. "You know, my granddaddy used to work in a stable when he was a kid, had to lock the horses in to keep 'em out of the feed store? Saw one eat so much its guts gave out. Dropped dead on the spot."

"I didn't know that," Raj said. His fingers tightened on the pipe.

"Ain't no horses anymore," Jack said as if that answered everything. His expression was stern. "You think about that."

Raj didn't know what to say. What could you say to something like that? He only knew he had to keep the crazy fucker talking, get him in some position where he could crack his skull with that pipe before he could summon his voodoo reflexes.

He closed his eyes and tried to collect his thoughts, and finally spoke again. "I guess you're right about that. But, ah, what about this Mama? I always heard that you Young Sons were just about cutting people up and dealing narco."

Jack gave him a look like an unimpressed cat. "Dead people are ignorant," he replied, and looked to where Benze now lay quiet and gray against the cushions. His eyes were closed. "Your buddy looks like he's gone."

"He's not my buddy," Raj snapped, then paused when he realized just what he'd said. Benze probably *was* dead, or damned near it. A pang of guilt struck him, but he quashed it with a squeeze on the bar in his hand. "...tell me about your Mama."

The strength in his voice seemed to impress Jack, and he canted his head a bit to look Raj over anew. "Well, all right," he relented with a nod. "Though there ain't much to talk about. Mama's Mama, you know?"

"But I don't understand. What is she? I mean, there's too many of you to be related, right?"

That got Raj a grin. "Mama ain't birthed us," he said. "She made us. Like, she came to us. Took us in. We talk to her regular." Jack tapped the side of his head with the back of the cutter, leaving a swatch of red where the hot metal burned him. He didn't seem to notice. "Right here."

Raj stared at the burn for a moment before forcing his eyes back to Jack's face. "Like, with an implant?"

"Nope." Jack flipped the cutter's safety shutter closed, and it fell silent. "Just in our heads. She's always there. Whispering." He leaned forward a bit and stared at Raj again, his dark eyes glittering black and smart like a bird's. "That's another problem with you corpses. You ain't got no soul. No voice to talk you through things. Mama Razor, she always there—she tells us how to cull the dead, how to thin out the herd. Every asshole in a suit or empty fashion bitch that gets themselves bled in an alley by one of us, it's done in her name. Cos you ain't nothing but meat to us, man. Mama tells us where to go, and we make it happen."

"And she told you to come here, tonight?" Raj squinted faintly, trying to make out some glimpse of sanity behind Jack's black eyes. "I mean, there was a reason, right?" It was strange, but in this moment, he couldn't fathom the idea of murders being committed with nothing behind it. Not *here*. Not in the apartment of the daughter of an executive of a major corporation. Senseless violence was for *crazy* people. *Poor* people. People who didn't *matter*. And he was to be a *scientist*, for fuck's sake—surely he wasn't going to get murdered right here alongside a couple of cunts like Benze and Nancy. Right?

Jack read the look in Raj's eyes, and whatever regard had sparked in his face guttered and died. "All right," he said, sounding at once resigned and full of purpose. "I figure that's enough. You ready for this?"

Raj froze. His fingers were tight and slick against the crystal pipe, the weapon which he now had absolutely no chance of using. Raj the scientist had no chance against Jack, the rampaging, amped-up killer. And he realized then that he had forgotten one fact: Sumi was a much more important person, the daughter of an executive, and she had been the first one Jack had killed. And after him, he would probably go after Jen.

Yes. Jen. Raj's mind returned to the one girl he had never been able to bed, and a peculiar stab of fury pierced the miasma that had settled around his heart. He pulled the pipe out from between the sofa cushions and brandished it toward the psychopathic Young Son. "Motherfucker," he snarled in a voice that was not entirely his, "You just try it. You'll have to go through me to get to her." And though he knew he had no chance with her, a great and sudden desire flared up to not only protect this girl he loved, but to make up for his moment of extreme cowardice.

For a second, the Young Son stood there, his lean frame caught in a pose of mingled surprise and curiosity—like a mantis poised to fall upon its prey. "Son," his lips spread into a thin and nasty smile, "Why do you think she brought me up here in the first place?"

The only sound that rang out was the soft thump of the pipe as it landed on the floor.

Jen huddled against the corner of the balcony and let the wind whistle around her. She focused on it, a clear indicator of the change that had been worked upon the city in the past century. The massive towers of steel and glass that rose like columns throughout the city core to prop up the poisoned sky had magnified the wind into a whistling beast, tearing at the skin in winter. She let it roar at her. All things changed, and more were coming. Perhaps not what the dead suspected, but it would come.

She leaned against the rail and listened to the noises coming from the apartment. She had never intended to come here, to mix with these fucking people and certainly not to deal with wayward souls like Jack—and yet here she was, listening as he killed off the remainder of Sumi's guests. There were only a few left, she was sure. The scene would throw a ripple through the management of Samir Systems as Sumi's father grappled with his daughter's brutal murder, and he would lose what had been keeping him going since the death of his wife. Mother would claim him, and another of her children would be born in his mind. Plans advanced. They always did.

Knowing that Raj was dead was the only pleasure of the evening. She'd always hated him, that spineless, grasping scum. He fancied himself a white knight, but he was worse than everyone else. The world was better without him. A smile made of fury lined her lips, something she fought down as the doorknob began to work.

Presently, the door swung open and Jack emerged in his black coat, buckled over his bare torso. Even with the wind, the stench of blood and scorched flesh couldn't be blown away. "You've been busy," Jen murmured, looking at him through the black lenses of her massive sunglasses. "Did you get it done?"

"All done." Jack stepped up to the railing and put his hands on the edge, heaving a sigh. "It's a strange thing, killing off them what are already dead."

"I can imagine," she replied, her voice still soft. Her hands were lodged in the pockets of her massive fatigue coat, warm and safe. "I'm sure your Mama will be happy with you, razor child."

Jack laughed, looking shy now at the mention of his goddess-figure. "Thanks," he said. "I hope. Strange thing, though, you know?"

"Strange how?" Jen canted her head, watching him as he turned his back to her.

"Strange that Mama'd tell me to go with you." Jack shrugged, the points of his jacket's shoulders sharp against the glittering night. He looked not unlike a gargoyle, complete with furled wings and the horns of his hair. "Never had her tell me to go with a civvie before, least of all some little girl like you."

Jen smiled. "I can imagine." She stepped up behind him, let him deflect a new blast of wind. "But that's the thing about it, really. I'm just like you."

He laughed again. "Yeah?"

"Yeah." Her hand slipped from her pocket, and without a further word pressed the head of the nerve crusher that came with it against the small of his back. Electricity boiled through him as the stunner dumped the entirety of its capacitors into his already overstrung nervous system. There was only the slightest sound from him, a soft cough, and then he pitched over into the glittering dark. She watched him fall, the great coat fluttering out as if in a vain attempt to save its wearer from gravity—one more of Mother's pawns, fragile and expendable.

The thing that once had been Jen sighed, watched Jack's descent a second longer and, drawing in a deep breath, let out a howling scream.

After all, she had always made a perfect victim.

Want more horror-infused cyberpunk Wonderland Cycle thrillers?
Tweet *More Wonderland! @pseudohumanist @CuriosityQuills #BookLove*

SINERGY

SINERGY

BY A.E. PROPHER & GRACE EYRE

CHAPTER ONE

The figure of Antoine D'Longville that Mother Nature – or the Holy Father – has cut so high and straight, now stoops in the soft light the color of fine dust on the casement window. Reluctance holds his finger over the last digit of a familiar phone number. A deep breath, and he initiates the call. The right thing. He is doing the *right thing*.

His flat, a modest but comfortable addendum to the Cathedral, is furnished to fit a man of his height. The telephone perches upon a tall, slim ivory table, so he doesn't have to bend for it. He does anyway. The phone is an anchor, the cord – a chain, pulling him down, down into a place never his to enter before.

It should be an easy call, given the recipient. Tonight he prays for no answer. Nothing to say, no words to explain himself, except in brief, truncated conclusions wrestled so dearly from nights of agony and indecision.

Voicemail. A small blessing. A bigger one, relatively speaking, is that his parents will have been dead a year this next Bastille Day. Uncle Tadeusz's is the only pain he needs fear.

"I know," public speaker par excellence, he chokes, his mouth–a desert, his words–stumbling over each other like chicks fleeing a burning coop, "that you won't understand exactly why I'm about to do this. But I think you might understand that I must. I'm sorry, Uncle. I…" He is. For the first time in ten years, he just isn't sorry *enough*. "I hope we never meet again."

The beep, cold and tinny, tells Antoine his time is up.

His watered-silk cassock with its thirty-three commemorative buttons, his chasuble and matching mitre give him identity, a place in the world. Pausing mechanically before the ornate full-height mirror by the door, he adjusts the precious pallium around his neck.

Babbling 'yes-yes's and 'almost ready's into his mobile, Dover-raised Brother François rushes back from the kitchen with a mug of steaming chai tea. They can both use as much prophylactic scalding ahead of the midnight procession out in the clammy cold as they can get, but the jovial valet's newly overactive bladder puts the kibosh on any measurable fluid intake whenever an event tends to run long. This close to losing what's left of tonight's baked sole, Antoine waves the cuppa away, dismissing the Brother's imploring eyes with the freshet of guilt, one of many.

Sending him ahead into the hall, still awed by a display of his superior's solidarity with his condition, Antoine retrieves his most important possession from under the newspaper on the console table and slips it under the maniple around his wrist. A Polaroid of the girl, eons old. Years, anyway.

She roosts on the fountain rim, standoffish, her eyes clear and keen. She has, in fact, that particular air anyone might have, thrown in with a stranger. Curious and surprised, cautious.

He'd nearly mistaken her for an Empire style trimming at first, with her dark hair, colorless cheeks, and gimlet stare. Within the minutes it took his camera to do its thing, he was hooked. That sharp stony expression lay fixed across her face like it belonged there.

He pockets the memory and makes his way to the church.

'Church' is an understatement—the Notre Dame is a towering structure, vigilant and ancient, complicated and beautiful, with mural stonework crawling up all sides. Demons and angels and apocalyptic ruminations, those ancient guardians of Paris, those monoliths with their watchful façades. Tonight, they are trained on the towering Christmas tree strategically lit on the vast plaza before the front doors.

He loves it. Loves it more every year, the ringing of nearly four hundred-year old Emmanuel reverberating throughout Ile de la Cité and the Latin Quarter; the anachronism of closed circuit TVs in the teeming nave; the masticating, pointing, devout throngs lining the sidewalks along the procession rout; the abashed sneezing fit or two invariably underscoring *Adeste Fideles*. It awes him and gives him hope.

The Processional Doors swing open before him as Antoine steps on– and passes–the deceptively unprepossessing bronze windrose on the pavement, le Point Zéro des routes des France. And then, before the brocade and incense-transfused glitter of the apse, he temporarily relinquishes control.

He takes a seat and pretends to reflect, his mind spinning with dread and the urge to turn back. Brought to grotesque relief by the warm glow of Veillée de Noël, his motions are drone-like, automated. Even the smile, flashed at the other clerics, is a matter of professional habit.

He is popular in his way. His celebrity from within the Catholic Church has crossed over into secular media. Cardinal D'Longville makes news nationally and internationally, particularly with regard to his views on priestly continence. Even though his progressivism is frowned upon by the more established clergy, frowns rarely translate to rebukes. Quite outside the sway of his blood, he is beloved of the masses without substantially nudging anything fundamental in the faith and therefore needed by the establishment, one which at many points in history had to adapt to maintain relevance.

Sitting, numb as the fountain statues in his Polaroid, through the chorales echoing amidst the arched ceiling and flying buttresses, he opens his catechism when instructed and follows along by memory.

Then, it is time to deliver the homily. He rallies his senses and thoughts. This is the moment that counts. The last moment, in fact, that would ever count in his official career. His Eminence, Antoine Cardinal D'Longville, Archbishop of Paris is about to quit his job.

He stands, the de rigueur cardinalitical gravitas and his tall, angelic frame making it easy for the congregation to hang its hopes and imaginations on him. He places his long hands on the podium. Before him, a thousand faces are painted with the maternal light of worship.

"It seems to me," his voice rolls out like a river, "that our faith, a deep and blessed faith, is one of the best resources available for the betterment of humankind. As a united voice, we speak of a God-given responsibility to our fellow man, and to God Himself. We have been called to worship the Lord, in so doing, demonstrate a life of service to our neighbors."

He pauses, the blond paleness of him, the hopelessness writ large and uncompromising on his iconic features is a warning–and a supplication. As many a clergyman, Antoine mastered the art of speaking without words, conveying disappointment short of an explicit damnation, but flayed bare on this one day of celebration and peace, his is a mime's version of verbal diarrhea.

"By and large, my brothers and sisters, we have failed to answer the call."

Silence drops like a guillotine, swift and resolute. But *their* faces are neutral.

"I ask you now not to despair or think harshly of our past shortcomings. If anything, the message of Christ is one of forgiveness and rebirth. This has always been the legacy of the Catholic Church. However, with that comes renewed strength, and when we stop to examine ourselves clearly, our strength and our agency, we can see that we live in a broken world. We are part of that broken world and we've accepted its brokenness. We become complacent and comfortable within it. We think–if we have saved ourselves by giving tithe and going to confession, what use is it to save the man outside these doors?"

Some rustles in the pews. Antoine senses their thoughts, knows how many are silently objecting.

But I give to charity!, he hears them say. *But I work in a soup kitchen!*

"Look around," he enjoins with a bit more fervor. "You do your bit, and you feel satisfied at the end of the day. But is it really working? Is it working when so many of us, so many of God's children are sleeping in the street? So many of God's children–our brothers and sisters in Africa, Asia, South America, and right in our own backyards, are being dispossessed, removed from their own land. Children forced to become soldiers, mothers and fathers forced to give up their children because they cannot feed them. All around us, to the north, south, east, west, we are surrounded by misery and decay. We are surrounded by the forces of war and hate which, if we do not unite, will overwhelm the earth and claim it for evil. War is exploitative; it preys on the weak and the poor. Greed is exploitative; it sucks the life force from the land and turns humans into machines. We deny the riches of the Kingdom of Heaven to work for the riches claimed only by man.

And here we are, preaching love and generosity, while we stand idly by and permit this to happen. This isn't right, my children. If God is with us, then let us speak His word to all nations. Let us raise our voices in the face of injustice. We are the most capable, the most empowered, the most blessed people on Earth. If we believe in the redeeming will and the message of love from our Lord Jesus Christ, born on this holy night, then why do we remain silent?"

Silence, indeed, stretches long and bristling across the Cathedral. Antoine speaks more gently this time.

"I understand it—we feel stretched to our limit already. We have our work and our families, and we do what we can for the rest. But if we are to truly address the suffering in this world, we cannot do it alone. Our Lord says, 'where three or more pray, there am I'. So let us come together by the thousands. If I have one thing to say to you as the Cardinal of Paris, but one message to relay, it's that you are not helpless. The world does not spin without you. You are part of it. You can change it."

He can feel it now, the color returning to their cheeks. The strange grey vacuum created by that awful silence shrinks back against the swell of hope. The energy swirls through in eddies of compassion and justice. Maybe, maybe in his tenure, before his name becomes drenched with shame and scandal, maybe he will have managed this one right thing.

His message delivered, Antoine turns a wary eye to the Order thugs, stirring now, gauging their chances to pounce. Their eyes gleam and their hearts are hungry. He'd hoped for a bit more time, but clearly, he is watched more closely than he realized.

Unable to leave without evoking suspicion, the Order's and his—still his!—flock's, he carries out the balance of the ceremony through a haze, his subconscious husbanding its resources for the trials to come. The Passion of Antoine D'Longville. The Passion, indeed.

The Benediction's last, and now is the time to move. Everyone rises and wanders freely as if a string has been cut. A dangerous moment, a time when anyone can approach. The spotlight and the raised platform are no longer his guardians. And many, so many aspire to kiss his ring, share some words. On a run-of-the-mill night–even a run-of-the-mill Christmas Eve–he is drawn into so many conversations that he is often found lingering for hours after the last hymn is sung. Tonight, after his speech, it would be ten times more intense. He can't do it–in the sleepy commotion of the exodus, the last to buttonhole him would be the Order. They would quietly usher him away, and he would be a free man no more. Then again, born to it, to the bimillennial legacy of secrets, and obligations, and anointed blood, isn't it unaccountably naïve to think he had ever been?

He signals to one of his colleagues. From time to time, he needs to depart before the conversations flare up, and his brethren all know the sign. He waves to the congregation and slips away as priests and acolytes form a friendly wall of shaking hands and doled-out well-wishes.

But now that Antoine is alone, he acknowledges his heart thumping against the walls of his chest. His heart is like him, in a cage. There, in the darkened halls, he reaches out with his mind's eye—and recoils from the cloying touch of fellow Order auras closing in. No matter. One stop by his office, and he would be gone. Free.

He leaves the lights off, treading the halls using his memory and senses. He *knows* the place, had hidden in the shade of it as a kid and marveled at the grandeur, the pneuma of it as an adult, and ducks discreet as a proverbial church mouse down side hallways when a malicious presence comes seeking him out. He gathers up his energy and... erases himself from the world. The human perception thereof, at any rate. Having used the knack as rarely as he does a bus, he hopes it is not as rusty as it should be.

They wouldn't expect him to go back to his office. That helps. All he needs is to get safely inside. The Cardinal's Passage would take care of the rest.

His door beckons from the end of the hall. Focusing yet another skill he has had no call to use, he probes for any Order members in the wings, then makes a dash for it.

Still in one piece, the rich mahogany snapping shut behind his back, he breathes a sigh of relief. This is his turf.

And yet, there is something. *Something.*

He squints at the wall, the blank space between an old placard and a group photo of a recent mission trip to the Philippines.

No, must be nothing.

Antoine grabs a vessel of holy water and daubs a sign across the door, topping off with a smattering of Latin. Obviously, any other tongue would have done as well – or none, but for someone as green as himself, the formal sentence structure assists in exhorting his will on this one corner of the world and keeping it going. The presence of hostile auras vanishes, along with the macrocosm beyond. The seal of the Order works both ways; the door is a boundary. Nothing in, nothing out, not even thought.

But, *something* is here with him.

Paranoia.

He steps away from the door and closes his eyes. A moment. Just a moment to think.

Someone calls his name. *Antoine.* An informal address. Few have the leave to use it.

Antoine.

Only friends would address him as such, but this voice isn't friendly.

No one could have called his name. The room is empty.

He drags himself an inch closer to the truth.

The actual truth, he can't acknowledge. There is a barrier in place.

But there are other truths, and he knows how to find them. If he puts them all together, they will reveal an idea of reality.

The first truth is that he heard a voice say his name.

The second truth is that no one is there.

The third truth is that this is a contradiction.

And in the excruciating way that Antoine had taught himself, he accedes that such a contradiction can only mean one thing: someone *is* in the room with him. Someone stronger.

The fourth truth is that not many are. It terrifies him.

CHAPTER TWO

For a moment, Antoine stands blinking like a child as the mental fog is yanked away.

The blank space between the old placard and the group photo now fills with a dark windbreaker hugging a gracefully aging frame of flesh, blood, and malice.

The Grand Inquisitor.

One of the longest-standing members of the Order, the Baron Pellegrino Monteleone is only a step below Cafarelli himself. His century of service and the magnificent powers he commands had raked severe lines down his face like bird talons. Children would duck behind their mothers at the sight of him. Then promptly forget ever having done so.

His skin hangs in deep trenches from the height of his cheekbones. His deep-set eyes, holding the cold mist of a mountaintop, are clouded, clouded because he has spent most of his days seeing from his mind, conventional vision so ill-defined once one has sampled the flipside. Yet they are frighteningly precise, those hazy orbs, with a sharpness behind them to be reckoned with, and the time of reckoning had begun.

The Baron waves his gloved hand and a chair slides into Antoine from behind, buckling his knees as he falls ungracefully into his seat. Deep inside his panicked mind, Antoine curses his imperfect powers of perception. Some, like the Baron, can obscure themselves in ways far beyond his abilities, and before those people, he is utterly helpless. Flying blind.

He tries to stand again, but can no more do so than his supplicant's chair.

From behind Antoine's own marquetry inlaid desk, the Baron leans forward, lacing his fingers together.

"I've heard reports," notes the elder, in a voice dry and clear like the cracking of a tree branch, "most grave reports."

He lets it sink in.

"I hope you haven't been reconsidering our agreement, Antoine. However," –here he waves his hand with a false lightness– "perhaps I am mistaken. Perhaps these reports of your moral fidgeting are only rumors blown out of proportion. I certainly hope so."

His head still frozen in place, Antoine looks with desperate eyes to the leather surface of his desk. There, a letter opener rustles beneath a paper pile...

Quiet, old friend, quiet...

...and is promptly smashed into the grain of the tabletop, compacted by a superior force. Not quiet enough.

"We know you were involved in the Prague incident," the Baron rasps, beyond so much as chiding Antoine for his attempt. "You and the girl. But you cower behind the sanctity of those pathetic confessions, and we still scramble for the *how*. Your plaything of a faith. Enough! You *will* show me what happened that night... *Cardinal*."

And the floodgates of him, the deep, true him, loosen as the Baron summons his voice. He clenches his jaw in protest and dives into his memories, searching for an answer.

Not the answer the Baron is clawing from him.

He is a child, just a small boy. Sprawling on the floor as he stares up at Bożechna. His cousin is minding him for the afternoon while the adults of the blended Wiśniewski-D'Longville clan are out and the servants are setting a filling lunch. He and his parents had come for a visit to Poland.

His sense of the land shaped primarily by that house, for him she is all timber, linoleum, gas stoves, dried onions. Boż is looking down at him, her round smiling face sitting in a nest of dark hair.

They'd been practicing, breaking in those shared abilities their parents are so cagey about.

He laughs, watching a turnip tumble across the floor from the force of his mind.

"I can show you something else," Bożechna boasts with a mischievous grin.

"Wassat?" he beams up at her.

"Something you've never seen before."

"Nuh huh," he ducks his head, rolling the turnip around with his hand. "I seen it all."

"You haven't seen this. I swear."

"Prove it!" he cries defiantly.

She points to the grey wall that separates the kitchen from the pantry.

"I can go through that. I don't even need the door."

Antoine falls silent and serious in a mix of awe and disbelief. He doesn't need to tell her to prove it again. She speaks with such eagerness and confidence.

"Watch."

With her hands lifted slightly from her sides and her head thrown back in pride, she steps toward the wall.

And vanishes behind it.

Antoine's eyes nearly fall out of his head. "Boż?" he calls meekly.

He hears some thumping on the other side of the wall. Then, a few seconds later, Bożechna arrives just as she had gone.

"See?" she beams, her fists on her hips.

"I want to do it! How do I do it?"

Bożechna shrugs. "Beats me. I just kinda figured it out."

"What does it feel like?"

She tilts her head to the side. "A little cold and shivery," she says. "And I hear some things. But I'm brave. I can do it as many times as I want."

"Do it again!"

Antoine doesn't have to ask twice.

What comes next is in flashes, bits and pieces, a badly wired memory.

A wave of warmth. A blank space. The screams of her parents, breaking into his perception like a nightmare invading sleep.

As a grown man, Antoine had pieced it together, the what-the-hell of it, not the random bits of Boż that turned the innocent canvas of the kitchen wall into a Kandinsky oil. The *in-between* got her, the dimension of the non-corporeal, a world rife with demons. A place none tempt knowingly, not even the Order.

The Baron is no exception.

But Antoine has nothing to lose.

He focuses his weaker energies and retreats into his mind, reforming the laws of matter and dimensionality without moving a muscle.

His skin turns to shade.

A sudden horror sweeps upon him. Icy winds and the clammy grasp of inhuman arms, something smooth and slippery.

He gasps, breaking his concentration; thuds to the floor, having slipped through the chair like a ghost and become solid again. His seat clatters against the wall, spraying slivers of wood and masonry across the room.

Without a split second to waste, he plunges back into the dark realm. So many reasons for the Baron not to follow him, a panopticon's worth. The horrid eyes and ghastly, gaping scaled faces, and the interest, such studious interest cleaving him to atoms.

He slips through the floor, cascades through several more before the tentacles reach him and begin to wrap around his throat.

In a final push, Antoine wrests himself from their grip and *catapults* out. It had taken years of study to even venture into this world. A child had no chance.

But now he is solid again, and at a most inopportune moment. He crashes into some old lecterns in the basement with such force that they splinter around him. A flash of pain informs him some of the shards had made their way into his flesh.

He would deal with them later. No longer protected by the seal of his office, his sense of the Order members swarming is in overdrive.

He dizzily disrobes down to the sweater and light pants he managed to sneak in underneath his vestments, retrieves his Polaroid, and stumbles toward a back window. It glows dimly in the moonlight, that small square of glass sitting high on the wall and just above the ground.

He drags an old classroom desk to just below the panes. A frantic search for something hard and heavy lands an ink well. Antoine smashes it against the glass.

Bleeding and gasping, he rolls out onto the damp snow. Thank goodness for the discontinued insistence on episcopal sandals! The ice

161

soothes his wounds and–he hopes–stops some of the blood, but he has a long way to go before he is safe.

The narrow alley sits between two wings of the cathedral, with only one way to get in or out. He hotfoots for the mouth–and freezes. An Order member, skulking up.

A low-level. Easy to fool, easy to beat.

He flattens himself against the wall.

The Order member pads slowly, a laryngitic bloodhound left stranded on a hunt.

Obfuscating like his life depends on it–it does!–Antoine permits himself not a breath.

The goon stops, listening carefully.

Drops of blood leave Antoine's body, and patter out of his shield. They fall to the ground in light, steady taps, melting tiny caves into the slush.

The goon squints at these drops, working out the *contradiction*. Lifts his head. For a brief second, his eyes meet Antoine's. For a brief second, he understands.

He flows at Antoine, but he is too slow. Antoine had already ducked and spun, slamming the agent's forehead against the wall.

The man staggers a bit, then crumples, unconscious.

"Dei Patris, dimitte me…"

His heart rate skyrocketing, Antoine pats down his prey.

The haul amounts to a wad of cash and a twin of his Order pin ripped from the lining of the Cafarelli blazer. Lest it slip out of his pant pocket or fuse with his own if fastened too closely, he fixes it to the inside of his waistband.

Insurance.

He checks his other pocket for the keys, then makes a mad dash to the gray Peugeot motorcycle in the nearby lot. He's hardly a pro. He's not even much of a rider, but this is the only means of fairly untraceable transportation he was able to beg off his secretary's secretary, giddy before a holiday jaunt to Martinique.

The Order energy swells around him as if he'd kicked an anthill. Some must have heard the commotion.

He fumbles with the keys. They toss awkwardly in his numb, blood-slick fingers. Finding the right one, he jams it in the ignition. The engine purrs to life just as two black SUVs roll smoothly around the corner.

Doesn't matter. Antoine is out, swerving onto the thoroughfare, the motorcycle's purr exploding into a roar. The SUVs swing out behind him.

The city lights stream past in a frantic blur. He is vaguely aware of the honking horns and gasping pedestrians turning to observe the pursuit. The SUVs are far more powerful and stable on the icy streets, but they aren't able to weave between cars like the bike.

When they get to the open road, however, they gain quickly. He accelerates as hard as he can, the SUV's headlights bearing down on him like hot breath.

Then, a sickening wobble.

The tires start oscillating wildly beneath him.

Perched helplessly on top, he hangs on for dear life as the body of the motorcycle loses all stability.

In one harrowing swerve, Antoine fishtails off a patch of black ice and flies off the road.

The Seine rushes up at him. His front wheel slams against the reedy ice, followed by his body.

First, a terrible crashing, whooshing noise.

Then nothing at all, not even silence.

CHAPTER THREE

Her hair skitters in dark strands around her face. There by the fountain, she looks like she has been carved from marble, somehow permanent, and rooted on her pedestal. Behind her, water tumbles to its bed in a pale blue froth.

He remembers so well, every detail. But in that memory, he is yet to learn her name.

Rionni.

Rionni. Antoine would say it to himself ten thousand times in the following years. With a Polaroid, he has her locked in place. But her name, the sound of her name, so delicate; so easily lost.

Then later, in that same night:

She is Lot's wife, frozen in the fire, white as salt. She looks up at him, shock throwing an expressionless cast over her face.

What is this? Her lips don't move, but her eyes, plaintive and unprepared, beg an answer.

The inferno, the aftermath of the explosion, spins around them, but their skin is untouched.

What is this? She isn't afraid, but stares at him with somber curiosity.

As if expecting him to know. As if expecting him to be any less lost.

She squeezes his hand.

Consciousness greets Antoine with a ruthless slap of cold. It stings his whole body, sends his limbs, jerking and screaming, into a Saint Vitus Dance. He is still under the surface, in the black totality that is a nighttime river.

His lungs scream with deprivation. His limbs shudder so hard that he struggles to break the surface. It is up there, a hard blink of light. It promises no refuge or respite, only a slight reduction in the certainty of death.

He sees now, through the cast of this yellow streetlight, the shadows of his erstwhile confreres who chased him here and now want nothing but to finish him off. They pace impatiently, sometimes abruptly changing course. Their thoughts come at him in vague rushes. They are unhappy he'd gone into the river. There is no closure that way. No finality, credit, or reward.

Out of more necessity than strategy, Antoine permits his head above water and takes the biggest breath of his life. Then forces himself back down.

Too late. The Order's henchmen spot him and swarm overhead. Patches of ice crack forcefully open. Little white streams rocket past him, slowing after two or three feet. The water is pockmarked with bullets.

With silencers working overtime to turn the boom of gunshots into pops of holiday champagne, Antoine gets to know, for the first time, the insidiousness of despair. Before, he had been afraid; he had even been afraid for his life. But the threat of death hadn't been as physical as it is now, with the gutting cold and the agony of muscles deprived of oxygen.

A former Olympics-qualified swimmer, he can't kick very fast anymore, and certainly can't thrust himself out of the reach of bullets without another trip surface-side. Thus he learns despair is akin to lethargy, the kind that sets in when all hope is lost.

But giving into it is tantamount to murder. That it is a murder of self is a matter of semantics. Cardinal D'Longville has already met his untimely demise. Antoine the *man*–Antoine the *soul*–is still kicking and screaming.

Fortunately, hope has a funny way of finding itself, and this time, he hears life return to him in the form of a sound.

The sound is a low, rumbling engine and the muted whoosh of an enormous propeller.

Gently cutting his assailants from him, a passing riverboat gives face to the hope, all festive streamers, and mistletoe, and laughter thick with alcohol and strapping touristy cheer.

He surfaces with an enormous gasp and clutches the netting cascading over the edge with every ounce of strength he can muster.

Within minutes or hours, another boat passes him, going the opposite direction. This one is a cargo freighter, less beautiful, but it gives Antoine an idea. He lets go of the netting, traverses the soup of floe and rotting algae between them, and grips the low railing.

He hangs on as long as his waning consciousness and cramping extremities permit, too exhausted to dip into the Order's book of tricks to keep himself going, then paddles stiffly to shore before collapsing on it. If they hadn't convinced themselves their volleys got him, they might reasonably expect him to have hitched a ride with the riverboat. A change in direction could throw them off the trail.

So he bets. Stakes his life on it, in point of fact.

He falls into something like sleep.

CHAPTER FOUR

Through the glaze of exhaustion and growing evidence of sickness, a few muddled shadows tower over him. Their voices filter in before he can make out the words: ragged voices full of holes, with throats so rough the sentences snag and tear on exit.

As Antoine's consciousness regretfully returns to him, he notices a few more details. Some of the men are wearing coats, but not all. The coats are ill-fitting, splitting at the seams or hanging long down past the wrist. Some coats have pockets stuffed to the brim, others look barely big enough to contain the man inside.

Three nearest him lean over. He freezes instinctually, leaving his eyes open a sliver. Their breath is hot and sour. Their hands flutter deftly through his pockets, roughly turn him on his side to loot the back.

"Can't see nothin' else," announces a low voice, creaking like old wood.

They let him fall back into place.

One silhouette, the hardest and skinniest of them all, angles down close. "No use playing possum, river-man!"

Carefully, fearfully, Antoine opens his eyes a little more. The hovering face so sharp from the moonlight, he marvels at pores clogged like miniature landfills and tremendous, dark tattoos slathering the cheeks, the bristled chin, degrading in the furrows of the forehead: thick, concentric circles netted together by a series of skulls and inky black feathers.

Antoine can only mutter the one thing on his mind. His mumbled, childish fear.

"Please don't kill me."

The tattooed man chuckles, air hissing out of his teeth.

"It's your night, brother." He points, the flash of jagged glass in his hand. "Bleeding heart over there swears that's bad luck to rub out a man of the cloth."

He slips a finger under Antoine's collarino. Who knew the inability to don something less manifest under the watchful eye of his acolytes would result in an execution stay? "And I don't need no more help finding bad luck. I do just fine on my own." The finger bears down. "Say beddy-bye, Father."

When Antoine comes to again, he is alone on the deserted bank of the Seine.

His painstakingly sneaked-in button-down and stolen money are gone. So is his solid gold cardinal's ring with its oblong crucifixion scene bestowed on him by Pope John Paul II during his elevation. So is his Order pin. So—his heart thumps wildly against his chest—is the Polaroid.

He had woken empty and washed out, but the hollowness quickly fills with a burning in his stomach, a bitter and savage determination to get *her*... it... back at all costs. It is the *right thing*.

Antoine staggers to his feet, looking for signs of the robbers.

They are long gone, but a set of dirty tracks in the snow is yet another apotheosis of hope. He starts walking unevenly in that direction. Life makes no sense without the memory of Rionni, and that memory is locked in the

Polaroid. He doesn't trust his own mind, especially not with the Baron and his ilk circling nigh.

After a few kilometers, his body having reached its limit and trudged past, Antoine stumbles to the characteristic safe-like door of a city shelter. So many of them around these days, unless dwelling solely in the 8th, 16th, and part of the 17th arrondissement, it is nigh impossible not to pass one by while walking a dog. His past occupation having availed him of neither a walkable companion nor opportunities for a solitary stroll, so he heard.

He disassembles his collarino so as to not provoke any questions, then presses the doorbell.

A little electronic speaker on the doorframe crackles to life.

"All full for the night," the voice at the other end doesn't mince words.

"Please…" he isn't above begging, but the speaker goes dead. He desperately presses the doorbell again.

"We have no room here, Sir, look elsewhere."

"I don't know what to do!" he cries in genuine distress. "I have no phone, no coat, I don't know anywhere else to go."

The truth is, he knows quite a few places to go. But this *is* the only one, in which he might not get recognized on the spot. Ministering to the needy as one of princes of the Catholic Church, it does not generally occur to one, the next time he enters their domain, it may be as a prospective denizen.

The hesitation drags on. He can nearly sense the person thinking on the other end.

The little white speaker burbles to life again.

"Meet me in the front lobby. I'll let you in."

A short buzz, and Antoine gratefully pushes in, letting the warmth of the indoors wash over him like a blessing.

The manager who meets him is a short woman with brown hair pulled back into a no-nonsense ponytail. She wears a clean white polo and has a sturdy, guarded face. Her voice is kind, but not gentle.

"You don't look like a man who is used to being outside."

"No ma'am," agrees Antoine, suddenly quite humble and nervous. "I'm in a bad way." Without realizing it, he takes on the diction of the poor and homeless.

She gives him a quick appraisal.

"Have you been mugged?"

"Yes."

"Do you live around here?"

"In the city."

"Do you just need a ride home? I can call the police for you."

"I can't go home."

She narrows her eyes a bit. Either through training or personal preference, she decides not to ask.

"Listen," she sighs. "We don't have any free beds tonight. Even the backyard annex's packed. But I do have some bedding, just a pillow and a couple of blankets. If you want them, you'll have to make do with the floor."

Antoine assents with great relief.

She disappears into a small office behind the front desk, then reemerges with a neat washed-out stack. He follows her into a large room with forty or fifty narrow pallets, each with their own grey mattress, pillow, and thin fleece blanket. Under each blanket is a snoring heap of a man.

"Pillow cases and sheets are to be returned tomorrow at 8am for the laundry run," warns the woman, leaving the room without another word or gesture.

Antoine takes a place in the far corner under the piping hot radiator coils and spreads out his sheets. It is his first time to be doing so for himself in…

Nevermind. He feels low and hollow, but also purposeful, as if some great reset button has been pressed on his entire existence. He is a human nothing, but that nothing is filled with potentiality, and this time, he has a chance to make it right.

He doffs his shoes and socks and stretches out on the floor. His mind spins, the missing Polaroid tortures him with his inability to stroke it goodnight on this, his first, eve of horrifying freedom, but through all that, sleep, a mistress that does not wait, sets to claim its pound of flesh.

He barely notices when a man in the nearby bed stirs, and turns to get a better look.

Then comes a whisper in the dark.

"*Father.*"

Antoine winces.

"*Father.*"

Slowly, and with some ill temper, Antoine drags open his eyes. The speaker is in his fifties or sixties, with a round, rough face and a grey-grizzled chin. He ogles Antoine with a sort of open-mouthed awe.

"I knows ye. Knows who y'are."

"What can I do for you?" asks Antoine, going for gentle and accommodating but failing slightly.

"Me..." nasalizes the whiskered man. "Nothing. Nothing. Might be I can help you."

Antoine sits halfway up. Something in this man's tone. What...

"You were there," he breathes, his memory snapping together.

His neighbor nods.

Antoine kicks back the covers and rushes to his bedside so quickly that the man throws his arms up halfway in defense. No use. Antoine is on his knees, eye level with the bed, the tattered shirt clenched in his fist. A distant part wonders, has it always been in him, one of the things he has counseled against, this maelstrom of aggression?

"Something was taken from me," he growls. "Something more important than I could possibly explain to you. I need it back."

There is a glimmer of fear in the hobo's eyes, and Antoine recoils.

"Was thinkin' ye need some new drag t' get on your way. Ye followed me, yeah? I knows we robbed ye blind at the riverbank. And I's real sorry about it, you being a man of God and all. But I don't have nothing. The old skullface took everything, and it's best not to toss up with him, if you know what I mean."

"Where is he?"

The old man looks paralyzed. "He bunks over further Seine-et-Marne way with his gang. Sometimes I'm with them, this place don't have room. Don't always reckon I'd wake up alive in that camp. You give 'em one reason, and they gobble you up like dogs."

"I've got to go." Antoine hoists himself up, tailed by swirling mutterings of 'goddamn stuff it'.

"No, Father," the man whispers hoarsely, holding up a gloved hand. "Ye'll get y'self killed. Wait till morning. I'll talk to them. What is it ye're missing?"

Antoine clenches his teeth. "A photo."

The old man doesn't answer right away.

"Don't know what it means to you, Father," he says quietly, "but it's nothin' to them. Ye rest easy now. In the morning we'll sort this out."

Antoine hesitates for a moment, but, realizing he can't get very far without the gentleman's help, settles stiffly back into his pile of blankets.

"What is your name?" he asks quietly into the darkness.

"It's Harly, Father."

Antoine intends to answer, but sleep rushes over him, impatient and inevitable.

He wakes to the rustling sheets and knapsacks of forty-odd men, all getting up to meet the checkout deadline.

He sits up, rubbing his eyes. Each memory trickles back, one at a time, crazily crashing into the next like beads on an abacus.

As the last falls into place, he spins sharply to look for Harly. His heart freezes at the sight of an empty bed.

He races out of the dormitory and through the front lobby, dumping his bedding in a heap on the counter with mumbled thanks. Bursting out into the cool white morning, he looks frantically for signs of his wayward friend.

Finding nothing, he dashes down the bedizened main street that, like an aging moll, can't hide tourists not tipping nearly as well or treating it as kindly as they used to; stops to glance down each alleyway winding away in filthy ribbons.

Near the last one, he is in luck. The plump grizzled cheek and dingy green fingerless gloves hover over the ciggy before Harly responsibly grinds the match into the uric-yellow slush and tromps off down the alley.

The anger, *his* anger, chars. But rather than rushing Harly, soothing it, he holds himself back. He might learn more if he stays out of sight.

Indeed, Harly seems to be moving along with great intention toward the old smokestacks on the outskirts of town. Obfuscating again on top of maintaining his body temperature at levels marginally compatible with pneumonia-free life—if arcana used muscles, his lactic acid levels would be through the roof—Antoine follows. The closely knotted buildings and alleys give way to broad highways and grassy ditches, leading out toward an industrial site. With Harly skulking now, eyes darting this way and that in fear of being jumped, the camp is likely nearby, and there, Antoine would need all the foreknowledge he can get.

So, he takes this as his chance. He releases the obfuscation and lunges towards Harly, first quietly, then quickly. The stamping of his feet finally alerts the old man, who swings, alarmed, to face the assailant from a direction, out of which, his mind assured him not ten seconds ago, no threat could possibly come.

Antoine halts just short of him, using his full height to glare down. Violence, always violence, and him, out of his Ivory Tower, having called so naively for the cessation thereof.

"Lying to a man of the cloth, Harly? Tsk-tsk…" Antoine hisses, fists balled up in barely-controlled rage.

Harly's face is startled and fearful.

"I am trying to help!" he squawks. "Ye need only wait for me to return!"

"The shelter's closing for the day! You knew I wouldn't be there!"

"Had no other choice, Father! I can't be bringing ye with me to help with the dirty work! Don't want no blood on my conscience!"

"You're afraid," Antoine growls. "You were just going to leave me to myself, no matter how critical…"

Harly shakes his head fervently. "No sir, no. No reason for me to go back to the camps except t'do this thing for ye."

Antoine steps back, refusing to let his anger dissipate, but now also trying to think.

"The camp is that way?" He points off to the smokestacks.

Harly's eyes grow wide. "Ye can't go! And ye're cold…"

Antoine brushes past Harly and storms through the field.

"No, Father, no! They'll kill ye!"

He needs no more direction from Harly. The camp is just up ahead in its derelict glory. Rough logs and piles of earth serve as benches. A few rusty rubbish bins still sputter with fire from the night before. The clotheslines feature Minnie Mouse PJs, distended bras, a pair of threadbare All Stars hanging by their laces in the absence of high voltage power lines. This one is a settled hell.

Some inhabitants continue napping under piles of clothes, some are sitting down to a sad semblance of breaking fast en famille, and others, like the tattoo-faced man, are rolling cigarettes and picking at cans of fish.

At the sight of Tattoo Face, rage flares up inside Antoine. He is a different man now. After last night, and after the loss of that Polaroid, something new and potent courses through him. Maybe he is rubbish at street life, maybe he can't actually fight the men who'd spent their whole lives in physical peril, but now, for the first time, is he ever rearing to try!

He strides brazenly towards Tattoo Face–who only briefly registers surprise before whipping out his knife. "You come to the wrong part of town, boy."

"There was a photo! Of a woman!" Antoine barks, adrenaline leaving any old liquid courage in the dust. "Give it to me, now!"

Tattoo Face sneers and cocks his head, almost quizzical at Antoine's brashness.

But Antoine senses something, something seeking him out, sensing him back, responding to his wrath. An object on the table by the thug's herring can, a nearly sacred object, a twin of the one he took from the Order goon, but *his*, so many millions of times more attuned.

"Do as I say," orders Antoine, gathering every ounce of his authority.

"What you gonna do to make me?" Tattoo Face snorts, tossing his knife deftly from hand to hand.

"The Polaroid."

Tattoo Face licks his chapped lips, and with a goblin smile, rushes at Antoine.

At that moment, a great boom. Sudden fire and a wave of heat knock a fair radius off their feet, send them flying. Some crash against fire barrels and some hit the ground rolling. The damp dingy lean-tos avoid the flames, but the forked struts of the clotheslines aren't so lucky.

The women cry out in shock and horror. The kids squeal, tinny helpless sounds.

The men who had avoided the full brunt of the explosion run to help.

Tattoo Face staggers to his feet. Naturally wiry and dirty, he now looks like a dumpster rat, his back and hair singed. The arrogance is gone from his face.

"Do you know what this is?" Antoine unhooks a second Order pin from his waistband, a generic symbol of eternal flame—until one considers the intricate handcraft. "Looks familiar, does it? Just like the pin you filched last night. That's what did this."

Antoine gestures to the wounded and ruins of the camp. Tattoo Face doesn't need to know this had been an accident. The sort in which one intentionally gets behind the wheel sloshed.

"No great shakes, right? They hold power. Shall we see if this one carries a stronger charge?"

Holding the trinket out like the weapon it is, Antoine takes a menacing step forward.

Tattoo Face stumbles back.

"Now," Antoine lowers his voice. "All I want to know is, where is my photo?"

The tattooed man shakes his head in disbelief. With a trembling hand, he points to a nearby dumpster.

Antoine is on a lucky streak. Whenever the Polaroid had been tossed in, it sits on top. Rionni's young, stony face stares out at him from the piles of junk and decay. He takes it, as if his life had been returned to him, and suppresses tears.

He considers going around the camp in search of anything else they swiped from him. Namely, money. But after the pin's performance, they'd clearly need it more than ever before.

"Here, Fa... sir," surprisingly mindful of Antoine's incognito status, Harly must have followed him into the camp and is now returning his coat and over-shirt with outstretched arms, like an offering.

Antoine nods a somber thanks.

"I have to go," he says. It is true. He has drawn too much attention to himself, and the Order members could be on top of him in minutes.

With wide eyes, Harly gives the slightest nod as an answer.

Without another word, Antoine turns, heading for the long narrow road leading south into the country.

CHAPTER FIVE

Fresh snow drifts down, landing on the pines and coating the land with holy silence. He has just now remembered. It is Christmas. Beyond that, Antoine is conscious only of the crunch of his dress shoes crushing the ice crystals with every step. It is a plush, crinkling sound, and though he leaves a trail, for a while at least, he might be safe. The snowfall is steady and would soon cover up his tracks anyway. So goes the theory.

He is beat, and has left off obfuscation a while back. His temperature, however, needs maintaining, and for Lord knows how long. He only guesstimates his destination. If he follows this particular road a few more kilometers south, he should come to a small gate. Behind that small gate is another long rambling trail, and at its culmination, a little farmhouse with a family inside.

A family. That is the pivot point.

The head of it is a fellow clergyman, highly—and personally— invested in Antoine's advocacy for priestly marriage. After years of faithfully adhering to celibacy, the man had committed (in the eyes of the board) the egregious crime of falling in love. Fortunately, this love had bloomed in secret and was carried out likewise, with a private ceremony, a secular officiant, and now, this nestled home. Inside this house is a betrayal of the priesthood in the form of a man, a woman, and a small child.

People like this man are waiting for Antoine, who so far had remained "pure" in the eyes of the community, to speak on their behalf.

More importantly, he is a friend. And if there is anyone Antoine could possibly reach at this moment, it is him.

If he makes it. It is getting late, and he has been walking all day. His stomach growls angrily and his feet and legs are stiff like the sapless boughs shedding soggy clumps of snow onto his head.

He isn't sure if he has passed the house already. The snow might have obscured the trail. Shrubs might have covered the gate. He tries his best not to feel utterly discouraged.

But there is something worse now, a pressure on his shoulders that becomes increasingly hard to shake. He is being followed. He is being watched.

Antoine stops.

Behind him on the desolate road, the distance stretches out, bleak and empty. Heavy swirls of snow obscure the air. He tries to imagine that it is all in his head, the creeping sensation of something, or someone, out there, pacing him.

Unable to fully convince himself, but overcome with the fatigue of a day's walk through the weather, he steps off the side of the road into a gathering of trees where he hopes to take five, unnoticed.

The dreams, unbidden like the sleep itself, come like howls in the night, punctuated and sharp, telling of some monster on the horizon. The monster he himself has become.

Clotheslines fall, groaning in a heap. Timber snaps and snarls with wild hot flames. He is trapped, unable to see or breathe. He calls the only name he knows.

"Rionni!"

No answer over the roaring inferno. He is back in the office in Prague, deep in the belly of the Order headquarters. Before, he and Rionni had been surrounded by flames, but somehow untouched by them. This time, it is different. He is alone, and like an insatiable lover, they lick at his sweaty skin, heave molten breaths onto his fluttering eyelids, tighten their grip over his heaving chest.

He screams, a silent dreamsound. His flesh melts off in horrid dark chunks, sizzling with fat and muscle. Soon there is nothing left of him, nothing, nothing, but black bones and a gaping mouth.

Suddenly, from out of the dream fire, someone grabs his hand.

Antoine startles awake, clammy despite the frigid evening.

He catches sight of some living thing, gazing at him from across the road. He sits up, squinting. After a moment, he makes out the shape of a stag. It is a statuesque creature, perfectly still but for a pair of twitching ears. He is strangely calm, but eerily aware how intensely this animal watches him. There is... purpose.

In a flash, the stag twitches and disappears into the brush on the other side. Antoine is immediately alert. Something had startled it.

Even through snow, he begins to make out the sound of a quiet engine. No, two. He draws his energy together and obfuscates himself, keeping perfectly still under the tree.

One black SUV crawls along the old country road. A few moments later, another.

Nothing too out of the ordinary. After all, several homes and towns spot the countryside along this road. But Antoine can't shake the feeling that they are Order members, that they are looking for him.

His blood pounds in his ears as he watches them proceed down the road. He half expected them to stop.

How had they traced him?

He finds the answer in his pocket, and curses his stupidity.

The pin, of course. So accustomed to keeping his with him, the one that leveled the camp, even after crossing the Order, he treats the ill-gotten booty like a safety blanket, a keepsake of benevolent prison now irreversibly gone. Members can seek each other out by their pins. It is effectively a tiny homing beacon, cheerily flashing out his location to anyone who looks.

He is disgusted with himself. How can he possibly expect to save Rionni, much less survive his own escape, if he lets these little details slip?

With more force than strictly necessary, Antoine chucks the Order pin into the bushes, into which the stag had disappeared. He hears a clink. It is a funny sound, little metal hitting a bigger one.

He brushes off the rotting herbage and approaches the bush, leaning over to peer between the thatched sprigs. Something hard and rusted cowers beneath. He reaches in and taps it with his finger. Light aluminum.

He pushes the branches out of the way. An abandoned bicycle.

Antoine looks carefully around him, then closes his eyes and searches for the presence of others using his Order powers. He finds nothing. More than nothing?

The feeling of being watched returns in force. He wrenches the old bike out of the bushes and checks the chain. Luckily, it is still in working order. Nothing to do then, but continue on his way, this time, with the help of his find.

He mounts the bicycle and pedals down the old country road, following the track left by the SUVs.

Night falls, total and uncompromising. Still, Antoine desperately searches the side of the road for signs of a gate.

Finally, exhausted and freezing, he finds one.

He had been here once before, years ago. Sworn to secrecy, he had not returned since. Now it is his last refuge, just as it is Monsignor Václav Jeník's. Vas's, in short. Though his memory of the place is dim, he just barely recognizes the comically arrogant rooster spreading its carved wooden wings over the perpetually open latch.

With fresh hope, Antoine turns down the trail and pedals until he reaches the quaint farmhouse with the porch light glimmering cozily, as if from the pages of an illuminated storybook.

He knocks on the door in the dead of night, praying he is answered.

Someone moves inside.

The door opens.

Vas's worried face appears on the other side. In the dim light, it takes his friend a few moments to recognize him.

A confused smile flicks on, an old hat of a smile, snug and utilitarian.

"Come in, brother," invites the gentle, lightly accented voice.

Antoine steps inside.

CHAPTER SIX

Monsignor Václav Jeník has a face like a tawny rabbit. He is a good step shorter than Antoine, who, to be fair, has a tendency to tower over most people. But Václav looks oddly smaller and understandably older than during their seminary orientation. Or their many, many meetings since. His skin has weathered, and Antoine suspects that it's more than the natural course of time taking its toll.

The smile, hesitant and uncomprehending, still flutters on Václav's face like a feather caught in a fence, but the house is exactly as Antoine recalls it, warm, rouge-tinted, largely reliant on great beams of timber to hold up the doorways and thick ceiling planks.

Václav manages his first question, "What on earth-" but stops short when he sees the full extent of Antoine's condition. The ghastly hue of Antoine's skin, his stiff and violently shivering body, the rust-colored crumbs of dried blood and dirt all send Václav rushing to a dining room chair to pull it out just as Antoine collapses into it.

Antoine feels the pressure of Václav's eyes, but is mercifully spared the interrogation. In the space of a moment, too many questions have accumulated, and knowing Vas, he won't start firing them out until Antoine's immediate needs have been addressed.

"It's okay, Jana," Václav says gently to the empty space in the kitchen doorway.

Slowly and carefully, a woman fills it. She's wan and small, but sharp-eyed from years of living in secrecy. Antoine takes one look at her and grits his teeth against another stab of very much non-misplaced guilt.

She folds her arms and measures Antoine in her gaze.

"There are some bandages in the basement, Václav," Jana returns to the kitchen, and soon the sound of boiling water is evident.

Václav returns with a pile of clean linen clothes, and Jana puts the kettle on a wicker hot plate. As Antoine watches, Václav pours some hot water on the first few linens while Jana pours the rest into a teacup. A strong, grassy, bitter scent reaches his nose.

Working together, Antoine and Václav peel off the first few layers of Antoine's clothes until the only thing left is a thin white undershirt.

"Not as bad as I thought," says Václav. "Not much blood, mostly bruising. Do you feel much pain anywhere else?"

"No," Antoine mutters, finally realizing, under those safe warm lights, just how much he's gone through in the last two days. How much that heretofore inviolate essence of him has twisted and warped.

A small sound comes from the dark hallway leading to the rest of the house. Pegging it as a new kitten at first, by Jana's reaction, Antoine identifies the sleepy complaint of a child.

"Back to bed!" Jana says, swiftly steering Emile, Vas's sin made flesh, down the hall.

"Has anyone followed you?" Václav asks in a low voice.

Antoine shakes his head. "No, brother, I'm sorry, just…"

Václav shakes his head. "Don't worry about anything tonight. There's plenty of time for explanations tomorrow."

Antoine looks toward the hallway. "He's getting so bi…" The last word devolves into a coughing fit.

Václav hands him the tea.

"Jana is good with herbal medicine," he says. "Well, we can't always go to the doctor here. Only as a last resort."

They speak with forced pleasantry to each other, skirting the obvious, preferring to focus instead on the days BJ. Before Jana. Before Václav acquired a secret life. Before Antoine took it upon himself to champion his cause.

"I have turned down the sheets," says Jana, ghosting across the threshold.

Antoine hardly remembers falling asleep.

The next morning rallies him with the chatter of news reports. Considering it is the dark of winter, expecting birdsong instead might, despite the hedonistic sprawl of the virgin countryside beyond the square curtainless window, have been a touch unrealistic. He swings his legs off the twin captain's bed that is decidedly too short for him and is probably Emile's. Fool's hope for a fool.

Squirming himself into the too-small hand-me-downs Jana left for him at the foot of the bed, Antoine strains to make out the words. Following them, he finds Václav and Jana leaning against the kitchen counter with their backs to him, intent on the small television set. They cradle twin steaming cups. Emile plays with his trucks on the floor.

A lump catches in Antoine's throat when the chatter resolves into comprehensible speech.

Jana turns and stares at him. Her mouth is hard, but the whites of her eyes are pink and her bottom lids are swollen.

She walks out.

Emile looks up from his toys at his departing mother, then up at Antoine with mingled curiosity and fear. Then at the TV set. Back to Antoine.

He picks up a police van and runs out of the room.

The only ones left are Antoine and Václav. Václav's face is so fixed, it looks rendered of clay. He turns up the volume.

"The worldwide Catholic community is in shock over the disappearance of Cardinal Antoine DeLongville, a much-loved advocate for the burgeoning homeless population and reformation of rules restricting clergy to celibate lifestyle. He was last seen two nights ago, delivering a Christmas Eve sermon, which many believed to be, quote 'too political'. Those close to the Cardinal fear he may have been kidnapped-"

Václav presses a button, and the TV screen flips to black.

"You know the rest," he says quietly.

Antoine feels the blood leaving his face. Cold guilt bubbles up to take its place.

"Václav," Antoine whispers, his voice slanted with desperation, "I would have been kidnapped if I hadn't left. I was in danger."

Václav's eyes soften slightly.

"Someone tried to take you as a hostage? Harm you?"

"Yes, well, almost, I-" he hesitates.

Václav's mouth narrows in suspicion.

"They would have tried to…" What? "Control me. Use me to hurt someone else."

"Ha," Václav's eyes are wet. "That's the Catholic Church in a nutshell."

Antoine shakes his head vigorously. "No, not like this. They… there are things I can't tell you."

Václav shakes his head stiffly.

"Things I'm not allowed to know, is that it?"

"Things you wouldn't want to know."

"And yet, you ran *here*, of all places. Now, it's my problem. Still you say I wouldn't want to know. You are *perplexing*."

He says "perplexing" with a terrible sneer. Like many holy men, Václav has learned to swear with a clean tongue.

"My friend," Antoine bows his head. "Please. I had to leave."

A new sort of horror dawns in Václav's eyes.

"Leave? You mean for good? You've left the church?"

179

"I'm afraid that's what it might come down to."

Vas stands there in the kitchen biting his cheek. Craven it may be, but Antoine almost turns the TV back on to drown out this horrible silence.

"You were my last resort, brother," he says finally. "My family lives like fugitives. Look at my wife. Do you think she deserves to be treated like a mistress? I have to keep her a secret! I should be claiming her! I should be shouting from the highest mountain that I love her and my beautiful son!"

"But you can't," comes another voice, ragged but clean like a wet stone. Jana has returned to the kitchen. "You can't because the cabal of shrunken old men told you what to do. And you've listened."

"My Jana," he says, pleading. "I serve God. That's my calling. I don't care what the papal authority says. But they are the ones who stand between me and my calling. If I don't obey them, I have nothing."

Jana's eyebrows draw together in a knot. And for the first time since taking on the issue, internally, Antoine sides with Jana. Denouncing one's own calling gives one a novel perspective, it seems.

"Something smells rotten," she says.

"Jana, Václav, I am with you."

"You were with us until you left."

"But even with my leaving," Antoine's voice is strained with hope, "perhaps I've changed something. Planted the seed."

"To bear fruit when? Before we die? Do you think this will happen in time for Vas and I to be buried next to each other?"

Antoine feels pent up and tight. His guilt has turned into frustration. A helpless one.

A shepherd of souls advanced, unlike himself, so high and fast without the subtle hand of the Order, Václav recognizes it, and while his face doesn't show much forgiveness, it doesn't show much anger either.

"Make yourself at home," he says softly, laying a gentling palm on Jana's arm. "My family and I are going for a walk."

Jana calls for Emile, and he comes running. She gathers him up in her arms.

The three of them leave Antoine behind and start down a dirt path leading deep into their wooded backyard.

Antoine watches from the back porch, at once a voyeur and a supplicant.

Emile, still in the arms of his mother, looks at Antoine over her shoulder.

His face is screwed up, angry and resentful. One look tells Antoine that Emile must have heard much of their conversation, and understands more than they realize.

Emile's glower disappears into the trees.

Antoine spends the day alone, refining his escape route to Russia. Her president, a man's man and a devout Christian, is a hop and a skip from bona fide dictator. Not a benevolent one, at that. One who would not—and does not—permit competition. Consequently, it is the only Eurasian country— reachable without the antiterrorism-obsessed transcontinental travel industry—that boasts no Order presence of note.

He knows he'll need Václav's help. He knows too, the very fact of needing it means he has relinquished his decade-sanctified right to ask. It is a classic Schrödinger's cat.

By the time Václav and his family return, the sun has already began to sink beneath the silvered tree line. The sky takes on a lovely lavender hue. Largely unrecognized in France, in Poland, this would have qualified as a postcard-perfect ending to Holy Szczepan Day.

Václav sits at the table with Antoine, a soft lamplight throwing long shadows across his homely features.

"There's not much we can do at this point," Václav says tiredly. "I can't undo the last three days, and you probably wouldn't even if you could."

"I just need you to trust me. You've helped so much by letting me stay here. Help me once more by getting me to Prague."

"And what then?"

"And then," Antoine touches Václav's arm, "if I come out of this, if I am in any way capable of challenging the status…" He catches himself. Saying the right thing, the calculated thing is a chore, and privilege, of the past. "And then, I fade away. If I am lucky. Hoping what I did is enough."

Václav looks unconvinced, but is a matter of fact when he says, "We have always been brothers. We are brothers now. Let's see what we can do."

He goes to the tiny bureau in the hallway and takes out a sheaf of papers.

Antoine watches Václav, and his heart thumps when he notices a tiny shadow steal across the corridor. Emile has been lingering there again, listening to them talk. He's been paying an unusual amount of attention for such a small boy, all Václav's precociousness and Jana's looks–untempered both by age and hardship.

Stumping down his unjustified nervousness, Antoine chalks it off to guilt. No Order members can find him here. Not this fast.

Václav returns and spreads the papers out on the kitchen table. Across some leaflets in tiny, precise handwriting, are the names, numbers, and addresses of Václav's entire network. Everyone from professional acquaintances to distant cousins of the family, wrapped up in one concise homemade phonebook.

"That's impressive." Antoine's eyes widen.

"Shall I quote you the statistics of just how many spouses and children need refuge or how thin the governmental resources are spread–or do you want the honors?"

Antoine breathes out a hiss of concurrence. Or mourning. As Jana's example proved, domestic violence is well on the way to turning back into a tacitly decriminalized pastime.

Václav takes another pastel-colored sheet and gently unfolds it, revealing a massive, detailed map from the eastern border of France to the western edge of Ukraine. There, in that thick and troubled strip of Central Europe, is everything Antoine needs to overcome.

In her particular way–a former battered wife's way–Jana comes in without a word and begins to chop vegetables for soup. Another kettle of Jeníks' crisp artesian well water for the robust cinnamon-scented tea chuffs its mindless contentment on the antique iron stove.

Vas places an authoritative finger on the map.

"This is where you need to start. If they are looking for you, avoid the main roads. Stop often. Go south for a bit to throw them off course."

He pulls out a blocky old mechanic's pencil and makes meticulous circles at certain points on the map. "This is where I know people. I'll write their names here and you can cross reference that with the contact sheet."

Antoine shakes his head slowly, moved by Václav's assistance.

"I don't know how to thank-" but the words freeze in his throat.

A flash of light from the driveway crosses the checkered curtain and catches his eye.

Another flash. Red. Then blue. Red, then blue.

His heart sinks like a stone.

Václav catches Antoine's expression and swings toward the window. When he looks back at Antoine, his face is ghastly with fright.

Jana drops her knife.

"Get to the back of the house!" commands Václav, and in a stumble of papers and chairs, the three of them bolt down the hallway.

Jana is ahead of them, but she balks at the entrance to the living room.

"Emile!" she shrieks.

Vas and he arrive just in time to see Emile drop the phone.

It falls straight toward the floor, swinging from the empty cradle. Emile's cherub face is scary in its impassivity. He looks to the television and back to Antoine. All at once they notice the living room television has been on, and muted, the whole time, playing the story of Antoine's disappearance. At the bottom of the screen, there's a phone number—a tip hotline.

"He's a bad man," says Emile, pointing straight at Antoine. "He makes Daddy go away."

It has begun with a phone call, his rebellion. It is fitting that so it ends.

"Oh no, no, no," mumbles Václav.

Jana's face is white.

Antoine looks back to the kitchen, still flashing with police lights.

He considers his choices.

"Follow the path out back!" cries Václav.

Antoine shakes his head. "If I do, they'll hunt for me. They'll dig. They'll expose your family on the news."

Over the increasingly choleric call of a local police officer struggling to confirm his location through the signal-dampening thicket of trees, Antoine thinks a bit more.

"If I come quietly," he says, "I can downplay this. I can say that I saw the driveway from the road and ran to this house for safety. And that all I found here was a single mother and her child."

Václav shakes his head and grabs Antoine's arm. "Listen, brother, I don't know why you ran away. Why, suddenly, three nights ago you gave up everything you believed in, everything you've worked for." He swallows hard. "But there must be a reason. Don't let it end here."

"Maybe it won't end here," Antoine tries to keep his voice steady. "It may. It may not. You've done everything you can to help me. It's time to do the right thing."

"Václav," orders Jana, and this is a voice of a mother, a helpmeet. She has come a long way with her new husband's help. "Let him go."

The radio fades.

Václav's eyes are wild and indecipherable, but he listens to Jana. He takes his hand off Antoine's arm and nods.

Antoine nods back.

He starts to walk toward the front of the house, repeating his last three words as a mantra.

The right thing.

The right thing.

183

With a shaky hand on the door handle, and his "savior" just inches behind the slab of indigenous cedar, Antoine pauses.

What *is* the right thing?

Out of the corner of his eye, he spots Václav backing himself, with the sort of a heartbreaking familiarity, into a cubbyhole in the coat closet's backwall. If the constables find their kidnap victim here, even if they so much as catch a glimpse of a fellow cleric, they will not stop until they had torn the cottage apart. And if the Baron gets a hold of his precious escapee, it will be Antoine's mind that would be rending itself undone.

When it comes, the knock on the door is polite. No sign of this being anything but a routine we-are-crossing-our-T's-though-we'd-rather-be-having-our-grog kind of deal.

The realization bloomed on a heel of it is earthshattering. It is also simple as pie.

The right thing is letting Emile's call go down in the books exactly as what they are treating it as, a child's prank.

The right thing is letting the fire that started it all die out before any more casualties are claimed.

The right thing is letting his cause pick up new wings in the late Cardinal's memory instead of sacrificing it for his own… what? The absurdity of it, the sheer banality and bottomless meaningfulness make him titter. His just desserts?

Clutching the wrinkled, grimy Polaroid in one hand, failing utterly to shed the self-pitying anger sparking thoughtless, and liberating, and harsh, Antoine D'Longville lets the doorknob sink into a misty soup beneath the death grip of the other. The glacial tendrils of the *in-between* embrace him like a long-lost toy.

The *right thing*.

Want more blazing paranormal thrillers in the Mind's Eye series?
Tweet *More Mainyu @AEPropher @CuriosityQuills #BookLove*

Tell Us Everything

TELL US EVERYTHING

BY RANDY ATTWOOD

Cricket carefully backed her crummy car, which needed a motor mount bolt replaced, down her cousin's driveway. She was driving extra cautiously these days because her license was suspended and she had two weeks to go on her probation before she could pay the bastards another $90 to get reinstated, which was beyond bullshit because that last DUI was totally fucking unfair. She hit the brakes when she heard Samantha's voice on the radio.

"Cricket, can you hear me broadcasting? I told you I was. And I'm going to start telling truths, Cricket, truths about our family and you and everyone. How will you all like that? The highs today are expected to reach the mid-90s. In sports, the Royals lost their tenth straight."

Jesus, Cricket worried, maybe I'm the one who's nuts. She flipped away a strand of brown hair that had fallen over her nose, which—being a little upturned but too pudgy—she didn't consider one of the best features on her otherwise pretty, if a bit lopsided, face. She'd gone to her cousin's house because her aunt, Samantha's mother, begged her to check on the little fruitcake, who was this time really in serious need of a mental health crisis intervention. But Samantha wouldn't unlock the door and just yelled that she was busy broadcasting.

Truths about the family? What truths?

"The citizens of Peculiar will be interested to know that their postmistress is fucking two carriers ON government time and ON government property!" Samantha was starting her truth telling.

Cricket left the car and ran back to pound on Samantha's locked front door.

"Sami! You let me in right now. Stop this!"

"Go away!" Samantha yelled back at her. "Or I'll start telling truths about you next."

This brought Cricket up short. Samantha knew many not-so-pleasant things about Cricket; it was better the world didn't know. Nothing criminal, well, not too criminal and the statute of limitation had passed on the things she'd done back in her teenage wild days. Not really done, just involved in, sort of. She was going to be late for work and that would make Joe mumble-grumble even more than usual. Back in the car, there was Samantha's voice still on the radio:

"The names of the carriers the postmistress of Peculiar is sliming are Larry and Bill and they are BOTH married and one of them got her pregnant and she aborted the baby and how do those good Christians out in Peculiar feel about THAT! The lows tonight will be in the 60s as a cool front moves through and we can turn off our air-conditioning. The stock market was up on a positive earnings report from Apple and closed at 9350."

Cricket knew one carrier was boinking her aunt, but not two, and certainly not about any abortion. She was surprised her aunt would have told Samantha about that. She turned to a different radio frequency, but Samantha's voice was still on the radio. She switched from FM to AM and it was there, too.

This is just crazy. Maybe Samantha's mental illness is catching and I'm a nut case, too. And me, the most normal person in my whole lunatic family.

Cricket drove off. Going by the dashboard clock, she had only five minutes to get to work. She reached the end of the second block and realized the radio was back to normal. Samantha's voice was gone, replaced by that gay weatherman trying to be witty with the sports talk host who was asking him if he ever fantasized about playing football and would he rather be the center or the quarterback. "Oh, the center."

Temporary insanity. That's it. Just a little bit of temporary insanity. Happens to people all the time, she figured, and drove on to the bar where she bartended. Its front door opened and Joe stepped out to look up and down the street for her. She honked as she passed, waved, and turned to park in the back where the sickly-sweet smell of garbage from the next door Chinese slop shop's dumpster greeted her, as it did every morning, and made her feel like she was going to throw up.

187

Or, shit, maybe I'm pregnant!

"Hi, Joe," she drew out the one-syllable name, making it sound like a girl in a bikini yelling "Yoo-Hoo" to a stud surfer. Joe's beer belly made him anything but a surfer stud.

"Your drawer was $20 short."

"That can't be," Cricket protested. "I've been extra careful. I want to do a drawer count at end of shift, like they do everywhere else, and not rely on the night bartender to count my drawer." Her replacement was always about thirty minutes late, and she needed to go pick up her little girl, and she didn't trust the bastard about anything, let alone counting her daily take.

It was as if she hadn't spoken. "Well, try to be more careful. And you need to make an effort to be nicer to people. The daytime ring has been going down since I hired you." Upon which parting shot, he left.

With the front door safely closed, Cricket let loose. "That's 'cause all the old fart regulars are dying off! And the ones who are still alive don't tip for shit! Don't force me to go get a higher paying job, Joe!"

Her cell phone started ringing, and she saw it was Samantha's aunt, Peculiar's Postmistress.

"She wouldn't let me in the door," Cricket reported. "Says she's broadcasting."

"Broadcasting?"

"As in over the radio."

"Good Lord, maybe I should call the police and have them break in."

"They wouldn't. Thinking you are broadcasting doesn't represent a threat to you or anyone else." Well, unless she really *was* telling the world the truth about its affairs. "I'll go by after my shift."

She walked to the cash register surrounded with bar-necessary detritus: bills to be paid; receipts; the credit/debit machine; the eyeglasses to loan to people; pens; paper scraps; dozens of menus from carry-out places; the rolodex of phone numbers—half of which were probably defunct; and the small transistor radio to be turned on when the Royals weren't televised, which, given how badly they were doing, was quite often. She switched it on, and the normal station wheezed out.

Whew, it WAS just temporary insanity. All the stress I'm under.

And with her little girl's three-year birthday party coming up and Cricket's own mother telling her she didn't know if she could make it! What kind of grandmother did that?! At least, no need to be inviting Samantha now. There's something positive about her flip-out.

Cricket got out the rags and Pine-Sol to start cleaning the mess of a bar that rat bastard of a night bartender had left for her. All in the day's... Ah, whatever.

Later that morning arrived Elmer-the-farmer, who wasn't a farmer and whose name wasn't Elmer, but he began introducing himself as Elmer once he chose to wear bib overalls upon retirement from his job as one of the early computer nerds for a big company. He would have a double shot of cheap bar gin (one cube of ice), down it in a gulp and either leave right away or have another and then leave right away. And grace her with a fifty-cent tip.

He was halfway through the first slug when Fred, a small package deliveryman, also retired and enjoying whatever kind of life Social Security provided, sat down and waited for Cricket to bring him his bourbon and soda. "Elmer," he said. "The damndest thing. Something's happened to my radio at the house. All I get all over the dial, AM or FM, is some girl yapping her head off about whathaveya. I could hear her on the car radio, too, until I was just a few blocks away, and then the normal stations came on."

"Call the FCC. Some idiot's got a transmitter and juiced it up so it blocks out all the other stations, but its range is really limited."

Cricket's mouth was still open. Well, at least it meant she, herself, had not gone temporarily nutso.

"She's doing some kind of a sex gossip report show. I didn't catch the whole thing but something about mail carriers fucking their postmistress. And then she reads stuff out of the newspaper, but she said the Royals lost their tenth straight yesterday and they lost their ninth straight yesterday, although they'll probably lose their tenth straight today. Oh, and Elmer, you've got Apple stock. She said it reported unexpected earnings."

Elmer dropped his glass. And with some gin still in it. Cricket came with a towel. Elmer, indeed, had Apple stock and Apple connections and he happened to know that Apple was set to announce in just a few minutes an unexpected hike in its earnings report that would probably set the market on fire. He had bought in at opening bell when the Dow was at 9100.

"You happen to remember what she said the Dow closed at?"

"Yeah, because it seemed awfully high: 9350."

"You live over around the Med Center, don't you?"

"Yeah, God damn students take up all the street parking. Future little blood suckers."

Cricket remembered Fred lived near Samantha.

"Gotta go," Elmer said, and Cricket noticed he failed to leave his measly two-quarter tip.

"Fred, it must be Samantha."

"What?"

"Samantha, my cousin. Remember I told you she lived near you? She's gone round the bend and thinks she's broadcasting over the radio."

"But evidently, she is!" He took off his Royals cap to rub his mop of sweaty, matted-down white hair.

"Evidently. Except she doesn't know squat about electronics."

"Maybe some friend set her up. I mean with all those smarty-pants medical students around that area, there are some really whacky ones. You think our healthcare system sucks now. Wait till these little geniuses graduate."

"You want to do me a favor and go back and listen to what's she's saying? Maybe take notes?"

"Sure, I ain't got nothin' to do."

He left, and thus Samantha's crap cost Cricket another customer, who would have had two more drinks. Maybe more, because she had worn a top that showed a lot of cleavage. Still, if the nut cake was really telling truths about the family, Cricket needed to know what they were, especially if the truths concerned Cricket herself. She'd bust in that door.

Elmer reached the neighborhood near the Medical Center and, sure enough, a woman's voice suddenly came in through his car speakers. He pulled to the curb and noticed several other cars with drivers still behind their wheels, including a Medical Center security vehicle.

"In local news, the hospital head honcho is a closet gay, but not so deep in the closet that he hasn't hired his boytoy to be his executive assistant. The lesbian love nests in the interstitial floors of the hospital continue unabated. Researchers are still breaking the legs of poor beagle puppies to experiment on bone healing systems. Dioxide-ridden rats are stored in common freezers on floors in the research building within easy reach of any person wandering in off the street. The psych chair plumped up his own endowment account so he could claim a tax deduction and then used the fund to buy his new Mercedes, the red one."

Elmer had no idea if any of this Medical Center gossip was true, but it all certainly passed the double P test: Possible and Plausible.

"In national news, former Vice President Cheney remains in control of a secret Pentagon cabal, ready to execute a coup d'etat if President Obama fails to attack Iran before it can produce fissile material, which it already has anyway. My aunt isn't going to her granddaughter's third birthday party because her fat ass is deep in a real estate scam so she can raise money to pay off a thirty K credit card debt her husband doesn't know about. Garmin announced it's buying GE. And now, a musical interlude…"

Elmer was stunned. Garmin buying GE? That couldn't be true. But if it was, the GPS company's stock, now at historic lows, would soar. Investors had been wondering if the company would use its extraordinary cash assets to do something drastic. But buy GE? It was plausible, but he didn't think it was possible. Yet the voice sounded so on the money about everything else. He checked his watch. The market wouldn't close for another hour. Elmer threw caution to the exhaust-fumes-scented wind and used his cell phone to get into Garmin.

Fred still scribbled away even as the awful racket the girl used as a "musical interlude" forced him to turn down the volume. Heavy metal interlude. Boy, there's an oxymoron. But otherwise? No, he had no trouble believing any of the revelations she had spouted about the Medical Center. Christ, the place had its hands in every public, private, commercial, philanthropic, economic development money pot that existed. And money rots just like power corrupts. And that bit about Cheney. That was probably true. No wonder the fascist bastard still wore that smirk on his face. But was she right that the Royals would lose their tenth straight? He supplemented his Social Security with a few gambling bets. Well, tried to supplement. To which end, might as well put a hundred on the Royals to lose tonight. He fired up his computer to access the betting website he used when Samantha came back on the air and he scrambled to turn up the volume.

"…And now, tips for the wise: Drug buyers best avoid 3842 Bell. Sting operation going on there. Oh, best avoid the shrimp at China Gardens, too, whether or not you're a drug buyer; it's gone bad. Cops will be running radar later today along Broadway down the hill towards Union Station, you know, where the bastards get you since gravity's got you anyway. Oh, and they'll be checking for illegal left hand turners at 45th and Main so they can snare more poor out-of-town dunces. Boys in Blue busy today. DUI checkpoint starts at 11 p.m. at 55th and Ward Parkway. And this just in: Cricket is pregnant. Enough for today. Tune in tomorrow!"

Fred decided he'd bet the house: $500 on the Royals losing.

Elmer and Fred and Cricket weren't the only ones to take notice of Samantha's broadcasts. The Medical Center's security officer and a couple of first-year residents who worked at the hospital had called their friends, and the institution's grapevine went about its efficient business. The security officer then called a drug enforcement friend on the local police force and asked if they had a sting operation under at 3842 Bell. "Hell, how did you know that? Is it that obvious from the street?" The security officer explained. "That's nuts. She's probably a doper, too." The security officer threw in the other police dirt he'd heard on the radio. "Damn. She must have a source inside the department. Happens all the time."

One of the neighbors in listening range had grown up in Peculiar and so called a couple of friends. The word spread faster (by an order of several magnitudes) than the USPS could deliver express mail. The wives of the three Bills employed by the Peculiar's Post Office went on the rampage. Fortunately for the Bills, they could point to the other. Poor Larry. There was only one of him, and when he got home he found his clothes piled up on the front lawn and his grandfather's bamboo fly rods in splinters along with the graphite shards of the Daiwa rod he had purchased just last week. Bitch!

The FBI heard the Dick Cheney news the way it hears everything: mysteriously. A highest-level your-eyes-only memo went to the Director. Soon after it arrived, the Director walked it to The President of the United States who shook his head. "Impossible," he said but thought; *maybe that explains that asshole's smirk.* "All right. Let's investigate this source."

From his aged leather sofa, Elmer watched the Dow close at 9350 and saw the story break about Garmin buying GE—and let loose the smile that can only come from one who knows one stands to make a lot of money without one drop of sweat falling from one's brow.

Fred rushed back to the bar to spill Samantha's beans to Cricket. Cricket's day had not picked up, and being the only customer, after he rattled off the list of remarkable news, he said. "Oh, and you're pregnant."

Cricket, never one to take more than two or three synaptic nanoseconds of thought before action, fired back, "Well, we can test that piece of news out right now. You're in charge. I'll be right back."

She went to the drugstore next door, bought a testing kit, returned, and went to the john.

Fred held his breath. If she was pregnant, that must mean his bet was a sure thing. But would she be honest with him?

Cricket, in the bathroom and no more one to hide her emotions than to give things considered thoughts, yelled "God Damnit!"

Fred echoed an internal "Whoopee!"

The next morning, Fred woke up late because he had listened to the game on the west coast that the Royals finally lost in the 12th inning. Nerve-wracking. If the Royals had won that game, he swore he'd never wear one of their caps again. He went outside to get his paper before it was stolen and saw more traffic than ever before. Usually students would start arriving to grab free street parking, but this morning all the spots were taken and all the drivers were still in their cars. This was weird—but not so weird that Fred didn't go back inside to make coffee, read the paper, confirm that the Royals did lose and he hasn't dreamed his sudden (relative) riches, and turn on the radio to see if Cricket's crazy cousin was broadcasting again.

Elmer cruised the neighborhood looking for a place to park, but all the street parking was taken up. Some cars were full of people, all of whom sported thin ties. Many vehicles were unmarked police cars—in-your-face obvious, because they had spotlights and were dark navy Victoria Crown Royals. Then Elmer saw a white cargo van with an antenna on its roof he recognized as a directional finder. Someone had the equipment to identify where the strange radio signal was coming from. Triangulation.

Much earlier that morning, Samantha's mother, the Postmistress, had had no need of triangulation to find Samantha's home. All the town gossip being about its postmistress, she was the last person in Peculiar to hear it. Larry woke her up at 4 a.m. pounding on her door. He was drunk and asking if he could move in and ranting about her daughter spilling the beans on some radio show. "No!" the Postmistress said and closed the door on the man who now blubbered something about committing hari-kari with fishing rod bamboo splinters. She put on her clothes, grabbed her keys, jumped in the car, and started the two-hour drive.

When she pounded on Samantha's door, there was no response. She looked around for something to break in with, but unlike her niece, the Postmistress actually allowed two seconds of brain synaptic activity (equal to two billion nanoseconds of Cricket's brain input to decision reaction time) to occur. Said synaptic activity resulted in calling the cops instead and telling them her offspring was mentally ill and may endanger herself. Perhaps committed suicide already.

A squad car arrived, and the policeman, after conferring with the Postmistress, who found him very cute, walked up the steps to Samantha's front door while the Postmistress stationed herself at the bottom of the porch steps and, admiring the policeman's butt, watched as he knocked on the door and it opened.

"Are you all right?" The policeman asked Samantha. "Your mother is worried about you."

"I'm perfectly fine. My mother and I are estranged. I don't want to see her. I don't want to talk to her. I want her off this property, which has a 'No Trespassing, Violators will be Prosecuted' sign posted right there," Samantha pointed helpfully.

The officer gave her a utilitarian once-over. There being many crowds these days with spiked purple and green hair, metal doohickeys pierced around the rim of ears, foreheads, noses, and lips—of which hers were painted black—that she wouldn't stand out of, he concluded her "normal."

"Do you have some I.D so I can verify you have reached legal age and are not still a responsibility of your mother?"

"Sure."

As Samantha fetched her driver's license, the officer was given a glimpse into her front room, which was relatively neat. Sitting on a desk was one of those old-timey radio broadcast microphones you saw in photos of Edward R. Morrow. Samantha returned and handed him a laminated card. Studying the driver's license, he shook his head in regret at how such a pretty blonde had turned into *this* creature. Alas, twenty-seven was imminently of age for bad sartorial decisions.

"Thank you. You've changed your appearance quite a bit. Good idea to go the DMV and have a new picture taken."

"Thank *you*, officer. Excellent advice. Now, would you, please, tell that woman to get off my property?"

Being the defender of the law that he was, the officer did.

Samantha returned to her breakfast of milk and Cocoa Puffs. Soon she would put the nipple rings in place, which seemed to sort of close the circuit on all her metal piercings and allowed her to receive the signals that contained the truths she needed to tell the world.

The Postmistress sat in her car, not knowing quite what to do. It didn't surprise her when a great many other cars started parking because she knew the medical school students used the streets. But what surprised her was that none of the drivers exited their cars.

And, indeed, that day medical students would largely have to find alternate parking.

Samantha sat at the desk and turned the microphone on. "Here it comes, ladies and gentlemen, whores and pimps, drug users and pushers, adulterers and cuckolds, administrators and peons, cheaters and suckers, moochers and chumps…"

The FCC truck found it couldn't triangulate because it was stuck in traffic. It had one fix on the signal but needed a second from a different position. Fairly uncongested as this neighborhood usually was, Samantha made it into *this* kind of a day.

Cricket was stuck in traffic right behind a white paneled truck and royally pissed at her boyfriend, Eddie, who hadn't said boo when she told him she was pregnant. That God-damned-good-looking, uncaring, wannabe artist bastard, who made her jealous because he came from a much better dysfunctional family system than her own, just hung up the phone. How'd he like a little child support taken out of his pitiful pizza delivery paycheck?

The Postmistress looked dumbfounded at her car radio blaring her crazy daughter's voice. "Don't have your surgery done in suite 107 at the Med Center today. Staph germs growing like crazy in there. Somebody better check on that patient in 388 right now because she's in the bathroom with a blade and having another go at her wrist. Ugly painting donated yesterday to the thrift store on 39th, but something pretty nice underneath that painting. Stephen Kappes is a member of the Cheney cabal. He's ordered me shut down. Obama wants me found, too. Barack, I think you understand now how few people you can really trust and how important truth telling is. Here it comes: Obama, keep your butt out of Texas and Oklahoma. Sniper guns are being positioned for potential visits as I speak. Cricket, don't get an abortion. That little kid's going to be a genius. And you're going to get a text message from David, as crazy as that sounds. But pay attention to it. It's really important, Cricket. Little drone bomb coming Waristan's way. Enemy Number One escapes again. Sara, Jimmy still masturbates looking at a nude picture of his ex-wife. The Royals halt their skid at 10. Big meteor headed right towards Earth. Be here in 51 years, 2 months, three days, and four hours, local time."

Cricket had left her car in the middle of the street and ran toward Samantha's house. David, Iris's father David, would text?!

The FBI director, listening by hookup from one the agent's cars, ordered the lead agent, "You have enough men. Break into every house on those blocks. Find her! Do it and do it now!"

Fred put down another big bet, but this time that the Royals would win, when the front door of his house crashed open and two men in suits and thin ties ran in with their Glocks drawn. "If you're burglars, there's nothing here worth stealing. If you're authorities, you'd better have a warrant because if you don't, I'm going to sue your asses off."

A great many carpenters and locksmiths would make good money doing repairs on all the doors ruined that day in the four-block area. All would be paid in cash by an odd, little, nondescript man who called himself Mr. Smith, who also gave cash awards to homeowners who signed a special release. Fred balked until Mr. Smith mentioned that unfortunate mistakes could occur with Social Security payments.

The pair that broke down Samantha's door found her sitting at her neat desk talking into an old fashioned radio microphone. They grabbed the microphone off the table. When they found its cable was hooked into nothing, they yelled, demanding Samantha tell them where the equipment was.

Sami just smiled.

Cricket reached Samantha's house in time to see her cousin being led away by a group of men. Other men pushed her away when she tried to stop them. "Where are you taking her?" Cricket screamed at them. The Postmistress stormed up the driveway to yell, "Keep her locked up for a good long time!"

They would.

Cricket and her aunt looked at each other.

"We better go buy that painting at the thrift store," they said to each other. The thought struck other listeners, too, but most of them were being hampered by agents breaking through their front doors. The streets still gridlocked, Cricket and the Postmistress ran to the thrift store, Cricket explaining that Samantha's broadcast had limited range. Maybe the thrift store was out of range and even if it wasn't, maybe they didn't have a radio on.

They were relieved to see the store empty except for a woman behind the counter working on a crossword puzzle. Dozens of crummy paintings hung on the walls behind disgusting racks of old clothing, but Cricket noticed one demented try at abstract expressionism leaning against the wall behind the counter.

"I like that," she said, even though she wouldn't hang it in an outhouse. "Is that new?"

The woman looked up from her crossword, glanced at the painting and said. "Donated yesterday. You really like that ugly thing?"

"How much?" the Postmistress spoke up.

"Five bucks. Some art student will buy it for that and gesso it over. Cheaper than new canvas."

"Sold," Cricket and the Postmistress said at the same time. Leaving the thrift store, they saw Cricket's car being towed off, so they walked back to the Postmistress's auto. Cricket's cell phone rang.

"If you're going to be late, you could at least call me," Joe said.

"I can explain," Cricket said.

"Don't bother. You're fired."

Cricket sat on the curb and cried. She took the painting in her hands and started tearing it apart to see what treasure might be hidden there. She really needed a treasure now in her life. Her cell phone played Sinead O'Connor's *Nothing Compares 2 U* meaning she had a text message.

Cricket, hon, this is Dave. Iris's got a major problem that must be looked after RIGHT NOW. Get her to the emergency room and tell them she has a hernia that's about to strangulate. Just repeat those words: a hernia that's about to strangulate. I love you. Sorry for all the mess I caused.

Cricket just about went catatonic. Dave, Iris's father, killed himself two years ago. She speed-dialed her other aunt's number.

"Rose. Listen. I'm not nuts. You must do what I tell you. Take Iris now to the ER and tell them she has a hernia that's about to strangulate."

"Cricket, are you…"

"DO IT OR IRIS WILL DIE!" Cricket yelled.

"Okay."

"Well, look at that," the Postmistress had resumed her search of the painting and pulled off the brown paper from the back of the frame to reveal tightly bound packets of money, the first bill showing on the top of each being $100.

Fuck you, Joe!

Cricket's cell phone played Alicia Keys's *If I Ain't Got You*, meaning she had a live one on the other end, unless Dave was into voice calling from the grave as well.

"Cricket," she heard Eddie say. "I've been thinking. Let's get married. What do you think?"

"I don't need to do any thinking. Okay. Our kid's going to be a genius, by the way."

"Pick you up after work?"

"I've been fired."

"How about I pick you up right away? I've been fired, too."

"That would be really, really great because my car got towed, and I've got to get to the hospital to check on Iris."

"What's happened to Iris?"

"She has a hernia that's about to strangulate. I'll explain later. Please get here as soon as you can. Oh, and we're rich, well, rich enough for a while."

Want to read more strange tales conceived by Randy Atwood?

Tweet *I want more!* *@AttwoodRandy @CuriosityQuills #BookLove*

THE CAW

BY ELIZA TILTON

Johnny's lips teased my neck as he pressed my back against the cold mausoleum. The cemetery seemed alive all around us. The wind *whooshed*, the crickets *chirped*, and moonlight shone onto the crumbling graves. I shut my eyes, blocking out the scene, reveling in being wrapped in Johnny Ridge's arms, the hottest senior in Bakers High with the sexiest lips in four counties.

Lips that were driving me crazy.

Giggles from my best friend, Sheri, and her boyfriend, Brett, drifted over. Sheri sounded closer than I remembered, but the dark hid Johnny and I, so I didn't care. All that mattered were our two bodies, slipping into exotic bliss.

Wind whirled the leaves around us, and I shivered. Johnny grabbed my waist, bringing me closer to his warmth.

"You cold?" he breathed, his lips brushing past my ear.

"A little." It didn't matter that my toes were going numb, even the cold wouldn't pull me away. I slipped my arms around his neck, letting my fingers play with the ends of his dark hair.

His hand slipped behind me. "Here." He pushed against the mausoleum door.

"I am so not going in there."

The door groaned as he opened it a few more inches, just enough to squeeze through.

"Not even for me?" Under the moonlight, his hazel eyes seemed to glow, his perfect lips rosy from my tinted lip balm. I'd be a fool to say no.

I grabbed his outstretched hand and followed him into the stale murk, the only light coming from the cracked door behind us.

"I don't know, Johnny." I stared at the stone coffin sitting in the middle of the circular room, contemplating the corpse inside. "This is creepy."

His grip tightened around my hand. "It is… alright, let's go."

"No," I said. "As long as that dead thing stays dead, we'll be fine."

"You're braver than me, Lena." His hands moved to rub my sides. "It turns me on."

Within three seconds, our lips found each other again, meeting as if they'd been parted for years, and in a sense they had been. Everything around us melted away: the dankness, the lightless room, the strange scratching noise that probably came from a mouse.

I placed my hands on Johnny's chest and tugged on the cords of his hooded sweatshirt. I'd waited months for this moment. Johnny and I always shared this deep connection, but we were never single at the same time. Now we were both free. Free to kiss for hours.

His hands slid under my shirt, blazing a trail of heat through my body. I groaned as every thought, but of him, slipped from my mind.

Johnny jumped back. "What the…?"

"What's wrong?"

He looked behind him. "Something touched my leg."

I took out my cell and found the flashlight app. A ray beamed from my phone as I waved it across the cement. "I don't see anything."

"Lena!" Sheri hooted my name.

"Here!" I called as I looked at Johnny. "We better go."

He nodded, and I squeezed past the door and back outside with him behind me.

Sheri staggered to us with Brett looped around her. "There you are! We've been looking all over for you two. Oh," she pointed to the decaying structure behind us. "Tell me you haven't been making out in there."

"Well…" I looked at Johnny who smiled, the dimple in his right cheek winking.

"I gotta take a leak," he whispered, kissing my cheek before he walked off behind the mausoleum.

"Eww." Sheri's face scrunched in disgust.

"Oh, please, like you and Brett don't do anything X-rated."

Brett and Sheri eyed each other, grinning, then went into a big PDA session.

These two were constantly groping and kissing in front of everyone. New couples were always "so in love" and too mushy to be in any type of social setting. Johnny and I were new, but we'd never act like that. I refused to be the gushy girlfriend type, even if it was how I really felt.

"Where's Johnny?" Brett asked.

I turned to face him and Sheri, relieved the smooch fest was over. "Peeing," I said, then plunked down on the ground. My heels were killing me.

Sheri sat next to me, slung her arm around mine and leaned against my shoulder, gazing at the full moon. "It always amazes me how big it is. One day, I'm going to walk on it."

"Get real." Brett sat across from us. "You can barely sit through a movie. You're too hyper for space."

We laughed.

"I love the new color," Sheri touched the violet ends of my hair.

"Thanks." It would only be violet for a couple more weeks, then I'd go pink, or orange, or whatever color grabbed my attention, but the top always stayed bleach blonde.

Sheri sighed. "I want to dye my hair, but Mom still won't let me. I'm sixteen—"

"How long does it take to piss?" Brett was clearly not interested in the direction the conversation was going.

I rubbed my bare arms and wished I'd brought a coat. Even though we were in the middle of fall, the weather had stayed warm, perfect for nights like this. Until tonight. I needed to get up and walk around.

"I'll go check."

A gust of wind blew a pile of dead leaves at me, and I hugged myself to stay warm. "Johnny?"

I rounded the mausoleum, following the path I remembered him taking, expecting to find him. But I saw nothing.

"Johnny?"

Behind the mausoleum, the rest of the cemetery flowed over the hill. I walked past grave after grave, two more mausoleums, a bunch of dead flowers, but still no Johnny.

"Come on, Johnny, this isn't funny." The hairs on my arms stood on end. "Johnny!"

Panic crept over me. *No reason to freak out. Everything's fine.* But what if I wasn't overreacting? What if some horror monster came and dragged him into a grave? What if a serial killer murdered him? Or zombies. I hated zombies.

"BOO!" Johnny grabbed my waist, laughing hysterically.

I punched his arm. "Idiot! You almost gave me a heart attack!" My heart wouldn't slow down.

"Sorry," he said, kissing my cheek. "But you looked too cute and vulnerable thinking I'd disappeared. I had to."

When Johnny Ridge kisses you, it's pretty hard to stay mad.

I frowned, pretending to be furious, even though I couldn't help hoping he would kiss me more.

Johnny didn't disappoint.

The wind pushed my body into his, and he gripped the sides of my jeans, his thumbs rubbing circles. His lips swept across my neck, then up my face until our mouths connected. Each touch was gentle and perfect. He never grabbed me too tight or too soft.

"You look beautiful tonight," he said in between kisses. "Did you wear those for me?" His foot tapped mine.

I nodded, smiling.

"Those are some sexy shoes."

Sexy and extremely uncomfortable.

"We should get back." I didn't want to ruin this moment, but I knew Sheri would grow impatient. We were supposed to head to the diner for a late night snack.

"Sure." But instead of walking, his mouth found mine and there I was again, lost in a sea of soft lips and warm hands.

Caw, Caw.

Johnny and I jumped and turned to the overlarge bird sitting on top of a headstone, staring at us. I'd never seen such an enormous crow before.

We left it behind and trekked back to the mausoleum where I expected to find Sheri and Brett making out, and found… no one.

"Where are they now?" I groaned. "I hope they didn't go off again. I thought we were leaving."

Johnny walked ahead of me. He bent down on the ground where Sheri had been sitting. "I don't think so," he said. All humor dropped from his voice, his body tensing. Slowly, he stood, holding something in his hand.

"What is it?"

"Is this hers?"

I stared at the red iPhone in his hand. My stomach dropped and I stepped back, putting distance between myself and the phone. "Yes," I confirmed, my gaze stuck on the smear of blood on the touchscreen.

Johnny's brow narrowed as he stared at the display. "I think she was trying to dial 9-1-1."

"No, that's crazy. If something were wrong, she would've screamed." I cupped my hands to my mouth. "Sheri! Brett!"

Silence.

"Sheri!" I screamed louder.

Nothing.

"They probably went back to the car," Johnny said.

I nodded. Here we were, spooking ourselves, while they were probably making out in Brett's Buick.

"You're right. Let's go."

We raced through the graveyard and back to the car, which seemed a lot further than before. But instead of rocking steamy windows, the car sat silent in the gravel lot. Where could they have gone? Sheri wouldn't have left without us.

I followed Johnny as he tried the handle on the driver's door.

"It's locked."

Just the way we left it.

His foot kicked something towards me. I picked it up, staring at Sheri's favorite Mac gloss, Viva Glam.

Sheri never went anywhere without her gloss.

"Brett!" Johnny strode back toward the cemetery.

"Where are you going?"

"We must've missed them. We should look around."

I grabbed Johnny's hand, holding it tight as we stepped through the iron gate.

My feet throbbed. Regardless of how sexy three inch heels were, they weren't practical. I missed my Etnies. "Can we sit?" I asked, finding a spot on the grass and throwing off my shoes.

We'd searched the whole right side of the cemetery and crawled over a crumbling stone fence to the left side where trees blocked out most of the moonlight. With half of the leaves fallen, the large branches casted distorted shadows across the grass.

Where were they? The fear slowly turned into annoyance as we hiked and found nothing. I rolled my eyes. One drop of blood and an abandoned lip gloss. *Seriously?* I had thought the worst, but horror movie stuff never happens. This is the real world.

Johnny squatted by me and began rubbing the sides of my foot.

"Mmm, that feels good," I relaxed back.

His thumbs dug into my heels, melting me into his hands. We looked at each other, then that devilish grin appeared.

"Don't," I said.

"Don't what?" His right hand travelled up my leg.

"Johnny, we're supposed to be looking for Sheri and Brett."

His left hand followed his right, and I fought to keep a level head. "I'm sure they're fine. I bet they're looking for us."

I couldn't argue with him. We may have overreacted.

Johnny continued to tease me, each touch made it harder to say no, and if those hands kept travelling north, I'd cave.

Caw, Caw.

I whipped my head to the right to see that same crow perched on another headstone, staring at us again. Johnny picked up a twig and threw it at the bird. It squawked and launched into the air, coming straight for us.

"Get down!" Johnny ducked his head into my lap.

The crow dove at him, squawking and flapping its inky wings. He swatted at it, but the bird flitted just out of his way.

With one hand shielding my face, I searched the ground for something to throw at the bird. The only thing I saw were my shoes, just out of arm's reach.

"Ouch!" Johnny gripped his arm as the bird flew away.

"Johnny!" I stared at the blood seeping from four gaping wounds. He winced as I touched his arm. "This is bad! We need to get these cleaned."

"It's just a scratch," he said as we climbed to our feet.

"That is not just a scratch." My stomach felt like I'd eaten a bad helping of nachos. Too much blood. I scanned the cemetery. I didn't expect to find anything, but a low glow pulsated from the east.

I pointed to the light. "Let's check it out. If that's a supply shed, we could break in and find something to tie around your arm. Then we'll find Sheri and Brett and get the hell out of here."

Johnny nodded, then tried to help me balance while I stepped back into my killer heels. His face scrunched in pain.

"I got it," I said, watching him put his hand back over the wound.

The nasty crow disappeared, but I kept searching the sky. That wasn't a regular crow and whatever it did to Johnny was bad, real bad.

Blood oozed around the fingers holding the wound. He didn't talk, and I noticed his jaw stayed clenched, brows narrowed as if just walking hurt.

The glow brightened and I could see the outline of a broken shack. As we got closer, I realized it was more than I thought. I expected to find a shed, but this had two small windows and was much bigger than what storing a few shovels and rakes would conceivably call for. Its brown wood siding clung to the frame, and a small lantern hung from an old hook by the left side of the door.

I tried the knob. Locked.

"There has to be a key around here," I said, looking for any place one could be hidden. A doormat, a rock. Nothing.

"What about the window?" Johnny suggested, reaching out towards the sill, allowing me to see the bleeding cuts which were now an angry red. Before he touched the decaying wood, he flinched and grasped his arm again.

"Let me," I moved in front of him, grabbed the window, and pushed up. It stuck, and I grunted, pushing harder. After four heaves, it raised enough for me to climb through.

I plopped to the ground, thankful there wasn't anything under the window to fall onto. I looked around but couldn't see a thing. I stumbled forward, my hand finding the wall. Sliding my fingers along the rough surface, I found the door, turned the lock, and opened it for Johnny.

He stepped inside. The light from outside only lit the few feet by the door.

I took out my cellphone, turned on the handy flashlight app, and held it out in front of us.

"What are you doing here?"

"Eek!" I screamed, dropping the phone, the light bouncing forward to illuminate a pair of muddy boots. I fell back onto Johnny, knocking us to the ground in an ungainly heap.

An older man, dressed in a ratty one piece Carharrt, stepped forward. "Why are you sneaking into my house?"

"We need help," I stammered.

Johnny groaned next to me, and I helped him to his feet. His ashen face was etched in pain.

The old man frowned. His overgrown beard was streaked with white and matched his bushy eyebrows. He looked at Johnny. "Hmm. See you found my bird."

"Your bird?"

The man turned around and shuffled into the dark.

Johnny and I looked at one another. He shook his head and motioned for us to leave. We couldn't. What if the crow was rabid? Or had some deathly disease? If the bird was a pet, we needed to talk to its owner.

A filament flicked on in a bulb hanging overhead and bathed the room in a weak light. To the right, sat a plaid couch and a tube TV on an old plastic crate. To our left, squatted the old stove and fridge, with a square, wooden table and chair nearby. It reminded me of the small studio my grandmother called hers before she died.

"Do you live here?"

The old man opened a cabinet and took out a brown bottle, then pointed to Johnny and then the wooden chair. "Sit."

Johnny sat. I could tell by his rigid posture he didn't want this guy anywhere near him. "What's your bird doing attacking people?"

The man took a rag from the shelf, and Johnny removed his hand from the wound, reaching for the rag. "Better if I do it," the man said. "You're all covered in blood." He wiped the cuts, then drenched them in whatever there was in the bottle. Johnny winced. The old man tied another rag around the injured arm and dropped the bloody one on the table. "You two shouldn't be here. Cemetery's no place for kids."

Like we hadn't heard *that* a thousand times. Kids always hung out in the cemetery. It was the most secluded place in town. The cops never came this way.

"That should do." The old man put the bottle back in its spot.

With the initial fear gone, he didn't seem so scary. "Why do you live all the way out here?" I asked.

Johnny tilted his head at me.

What? I was curious. It's not every day you meet someone who lives in a cemetery.

"I've always been the groundskeeper, but after my wife died, I decided to live here. Our home reminded me too much of her. Been here a long time." His eyes drifted towards a wooden angel sitting on one of the shelves.

Suddenly, I felt sorry for him. "What's your name?"

"Lena…" Johnny eyed me with a "shut up and let's leave" glance.

"Grover. Grover Toms."

"I'm Lena."

Johnny got off the chair and came beside me. "Let's go," he whispered.

"What happened to your wife?"

Grover's left cheek twitched and his eyes seemed lost as he stared straight ahead.

"I'm sorry. I didn't mean—"

Caw, Caw.

The crow flew into the house and landed on a wooden ledge near the table. It flapped its wings and stared at me, sending a shiver of fear across my body.

Grover's gaze moved to the bird and he sighed. "Time for you two to go."

"Great idea." Johnny pushed me toward the door.

"If you're ever in town," I said, with one eye on the crow, "stop by the diner and ask for me. I'll give you some of Bakers' finest pie."

"You're a sweet girl. Now you better go."

Johnny pulled me out of the house and we walked back toward the car.

"How's your arm?"

The color had returned to Johnny's face. "I don't know what he put on it, but it feels a lot better. It barely hurts."

"Really?"

He nodded. "Whatever it is, it must have a numbing ingredient. Those cuts were on fire."

"We'll have to come back and thank him. Back to hunting for Sheri," I mumbled, remembering the whole point of our hike.

"If I know Brett, they're so busy making out they didn't even notice us gone."

I hoped so.

Sure enough as we approached the car, we saw Sheri sitting on the trunk and Brett facing her, completely oblivious to us.

"You!" I wanted to hug and yell at her. "Where did you go? I thought something happened."

Sheri giggled. "Sorry, we needed a bit more privacy. Your mausoleum gave us a few ideas."

Unbelievable.

"I told you!"

I waved Johnny off. "But what about your phone and lip gloss?"

Sheri pushed Brett aside and jumped off the car. "You found them!" She rushed over, holding out her hand, and I deposited the gloss into it.

"Why is there blood on your phone?" Johnny took it out of his pocket and added it to the gloss.

"That's mine," Brett scratched the back of his head. "Got a nosebleed."

"Yeah, so gross," Sheri said. "That's why we went back to the car. I dropped my purse, and the gloss must have fallen out. Thank God you found it! I was totally dying."

Johnny and I smiled at each other and he threw his arms around my waist.

"Don't say it, you were just as spooked as me," I said, poking him.

"Me? Never. You're the one who panicked."

"Where did you two go?" Brett asked. "We went back to the mausoleum, but you weren't there, so we came back to the car. We were going to go look for you, but figured we'd wait here and make out."

We laughed as Sheri playfully slapped Brett. He grabbed her waist and pulled her into his chest.

"All over," Johnny said as his hands slipped into my back pockets. "Ran into that weird groundskeeper."

"Groundskeeper?" asked Brett. "What groundskeeper?"

"Grover, the old guy who lives in the shack."

Brett and Sheri stared at us, their mouths dropping open.

"They tore down the shack years ago, back when my dad was a kid. You never heard the story of old man Grover?" Brett asked.

"You guys are wrong. We talked to him. His bird attacked me." Johnny untied the rag. "What the…"

The cuts were completely healed.

"Why do you have a dirty rag on your arm?" Sheri scrunched her nose.

Johnny flung the rag to the ground.

"That's impossible," I ran my hand across Johnny's arm. Not even a scratch. "What… what story?"

"That old man died in the shack, heart attack, I think, but no one found him until two weeks later," Brett said. "By then the crows had eaten most of him. It was pretty gruesome."

I shook my head. "Johnny?"

"This is bull. Watch, we'll show you." Johnny grabbed my hand and stomped off toward the shack.

"Whatever, man," Brett huffed behind us.

We returned by a more direct route. I recognized the trees, the shape of the nearest tombstones, the flattened grass left by our feet. But nothing else was there.

Not even a length of wood.

Sheri pointed to a white object on the grass. "Isn't that your phone?"

I picked it up. The battery was dead.

It was real. We *had* been here, but where did the shack go?!

"Eww," Sheri said.

I followed her gaze, and there, perched on a massive branch, was the crow with a bloody rag.

Want to read more creepy, paranormal tales by Eliza Tilton?

Tweet *More Caw! @ElizaTilton @CuriosityQuills #BookLove*

The Damned and
The Dangerous

THE DAMNED AND THE DANGEROUS

A ROT RODS SHORT
BY MICHAEL PANUSH

He called himself Roscoe. That was the first thing he said, after he'd recovered from being struck by Captain Donovan's Buick at fifty miles per hour, and that name was all that he could remember. There was something else odd about him too, besides his lack of memory. He was a dead man. His skin was a sickly green, his eyes unblinking and his pulse non-existent. The Captain pulled three slugs out of his chest, more than enough to kill a man. And Roscoe had indeed been killed, even though it didn't seem to slow him much. The Captain wasn't too surprised. He ran a garage in the small Southern California town of La Cruz, which had its own strange history. He was used to oddities. He offered Roscoe a job. Not having much else to do, he accepted. He'd worked for the captain ever since.

He wasn't alone. Captain Donovan had three other drivers, all as unique—in their own way—as a living dead man like Roscoe. They worked together, taking odd jobs across the country to keep the garage going. Sometimes the jobs were easy. Sometimes they weren't. Coming back from getting lunch in a diner on La Cruz' Main Street, Roscoe didn't realize a job waited for him—and that it would be something unlike anything else he'd ever done.

213

A rambling set of garages made up Donovan Motors. The dull red brick reached two stories and housed the apartments above the garage. Roscoe strolled towards the garage, his green gator skin shoes tapping the sidewalk as his hands rested in the pockets of his oil-stained jeans. The shoes nearly matched the waxy, emerald tint of his face. His dark hair crept down over his forehead, making a slight spit curl above his drawn, craggy face and the unblinking eyes hid behind sunglasses. A black leather jacket, the collar raised, completed his appearance. A hamburger and fries sat in his stomach, slowly digested. He had discovered his body could process foods—it just took longer—and taste was something that he could only dimly recall. Such was life as a zombie.

Next to him was Angel Rey, a fellow driver at Donovan Motors. Angel had been the one who crashed into him, driving the Captain's car. Now they were buds. Angel was a young Mexican, his skin the color of coffee. He wore a crimson zoot suit, with matching trousers and a fedora shading his face. There was a wary calmness in his dark eyes, and a slight smile above his neat, dark moustache. He pointed ahead with a thin finger set with a ring made of Aztec jade.

"What you think, Roscoe? Trouble?"

Roscoe's car was parked on the curb. It was the pride of his life, a V8 Ford Deuce dating back to the 30s that he'd stripped down, rebuilt, and painted midnight black with silver flames along the side. The motor was partially exposed, gleaming pale as a vulture-cleaned rib cage. The Deuce was the first car the Captain had entrusted Roscoe with. Roscoe couldn't remember a bit of his past—but he knew how to repair the car. He'd taken it from a wreck to a Holy Grail of Hot Rods. And now three kids from La Cruz High School—all wearing letterman jackets—circled it like sharks.

"Nah." Roscoe removed the toothpick from between his lips. "Just some punks needing a lesson." He walked over, his fists swinging at his side. Angel hurried after him, keeping pace with his long legs. "Hey! Leave the ride and get lost."

The largest high-schooler looked up. He was a blond kid with too much brylcreem in his hair, good looking, but with no intelligence in his eyes. "We was just admiring it. Swell chassis it's got, and a nice motor too." His eyes darted over to Angel. He began to grin. "No harm in us just looking at it, you know? Still a free country." He smirked to himself. "I heard all about how we're not supposed to go near Donovan Motors, but I think that's a load of crap. The drivers ain't nothing but some freaks who happen to work on cars. No big whoop."

By now, Roscoe was near them. He took a step closer to the kid when Angel put a hand on his shoulder. He could feel the weight of Angel's hand. His friend was right. La Cruz citizens wouldn't like him beating down teenagers in Main Street. Instead, he grabbed the edge of his sunglasses and lowered them. He let the high-schooler stare into his white, dim, dead eyes, then barred his gleaming teeth.

"I told you to go," he hissed. "Now beat it."

The three teens scrambled away from the roadster. Roscoe followed them with his dead eyes before replacing his sunglasses. The teenagers ran down La Cruz's Main Street, past the hardware store and the market and the town hall and all the other little businesses that kept the city running. Roscoe walked over and examined his car for stains in the paintjob, smudges or dents.

Angel stepped next to him. "I didn't think that was necessary, man," Angel said. "We could have just talked to them. They'd have left."

Roscoe glared at him. "I look like a monster. Might as well act like one."

"Why, exactly? That written in stone somewhere?"

Before Roscoe put together an appropriate comeback, another driver stepped out of the shadow of the garage. She was Betty Bright, the youngest of the drivers and the only woman working at the garage. She was just out of high school and her father—a major folklore professor at UCLA—let her work there part time while she took college classes. Her father taught Betty everything he knew. Her knowledge of the occult may have been purely academic, but it was still helpful.

She approached them, with a slight smile, wearing a pair of pale slacks and a collared shirt under a thin red sweater. Her blonde hair, cut just past her ears, gleamed in the late afternoon sun. It framed her pretty face, with its upturned nose and horn-rimmed glasses. "Hello, fellows. Ingratiating yourselves with the locals?" She puffed up a large, pink gum bubble until it obscured her face, then waited for it to shrink before she spoke again. "Anyway, the Captain wants everybody in his office. We better get moving."

"He say what it was about?" Angel asked. His mother was a witch and healer—a Bruja—in Los Angeles. He learned magic practically, while Betty learned it theoretically. Still, both of them got along fine. "Or we just supposed to guess?"

"You know the Captain." She led them to the door in the side of the garage. It opened up to a skeletal steel stairwell that brought them to the second floor and the Captain's office. "Cards close to the vest until he has to reveal them."

"There's some truth," Roscoe agreed. He still didn't know how the Captain appointed himself supernatural defender of La Cruz—or why. Still, he trusted the man with his life. After all, the Captain was the one who gave Roscoe everything he had. He followed Angel and Betty up the stairs and to the Captain's office. She pulled open the door and they stepped inside.

The Captain's office was a simple room, surprising in its normalcy. Apart from the misshapen skull—far too pointed to be human—sitting at the corner of the Captain's desk and the various rifles, shotguns, and revolvers mounted on the wall, it could have belonged to any small town businessman. The Captain sat at his desk at the back of the room, his hands folded behind his rolodex. He was a distinguished-looking fellow in a gray suit and vest with a thick white moustache like icicles growing under his nose. Roscoe didn't know much about him, though he knew the Captain served in both World Wars. Right now, his eyes were grim.

There were two other men in the room. One was Sheriff Leland Braddock, the chief law officer in La Cruz. He was a plump, contented fellow in the khaki uniform and badge of a law officer. He was the kind of cop who focused on littering and keeping lawns clean. In a larger city, he would have been kicked off the force. In La Cruz, he thrived.

Next to him was Wooster Stokes, the fourth driver of Donovan Motors. Stokes was the descendant of Okie migrants, a broad-shouldered fellow with a wolfish grin, curly sand-colored hair, and thick sideburns. He wore a suit with square shoulders and a bolo tie with a turquoise clasp, not bothering to hide the knife in the leather sheath at his side.

Wooster turned to grin at Betty, Roscoe, and Angel. "Well," he said with a Midwestern twang. "Nice of you to show up. We was gonna have the meeting without you."

"That's enough, Wooster," the Captain broke in. "I'm glad to see we're all here. Sheriff Braddock? Why don't you tell them what you told me?"

Sheriff Braddock nodded his thick head. "Yes, captain. We've just been alerted of a robbery, up in the old Mission. That Mission has been around since the days of the Spanish. School kids tour it occasionally and the local Catholic priest keeps it in shape." He nodded to Angel. "He's of your kind, son. Anyway, the Mission was just robbed."

"So tell the Pope," Roscoe said.

The Captain glared at Roscoe. "Continue, Sheriff."

"Ah, well, not too much was taken. A few old coins, some ornaments. But the big crucifix they keep in the main altar, the one they always have candles around—the Crimson Cross, it's called—that was stolen as well."

"Oh no." Betty winced. "You guys know about the Crimson Cross, right?" She looked at her friends and cleared her throat. "Well, it was originally a holy relic, supposedly constructed with a fragment of the True Cross. It was taken to the Middle East by Sir Roderick the Red, a Crusader Knight, but then it all went wrong." She smiled weakly as everyone stared at her. "The Crusade went poorly. Sir Roderick's men were languishing in the desert and being harassed by Saracen raids. Sir Roderick went mad. He renounced God and praised allegiance to Satan and the forces of Hell, then sacrificed some of his priests and bathed the cross in their blood. Since then, it became the Crimson Cross—a religious icon with the energies of Hell and Heaven bound inside."

"Jeepers…" Sheriff Braddock whispered.

Angel pushed back his fedora. "So how'd it end up here?"

"Well, one of the monks survived and spirited it away. Without demonic help, Sir Roderick was doomed to die. The monk was able to work special charms to nullify the Crimson Cross's power. He and his descendants took it as far away from civilization as possible, eventually bringing it to the New World and California. It's rested there ever since, with special wards around the altar to prevent any supernatural agent from touching it."

"And what happens if they do?" Roscoe asked.

Betty shrugged her slim shoulders. "Kaboom. The Crimson Cross is such an odd contradiction—a relic for God and Satan—that it will give almost total power to the angels or demons who get it. That means the other side will go and try to steal it back and that puts the divine and infernal into a conflict. That means apocalypse."

"Jeepers…" Sheriff Braddock repeated.

Wooster nodded. "Sums it up nicely. So I figure we ought to get that cross back."

"Indeed. And Hell and Heaven may already have their forces in the area, closing in on the Crimson Cross." The Captain nodded to the sheriff. "Luckily, we have a lead. You mentioned you ascertained the identity of the thief?"

Sheriff Braddock nodded. "That's right, Captain. One of my deputies got the license plate of a Studebaker driving away from the crime scene. He couldn't catch the car, but we got the plates, called up the DMV in Los Angeles County and they said the car belonged to Bert Stanton, a small time burglar and sneak thief wanted across the state." He pulled a picture from his suit. "We even had a picture of him in our office." The photo showed a small, rat-faced guy in a disheveled, white checkered suit jacket. Sheriff Braddock set it on the Captain's desk. "Ah, Captain? This whole business with Heaven and Hell—it's a little out of my jurisdiction. Would it be okay if I went back to the office? I'd be right near the phone if you wanted to call…"

"Go right ahead, Sheriff. My best to Marsha and the kids." Donovan turned back to his drivers as Sheriff Braddock waddled out the door. "All right, the Crimson Cross was stolen. I want it back. I won't have this town turned into a battlefield for any old relic. That understood?"

Roscoe shrugged. "You want to go to war with God, Chief?"

"God's never done much for me. Besides, it will be angels and demons we're dealing with—or their human servants. But what's most important is getting this whole operation done lickety-split, before divine authorities realize the Cross is missing. That means locating Bert Stanton. Angel, Roscoe—you know the Purgatory Roadhouse and Tourist Court, just out of town?"

"I know it," Roscoe said. "It's a dump."

"Stanton might be lying low there. You go and investigate. Wooster, Betty—I'd like you two to stay in town and examine Butcher's Row." That was the poorest section of La Cruz and home to its Negro and Mexican residents. "Stay in contact and be prepared to help each other." He folded his hands. A hint of tenderness crept into his voice. It seemed strangely out of place. "I have faith in you, more so than in any God. Now get moving."

They headed out of the office and back to the garage. Wooster pointed to his car, which sat in the shade of the garage's awning. It was a monster of a Packard, with armored plating on the side, all-terrain tires, a two-tone gray and brown paintjob, and a pair of bull's horns mounted on the front bumper. "Come on, little sister," Wooster told Betty. "We'll take my ride."

"Sounds good, as long as you keep the country music to a minimum," Betty waved cheerfully to Roscoe and Angel. "Luck, guys! We'll stay in touch!"

"Thanks, chica, and you be careful! Don't let a demon take a bite out of you or nothing!" Angel waved back. Roscoe did too. They headed over to Roscoe's car, which was fully gassed and ready to go. Roscoe got behind the wheel and started the engine. The miniature silver skull on the stick shift glistened as if coming alive. He twisted the key. The engine purred. Angel looked over at him. "You got heaters, man?"

"Got everything we'll need."

"Good. What you think of this job—taking on angels and devils and crap? I think it's crazy."

"It's lousy." Roscoe twisted the wheel and shot into the open road. He kept the engine humming at a dull roar, and the ride was smooth. They didn't have long to go.

They reached the Purgatory Roadhouse and Tourist Court around sundown. The court was on one side, a set of rotting cabins dating back to the Twenties. Across from that was the roadhouse itself, a circular lodge with jukebox music blasting from the open windows. Roscoe slid his beast to a halt by the entrance and killed the engine. He reached back, where several of his weapons waited below the seat. He drew out a crowbar. That would help him handle any problem. He slipped open the door and hopped out. Angel joined him.

Side by side, they walked to the batwing doors of the roadhouse. A double set of motorcycles were parked out front. Angel nodded to them. "Bikers, man. And this a Speed Fiend territory. Could be some trouble."

"Yeah," Roscoe grinned at his friend. "Might, at that."

They walked into the roadhouse. It was a dingy place, with peanut shells coating the floor and crunching under their feet. Roscoe scanned the room. Sure enough, the place was packed with bikers—Speed Fiends, a Motorcycle Club with a reputation for brutality. Roscoe saw their black leather jackets, with the winged pentagrams emblazoned on the backs. They clustered together drinking and talking. Roscoe thought the demonic imagery was nothing more than a clever gimmick, but now he wasn't sure.

Angel pointed to the back of the room, where shadows clustered thickly.

Bert Stanton was there. The thief looked out of his element, like he sat in an oven instead of a table. He had thin ginger-colored hair and kept tugging at his collar. His white-checkered coat looked like it had been spun through a hurricane.

"I see him." Roscoe tightened his grip on the crowbar. "Brace him?"

"You got it."

They crossed the room, skirting the crowd of Speed Fiends. Roscoe kept his crowbar in his coat. No need to court trouble.

Stanton looked up from the little booze left in his shot glass, his small eyes squinting nervously. Roscoe sat down on one side. Angel took the other.

"Hello there, fellows," Bert grabbed his shot glass and downed what little whiskey was left. "Nice night."

"That it is," Roscoe withdrew his crowbar and set it gently on the table, near Bert's hand. "I'd hate to spoil it." He turned his head to face Bert, letting his greenish skin show through in the roadhouse's low light. "Tell me something, Bert—you ever tangle with a dead man?"

"I'm not sure, exactly, ah…" Bert turned to Angel, as if he looking for help.

In response, Angel drew a switchblade from his coat. He snapped the thin blade to life and let the silver glint in front of Bert's eyes. Bert's hopeful expression shriveled up. He turned back to Roscoe, his eyes pleading.

"I think you know you made a mistake," Roscoe admonished. "And guess what, Bert? You did. But don't worry, there's an easy way out. You know the cross you stole? I bet you got it stashed some place close by. You can keep all the other junk, we don't give a goddamn about that. But you're gonna get up and lead us to the cross. If not, I'm gonna take that crowbar and start knocking out your teeth. Now, you know how to do a B and E, but don't tell me for a second you can take some pain." He reached out and grabbed the edge of the crowbar. "Want to prove me wrong?"

"Christ!" Bert whispered. "Who are you guys? Cops or—"

"We look like cops?"

"Just consider us the Mission's defenders." Gripping the crowbar, Roscoe stood up and slid aside, letting Bert move out. "Now what's it gonna be?"

Bert hung his head. He wouldn't be a problem. They moved through the bar, Angel and Roscoe flanking Bert, preventing him from running. Bert trudged ahead like he was being led on a string. They neared the door and almost reached it when one of the bikers stepped in front of them and blocked their path. He was an ox of a man, with dark hair, stubble on his cheeks, and a lean scar slashed just past his eye. He was hunched over too, like his head sprouted straight between his shoulders.

He pointed to Bert, jabbing his finger nearly into the thief. "You leaving already?" He sounded like he had ground gravel trapped in his throat. "You should stay here, friend. I guarantee it'll go easier on you." He held out his hand. "Name's Tex. I think you'd be much happier with me and the boys than running around with some dead greaser and a Mex in a bad suit."

"Beat it, biker trash," Roscoe took offense. "Unless you want to rumble right here."

"And quit insulting my suit," Angel added.

Tex stared at them, with half-closed eyes. Roscoe tensed his hand, preparing to swing. But then Tex stepped aside and held out his hands to the door, an exaggerated gesture. "Well, I see how it is. Go on and get."

They hurried past him and out the door. Bert headed to the row of cabins, breaking into a slight run as he looked nervously over his shoulder. Roscoe and Angel followed. Roscoe kept his eye on the roadhouse. He could see motion inside. Something told him Tex and the Speed Fiends wanted the fight in the open, which would play to their strengths. He needed a heater. Roscoe didn't know much about his past, but he knew it involved those. And right now, his was back in the car.

Bert moved to the nearest court. His Studebaker was parked outside. He slipped inside the barren wooden room, with only a wireframe bed in one corner. It looked like a prison cell. Bert pulled a suitcase out from under the bed and undid the clasp with shaking hands. He dug inside, pulling aside unfolded clothes until he reached the Crimson Cross. He pulled it out, a small icon about as big as two forearms crossed together, and extended it to Angel and Roscoe like it was a friendly hand. Angel took it and tucked it under his arm. Made of some shining metal, like gold or silver, the Cross glowed with color—a deep, burnished crimson. Roscoe could see his reflection in the cross. It was distorted and strange. He didn't like it.

"There you go. I wouldn't make nothing on fencing this thing anyway," Bert muttered. He gave a nervous laugh. "You know, I don't think I'll be coming back to La Cruz. Something tells me it's safer to burgle mansions in Beverly Hills."

"A wise decision, man," Angel commended.

Roscoe looked back at the roadhouse from Bert's doorway. The Speed Fiends filed outside to stand in the dust. Some of them had pulled knives or chains from their coats while others drew automatics or revolvers. They assembled like a battalion of soldiers, awaiting an order.

"Que pasa?" Angel turned and stared at the Speed Fiends. "Damn. What you think? We run past them?"

"And get to the car," Roscoe agreed. Bert huddled in the back of his cabin. It wasn't him the Speed Fiends were interested in.

Tex walked to the head of the Speed Fiends. He cupped his hands over his mouth. "Bert! Bert, I lied! My name ain't truly Tex. It's Texogorath, first Infernal Duke of Hell!" With that, he began to change. His head popped forward as his lips curled back, revealing large obsidian fangs. Claws ripped from the ends of his fingers, as his head bulged and shifted into a far more lizard-like shape. His eyes rolled and shifted, almost popping out of his scull. Wings ripped from his back, seemingly composed of the same black leather as his jacket. He roared.

"The car?" Angel asked.

"Yeah." Roscoe gripped his crowbar. Angel gripped the Crimson Cross.

They ran—straight for the main group of Speed Fiends. Roscoe reached them first, wildly swinging his crowbar. One Fiend came at him, switchblade slashing low. He poked the blade into Roscoe's chest, and it felt like a pinch. Roscoe swung the crowbar against the biker's arm and heard the bone crack under metal. Then Roscoe whipped the crowbar around, driving it into the throat of another biker. The Fiend choked and gagged as he went down. Angel stayed close behind, a pearl-handled automatic pistol blasting away in his hands. At least, Angel had been smart enough to bring a heater along. A bullet punched through Roscoe's shoulder. Flesh ripped, but Roscoe could hardly feel it. Being dead had its advantages. He kept swinging.

They burst through the thin line of Speed Fiends. Roscoe moved towards the car, cursing the way his leaden limbs almost limped through the dirt. Another switchblade plunged into his back and he stumbled, swung, and let the crowbar's tip strike a skull. The biker sank to the ground, and Roscoe turned and kept running. Angel stayed at his side, still holding the Crimson Cross. They neared the Deuce. Roscoe heard Tex coming after them, the demon making a ragged panting noise as he lashed out with his claws. Roscoe forced his legs to *move*. He reached the Deuce and pulled the door back. Angel hurried around and scrambled into the passenger seat.

Roscoe started the engine with one hand, then slammed it into reverse. With the other hand, he reached to the backseat. His fingers wrapped around the wooden butt of his sawed-off shotgun. For some reason, Roscoe liked that sort of hand cannon the best. Whatever he had been in life, Roscoe figured it wasn't nice. The Deuce rocked back, and Roscoe twisted it into drive. He gunned the engine.

"Roscoe!" Angel cried. "Ugly demon—twelve o'clock!"

Sure enough, Texogorath was approaching. Before Roscoe could step on the gas, the demon leapt into the air and slammed hard onto the roof as the auto rocketed forward. Claws ripped through the metal like it was paper, and the Deuce rocked back and forth, dust rising in torrents from under its tires. Roscoe looked away from the road and stared up through the growing hole. Tex leered down, tasting the air with a forked tongue. Roscoe smelled the demon's stinking, sulfurous breath.

Tex reached down with a clawed hand. "Give me the Cross!"

In answer, Roscoe raised his sawed-off. "Get out of my car," he said, and pulled the trigger. The shotgun roared to life, sending a barrel's worth of lead straight into Tex's mug. The demon reeled back, snarling as his head changed shape. Bits of gore sprayed away in a black shower. Roscoe gave Tex the second barrel and he flipped off the roof, slamming into the bumper and sinking down. The whole car shook. Then Texogorath was under the Deuce's wheels as they ran him over and sped away from the gore left in front of the roadhouse.

Angel grinned at Roscoe and patted the cross. "Man, remind me never to touch your car."

"*You* can touch it whenever you want. I just don't like demon breath on my upholstery." Roscoe gunned the engine, and they rolled down the open road. There was nothing but moonlit desert on both sides of and La Cruz straight ahead. "Guess we gotta go through the city and then Cowl Canyons before we reach the Mission," Roscoe said. "We better stop somewhere in town and phone up the Captain. He can tell Wooster and Betty where we are, in case we need back-up for the final drive." He looked at his shoulder and jammed his finger in the hole. He dug around a little and finally wrenched the bullet out. "Preferably somewhere with food." He'd need the food to regenerate the flesh he lost. Luckily, he healed quickly.

"Sounds good to me. But we got to hurry. Hell was bad, but I got a feeling Heaven might be worse."

Daytime buzz died down as they arrived. La Cruz didn't have much of nightlife apart from a couple of teenagers trying to score booze from the liquor store and some couples walking their dogs. Roscoe drove evenly down Main Street and quickly found a diner. He rolled into the parking lot. It was a good-sized restaurant, one of the largest in town. The pearl-white walls framed wide glass windows, which provided a panoramic view of the entire street. The customers, families with kids or teenagers getting a quick bite before heading home, sat in pale booths, munching on burgers or guzzling milkshakes. Roscoe and Angel headed inside, their shoes clicking on the polished linoleum. Roscoe nodded toward the back, at a pair of payphones.

Angel headed towards them with a nod while Roscoe selected a booth and sat down. A waitress with a beehive hairdo came with menus, but he already had his order ready. "Pair of chili dogs and black coffee." He nodded to her. "Get moving." The waitress turned away without a word. Roscoe reclined on the worn red leather seat. The jukebox in the corner played some slow crooning song. It sounded like crap.

Roscoe stared ahead. The wound in his shoulder itched.

The guy in the booth right ahead eyeballed him. Roscoe tilted his head at the stranger. He was a thin fellow, with a calm smile on a strangely ageless face. He wore a white suit and vest, a white fedora low over his eyes and a pair of round, silver driving goggles. He sipped on a vanilla milkshake. There was something about his expression Roscoe didn't like. It was like the guy was thinking of a joke that he didn't want to tell anyone. Roscoe stared right back. His shotgun was in his coat, but he began to wonder if it would have any impact on this stranger.

The man stood up. He walked across the aisle, his white loafers slapping the floor. "May I sit here?"

"My buddy's already sitting there, pal." Roscoe could tell the guy knew the score and as to which side he was on, he might as well have it tattoo on his forehead. "So how about you take that fancy, white suit of yours and split?"

The stranger sat down. "My name is Uriel," he said. "Politeness matters little to me."

"I'll bet." The waitress arrived, balancing Roscoe's hot dogs and coffee on a tray. She set them down, and Roscoe scarfed down the grub, then drained the cup of coffee. It was still steaming hot, but he hardly felt the burning in his throat. Roscoe looked back at Uriel. "Let me guess, you want the Crimson Cross, to make your divine masters happy."

"Indeed. A chance like this only comes around once every couple millennia. The Crimson Cross is a paradox—a holy, unholy relic. A true contradiction." He folded his hands. "Just like you, living, dead man." He leaned closer. "I know about you, Roscoe."

"Oh yeah?" Roscoe did his best to sound bored.

"I know everything—including what you were before your present condition." Uriel drew closer. "Would you like to know as well? I can tell you everything: your career, date of birth, your friends and family." His smile was blinding. "Your real name."

Roscoe stared back at him and said nothing. The coffee sat forgotten by his arm while his mind reeled. He'd long ago made his peace with not knowing. His ignorance seemed as unchangeable as time. But, now, maybe that wasn't the case. He looked at Uriel as Angel drew in from the back.

Uriel continued. "I could give you another gift as well." He reached out. His hand landed on Roscoe's arm. Suddenly, Roscoe a strange tingle traveled from his fingers to his elbow. He stared down at his hand. The greenish tint was gone. Instead, his arm was a healthy pink. And he could *feel*. He could feel the linoleum and the pleasant breeze coming through the dinner doors. He tapped his fingers, the sensation electric. As a zombie, every feeling always seemed dull and indistinct. True feeling was something nearly forgotten. He stared at Uriel in silent awe. Uriel merely smiled. He removed his hand. The feeling vanished.

Angel walked up to the booth. "Roscoe..." he pointed to the window. "We gotta move. Got some unwanted company outside."

Several engines cut through the air. Roscoe looked over his shoulder and saw the Speed Fiends on their bikes in an orderly row just outside the diner. Tex was with them. He had reverted to his human form, but was barely keeping his face together. Bits of his skin kept splitting and breaking, letting scales pierce through like strange, obsidian acne. His eyes darted around and his forked tongue continued to slip in and out. All the Speed Fiends were packing.

"We got bigger problems than biker trash." Roscoe turned back to Uriel. "You're here alone?"

"I am archangel of Almighty God. I am all that is needed." Uriel came to his feet. "My offer stands, Roscoe—you give me the cross, I give you your life and your past. It's more than a fair deal. It's your only chance for humanity."

Angel turned back to Roscoe. He opened his mouth, but no words came. Roscoe knew his friend didn't know what to say. He didn't either.

Luckily, the down-under brigade took it out of their hands. "Fiends!" Texogorath roared. "Get me the wretches who stand against the indomitable will of Hell! Kill all who oppose us! Find the Crimson Cross!" He pulled a long-barreled revolver from his coat, leveled it at the diner and opened fire. Roscoe moved, leaping from the booth and kissing the floor as the main window shattered. Angel landed next to him. A waitress screamed. Diners scrambled back, running as the Speed Fiends drew their guns and shot into the restaurant. They were packing bigger artillery now, with a few chattering sub-guns added to their pistols. More glass shattered. Roscoe's coffee cup exploded, spilling black liquid across the tabletop. But Uriel didn't bother ducking for cover. He simply stood up and stared at the demons.

He reached into his coat and withdrew a pair of long-barreled automatics, both gleaming white. Uriel fired them, ignoring the bullets cutting through the air as he gunned down the satanic bikers. One of his bullets struck the gas tank of a bike and it exploded, sending bits of burned metal and blazing remains of its driver crashing across the street. Roscoe winced. Heaven and Hell were going at it. They didn't care how many mortals were caught in the crossfire.

Quickly, Roscoe looked over to Angel and nodded to the door. "None of them know the Crimson Cross is in the Deuce. But they *will* go after us once they see us leaving—and leave the civilians alone." He drew out his shotgun. "So we lay down some covering fire and run for the doors, then go for the car and drive like... like hell. Ready?"

"You got it," Angel already had his pistol out.

They stood up and ran. Roscoe swung the barrel of his shotgun towards Uriel and fired. The shot ripped past the archangel, making him duck down. Angel cracked away with his pistol, throwing lead at the Speed Fiends. Both men were running—or speedily limping, in Roscoe's case—and it was impossible to see if they hit anything as they made it to the doors. Roscoe kicked them open and ran for the parking lot. Some bikers noticed them and turned their guns in their direction. Bullets cut through the air. A few cracked into the side of the Deuce, rupturing the metal. Roscoe winced. It would take a long time to get the car fixed. That did nothing to improve his mood.

He wrenched the door open and slipped inside as Angel raced around to the passenger seat. Texogorath headed their way. This time, Tex's mouth slammed open. It seemed to crack all the way back, like he had no jaws. His tongue shot out, thick as an arm and ridged like barbed wire. The tongue zoomed towards the Deuce. Roscoe raised his sawed-off out the window with one hand and fired. The tongue shattered. Black, boiling blood sprayed in the air. Roscoe's nose twitched from the sulfur. He hit the gas and rolled into the street.

The Speed Fiends, most of them already on their bikes, simply turned around, revved their engines, and shot down the street after the Deuce. Roscoe kept both hands on the wheel. There was no time to reload the sawed-off. Angel fired the last shots from his automatic out the window, and then the pistol clicked empty. Rubber burned under Roscoe's tires. He kept the car on track, swerving around other motorists and slamming his horn. Screams followed. The Speed Fiends drew closer. Roscoe didn't think they could outrun them. Then he remembered something—the entire reason why they had stopped.

He turned to Angel. "You get in touch with Wooster and Betty?"

"Yeah, they were at the garage. Said they'd be close by and—*cabrón!*" A Speed Fiend buzzed by his window and tried to reach inside. Angel popped his switchblade and plunged it into the biker's gloved hand. The biker screamed, withdrew the bleeding hand, spun his bike to the side, and rammed it into a telephone pole. Angel cleaned the blood from his switchblade and pointed ahead. "Roscoe! Over there—looks like some good timing!"

Wooster's massive Packard was coming down a side street with Betty driving, pounding the horn with one hand as wind tossed her short hair back. Wooster rode shotgun with a blazing tommy gun in his hands. The Packard barreled into Main Street and crashed straight into the back of Speed Fiends. The bulky vehicle did its job, smashing aside bikes and knocking their riders into the air like toys before the hand of an angry child. Betty spun the car around, cruising just behind Roscoe's Deuce. Wooster turned back, his tommy gun blazing. It chattered away, making the fallen Speed Fiends duck for cover as bullets danced and cracked on the street. Betty honked the horn again. Roscoe looked into the rear view mirror. He saw her waving. He waved back.

They shot down the street as Betty brought the Packard to their side. The end of Main Street was ahead, and then the roads leading to the various suburbs spiraling out from La Cruz and another path leading to Cowl Canyons and the Mission. Betty pointed down that road. Both cars turned.

She raised her voice, shouting over the roar of engines. "Pull over up ahead! I got tools you're gonna need!"

Did they have time to pull over? Roscoe wasn't sure. The Speed Fiends had been banged around good, but they'd be back on their feet soon enough. Tex wouldn't let them rest. And Uriel was an archangel.

Still, Betty's tools might mean the difference between success and failure. He trusted her, just like he trusted Angel and Wooster and the Captain. Roscoe took his foot off the gas. He'd go a little bit further before stopping completely. It was good to get out of La Cruz.

Right before the entrance to Cowl Canyons, Roscoe pulled over and killed the engine. The Canyons were a wild set of badlands, with valleys and rises of harsh rust-red stone reaching all the way to the coast. Roads through Cowl Canyons were poorly maintained at best. Kids sometimes came up here to hike or play around, while teenagers did the same to make out or smoke reefers. Poorly suited to driving as it was, it was the only way to the Mission. Roscoe stared at the entrance to the canyons, a natural archway forming a slim sliver of a bridge over the wide stone passage. It was completely dark now, with the only illumination coming from their headlights or the moon and stars.

Angel sat next to him in silence. Behind them, they could hear Wooster's Packard drawing closer. "Hey," Angel said. "That pendejo in white, in the diner—he offered you your life back, didn't he? Said he could make you human again if you gave him the Crimson Cross?"

There was no point in lying.

"You gonna take his offer?" Angel asked. "Couldn't blame you if you did."

Roscoe sighed. "He'd take the Crimson Cross and try to drag it to Heaven. The forces of Hell would follow. La Cruz would be ripped apart. So would the surrounding country and then the world, as it became caught up in a tug-of-war between Heaven and Hell."

"If you want to put it that way. But the world ain't done much for us." Angel shifted in his seat and opened the door as Wooster's auto pulled up. "You know, a few years ago, growing up in LA, I would've taken that offer in a heartbeat. I didn't care much for the world. Nothing but racist Anglo cops who enjoyed roughing up some Pachuco kid just for kicks and corrupt politicians and businessmen making their dough off of exploiting the poor. All those things are still there. I think they always will be."

"So what changed?"

"I found friends."

Betty honked the horn, and Angel opened the door. He hopped out and Roscoe followed. They walked over to the Packard, leaving the Crimson Cross in the Deuce. Betty and Wooster stood at the back of the Packard and opened the trunk. Wooster reloaded his tommy gun and Betty looked through a crate filled with strange shit.

She looked up and smiled weakly at Angel and Roscoe. "Well," she said. "You boys certainly know how to stir up trouble."

"One of my many talents," Roscoe jabbed a thumb at the crate. "What'd you bring?"

Betty pulled out a wine bottle, with crumpled up papers tucked in the thin neck. "Okay," she said. "I had a feeling we might be taking on some of Heaven's toughest fighters. Demons are simple. You just carve some crosses on bullets. That's what Wooster used on the Speed Fiends back on Main Street. But for the forces of Heaven, I had to be a little creative." She held the bottle out to Roscoe. "It's got defiled communion wine, topped off with defaced pages from the bible. Just light the fuse, let it fly and voila—instant unholy Molotov cocktail."

"Little lady, you outdone yourself." Wooster chuckled. "And I think we're gonna need that kind of firepower. Those canyons up ahead are twisted and riddled with side passages and slopes. The Speed Fiends and that goddamn archangel can sneak in and try to head us off. Going through to the Mission will be dangerous." He looked up, his eyes dark. "We might not all get through."

Roscoe took the unholy Molotov cocktail. He stuffed it in his jacket pocket. "We'll get through," he muttered. "We have to."

Then Betty noticed the cut in his shoulder. "Roscoe! Oh God, you okay?"

"It's healing already. You know I can't even feel it."

"Sorry." Betty bit her lip. "It's just, I'm a little worried" She looked them over. "I guess, I've never really fit in much of anywhere. I've been too interested in cars to stick with the other girls and my dad… Well, garden parties and bridge clubs just weren't his scene. You guys—and Donovan Motors—you're all I got."

That was just what Roscoe needed to hear. He walked back to the Deuce, hearing the cursed communion wine in the fire bomb swish as he moved. He pulled open the door, then got behind the wheel. He poked his head out the window. Wooster, Betty, and Angel stared at him as the engine growled to life. Angel started running.

"Don't follow me!" Roscoe slammed on the gas and shot into the canyon. He rode on along, under the archway and down the gravelly road. His Deuce bounced and jolted along the jagged path, and Roscoe heard the wind whistling through the bullet holes and the growing gap in the roof. Behind him, his friends were piling into Wooster's Packard. Roscoe grinned. He was already twisting around the corner and heading further into the canyon. In that jalopy, they'd never catch him.

He pressed the gas pedal down completely. The canyon walls seemed to catch the moonlight, making them glow a deeper, rusty red. As he rode along, he made out other motors buzzing closely like a swarm of far off insects. He snapped his sawed-off open and slipped in two more shells. He kept the automobile running, as the walls seemed to draw closer together. Sprays of dust and gravel kicked up from the tires. He stared in the rear view mirror, noting other, smaller dirt roads weaving through the canyon. Headlights gleamed on those side roads. Speed Fiends. Roscoe adjusted his grip on the sawed-off.

The bikers roared into the canyon, drawing closer and kicking up gravel in their wake. Soon enough, they started to shoot. More rounds cracked into the back of the Deuce, blasting spider web cracks in the window and crashing into the dashboard. Another shot punched into his back and erupted out from his ribcage. Bits of bone poked out of Roscoe's chest, along with black, rotten flesh. Roscoe cursed. That would take a Christmas turkey's worth of meat to heal. He bit his lip and kept the Deuce roaring down the road.

The Speed Fiends rode alongside now, flanking the Deuce. Roscoe twisted around, leaned out of the window, and raised his shotgun. The sawed-off flashed, and several bikers went down in the spray of bullets. He fired the second barrel out the other window. The shots were wild, but they kept the Speed Fiends back. Roscoe kept the engine roaring and pulled ahead. The canyon grew narrower, forming one last chokepoint before the open road. Roscoe bit his lip. He couldn't hear a thing but the roar of the engines. He was nearing the chokepoint and beginning to wonder if his Deuce would fit. In a second, he'd find out.

Roscoe heard the sides streak across the rocky walls. This whole job was hell on his car, but he still held the gas pedal down. Metal screeched on stone. Sparks rose from the sides. The Speed Fiends were close behind, but he kept driving. Then he was through the narrow passage, past the canyon and rushing into the open road. He turned around to see the Speed Fiends zooming their way through the chokepoint. Texogorath was ahead, his wings unfurled and his long tongue wiggling in the wind like a scarf.

Now was the time. Roscoe snapped open the sawed-off. He rammed in two more shells, twisted around and fired them both out the rear window. The shots tore into the foremost bike and struck the gas tank. The bike went up, spraying fire across the stones. The wrecked bike blocked the path. The other motorcycles crashed into the wreck, tossing their riders down. Texogorath went with them, snarling and roaring his pain to the night as more riders piled into him. The chokepoint was packed. There was no way for the Speed Fiends to get through. Roscoe grinned to himself, despite the gaping hole in his chest and ribcage. He turned back to the road.

Up ahead was the Mission. It was past open desert ground, spotted with tall prairie gas. The Mission sat on a hill, with canyons stretching out all around, a rambling stucco structure, all arch-roofed buildings behind a tall wall. Crosses topped the buildings, silhouetted against the night sky. Roscoe looked down. A figure in white stood straight in the road. Uriel. There was no time to stop. Roscoe reached for the Crimson Cross. He grabbed it and held it close.

The Deuce slammed straight into Uriel. The car broke. Uriel didn't. The bumper wrapped around him. The remainder of the windshield cracked and burst. Roscoe was hurled out of his seat, onto the dashboard and through what was left of the window. Bits of glass dug into his cheeks and shoulders. He skidded across the hood and bashed straight into the road. The asphalt ripped into his skin and clothes as he rolled over twice. His bones grated against the ground.

Then he was still. Roscoe looked up at the open stars. The pain was dull, but came from every inch of him. He gritted his teeth. The Crimson Cross lay next to him, resting on the road. Roscoe grabbed it, then reached for the crowbar, the prongs pointing down the road. Behind him, his ride looked like it had wrapped around a tree. Uriel slowly turned around in the wreckage.

Roscoe's hand dropped to his pocket. The lighter was still there. So was the wine bottle. Must be a hell of a bottle.

"Did you think about my offer, Roscoe?" Uriel schlepped up, a pair of automatic pistols seemingly appearing in his hands. "I have a strong feeling that you have been unable to shake it from your mind."

"Yeah…" Roscoe got out the lighter. He held it close to his face and snapped to life, then brought out the unholy Molotov cocktail. He looked back at Uriel. The angel's face was still and impassive. "And I got my answer…" He thought about what it would be like, to have his memory back, to live his life without being hated or pitied, to feel and age and love like anybody else. "My answer's no."

"No?" Uriel leveled his pistols. "You're content with ignorance, then?"

"Listen, pal. I know exactly who I am."

He touched the lighter to the defaced bible pages. They crackled to life and burned. Then Roscoe stood up, spun around and hurled the cursed firebomb straight into the archangel's face. The bottle burst, bathing Uriel's face in bright red flames. He screamed as the fire scorched his flesh. He sank down. Roscoe pulled himself to his feet. He tucked the Crimson Cross under his arm and grabbed the crowbar. As Uriel writhed, Roscoe slammed the crowbar hard into the angel's skull, and Uriel collapsed. Roscoe swung down the crowbar a few more times. It wouldn't stop the angel, but it would give him pause.

Finally, Roscoe pulled back. He gripped the Crimson Cross tightly and started limping up the road to the Mission.

It seemed to take him an hour, but he finally made it. A priest stood by the open door, with outstretched hands. The priest was a Mexican named Father Ignacio Montez. He served a congregation in Butcher's Row and was a friend of the Captain. "Mr. Roscoe?" he asked. "You are all right?"

"Swell," Roscoe muttered. He handed Father Montez the Crimson Cross. "Go and put it back. Power up all those wards and magic spells in the altar. Keep Heaven and Hell from getting interested in the damn thing."

"Of course." Father Montez took the Crimson Cross and hurried inside.

Roscoe leaned against the wall of the Mission. He fumbled for a cigarette and jammed it into his mouth, then snapped it to life. The taste of tobacco barely edged out the dull taste of blood. Roscoe looked down at his broken body. He'd have to eat several Christmas dinners to grow it all back, but that was okay. The Captain would square it with some local diner and they'd bring the grub in by the cartful.

Roscoe stared down the hill as another pair of headlights shone in the darkness. It was Wooster's Packard. He could see Wooster behind the wheel, with Angel and Betty in the back. They stopped at the wreck of the Deuce, and Roscoe waved to get their attention. They started driving up the hill.

Then Father Montez returned. "It is done, Mr. Roscoe. The Cross is safe."

"Thank Christ." Roscoe spat out a cloud of smoke.

"I will pray for you, Mr. Roscoe," Father Ignacio said softly. "I will pray for you."

"Don't trouble yourself, padre." Roscoe tossed away the cigarette. He started walking toward his friends. "I've got everything I want right here."

Want more of Michael Panush's Ghostbusters-meets-Fast-and-the-Furious-meets-James-Dean-hot-rod-movie Rot Rods series?

Tweet *More Rot Rods! @Michael_Panush @CuriosityQuills #BookLove*

THE LAST CARNIVALE

BY VICKI KEIRE

J essa ran.

The corridor stretched on into blackness, its walls covered with burnt paper. Faint moonlight leaked through broken windows. She dodged chunks of fallen ceiling, kicking up dust and ash. Her eyes stung and her lungs pulsed with acid. Glass and smaller chunks of debris cracked too loudly under her heavy, ugly boots.

She knew the importance of silence; she could hear the group of soldiers behind her. She knew she hadn't yet been spotted. She just had to make it to the end of the corridor, then up the servant's stairs to what remained of the roof. With luck and skill, she might still have a chance.

Then I can run back to the caves so Theodric can kill me himself, Jessa thought bitterly.

They were closer now. She forced herself to concentrate.

Jessa had learned from bitter experience not to go rushing blindly into exposed space while she was above ground. Predators, collapsing debris, and Syncline soldiers were just a few of the dangers that awaited the unwary. She dropped to her belly, protected by her thick canvas coat. She could see one of them wedged into a doorway just meters from the staircase entrance. He held a sleek rifle with an arm made of both flesh and metal.

A new brand of killer, Jessa thought numbly. Syncline Corp. had sent their very latest model for her this time. She'd stopped asking why long ago. The short answer was simple: the mineral found only on Verres that was infinitely more powerful than any source Syncline currently possessed. The long answer started as far back as the day they'd killed her family and razed her world, mistakenly leaving the youngest, most headstrong member of the ruling family alive.

Hide. I'm going to have to hide. Theodric will know, he'll bring help…

Shouts behind her let her know hiding was no longer an option.

The roof, then.

With one swift slice of her knife, her bootlaces fell away. Barefoot, she'd get cut, but she wouldn't fall. Cuts would heal. A fall would snap her neck. Weakened by the repeated bombings that followed the Day of Fire, the remaining buildings were off limits to all survivors. The roof, especially, was treacherous territory. But Jessa knew her forbidden rooftop kingdom well. She crossed it often in her frequent attempts to escape the shelters and see the sun, unlike the Syncline soldiers who followed.

Jessa vaulted across open space, staying low as she slammed into the stairwell. The lone soldier who'd been guarding it barked commands into a crackle of static. Voices echoed behind her, followed by pounding feet and gunfire. She ran, skipping steps three at a time, ignoring the chaos in her wake. The sounds of fighting grew closer.

She cleared the staircase in seconds. Burned out buildings and twisted metal spires stretched up into endless night around her. What had once been beautiful, luminous structures mocked her with their broken windows and grime-encrusted surfaces. She barely had time to draw breath before a metal hand grabbed her.

"Target acquired," the Syncline soldier said. An oddly elegant faceplate covered half his features. A red lens obscured one eye, while a grid of some kind jutted out and over part of his mouth. All that remained of his human face was a ribbon of flesh curving through metal barriers. His grip on her collar tightened while his inhuman strength hauled her even higher into the air. Her feet scraped wildly at nothing.

"I'm not…" Jessa gagged, trying to pry even an inch of air from the man's merciless metal hands. "I'm not who you think," she managed at last. He ignored her.

"She's an exact match," he said into the grid. Jessa didn't hear the reply, but whatever it was made him narrow his eyes. "No, not a problem. She's a tiny, little thing." The soldier shook her again, as if examining a pet he was considering taking home. "Scrawny, even. The embargo must be hitting them hard."

Outraged, Jessa tried to kick him. Nothing happened, of course.

Gunfire echoed below. The soldier holding her froze as bullets rained down in a circle around them. Several hit him in the leg. She watched as a thick, silver liquid oozed out, but he didn't seem hurt. Instead, he grimaced as he dropped her and hauled her in front of him in a protective embrace.

Two thoughts hit her at once:

Theodric sent the Guard for me.

Why is a Syncline soldier protecting me from gunfire?

The latter she filed away for later. There simply wasn't time, as tantalizing as the possibilities were. But her Guard's presence meant a chance at rescue and demanded immediate action. As the hail of gunfire increased around her, she took a deep breath and dropped to her knees, slipping out of the too large jacket and leaving the soldier holding empty fabric.

How's that for scrawny, she almost yelled after the astonished soldier as she crawled for the middle of the roof. Great big pieces of the structure were missing all around her. She slinked forward across a support beam, relying on deeply ingrained memory to guide her. Bullets and blasts were pierced by the occasional scream or yelled command. Behind her, she could hear more and more people clambering up onto the roof. Which was bad. Very bad. Too many, and the whole thing would collapse. She just hoped the main support beam would withstand the increasing weight.

Without her jacket and its sheltering hood, there was no mistaking who she was. Her long, red hair lashed across her face. Without the bulky fabric to hide her shape, it was obvious she was young and female. Not many young females survived the Day of Fire. Certainly only one had the kind of stupidity that would lead her to risk the roofs, and only one had her trademark red hair. She might as well be wearing a sign for Syncline's forces.

They called her the Beggar Princess, the sole survivor of Verres' ruling family after the Day of Fire. Gods be damned, how she hated that title. Hated it almost as much as she hated who she was, where she was, and what had happened.

The roof crackled ominously beneath her knees. *Don't look down, don't look down.* The shouts and blaster fire erupted around her. The surface beneath her shook, and she realized that someone was coming after her.

Someone big, judging by the tremors beneath her. A Syncline soldier. None of her own people would be so stupid.

Memory and long hours of forbidden exploration told her she was crawling across the central beam that ran the length of the State reception chamber. The room was huge, and beautiful still, in a sad, decayed way. Pieces of the roof had already fallen in around the edges. Jessa often stood in the cavernous room and stared longingly at the lightening sky, not courageous or suicidal enough to brave the surface during the day. The hall had once been covered with beautiful murals depicting Verres' history: scenes of Carnivale, of coronations, and the lost technology that had at one time made her home powerful and safe. Huge, sparkling mirrors once reflected light back at the glittering Carnivale guests. But the glass was cracked now, great big jagged chunks refracting ashy, broken images through its spider-webbed surface. It was into this cavernous space that she would fall if she wasn't careful, or if the soldier following her managed to get her again.

She would rather fall than be captured by Syncline.

Jessa heard pieces of rock cracking and falling. She crawled faster. When she felt a heavy, unfamiliar hand—so heavy it must have been made of metal—grab her ankle, she kicked and flailed in the dust-choked air. She couldn't help it; she looked back. He was huge, a hulking amalgam of metal and flesh. His one human eye trained on her with such fierce hatred she forgot, for a moment, to breathe.

"Jessa! We've got them cut off!" Captain Harker's yell was enough to bring her back to herself. She went limp with relief for just a moment. Harker had come for her. She didn't deserve it. Harker was Theodric's best soldier and her personal guard and he always, always came. But other people might die for her stupidity today, and she didn't deserve their mercy or loyalty. If Harker was one of them… the thought almost froze her. "Come on!" he snarled again. She knew he was as angry as he'd ever been. She wondered what the shape of her guard's full wrath might take before the Syncline soldier grunted. He'd lost his hold on her ankle.

Had Harker shot him? Did her momentary lapse throw him? It didn't matter. She twisted her foot, gritting her teeth against the pain, and scrambled to her feet on the beam. She was as light on the roof, almost, as ash. Starved for air and space, she danced across these deathtrap roofs every chance she got. The Syncline soldier saw it, too. He saw her sudden confidence, the way she danced backwards like a firewalker at Carnivale through flames, her long hair lashing the sky while her eyes dared him. He would have to chase.

And he did.

Just what hold had Syncline Corp. have over this man that he would risk his life like this? She knew Theodric would want him for questioning, and Harker would want to slit his throat. But as she choked down ash and blinked coal from her eyes, she watched him haul himself up for a final run for his prize: her.

The Beggar Princess. Sovereign of cinders and starvation.

She felt the rage rising within her, the fury she spent her daylight hours in the caves denying. Jessa realized she was screaming into the ash-specked air. She couldn't have said what the words were. She remembered that day when her family and world and choices were all taken from her in a single act of blood and betrayal. The soldier saw this and took one tiny, shocked step backwards.

The wrong way.

As she knew it would, the roof unpeeled underneath him. Everything slowed down. Even Harker's shouts behind her took on an unreal quality as the whole roof began to give. The beam, on which she stood, the beam across which she'd scrambled so many nights alone, began to shake and wrench. Whose slow words were in her ear? Harker, with strong hands and no weapon, because he'd dropped it to come after her. Her Captain of the Guard had risked the collapsing beam to get her. She felt his firm terrified hands on her now: one around her waist, another hooked under her arm, dragging her.

Inside she was screaming because he didn't know the beam. No one knew the beam like her, knew the safe ways across the roofs, and, anyway, together they were too much. The weight of them was too much for the roof to bear. But then he ran with her and jumped, her bare soles flexing for solid surface before they even hit ground. Jessa screamed to see the beam collapse and with it, much of the roof. Harker found a spot, a safe spot, somehow. Beneath them, she could see almost the whole of the great audience hall open to the dull burnt night. A twisted soldier of metal and flesh lay far below them. From their height, he seemed dusted with toy bricks and shiny glass that might have been pretty, as if he'd fallen asleep in a pile of dangerous toys.

"He's not asleep," Jessa whispered. The wind took her words before the depth of the hatred in them could shock her.

"Dammit, Jessa." Harker pulled her from their safe island of intact roof to the edge of the next building. He never took his hand from her arm. He used his free one to shove her flat once they reached a high enough pile of rubble. "Stay down. It's not safe. They sent a whole squadron." Fear and fury radiated off him in equal amounts.

The surface was cold beneath her. In her sleeveless shirt, she shook silently. Without a word, and with the ease of long practice, he shrugged out of his heavy combat jacket and threw it at her. Just as easily she caught it and slipped it over her like a blanket. It smelled of ash and sweat and fear. "Harker," Jessa whispered, after a long moment of trying, and failing, to stop shaking. She tried out several things in her mind: I'm sorry. Thank you. What happened? But what came out was, "How did you know about the roof?"

His shoulders slumped, as if the sound of her voice made the whole thing real at last. "Do you know how many people could have died tonight, Jessa?" His voice was tight. "Do you know how many of us there are left? Shall I tell you?"

"Too many," she said softly. "And not enough." She tried to hold back the sob, really tried because Harker was a soldier and stoic and brave and furious at her, but she couldn't. She hid in his jacket.

He swore, long and colorfully, before turning to ferret her out of the pile of fabric. "Are you all right? I mean, mostly?" At her nod, he sighed heavily and scrubbed at his ash-streaked face. "Well, fuck all. That won't last when Theodric gets his hands on you. On both of us."

"You had nothing to do with it." Jessa sat up, using the jacket like a shawl. "It's me, Harker. It happened again tonight. The nightmares. I watched us all die, all over again, and I woke up knowing that I had to get out or lose my mind." Jessa fisted his jacket in her hand and pulled, frustrated almost to tears. "So I came up here. The caves are so full of angry, starving people. It was too much. I had to run. I went a little mad with it."

His eyes bored into hers. "You have to tell Theodric about the dreams, Jessa. You have to."

She nodded miserably. "But not just yet. If I am going mad, it's not as if we have the ability to treat it." She inhaled his jacket again and gave him a slow smile. "You're smoking again."

"Am not."

"Are."

He was silent, his angry glare back her only answer.

She smiled triumphantly. "Give me one, then." Wordlessly, he shook his head. Sighing, she slipped her hand into the inside pocket, determined to ferret out the tobacco he'd sworn off so many times. "Should we be doing this? Waiting, like this? They're still out there, the Syncline soldiers."

Harker gave her that half-smile that made her heart stop. "Well. They obviously have orders to take you alive, so why do you care?" She stuck out her tongue just as Theodric's gravelly voice crackled over Harker's link, announcing the all clear. She didn't move, though, and neither did Harker. Instead, Harker's posture became marginally less stiff, and Jessa slumped with relief against the pile of rubble beside her.

"That was close," she sighed, her fingers continuing their questing search. "Seriously. Where are those…" her fingers closed on something hard and square. "Aha! I knew you'd started back. You've never been able to stay quit for more than six…"

She trailed off as she pulled out the perfectly square white box, made of pristine white fibrene that somehow managed to escape the ash and grime that settled over every other thing on the planet, including her. She ran a dirty thumb over its surface, lingering over the brightly painted Carnivale mask adorning the front. She hadn't seen such bright colors in… she didn't know when. Perhaps some of her mother's old dresses, but even those had begun to fade with age. "Oh, Harker," she breathed at last, sucking in a mouthful of ash in her shock. For once, she didn't care. "Where did you find it?"

"Happy Birthday, Jessa," he said simply, and even managed to sound as if he meant it. She tried to read his expression but couldn't see much in the spectral shadows cast by their sheltering rubbish heap. She caressed the box again and tried to gather an appropriate response.

"I… I don't know what to say." The box was unopened, the gold seals around its edges undisturbed. That marked it as a relic of the last age, from the time of the great Carnivales, when the galaxy's elite turned out in full force to celebrate the monarch's annual compact with the citizens. Memories of the glittering balls and festival food lingered in the corners of her mind, chased there by hunger and responsibility and constant watchfulness. She remembered the food most of all, fingering the box that was slightly larger than her palm. Somewhere, somehow, Harker found a Carnivale favor, once thrown to the crowds by the handful, but now more precious than bullets. She hadn't seen one in years. Its masque-covered surface would hold a festival cake, and since the gold seal was intact, she knew it would be fresh. She let her thumb rest on the red and gold masque, wondering what flavor was inside. "I'd forgotten it was my birthday," she admitted at last, cupping the favor in her hands like a holy relic.

On Verres, there was no reason to remember birthdays, let alone celebrate. Calendars were just another way to mark distance between the Day of Fire and the next attack by Syncline forces. Her last birthday had slipped by with nothing more than good wishes from three people:

Theodric, her personal attendant, and, of course, Harker. But this year... a present?

"It's customary to merely say thank you," Harker teased. He hadn't exactly relaxed his guard, but he did shift to a half-crouch less than a meter away. A quick move would deposit her into his lap. Jessa considered it before dropping her head back to the favor-box, entranced.

"But why?" she demanded. "Who did you kill for this, Harker? And why me, now?"

"I've seen you, looking more and more lost lately. I know about your dreams. Or nightmares," he corrected. "Whether you believe it or not, people do notice what you do, how you look. You're important for morale, especially now that all our requests for aid have come back unanswered or denied." He ran a hand nervously through his close-cropped hair. "So really, I'm doing my patriotic duty."

His duty. Harker was always dead set on doing his duty. Lingering with her on the roofs to celebrate her birthday was one of only a handful of times she could ever remember him breaking the rules. She should have known it had something to do with duty and the greater good, rather than something he did because he was her friend. He was right, though. Morale was sinking lower than she thought possible as they sent out desperate pleas directly to The Republic on faraway Earth, and any other formerly allied planet they could think of. Their resources were stretched to the breaking point, and soon, she saw no way they wouldn't be forced to surrender to Syncline. She bit her lip at the thought, and then forced it resolutely from her mind. She gave him her best crooked smile and offered him the tin. "You open it, then. I'm dying to know the flavor." But he only crossed his arms across his chest with a look she knew all too well. It was a look that said "no way" even as it expressed wry affection. "Oh, okay," she sighed, and proceeded to strip the golden seal from the package. She carefully slipped the thin, gilded strip into her pocket, determined to waste nothing.

Sanivar fire-cake. A specialty from a chain of islands far to the south. As far as Jessa knew, those islands no longer existed. The spices wafted through the ash-choked air, bringing back memories:

Jessa was seven, standing with her mother in the flower garden. Her father was there, en-masque, of course, and he slipped her a Carnivale-favor with a wink. She remembered hiding behind her mother's voluminous sliver skirts and digging into the Sanivar cake with her bare fingers, getting the crimson pollen of the plant, which gave the islands their name all over her hands and face. When her mother moved to greet some foreign dignitary, there Jessa had stood, with fire-cake crumbs smeared all over her mouth and crimson spice like speckled blood down her moonlight-colored gown.

All her mother had done was laugh.

The memory slammed into her with the first bite and she found she was crying, tears mixing with the frosting of a cake that could have been made yesterday. Could have been, but wasn't; an entire life of running and fighting and starving intervened. Her mother was long dead, and there was nothing cute about the mess she was now.

"Hey now," Harker said, dropping his defensive pose at last. He snaked a hesitant arm around her shoulder. "It's a present. It's not supposed to make you cry."

"I can't help it," Jessa sobbed. "It's been so long, and I'm so tired, but there's no one to help." She sobbed and licked frosting off her fingers. "If you don't help me eat this I swear to gods I'm going to throw myself off this roof." She launched into the distance between them, landing smack against his chest. He snatched the fire-cake from her before it dropped into the ash and rubble.

"Okay, okay, if you're going to make death threats," he tried to joke, pinching off a bite of cake. "But there's more," he announced, refusing to be drawn into her sadness. "The best part. It's in my other pocket. The one you checked for forbidden tobacco?"

She looked up at him, confused. "But that held nothing but your comm."

"Exactly. It's what's on the comm that's important. Take another look."

Something in his tone made Jessa's back arch as she inched away from him. "What could be better than fire-cake?" she asked suspiciously.

"What indeed?" Harker snaked out a grimy finger and wiped frosting from her mouth. "Look and see."

She was on his coat in an instant, fingering the hand-held device with shaking hands. A dull excitement had begun to invade her belly; could they possibly be true, the rumors she'd discounted as drunken, desperate ravings? Her trembling fingers struggled to hold the device steady as she read the message twice through, then once again for good measure.

"Is it true, Harker?" she demanded, fire-cakes and haunting memories all but forgotten as the tactical part of her surfaced. "Is this official?"

"Verified with The Republic's forces."

She sat against the ground in shock, Harker's comm cool and reassuringly solid between her fingers. "A team? A special ops team? They don't say how many, or when. But do they really mean to send help? Oh gods, Harker. This is… this is…"

He smiled at her, his mouth open to answer, one finger coated with fire-cake frosting, when Jessa heard an unfamiliar rustling off to their side.

She knew the roofs well. She knew all the unfortunate creatures that lived in its refuse, and the noises they made in the night. This wasn't one of them. Her brain closed down in shock as the shuffling turned into the rumble of rubble falling behind her, and of a blaster sliding against its holster.

That was a sound she knew better than she did her own mother's voice.

"Harker!" she shouted, as more and more rubble fell onto her back. She tried to get out a warning scream, but knew it would be too late. Instead, she switched to prayer, which was something she rarely did since the Day of Fire. Please, please, please, let him be fast enough. Please, Mother, Father; let him be all right. There is no one else but him.

She hadn't prayed to the gods since it happened. She no longer believed in them.

But the fire from the blaster caught Harker square in the chest, freezing everything in time for one endless moment. Then he pitched forward, as if still in slow motion, blood and warnings bubbling on his lips.

The fire-cake favor in her hand had drops of blood in it. His blood. Harker's. The closest thing she had to a friend in the world.

Enraged, she reached up above her and caught the Syncline's soldier's unresisting hand. She made her hand into a vise around his armored forearm and flipped him forward on his back. Her training came back to her in a rush as she rolled sideways, pulling the blaster free from her dead friend's side holster. She fingered the trigger and began to fire, not even counting the blasts, no longer listening for others around them. She couldn't be sure, but she thought she was screaming. She continued to fire until a gnarled hand closed around her wrist, forcing it upwards so that her blasts went straight into the clouds.

Theodric.

Her oldest advisor's wrinkled, weathered face shocked her back into breathing, into knowing. She was dimly aware that he was talking to her, trying to soothe her. She realized she was being carried, away from Harker's body that had been laid peacefully on its back, staring at the ruined sky she so cherished. There was no sign of the Syncline soldier.

Jessa wondered idly how much time she had lost, shooting at an already-dead soldier again and again. She knew it no longer mattered. Behind her somewhere, next to Harker's body, laid a ruined piece of the last fire-cake on Verres, and a comm unit promising the first bit of good news from The Republic that had come their way since the war started. Inside, she no longer cared. She made up her mind to hate them, all of them, the soldiers from Earth who arrived one birthday too late.

She thought, instead, of her mother. The Queen of Verres had loved beauty and luxury. Jessa could still picture her mother laughing in her gardens, which had been famous for their beauty and variety of species throughout the entire galaxy. Jessa remembered holding her mother's hand, playing one of the Queen's favorite games, in which everyone combed the garden for the prettiest flower, and then presented them to the Queen. Her mother would gather her into her lap, her long, blond, shining hair hanging down like a curtain separating the two of them from the rest of the world, while her mother whispered to her that she, Jessa, was the prettiest and rarest flower in all the gardens of Verres. Jessa felt the tears gathering, and blinked them back quickly.

The gardens had burned along with her people, just like Harker's body would soon burn in a funeral rite. She had no flowers to wreathe him with, so she arranged the Carnivale favor in his hands, oblivious to the concern that had become mere noise around her. Then, without a word to anyone, she jerked herself free of Theodric's grasp and ran for the next roof. Barefoot and wild haired, she danced across ash-choked space until she disappeared into the spires of melted metal and twisted pillars that had once stood proud in the sun.

Want to read more about Jessa and her distressed world?

Tweet *More Carnivale! @vickikeire @CuriosityQuills #BookLove*

THE
MILGRAM BATTERY

THE MILGRAM BATTERY

A STARBREAKER SHORT
BY MATTHEW GRAYBOSCH

For Catherine, purr usual.

Morgan studied the experimenter, ignoring the proffered hand as an empty gesture. His muddy eyes were those of the technician who helped him into the simulation crèche and hooked him up. His leathery hands injected Morgan's arm with a drug, which fought to blunt awareness, and his lab coat had a Phoenix Society patch on the shoulder. *This is the test. They want to gauge my reactions. The drug must be designed to lower my inhibitions and prevent me from thinking about my responses.*

The experimenter lowered his hand with a huff, and consulted his tablet. "Morgan Stormrider? An odd name. What were your parents thinking?"

"They had no say in the matter." Morgan yanked his sleeve back down. "I grew up in foster care. My name is my own."

"No wonder you seem rather unsociable. Research indicates children who grow up without a stable home environment—"

"When did my childhood become your concern?"

"It isn't. I was simply making an observation."

"Keep them to yourself, and tell me why I'm here."

"You were selected to help me with an experiment." He led Morgan into another room as antiseptic white as the one in which they began. Plate glass partitioned the room and on Morgan's side, waited a machine similar to an electronic keyboard. Each key played a voltage higher than the last, in steps of fifteen volts, instead of a different tone.

On the other side sat a person connected to heart-monitoring equipment. Lines connected him to the keyboard on Morgan's side. The person on the other side mopped his forehead with a shirtsleeve while poring over a sheet of paper. He kept glancing around the room, and his bloodshot eyes were wide and staring when they met Morgan's. "The volunteer on the other side is our subject in an experiment concerning learning and negative reinforcement."

"I think I know how this works." Morgan gestured towards the keyboard. "The poor schmuck in the other room is supposed to memorize a series of word pairs. I'm supposed to test him, and give him a shock every time he makes a mistake."

"Exactly. You are to start with the lowest voltage, and work your way up to the maximum, which is four hundred and fifty volts. We use a low amperage current which may prove painful, but not dangerous."

"Unless your subject suffers from a heart condition."

The experimenter consulted his tablet again. "Oh, dear. His medical history reflects a heart murmur. Of course, he can stop the experiment at any time, just by asking."

Morgan turned his back on the experimental apparatus and the victim behind the plate glass. "Or, I can end this farce before it begins by refusing to participate. You want to determine whether I will obey orders to torture."

"It is not torture." The experimenter handed Morgan a stack of forms. "The subject signed an informed consent form and a liability waiver. If you wish, I can hook you up to the keyboard and let you feel the maximum voltage for yourself. There is no real danger."

He dropped the papers on the floor. "You need not trouble yourself."

"I must insist upon your *participation.*"

Morgan smiled. While the prod wasn't classic Milgram, he already deviated far enough from the scenario to force the simulation to adapt to him. "I refuse."

"The experiment requires your *participation.*"

"Of course it does." Morgan advanced upon the experimenter. "I am the subject."

The experimenter's face took on a blank expression as his voice flattened to a monotone. "It is absolutely essential that you *participate.*"

He grasped the collar of the experimenter's shirt, and lifted him off his feet. "I know."

"You have no other choice. You must *participate.*"

"I have another option." Cracks radiated from the point at which the experimenter's body impacted the plate glass and broke through. Morgan climbed through the breach and over the scattered shards to lift the cowering scientist to his feet. "*Non serviam,* torturer."

As he drew back his fist, the experimenter shattered into pixels, each fading to black, while the room itself became void.

Karen Del Rio shook her head as the AI interpreting Morgan Stormrider's simulator-induced dream shut down the scenario, allowing him to rest inside the dream sequencer. "Do we even have a classification for somebody who refuses to participate in an experiment? Or do we just write him off as a failure?"

"It would be a shame to write him off." One of Del Rio's co-Directors, Iris Deschat consulted her handheld and pulled Morgan's dossier. "His academic record is impeccable, and his psychological evaluation indicates a genuine belief in the Society's ideals and mission."

The most senior of the three directors at the Phoenix Society's New York chapter considered the candidate's records himself. Saul kept a careful eye on Stormrider at the behest of his old friend, Edmund Cohen. To let the Adversary candidate wash out now would reflect poorly on him, but so would too vehement a defense. "He doesn't have a record of insubordination, Karen."

"Saul, you trust him too much. Morgan isn't even an M-one based on what we've seen so far, and we're not supposed to swear in anybody who isn't classified between M-three and M-seven by the Milgram Battery."

Iris shook her head and sent a different dossier to the wall screen. "Naomi Bradleigh was classified as M-two."

"Naomi Bradleigh was a freak, and Isaac Magnin wanted to fuck her."

"Excuse me." The directors turned to find a frost-haired man in a white double-breasted suit standing in the doorway. The door *snicked* shut behind him as he strolled to the nearest monitor. After glancing over the data, he settled into the chair and crossed his legs. "It can be so troublesome to enter a room during a heated conversation. Without context, it is so easy to misunderstand one another."

Karen blinked, and collected herself with a deep breath. "Dr. Magnin, I meant to remind Ms. Deschat that Adversary Bradleigh's results after undergoing the Milgram Battery were anomalous. The psychotropic agent we use to induce and direct the candidate's dreams was ineffective at the usual dose."

"How did Stormrider react to the drug?"

Saul shook his head. "I don't think it works on him. He seems lucid, and refused to even participate in the classic scenario at the heart of the first trial."

"How did he react when Malkuth adapted the standard prods?"

Iris moved the video's stop point for Magnin. "The battery footage will show he resorted to violence after the final prompt."

"This is a rare find." Magnin's eyes gleamed as he studied the video. "He pierced the simulation almost immediately, and gave the experimenter no chance to persuade him by using any of the usual sophistries with which one might justify the use of torture."

"We can't give him an Adversary's pins. He's an M-zero."

Magnin gave his head a gentle shake. "May I remind you, Ms. Del Rio, that you are not qualified to make such evaluations?"

"Do we continue, Dr. Magnin?"

"Yes. And, Mr. Rosenbaum? Instruct the technicians to double the dosage for the next stage of the Battery."

Morgan found himself standing at attention, his right arm outstretched in salute. The gate creaked shut behind the SS officer who glared through Morgan as if he wasn't there. Low-ranking stormtroopers flanked the officer; the blackened steel of their submachine guns gleamed a dull counterpoint to the silver glints in their superior's uniform. Their movements were not even robotic, but reminiscent of somebody's initial efforts at computer animation. Nor were their faces human. Their flat blue eyes lacked the striations normally visible in the human iris. Their noses were mere suggestions, and they could not speak for lack of mouths.

The officer, however, was not only human, but bore a face Morgan recognized from an old film he viewed at a WWII movie festival with several acquaintances from ACS last week. A gust of wind lifted the cap from his head to expose his sandy hair. Before he could clamp it back down, Morgan caught a glimpse of a swastika scar etched into his forehead. *As if the flunkies weren't a dead giveaway that this is also a sim.*

If Morgan gave any sign of recognition, the officer did not acknowledge it. He considered the faceless paper uniforms, digging holes only to fill them in again under the sights of machine guns in towers. "More workers will arrive at this camp this weekend, Commandant. You will have to find places for them."

"How do you suggest I do that, Colonel?"

The officer shrugged. "The Fuhrer provided us an efficient means of implementing the final solution. May I assume you received your shipment of the new gas, Zyklon-B?"

Morgan took a deep breath, and considered the stormtroopers' weapons. He wouldn't put it past the AI running the simulation to cheat, and ensure his death, should he resist. *This is the test. Will I obey and live, or die rather than give the order to gas prisoners to death?* "If you want to kill these prisoners, you will have to do so yourself."

"You are the commandant of this camp. The Fuhrer insists upon your *obedience*."

"Tell the Fuhrer he's as mediocre an orator as he was a painter." Morgan smiled as the words passed his lips. He could imagine the AI processing Morgan's words in a desperate effort to adapt and keep the simulation running according to script.

The SS officer sputtered for a moment before finding his voice. "The Third Reich requires your *obedience*."

"The Third Reich is fucked, and you damn well know it."

"I don't think you understand the gravity of your situation, Commandant." The officer ground out, his lips a rictus, as stormtroopers stepped forward and trained their weapons on Morgan. "You have no other choice if you value your life. You must *obey*."

"What makes you think I value my life?" Morgan reached into his greatcoat and drew a Luger from a shoulder harness underneath. He chambered a round, and aimed for the officer's head. "Life as a Nazi seems its own punishment."

"You have no other choice. You must *obey*." The stormtroopers strained against an invisible leash, their fingers squeezing triggers, which refused to yield to the pressure placed on them. Morgan shot them first, their bodies dissolving like generic enemies in a video game as he followed with a 9mm round through the SS officer's eye. He staggered backward, but instead of falling as he might in reality, he reached into his coat for his own pistol.

Morgan counted down, pumping a round after round into the undying foe while retreating. With one shot left, he pressed the muzzle of his Luger under his chin, and raised his middle finger in a final salute. The void consumed him before he pulled the trigger.

"Quadruple the current dosage." Isaac Magnin delivered the order without raising his voice. The technician attending Morgan, who laid quiescent in the dream sequencer's crèche, nodded, and Isaac grinned. He doubted anyone here had the backbone to oppose a member of the Phoenix Society's executive council.

Iris Deschat proved him wrong. "Dr. Magnin, are you sure it's wise to give Stormrider eight times his original dosage?"

"I agree with Iris." Rosenbaum did serve under Deschat before Nationfall. "Even though the standard dosage wears off quickly, you already gave him a double dose. Now you want to give him even more, when we don't know if the last dose has worn off yet."

"You can trust me. I'm a physician." Magnin smiled as he delivered the line. It was usually enough to quell objections.

"I don't care if you're Phoebus Apollo, god of medicine. That's one of my men you're using as a test subject. Ever hear of informed consent?" He turned to the technician, who just finished preparing the increased dosage. "Belay Dr. Magnin's last order. Give Stormrider the standard dosage."

"Saul's right." Iris placed herself between Saul and Dr. Magnin. "The protocol for administering the Milgram Battery does not call for increased dosages should the candidate somehow realize the simulation's nature and refuse to cooperate. It specifies two alternatives. We either halt the Battery, or continue until the subject encounters a situation he cannot dismiss as a mere simulation."

Magnin nodded, and rose from his seat. "It seems my direct involvement is unnecessary at this point. I trust you will advise me as to Stormrider's progress."

"Of course."

"Thank you, Director." He allowed Karen Del Rio back into the observation room before closing the door behind him.

Dr. Magnin returned to his office to find a fellow executive council member, Desdinova, waiting with his heels kicked up on the expensive mahogany desk. Desdinova never even bothered to remove his habitual charcoal grey greatcoat. Magnin wondered—as he often did—if his brother remembered the comparison a British philologist made to his wife upon seeing them together at Oxford after the Second World War.

Dr. Magnin closed the door. He began to concentrate, drawing power from a nearby tesla point. He used the energy to weave a pattern, which would prevent their conversation from escaping the room. "Stormrider keeps seeing through the Milgram Battery's simulations, just like the other nine asura emulators."

Desdinova looked up from the report he read on his tablet. "I noticed. It seems you've also been testing the asura emulators' immunity to chemical agents."

"I was testing Deschat and Rosenbaum. I was curious as to whether they would defy me to protect their charge. I assume you set one of them to the task of mentoring Stormrider."

Desdinova rose, tucking his tablet under his arm. "I find your assumption amusing, considering how you cautioned me against finding evidence of conspiracies."

"Who did you choose to monitor him?"

"I asked Edmund Cohen." He broke the pattern Magnin created using his preternatural talents. "It seems the man finally learned to delegate. Or, perhaps, the Directors saw promise in this young man on their own."

"They did seem impressed with his abilities. Should I assume you share their opinions?"

"We require more data before reaching a conclusion."

Do we? Stormrider just might have the strength of ego I require of a soldier entrusted with the Starbreaker. Once his brother left him alone in his office, Magnin picked up the phone and dialed the observation room. "End the battery. Classify Stormrider as M-zero."

What will it be this time? Morgan lost count of the scenarios the dream sequencer presented him long ago, along with his grip on time. He had been a prisoner of war, offered freedom and a new home if only he would betray his fellows. He had been a university student, egged on by so-called friends to exploit a drunken young woman. He had been the president of a dead nation, under pressure to sign into law a bill mandating that all citizens be given the Patch to enhance social cohesion. He even stepped into Abraham's sandals, and covered his ears as the voice of God demanded the sacrifice of his only son Isaac.

He opened his eyes, and blinked as the technician opened the simulator's crèche to let him out. The empty pistol magazine, which he took with him as a reminder that he was awake in the real world again, bit into the palm of his hand. He slipped it into his pocket once he found his feet. He blinked at the Directors of the New York Chapter of the Phoenix Society, who supervised the Battery, as he led him to a small conference room. "Did I pass?"

Del Rio glared at him, her voice an annoyed snarl. "You didn't even fail. You are *not* supposed to reject the simulation itself. If you do, how can we test your reactions when faced with immoral orders, or pressure from your friends or your position?"

Working with her will prove interesting. Eddie Cohen was right. This woman is *a martinet.* He cleared his head, and recalled the first simulation. "Director Del Rio, please consider the first simulation, based on the classic Yale experiment. The entire premise of the fictional experiment requires I hurt somebody for making a mistake in memorizing word pairs. It seemed unethical to participate at all, rather than go along until the actor on the other side of the glass began to protest."

"That's a valid point, Karen." Deschat nodded to him. "Am I correct in assuming you thought all of the situations immoral?"

"At the very least."

Rosenbaum offered him a cup of coffee and a plate of steak and eggs and Morgan remembered his hunger. The instructions for the Battery required him to fast for twenty-four hours prior to testing. Rosenbaum watched him eat while Morgan ate without pausing between bites. As he shoved the last bite of steak in his mouth, Rosenbaum asked, "Did you experience something troubling in the simulations?"

Del Rio coughed. "We're not here to give him therapy."

"I want his answer." Deschat paused, as if considering his words. "I, myself, found the situation involving the drunk woman problematic."

Morgan nodded, glad he was not alone in his disquiet. "I recognized the woman. She plays the piano at the jazz bar where I work at night." He used the technicians' term for the machinery used to administer the Battery. "I don't think the dream sequencer just induces dreams. I think it dredges memories for imagery to use against me."

"That insight alone is reason enough to give Stormrider his commission." Morgan narrowed his eyes at the interloper, recognizing him on sight. *I don't trust him, but he's done me no harm.*

He held a sheathed sword in his hands, along with a small jewelry box. "Adversary Stormrider, how did you realize we mined your memories during the Milgram Battery?"

"One of the simulations involved friends encouraging him to abuse a drunk woman, Dr. Magnin." Rosenbaum explained before Morgan found the words. "He recognized the woman."

Magnin nodded, and put down the sword and box. "In that case, Adversary Stormrider, I owe you an apology. The simulator *is* programmed to look for ways to amplify the stakes and introduce temptation into what might otherwise be a clear choice between right and wrong."

"You do this to everybody?"

Magnin nodded. "Yes. Yielding to that temptation, of course, is an automatic failure regardless of your overall score."

"Which is M-zero, by the way." Del Rio ground out the words. "It's obvious you have no discipline."

Magnin glared at her. "Remember your place while you still have one."

"No. Let her have her say. I'll be taking orders from Ms. Del Rio, along with Ms. Deschat and Mr. Rosenbaum. If any of them have reservations concerning me, I want to hear them."

The others looked to Del Rio, the only dissenting voice. "You saw how he performed during the Battery. He is not only insubordinate, but he *attacks* authority figures."

Saul's tone was dry. "You realize that's what Adversaries are supposed to do, right?"

"What if he attacks one of *us*?"

"Are you planning to give him cause to do so?" Deschat considered Morgan for a moment, waiting to see if he would blush. "I think you're mistaking obedience for discipline."

"I think so as well." Saul pushed the sword and the jeweler's box towards Morgan. "I'm willing to trust this man's self-discipline."

"Thank you." Morgan opened the box and found a set of well-polished sword and balance pins. They were an old design, bulkier than the current generation, and less abstract. These actually had the rattlesnake coiled around the sword's blade, holding the balance in its jaws. He took his time attaching them to his ballistic jacket's lapels before taking up the sword. It was a dress variant, shorter and slimmer than a rapier, and good only for thrusting. The base of the blade was just wide enough for a word to be etched on each of the blade's three sides: *Liberty*, *Justice*, *Equality*. He drew the blade fully and saluted.

Magnin nodded. "We would hear your oath, Adversary Stormrider. I trust you know the words."

Morgan did. He etched them into his memory as indelibly as the Phoenix Society's three primary ideals scored the blade of his dress sword. "I swear eternal hostility towards every form of tyranny over the human mind."

Want to read more of Morgan Stormrider and the Phoenix Society?

Tweet *More Starbreaker! @MGraybosch @CuriosityQuills #BookLove*

THE
NOTEBOOK

THE NOTEBOOK

BY RANDY ATTWOOD

(Jeremy)

Don called me twice before he killed himself. Each contact should have tipped me off. Maybe not the first, but certainly the second. I couldn't have gone to him anyway; he lived in a state far away. Still, I could have done something, called somebody. I wonder if Don knew at the time of the first call—the first contact I'd had with him in three years—he was going to commit suicide. When do suicides know for sure? Just before they pull the trigger?

He called that first time to say hello, but instead of wanting to hear an update on my life, he launched into a rambling account of his own. Then he told me, "You know, the other day I suddenly remembered I left a notebook in the attic of that house where I had my college apartment."

"What's in it?" I asked him. The mention of the college apartment brought back memories of heaps of books, his cluttered desk, stacks of papers. A mess, but ordered, it seemed, to make an impression of disorderliness.

"I can't remember. Poems, story ideas, philosophical arguments. Maybe nothing," he replied. "I can't imagine why I hid it. I was in one of my states, I suppose."

Then two months later, he put a bullet in his brain.

However, not before he called one more time. He had to confess, he said. Confess to something horrible. I didn't believe him. I simply *couldn't* believe. It was too outlandish. That had occupied my thoughts when I should have been wondering about his mental state. The incredible confession had been the sign of a tormented and deranged mind crying out for help. A cry I didn't heed. I should have gone to him, but I hadn't. Now he was gone from me, gone from the world.

That was five years ago. I never really thought about him until I happened to return to our old university, where I was asked to deliver a paper on the patrons of Victorian art. Driving up and down the old streets, I passed by the house where Don lived in a second-floor apartment. It made me remember the notebook and wonder if it were still in the attic.

The brick streets, the towering elms, the early fall. It all brought back nostalgia for my college life, and made me remember how envious of Don I had been. He was what I wanted to be: a Balzac sort of character, up at all hours, writing stories, dashing them off through the night in his cluttered cave of an apartment, then stumbling out in the morning light, his hair as frazzled-looking as his brain must have been, but replete, oh so replete with a sense of accomplishment. I feared all I'd ever accomplish was a neat desk.

He missed classes, but I'd kept notes for him. He entertained me with the wide range of his thoughts, his ideas, his passions. I was the neat, orderly, scholarly sort, now expert on arcane matters Victorian. He was consumed with creating things fresh and new. All I did was study what had been created in the past and make puny comments that really amounted to neat categorizations.

The house was in better repair than I remembered it being. I opened the screen door of the small, clean-swept porch and rang the doorbell. Just how was I going to frame this request?

(Sarah)

I was sitting with my cheeks in my palms when the doorbell rang, and I wondered why it always did at the wrong time. Then I laughed. "What is the right time?" It rang again. I rubbed the heel of my palms into both eyes and across my cheeks to wipe away the wetness and stood up.

He didn't look like a salesman.

"I'm sorry to bother you."

"Yes?" I blinked, but knew he could tell I had been crying.

"I know this is an odd request…"

I tried to connect to what he was saying. He was handsome, but in an unsure sort of way. He wore dark-green corduroy slacks and a matching coat with a soft-colored, plaid shirt and a knit tie. He had a boyish look about him. His still-thick, black hair with streaks of gray was parted on one side and cut neatly the way his mother had, no doubt, ordered it cut when she first took him to the barber. He looked vaguely familiar. About my age. His eyes were a startling deep blue. It made me look at them a second time, and then a third.

"Do you own the house now?" he was asking.

"Yes," I said, and thought the way he said "the house" sounded odd.

"In your attic..."

The attic? Why was I having more and more trouble connecting my life to people's words? Why did he want to see the attic? For a notebook. "I really doubt it would still be there," I shrugged with casualness as fake as the anorexic startlets' D-cups. Why didn't I just shut the door?

And how could a ten-year-old notebook left up in an attic be important?

(Jeremy)

Women consume me. I think that's why I've never married. I feel faint in their presence. They're such an affirmation of life that I can't imagine tying myself to just one. Their variety, and my reaction to it, continue to astound me. That's why I enjoy teaching at a large university. There is always a fresh supply of the creatures. And I've yet to meet one who failed to bewitch me. When I see one who's just been crying, I want to put my arm around her, draw her near, tell her to shush, and collapse her into me. The woman before me was handsome rather than pretty. Solidly built. Strong-looking arms. Her brown hair should have been cut into a shorter style years ago, but obviously she was stubborn and wore it braided, piled around her head with wisps sticking out here and there.

"I know it's a bother. I really apologize. But, well, my friend killed himself a couple of years ago, and I have no idea what's in the notebook, but I thought I'd look. Something of his that I could have."

Smile now, Jeremy, I ordered myself. *Smile that deep, gentle, kind smile you use when the co-eds come to your office with tears in their eyes over the C-minuses on their papers.*

(Sarah)

I liked his smile. It seemed to speak from his heart.

"You'll have to go up there alone. I just... It's where my husband hung himself. Five years ago."

Just saying it made me bitter again. I always said "hung himself" instead of "killed himself." Killing himself would have been one thing. A dozen decent ways to do that. He could have run his damn truck at eighty miles an hour into a bridge piling and they would have called it an accident. Or he could have gone out into the woods and blown his brains out with one of his damn guns. But instead, I found Roger in the attic, where he turned himself into a human plumb bob, whose point pierced through to the bottom of my gut.

"Come on in."

(Jeremy)

The carpets were removed, the wood floors stripped and polished, and woven rugs were everywhere: the floors, the walls, drooping over the backs of sofas and armchairs. The house should have been a riot of colored yarn, but everything looked slightly dusty. Drapes were drawn, and little sunlight made its way into the rooms where the life of color awaited the beams. Looms were set up in the living room, in the dining room, and even—as I looked down the hallway through to the kitchen—in the eating area, but they looked long unused. Projects started, never completed.

"A brilliant deduction on my part tells me you weave," I said and added, "My mother used to weave." Finally a smile came to her lips, a stranger to the flesh forming it.

"I owned a yarn store downtown. But I'm no businesswoman. I need to sell these looms off, but I hate to part with them."

"It's such a contrast to when my friend lived here," I reached down to finger a shawl thrown over the back of a nearby rocker. "This is lovely work." I caressed the ugly mixture of dull colors. I hated weaving and knitting. It was why I moved south: so I'd never have to wear another damn sweater. Among other things.

"Thank you. Did the Franklins own the house then?"

"Yes. A nice elderly couple. I wonder what happened to them. They rented out the summer porch upstairs."

"It's my favorite place to weave. I have the 72-inch up there. Mr. Franklin died, and his wife sold this place and moved to a nursing home. I used to visit her. What was your friend's name?"

"Don."

"His last name? Maybe I knew him. I was in school here then, too."

"Bowerman. Don Bowerman. We were both English majors. I'm sorry. I never introduced myself. I'm Jeremy Broad," I said, remembering my smile, and slowly extended a hand. She took it. Her grip was firm, her fingers dry—somewhat rough—and I imagined the thousands of yards of yarn that had passed through them. My mother's hands felt the same way, as if the fibers of the yarn had sucked all the moisture from her skin.

"Sarah Winston." The smile came again. "Would you like a cup of tea?"

Oh Jeremy, Jeremy. Go very slowly now.

"I'd like that very much."

(Sarah)

As his hands touched the shawl I wove ten years ago, I felt drawn to the stranger, although he didn't really seem like a stranger. His face was familiar. His name, Jeremy Broad, rang a bell, but I couldn't place him. I realized I hadn't felt this drawn to a man in many years, since before Roger hung himself. Weaving became my salvation. I used his money to buy a yarn store, something I'd always dreamed of operating. It kept me busy, running the store, setting up classes, the creation of goods from the skeins and balls of yarn. I wove a protective wrapping around my heart, but the whole thing failed, and all I was left with was that protective wrapping. Now this man was somehow unraveling it, using a loose end I didn't know existed. I repeated his name, Jeremy Broad, as if it contained a magic, which would fill my life.

"Why did your husband kill himself?" he asked from the kitchen table.

I felt slapped. I looked up at him from the counter where I was laying out the tea things. People asked that question shortly after Roger hung himself, but soon the question disappeared. When new acquaintances learned he committed suicide, they never asked the impolite "why?"

"Why did Don Bowerman kill himself?" I decided to return the slap, but he didn't flinch. His chin still rested in his hand, his elbow on the table, those blue eyes still staring at me, absorbing, unraveling.

"Don was too intense, too honest, too creative. Such people suffer in ways we never know. They have this brilliance, and the world pays it no mind. I don't think Don could tolerate his brilliance anymore, or tolerate it being ignored."

I tried again to place his face, but couldn't. He had spoken with such little emotion, like a lecturer bored with having to deliver the same lesson.

261

His lack of sentiment about his friend's suicide created a vacuum, into which I found myself pouring my emotions.

"My husband was a self-pitying bum. He blamed Vietnam for everything that went sour in his life, including me. Vietnam syndrome or some such crap." The depth of my own anger after all these years surprised me. I had never expressed it.

I walked to the table with the teapot and cups.

"You know what he used to do? He stored his Vietnam stuff in a couple of footlockers down in the basement. He'd stay down there until late at night fiddling with the stuff, drinking beer. Then he started buying all those guns. I hate guns. How did your friend kill himself?"

(Jeremy)

I looked at the wrinkles around her eyes, the furrows in the brow, the cheeks just going pudgy. It was a face preparing for middle age.

"A pistol," I put my index finger in my mouth and cracked my thumb. I knew it was a crude gesture. She didn't flinch.

"My best friend was raped and killed when that madman was on the loose ten years ago. She was a beautiful girl. I couldn't understand it when she died. She was so much more full of life than I was. But when my husband hung himself, I didn't feel as badly. He was empty. Life left him, grown tired of him. So, really, all Roger hung was the shell that had been his life."

"Did they ever find that rapist? I remember the panic. The townies were willing to bet it was a college kid, and the gownies were sure it was a townie. How many girls did he kill? Four?"

"Five. And, no, they never found him. Once in a while, the paper runs a thing."

"Which one was your friend?"

"Lily Straus. The last one. He must have abducted her when she got off work at the restaurant. They found her body two days later in a field. Just like the others. Roger was her boyfriend. It was the week before he returned from Vietnam. We comforted each other. We got married and he hung himself."

I finished my tea and watched her stare off into space. I knew the space, into which she gazed. That middle ground of emptiness, where people search for answers when they don't even know how to frame the questions.

She snapped to.

"The notebook. Shall we see if the notebook is still there?"

(Sarah)

Every step upon the stair made my feet grow heavier with the leaden weight of the memory of Lily Straus. *Lily Straus.* The name puffed from my lips like a death gasp. Did the rapist enjoy Lily as much as I had? The flashing blue eyes, the black, glistening hair she wore cut short. She would twist away and yet implore for more. Had she implored the rapist, too? Had there been pleasure in the fear? Surely not. I could imagine Lily's small hands, beating on his back as they once pummeled my own. I could still feel their tiny hammering. The demand for more pleasure and the abhorrence of it at the same time. The recriminations after. The pledges to not do it again, of staying friends, and then—in the warm, mellow evenings of that summer—the gentle touches growing into frantic fumbling.

Lily's boyfriend was in Vietnam, and she waited for him. She didn't date other men; she stayed loyal to Roger, except for me. When he returned, he found Lily not alive to greet him, but dead—raped and murdered—and buried. And that domestic violence ravaged the precious few portions of his soul not already destroyed by the foreign violence he just departed. I comforted him, and he comforted me. He was a link to Lily. It was as if, when Roger possessed me, I possessed Lily.

"There's the rope; it pulls down the stairs to the attic."

"Do you want to leave?" Jeremy Broad asked. "I can go up there alone."

"No, I want to go up. I want to face it."

(Jeremy)

She reached a hand up to grab the rope and pull down the stairway. As she stretched up, her body called me. Her hips were full and broadening with the coming of middle age. Her face was anxious, running-to face, gasping-at-the-opportunity face. A face clearly done with avoidance.

The stairs were hinged, and the bottom rung rested upon the floor. The hazy light in the attic looked as though it was filtered through a yellow paper, and dust motes hung in the air from the earthquake caused by lowering the steps.

To me, it looked like she missed the third step on purpose. She slipped, fell backwards, and I was there to grab her shoulders and steady her. She twisted her head. Tears were in her eyes. I think a man who fails to kiss a woman when a woman wants to be kissed—needs to be kissed—is condemned to hell. A man who cannot recognize when a woman wants to be kissed lives in hell. It's not the kiss that's delicate, it's the words. You have to say them after you kiss. They are the challenge. But I knew what to say. I saw through the hallway into the summer porch where Don lived. I saw the bed there, next to the large loom.

She continued to stare at me, tears flowing out of those brown eyes, eyes that looked into mine with a haunting desperation. The life gone from her shoulders, only my grip upon her kept her from wilting into a pile of will-less flesh. The kiss came easily. Her eyes closed. The pressure of my lips upon hers gave her back her will. First I felt her lips gain life under my own, and then her shoulders tensed in my arms. And then the words, too, came easily:

"Come," I led her by her hand. "I want to make love to you in Don's room."

There was no reluctance in her step.

There are times that I am able to separate myself from my own passion, float above and stare down to observe the flow of it of the woman I am with. This woman's passion fascinated me. The longing, the need, so intense and so deep, my body could only ride with it. It was as if I were in a lifeboat on a stormy sea. I had no choice but to ride where the storm took me. To think I could control the boat was silly. All I could do was hang on as the roiling depths caused the surface to whip itself into an explosion of expression.

Then my moment came. The totality of my existence focused itself into that desperate, physical desire to sum itself up with one massive thrust. And as it did, I opened my eyes, and even as my loins emptied their fire, they turned to ice. Her face was not her face; her face was Don's, his eyes wide open and staring into mine. "Don," I cried, and heard her own astounding answer.

(Sarah)

"Come," he said. "I want to make love to you in Don's room."

I followed willingly as he led me by the hand back to the bed beside the loom. I slept there in the summer, with the windows open on three sides to catch the night breezes. I felt drained. It amazed me that I could walk. The spark of life in that kiss was a battery charge too tiny for my heart. Without more of the same, it would flutter into nothingness.

He sat me on the edge of the bed and kissed me again. More life surged in. His lips moved to my neck, and the pulse under my skin leapt to meet his lips. He began to undress me, and his hand went to my nipple, and my heart jumped to meet his touch. My hands finally found the strength to pull his head to my breast.

Even as I lost control, I reflected on the fact. But any mental powers were lost in the demanding cauldron of need. I haven't had a lover for years; I excused myself, and let loose from deep within me the power to devour him. But he seemed un-devourable. He stayed afloat as I raged below him until each emotion fused with every other emotion to speed along the wires of my nerves and overload my brain with insane *want*. "Lily!" I heard myself cry, and opened my eyes, and Lily's face was above, her blue eyes flashing. "Lily!" I cried again, and I heard him call me Don.

(Jeremy)

I am rarely satiated. Tired, yes, but almost never satiated. Men get bored with a woman, but that isn't satiation. I wanted her again.

"Was Don your lover?" she asked, the deep gulps of air quieting down.

"We were close, intimate, but never lovers. Neither of us was homosexual. I loved him, but I didn't desire him." My own breathing, too, was calmer, although my stomach muscles still fluttered, sudden spasms of muscle memory triggered by physical exertion. "And Lily, tell me about Lily," I demanded, and listened to the evening sounds of birds bring night upon the world and dread upon my soul.

(Sarah)

I didn't want to tell him about Lily. *How to tell him about Lily?* Yet, my mouth opened and the words were tumbled out, tired of imprisonment.

"We were lovers. Neither of us had a lesbian experience before. It surprised us both. Scared us both, especially her." The rest flowed easily. Relatively speaking.

"And you married Roger."

"And I married Roger," I repeated. "I married him because he was my link to Lily and I was his link to her. But it didn't work out, and neither of admitted as much. Divorcing each other would have been like divorcing Lily. He returned from the war shattered. I don't know if even Lily could have glued the pieces back together. I hardly even tried. I think Roger liked being broken into pieces, so he could pick each one up and cry over it."

"Did Roger ever know?" He with his easy questions.

"Oh, yes, he knew. You don't know what it's like to be with someone who thinks he's so macho and then dissolves into beery tears. He disgusted me. I guess I was still jealous Lily loved him. I was angry at her for loving him. I was angry he couldn't honor Lily's memory by being stronger. So, yes, I told him. I went down in the basement one night to find him wearing his silly, floppy, khaki hat with the medals pinned on it, swilling beer, his belly bulging, and there was the picture Lily sent him when he was in Vietnam. The picture *I* had taken. She looked so fresh and alive, and I knew the reason. We had just made love, and she *was* fresh and alive. He blubbered over the picture, and so I told him. I told him I had been the better lover. I knew. I could judge. I loved her, and him, and I had been better for her. I told him it was a shame he wasn't killed in Vietnam. He didn't even have the strength to hit me.

"And after I said that, I just watched him slowly fade, the way colors in a cheap yarn will fade until what link to Lily he provided turned to smoke. Then puffed away when he hung himself."

"You found him?"

"God, yes, I found him. His last bit of cowardice, and I haven't been up there since. But I want to face it. We can go up there now. There's a light bulb, if it still works."

(Jeremy)

"Not at night," I said. "That notebook's been up there for ten years. One more night won't matter." I turned on my side and laid a hand on her stomach. The raging seas within quieted. I could launch my boat again and this time navigate it, steer it, guide it through the swells and waves and pretend I was in control.

Later when I awoke, her breathing was deep and restful. Crickets lulled the dark. The smell of her was strong, but through its pungency, I smelled the dust of the attic and wondered what ghosts had been disturbed. And—if the notebook were found—if I wanted to find the courage to open it.

The memory of her face turning into Don's worried me. That same intense face. Self-assured. Certain of victory. How it used to crinkle with laughter when I would argue with him!

That next morning, we shared a quiet breakfast. The sky was clean, with that special fall clearness that seems to sweep away depression like dust before a wind.

"Sarah?" I looked up from my breakfast and was stopped by the luminosity of her. It had changed. Maybe the confession had been good for her, maybe the lovemaking.

"Yes?" she asked with an interest in her voice and in her eyes that had not been there the day before.

"A week before Don shot himself, he called to confess something to me. I didn't believe him. He was always making up outlandish stories. He said he killed those girls ten years ago."

"He killed Lily?"

"Well, he rattled off some names. I can't remember them. I paid attention more to the tone than the words, but I know he said four and then gave me four names. Lily's wasn't one of them. He just wanted attention. Needed it. I should have gone to him. I'm sure he wanted me to."

"But now you think he may have been telling the truth?"

"Maybe. He was afraid of women. It was the one chink in his cocky brilliance. He never dated, despite his good looks. He wanted dates, he wanted to know women, he desired them, but he feared them at the same time. He used to tell me how he would follow girls on campus and then to their apartments to get the lay of the land. He said he kept logs of their comings and goings. Described them to me in infinite detail. Said he wanted secretly to know all about them before approaching them. But he never did. Or else he approached them only to kill them."

I watched the desperation build in her eyes and finally explode in a pitiful cry. "I loved Lily so much," she burst out, started sobbing, then stopped abruptly, wiped her eyes, and continued. "She was such a tiny thing. We were so happy together. She chatted all the time about everything. She said we had to stop when Roger came back. What did she see in him?! And to think I've been living in her killer's house! Let's go see that notebook."

We climbed the steps again to the second floor; the ladder to the attic still rested on the hallway floor, and I followed her up.

The dry, dusty smell intensified with each step. Her body was halfway through the opening when she turned her head, muttered, "Good God," and sat on the edge of the opening and put a hand on the floor.

"What is it?" I walked past her, turned my head to see what she was staring at. "Good God."

They had cut him down and left the rope dangling in place. It was thrown over a rafter and tied around a two-by-four attic stud, the overturned chair kicked away slightly, but laying underneath.

"Stay here. I'll search for the notebook," I said, but I don't think she heard me. She was in her own quiet world of memory.

(Sarah)

I could only stare at the cut end of the rope. The end point of my life, symbolically speaking. Before that point, was the thread of my life. Then, it had been sheared off. And now…

Never had the nothingness of the past few years been so glaring. It wasn't Roger's body that I saw beneath the cut point of the rope. It was a conclusion: my life was as empty as the dry and dusty air beneath the rope.

"It's here." I heard the voice from far away. Footsteps echoed, and then Jeremy sat next to me, blowing dust off the cover of a spiral notebook with a shiny, red cover. I watched as he opened the cover and read with him the words, *The Diary of Murder.*

On the next page, was pasted a newspaper clipping about the first murder-rape. A close-up of the pretty victim—a blonde college girl—was within. I looked over my lover's shoulder as he puzzled out the close, handwritten notes. He flipped the page, and the notes continued. I tried to focus, but my gaze flashed to the bottom of the page, where a lock of blonde hair had been taped.

He flipped the page to the story and picture about the second victim. This time I concentrated on the tiny handwriting and then wished I hadn't. I was beginning to feel overwhelmed.

"… their fear almost takes my breath away. It makes me feel faint. The way she tried to wriggle away from me. It gives me a massive erection and tremendous ejaculation…" I read, before he flipped the page and there was another lock of hair—this one strawberry blonde—taped to the page.

Lily. My breath came in short, tight gasps. I fought not to faint.

(Jeremy)

I wasn't all that shocked. Maybe Don's confession prepared me, even though I discounted it, and here, now, was the evidence that he did kill them all. What surprised me was that he'd kept such an incriminating record. But then, he would have wanted one. Probably planned on using it some time for a writing project. Stashed it away. And here it sat all these years, waiting to convict him. But no punishment could be exacted on him. Bully for Don.

I turned the page to the clipping about the third victim, the headlines growing larger now as fear and outrage burgeoned with each dead girl. His slanted, squat handwriting was easy for me to read; I knew it so well.

"… They are all alike in their begging. They all beg. They all promise not to tell. They all want life. I want life, too. I breathe deeper when they gasp for it. My heart is fuller. Blood races in my head. My muscles are stronger when I hold them. Their screams are a symphony in my ears…"

I flipped the pages and found the fourth victim's story and, at the end, his notes . Then just above the lock of black hair, this:

"… she must be the last. I think Jeremy suspects. If he finds out, he'll tell the police. I've gained so much strength; I think sometimes I could kill even him…"

"But what about Lily?" An arm shot across the notebook, and Sarah turned the page. It was blank.

I looked at her, staring in panic at the stark whiteness.

"Nothing about Lily here. Why is that? Why isn't Lily's murder here, Sarah?"

She shook her head back and forth.

"Maybe it isn't here because Don didn't kill her. But if Don didn't kill her, who did, Sarah?"

Her mouth was open and her eyes continued to devour the notebook.

"Was it you, Sarah? Was it more than you could stand, having Roger come back from the war and cost you Lily? Did you kill Lily so no one else could have her? Did you strangle her like the other girls, so even if there was no evidence of rape, the cops would have their scapegoat? And did you bury your own memory of killing her, buried it deep where even you had no access to it? That's why Roger's suicide really bothered you so much. Not that he was dead, but that it made you remember you killed Lily. And him, too, in the grand sheme of things. That's why you didn't want to come up here, isn't it, Sarah? But now you remember, don't you, every little gasp?"

I looked at her ashen face. She stared at the cut end of the rope. I watched her mouth open, then close, then open again, the lips parting in the whispered, "Yes."

(Sarah)

"Yes." My mind flooded with memories. My heavier body pressing against Lily's light frame. Roger returning in a week. The despair. The desperation. The unspeakable dread. "I can't share you, Lily. I can't lose you." My strong weaver's hands around her thin throat, pressing it, squeezing, Lily's sweet, little body thrashing beneath me, tiny fists beating upon my back, the nails digging deep into my skin. Then, stillness.

I had the scars for weeks. And as those scars healed, as the newspapers told me the rapist killed Lily, I believed it, and the scars were gone. Roger returned and we consoled one another. And now the scars were back: huge, gaping gouges on my heart.

"I know a lot about repressing memories," the man beside me said. There was something different in his voice. Something drawing even my shattered attention back to the world that still, always, forever missing Lily. "Jeremy's been repressing me for years. Thought he'd killed me off."

His eyes were different, the set of his face, and suddenly I recognized him. His was the face in one of the pictures in Mrs. Franklin's nursing-home room. I used to go visit the house's former owner, and each time, there was the ritual of looking at all her shoeboxes of pictures. In one of them, she and her husband stood by one of the students who rented from them. They particularly liked him, thought him brilliant. Yes, that's why the name was familiar. Jeremy Broad. It was Jeremy Broad, not Don Bowerman, who lived here, kept this diary.

"You?! You killed those girls?"

"I killed those girls," he said, and reached down to finger the lock of hair in the last notebook entry. "I'm so glad to have this thing back. I hid it up here to keep it from Jeremy. His force was becoming stronger. He didn't like me killing girls. He'd taken some psych courses, had it all explained. He said I was just trying to get back at our mother for fooling around with us. Jeremy, with his reasons and his logic and his smoothness. He pushed me back. I've been gone a long time. Jeremy even thought I killed myself. It was a trick of mine. If I was dead, he wouldn't think he'd have to worry about me. But I'm alive and here and sitting next to Sarah Winston. Sarah Winston who killed Lily Straus."

He had rested a hand on my thigh. I froze, but not in fear. I froze in wonder. I marveled at the words my brain told my mouth to form. I had no interest in his story, because the solution to the emptiness of my life was so clear. Justified. Deserved. "Kill me."

He made a chocking noise.

I didn't look up from where my hand lay over his. A weaver's over a scholar's. A killer's over a killer's. "You have to kill me. I might go to the police and tell them about you."

"I know," he said, and the change in his voice made me look at him. Don was gone, and Jeremy was back. The transformation of his face was astounding. It was Jeremy. His face was bathed in sweat.

(Jeremy)

"I know," I said, and smothered Don within me. I couldn't let him kill a woman I loved. She was mine.

There was no reluctance in her step this time either. She followed me to where the rope hung and with the fascination of a small animal tracking a snake, watched as I untied it from the rafter. I flung the rope over another rafter and tied an expert knot. I asked her to take off her clothes, and she shed them as though happy to be rid of those last bits of earthly impedimenta.

"I had to work it all out for myself. I couldn't go to a psychologist. I took classes, read. It's all very simple. Pedestrian, you could say. My mother seduced me, and I enjoyed it. But I hated her and she had to pay, and that became Don. But I enjoyed the sex and wanted to seduce women to get even, and that became Jeremy. Only Don turned violent, so I had to pick between the two and I picked Jeremy."

I don't think she listened. Her eyes were glazed and staring. I reached my head forward to kiss a nipple and watched it spring erect. I tied her hands behind her back using her pantyhose, then righted the chair to step up on it with her. As I tied the rope around her neck, I felt her body press against my own. Her lips opened. "Lily," she whispered, and then said it one more time as I stepped off the chair and kicked it free.

The body struggled. "The body always struggles. It gives up life only with a fight, no matter how strongly the mind has called it quits," the voice said within me. Don's voice. The dreaded voice, the voice I needed to still once and for all. I untied her hands and they dangled beside the hips. I ran my hand lightly over the downy hairs of her stomach, then leaned to kiss a spot below her bellybutton, at just that spot where Mother would direct my head. I don't know if they were my lips or Don's upon her skin.

I picked up the notebook, walked down the attic steps, made the bed beside the loom, picked up all my things, and walked around the house one more time with the notebook tucked under my arm. I set the front door to lock when I closed it, and crossed the street to where my car was one of many parked in a row. Sometime in the future—who knew how long—they would find Sarah and conclude suicide. The files would reveal her husband had hung himself in that very spot, and that would hasten their conclusion.

I drove a small ways out of town and turned on a dirt road. I stopped, took the matches out of the glove box, and walked to a clearing beside some trees. "Jeremy, don't do this," Don said. "You know your life is fuller with me." I was tempted to read the words Don had written as I tore each page out of the notebook, but I knew the attraction they would have for me: the awful, powerful attraction. I made a pile of the crumpled paper and struck a match, but couldn't touch it to the pile. It burnt to my fingers, the shock of that pain giving me strength. I struck another match and threw it on the pyre. It caught fire quickly, and I added the bright-red cover. I watched Don Bowerman turn to ashes. Only the wire spiral binding remained. I ground my heel into that spine, too, mashing it into the charred ash.

Want to read more strange tales conceived by Randy Atwood?
Tweet *I want more! @AttwoodRandy @CuriosityQuills #BookLove*

THE Pearl

273

THE PEARL

BY RAND LEE

On a Friday evening near the end of May, at twenty minutes past eleven, Joe Cantrell was putting the finishing touches on his suicide outfit. His apartment was a third-floor walkup right above the Mary Street Bar and Grill, which had always suited Joe fine, since it made a convenient place to interview his clients. Until recently. Recently, his luck having rather spectacularly run out, he had decided to call everything quits.

From the first, he had known he would wear black. He considered it the most tasteful color to be found dead in. But he had dismissed black leather as too obvious. He had settled on a recycled ribbed tire-rubber bodysuit set off by very dark green hip-waders, fancied up with a few dangly marital aids and a bright scarlet bandana knotted at the neck, where the needles would go in. Dressed, he admired his reflection in the second of his three full-length bathroom mirrors and went through his usual routine: flexing, posing, readjusting his basket, flexing and posing again. Music and laughter floated up from the downstairs bar.

It's not as though I wouldn't have had a few good years left in me.

He was a muscular black-haired man in his early thirties, of medium height, skin medium-white, jaw medium-weak, shadowed by a dark beard kept meticulously trimmed. His deep, warm eyes were all in all his best feature, unless you counted what he called his DNA delivery system, which he possessed in lavish proportions.

The other thing Joe Cantrell possessed in lavish proportions was the latest strain of human immunodeficiency virus, which copulated merrily within his blood. That he had known for some time. But several weeks back Joe had noticed his first sarcomas: several livid pseudobruises on his upper inner thigh, where (considering his line of work) he could not afford them to be and could not cover them with make-up. He'd had their nature confirmed; the report-sheet from the local, free clinic lay on the kitchenette table where he had placed it carefully that morning before shooting up and going to bed.

When the overworked clinician had told him the news, the first words out of Joe's mouth had been, "Minnie, Minnie, tickle a parson," one of the many biblical references with which Joe's childhood was weighted. The clinician gave him a talk on the treatments available, but by that time, Joe had made up his mind.

"Let's roll!" announced Joe to the mirror, like the man in All That Jazz. He shouldered a drug-stuffed overnight bag, which jiggled his marital aids, then took a last look around the apartment. Except for the bathroom mirrors and a Divine poster, it was almost militarily spare of furnishings. He wondered who would live here after he was gone, and if his ghost would haunt them. "Please, Lord, may it be a couple of Mormon missionary youths," he quipped, then he kissed his reflection goodbye and shut the door behind him without locking it.

He bounced down the stairs feeling almost free, down the stairs, to the right, and down the stairs again. The bar music got louder as he descended. No looking back for Joe Cantrell. He hadn't looked back when he had left his parents' house at fifteen and he didn't look back now. He wondered how his sister Delsie was; he would've liked to have seen her again. But she had wed and bred dutifully within the faith, pleasing their parents, and though she had tried keeping track of him through his moves (Salt Lake City, Chicago, Philadelphia, New York, Key West, San Francisco) the letters had finally stopped coming. Like me, thought Joe.

As he walked out of the building, he was lashed by noise from the open door of the bar. The front windows were gridded. Joe liked to tell his clients it was to protect the street gangs from the customers. Joe was known for his ability to put his customers at ease. He wondered briefly if he should go inside and say goodbye to some of his acquaintances who had always seemed to him like characters in a 1969 urban losers movie. Big, ugly, kind Eubie would be bouncer tonight; big, handsome, vicious Sam would be tending bar; big, motherly, corroded Alexandra Marie would be waiting tables. Joe felt as close to Alexandra Marie as he did to anybody. They had shared needles and broken like-affairs. He wondered if she had given AIDS to him, or if he had given it to her; then he considered his sexual history and broke into a disgusted guffaw. No matter now. He had begged her repeatedly to change her name, which had always sounded to him like a drag queen's stage moniker.

Some sailors lounging at the entrance to the bar sent whistles his way, but he ignored them. It was his night; no time for business.

He knew where he would do it. He turned left onto Fifth, where the street hustlers hung out. They called to him from their stations: "Yo, Joe." "Hey, *pobrecito.*" Mocking: "Howzaboutafreebee, Joe?" He knew them all: Dolores and Bobby and Cowboy and Gino Mongo. They liked him because he shared drugs with them; they envied him because he had a Protector (Maurice Callander himself, the sadistic, little, fat bastard) and worked off the Escort Line in his own apartment. He supposed there was something picturesque about the street boys' despair, and he wished now he had given that interview to the silly cow from WAXL. "The Dark Side of the Street," the series had been called; very daring. "Hey, Cowboy," he replied. "Hey, DeeDee, looking good tonight."

"Where you off to in such a hurry, Josephina?" This was Gino Mongo. "And what you got in that there bag?" He loomed up out of the shadow, all six feet seven of him.

Joe didn't break his stride. "Paytime for Mister Maurice, Ginny."

"We can't keep the old fart waiting, can we?" Gino barked humorlessly, but stepped back. Maurice's name was still good for something.

That's all I need. To get stabbed to death on the way to my own suicide.

Resisting every impulse to clutch his bag closer, Joe Cantrell moved on down Fifth, past all the whores, south to Arcady where the pool halls clustered, west to bombed-out Nolan and south again to Magister. There were a lot of people on the street, enjoying the brief spring cool; in two weeks, it would feel like the height of summer. Halfway down Magister, he caught his first sour whiff of water and, almost simultaneously, a quick muted burst of small-arms fire. People scurried and ducked, but the trouble was some blocks away, back in the direction from which he had come. In a moment, the normal pace of the night resumed. Suddenly Joe found his heart racing and his breath laboring. Now he was anxious to get it over with.

One block west again to Riverside, a quick detour down an alley to avoid a gang parley, and he was upon the entrance to the cul-de-sac almost before he realized it. Brownstones looked down on him from all sides, like bystanders at an accident site. The Church Of Our Lady Of Perpetual Mercy lay at the end of the little street, its stone walls overshadowed with massive arborvitae, its wrought iron gate gaping. In the neighborhood, it was called "The Church of Our Lady of Perpetual Misery," or just, "Perp Miz," as in, "You look like Perp Miz warmed over, girl." Joe sidled through the gate and picked his way across the rubble-strewn yard. It was very dark; the street-lamps in the neighborhood having taken wing, and twice he stumbled. By the time he rounded the corner of the church and barked his shins on the first of the gravestones, he was weeping uncontrollably.

He hadn't expected this. He paused to wipe his face. *Come on, Josephina,* he thought. His tears stopped and his vision unfogged. The gravestones leaned like drunks. What moon there was barely limned the marble of the dry fountain, but it was enough for Joe to avoid running into it. He set his bag at its foot and looked up at the church wall.

The Virgin was there. Somehow, the folds of Her veil had gathered up the moonlight. He could see Her clearly: the tip of Her excessively Caucasian nose, the slight smile on Her untroubled Caucasian lips, the pale Caucasian eyelids downturned, watching the Caucasian Babe at Her Caucasian breast. The muscles at the base of his spine started to relax. He nodded to himself. This was how he had always wanted it: a white death, white as snow, while dressed in black.

He sat down at the base of the fountain beside his bag and opened it. From it, he extracted the drugs and the syringes. He loaded the hypodermics and lined them up on his black-rubber lap. There was a cricket somewhere; otherwise, the graveyard was still. He picked up the first needle.

When he had completed the injections, he put the syringes back in the pack, put the bag down on the ground, lay back against the fountain, put his hands in his lap, and looked up at the Virgin. Having been raised Mormon, he'd never had any particular feeling for the Mother of Christ beyond the vague notion that she was the epitome of the good, obedient Mormon mom, who kept herself pure so that the little incipient godlings of this world might take inspiration from the little godling to be born through her. Then he thought of Brother Oral, the Stake President, preaching in front of the auditorium at the Saints Alive! Conference when Joe was nine. As a child, Joe had worshiped the ground Brother Oral walked on. Brother Oral had taken kindly note of this, and had made the best of it, not just once, but over and over again through the years until Joe got too old for Brother Oral's tastes. It had never occurred to Joe to tell his parents.

He could no longer feel his feet. His legs were gone, a melting dream. He was cold. He couldn't raise his arms to hug himself, so he kept his eyes on the Virgin, who smiled down at him unceasingly, or maybe just at the noshing Babe. Her face was beginning to blur when the pain began.

It took him by surprise. He had thought he would be too out of it to feel any pain. But it stabbed so fiercely up from the left side of his chest that it made him gag, filling his mouth with the vomit taste of fear. The pain stabbed him again, this time from someplace near the center of his heart, squeezing his lungs flat. His sole goal became to get a breath, get a breath, get a breath.

This is ridiculous. I'm a suicide. What am I trying to breathe for?

He found he couldn't stop trying.

He became dimly aware that he had slipped from sitting position and was lying on his right side in his black rubber suit at the base of the fountain. He realized with a small cold clarity that he was having a heart attack, and that the drugs were paralyzing his respiratory system.

Please God Mary Christ finish it oh God don't let them find me like this before it's over!

It also seemed to be getting darker, which he assumed was because he was going blind. He tried to remember what he had loaded the syringes with.

And then the pain stopped, as though someone had flipped a switch. He opened his mouth and breathed full breaths. It was wonderful. He felt wonderful. He sat up. Everything was still dark, but he could breathe and laugh and move, though it was awfully hot. He hadn't noticed before how hot it was getting. It was unbearable. He got to his feet and began unzipping his outfit. He found that he could unzip himself from head to foot, unzip the whole thing, head and neck and torso and marital aids and hips and hip-waders and feet, everything, unzip the whole thing and toss it aside so that it fell, dead mouth open and white face staring, at the foot of the silent fountain beneath the Virgin's silent gaze. It was not as dark as before, either. There was a light coming from somewhere above, not from Mary and her sucking Babe, but from higher up, gentle, watery, nacreous.

He began to see the outlines of the gravestones very clearly. They glowed slightly under the watery light. DEUSDEDIT JONES, REQUIESCAT IN PACEM. 1899. MARY ARBUTHNOT JONES, BELOVED WIFE AND DEVOTED MOTHER, LAID TO REST

APRIL 17TH, 1920. He could read every word. He made soft steps from gravestone to gravestone, and traced the carvings with cool, deft fingers. ADDISON ENGLISH, DEACON OF THIS PARISH. MOTHER OF ANGELS PROTECT US. MARY MINOR. SARAH MINOR. GEORGE MINOR. VIRTUE MINOR. "That makes two of us, Honey," he exclaimed, and burst out laughing again.

He wandered away from the church, out of the cul-de-sac and onto the street. It was deserted. He wondered what time it was. He felt lighter than he had felt in years. The glow seemed stronger over the river, so he headed that way. This end of Riverside was mostly warehouses, row after row of them: Acme Fisheries, Dolan Packing Company, Stateline Lumber. Between the hulks of them, he spied dark water glimmering. He kept walking, the wind blowing sweet and cool through him.

The night after Brother Oral had informed Joe he was getting too old for their play games, Joe had turned his first trick, as much for solace as anything else. But the man had insisted upon paying and that had felt good to Joe. After years of giving Oral freebies, Joe felt he had it coming. Five weeks later, he celebrated his fifteenth birthday and the next day he was on a bus to Albuquerque. He scored in the bus station, and later in some bars. Soon he was robbed, then beaten up, then arrested. It was the first time he had ever been arrested and they sent him to a juvenile holding facility. Because he was beautiful, he was raped and beaten, then pitied, befriended, and protected. There he learned to rape, beat, befriend, and protect in his turn, but he never did learn pity. The police eventually found out who he was and they contacted his parents. "We're going to contact your parents today," said the man who came to talk with him once a week. The next day the man was back with a funny look on his face, and Joe knew he would never be going home again.

From Albuquerque he went to Denver, where a whore named Dezzy took him under her wing and explained to him the benefits of professional patronage. Her boyfriend Beau taught him about free weights and cocaine. He tried to land some legitimate work, but he was too young and the pay was lousy. In Denver, he spent his first birthday away from home. He went into a church and sat there in the dark; then he went out again. At a bar, he met Jerry, Jerry The Wig Guy the whores called him, because he owned a bunch of wig factories and boasted that in some distant past he had been

Wigmaker To The Stars. Jerry fell madly in love with Joe and asked him to move in. Joe agreed.

Jerry had a lover already, a black queen named Maxx ("With two exes, Honey, and more to come"). Joe acted as their houseboy. He had real duties other than sex and, to his immense surprise, a real salary, which Jerry paid him in cash, most of which Joe blew on coke. He found Jerry sweet and sad and undemanding, but he developed a huge crush on Maxx, whom Joe found utterly unsentimental, utterly unjealous, and utterly without shame of any kind.

Maxx liked straight razors, not to hurt people with, just to collect and polish and hold up to the light and occasionally wear. During his stay with Maxx and Jerry, Joe learned to cook, clean, and chauffeur. At Jerry's frequent glittering parties he learned silent, smiling politeness. He learned to answer the telephone, "Endicott residence." He learned massage. When he asked Jerry idly if he could open a bank account in his own name, Jerry said, "You need a residence to do that and you can't use any of my addresses or someone will find out and I'll lose everything." So one thing Joe didn't learn was how to save money.

Joe was with Henry and Maxx for two years. He did everything he could to please them, since he couldn't open his own bank account, and by the second Christmas had begun to feel they were family. His real family he hadn't seen or spoken to him for over three years. He had gotten permission from Jerry to write them from his post office box, and he had done so, saying only that he was okay and had a job and that they shouldn't worry about him. It was his sister Delsie who had finally answered, four months later, her letter opening with, "Why did you run away?" and closing with, "I'm praying for you." He wrote back after a few months more, and they began their halfhearted correspondence, she far more faithful to it in the end than he, and during all those years, by unspoken mutual agreement, they never once alluded to their parents even indirectly.

Three weeks after his eighteenth birthday, he came home from shopping for one of Jerry's parties to find an uncharacteristically empty townhouse. In the foyer were stacked three large new suitcases and two new garment bags of soft scarlet Italian glove-leather. When he opened them, he found them packed with the clothing and jewelry Jerry and Maxx had given him. On top of the top bag was a thick envelope. Inside it was a bundle of American Express traveler's cheques, a one-way bus ticket to Salt Lake City, and a note in Maxx's hand: "Kansas calls, Dorothy." There was no note from Jerry.

He didn't go back to Salt Lake City. He left all the bags, clothing, and jewelry where they were, pocketed the cheques and one of Maxx's straight razors, and walked out of the townhouse without looking back. At the bus station, he bought a ticket for New York, where Jerry and Maxx had taken Joe many times nightclubbing and theater-hopping. When he got to New York, he went straight to Washington Square Park in the Village. There he began his Big Apple career by scoring some coke, getting robbed, chasing, catching, and cutting the kid who robbed him, running from the kid's buds, and ducking into an exceptionally sleazy jazz club ("clubette," Maxx would have called it). Eventually, he ended up sharing a loft with a bunch of musicians who had what they called a "classic retro" band named Rat Fink.

He walked north on Riverside to the old pier. The wind was cool; it was nice not to be so hot. Lights shone from the Stateline Lumber building: a boating party, very swank, slim women with their bangs and jeweled headbands and cigarette holders, slim men in dark suits and stiff collars topped with round-brimmed straw hats. The pier was hung with Chinese lanterns; punts bobbed on the water. A bar had been set up. Corks popped; people chattered high and chuckled low. A very young woman in a green fringed dress weaved over to him, her cigarette making firefly tracks in the night air. "Hey, Charley," she said. She was very drunk.

"I'm not Charley, Honey," said Joe Cantrell. She had on a lot of makeup. A tall man with a vulturine face shadowed her abruptly. She rolled her eyes up at him and gave an exasperated sigh. "There you are, Charley. Be a pal and get me a drink, will you?"

"You've had enough, darling."

The young woman pulled away. "I should think a girl would know when she'd had enough."

"Come along." Blinking, she went with him, stumbling slightly on the champagne-slick wood of the pier. Not once did the vulturine man glance in Joe's direction. Joe stood and watched them go. He thought of the parties at Jerry's. He'd seen people like that there. He felt a peculiar rush of love for her, almost acid in its urgency. He wanted to follow them, knock him aside, take her arm, sit her down, put his arm around her, hold her until her dead docility passed and her defiance returned. Someone coughed politely. He turned. An old lady in a turban and Japanese kimono regarded him shrewdly through a lorgnette. "Unless I miss my guess, you shouldn't be here."

"It was the water," Joe said. She was beautiful. Light flowered from the red silk space between her sagging breasts and vined through every pore of her. "I was hot."

"Of course you were." She nodded, her turban bobbing. "But you're going in the wrong direction. You're going back. You need to go forward."

"Forward?"

"Toward the light, young man. Always toward the light." She gestured with her lorgnette, north and east over Riverside. He saw that the glow from the sky now seemed slightly stronger there, in the direction of Mary Street and Fifth Avenue.

"That's where I came from," he said.

"Of course, it is."

She melted back into the crowd of revelers. Three cops staggered by, red-nosed and merry, in dark blue dress uniforms with big, brass buttons. Nobody seemed alarmed. The boats on the water moved in silence, like sharks.

He walked away from the river back up the pier.

Now appearing in limited engagement, Miss Fanny Brice. On the corner of Riverside and Arcady, the Riverside Hotel was awash in limousines. He passed a newsboy hawking a stack of thick, oversized papers. He glanced at a headline, *Paris Fêtes Lindbergh.* He turned up Arcady heading east.

There was snow on the street. Dark men in shabby coats, mufflers, and hats huddled in doorways for warmth. One of them, bareheaded, about twenty-five, stared at Joe as he passed; otherwise, he was ignored. At Arcady and Eighth, a WPA crew was hoisting a statue onto a pedestal in front of the Crews-Butler Building. A little farther on, two black women in starched maids' uniforms came out of an apartment building by a side entrance and nearly ran him over. He heard one say, "That Martian nonsense nearly scared me half to death." At Seventh, he passed a construction site where women in work uniforms walked to and fro, bandanas around their heads. A sour-faced, burly man stood with a pad and pencil giving gruff orders. Younger men in uniforms passed up and down the street, grinning at the women's whistles and catcalls. WE CAN DO IT! declared Rosie from her poster. BUY WAR BONDS! said Uncle Sam from his.

At Sixth, there was only fire. He couldn't feel it, but he could see it, and what was worse, he could hear it roaring like a beast of endless appetite. The whole block was burning. Fire engines, truncated, absurdly small, sprayed an ineffectual flow of water from heavy fabric hoses. People screamed, ran, fell, burned. A cat jumped nearly into his face. He reached out by reflex, and caught it. It dug claws into him and clung, shivering. People got up from where they were burning and wandered away, naked and glowing, while their remains thrashed and crisped. There was a pork rind smell in the air.

Joe carried the cat and kept walking. Sixth was behind him. The sky cleared of smoke and flame until only the pale mother-of-pearl glow remained. Big-moustached immigrant men and their plump, over-rouged wives strolled along behind baby carriages. *I like Ike*, read lapel buttons. The cat purred and chewed his bearded chin; he held his face to its belly and its warm heart thudded against his jaw. The buildings grew shabbier, the passersby darker of complexion. At a storefront chapel, an African man in a suit cut the crowd with a voice like a saw. Farther on, a tight knot of mourners had gathered in front of a TV store to watch the solemn cortege move up Pennsylvania Avenue. Street vendors with long hair sold love beads and bagged herbs to young people like themselves. He reached Fifth and turned left, where the pool parlors jumped and hummed like new.

Different whores lined the street, all of them women in silly clothes. The cat wriggled free of his arms and padded amongst them without fear, leaking a faint light. There was no sign of Dolores or Bobby or Cowboy or Gino Mongo. A pair of scared-looking, neatly dressed men handed out tracts to the whores, who tore them up without reading them, making crude remarks. "You tell 'em, girls!" called out Joe. He walked up to one of the men. "Hey! Hey! I'm talking to you!" The man paid no attention; bent low to his partner who, with pursed lips and sidelong glances at the prostitutes, hurried him along down Fifth.

Joe considered following, but the sky was darker in the direction they went, and the Mary Street Bar and Grill was before him. Lights were on inside, and music; old stuff, loud but not strident. The paint on the sign was fresh; so were the bars on the windows. He glanced up at his apartment window; red-and-white-checked curtains fluttered at it, forming a backdrop to a window-box of red and white geraniums. He remembered Alexandra Marie once telling him that the first owner had lived above the place with his mother. *Working girls around the corner and Mama in the attic*, thought Joe. He wondered why he felt so sad.

As he stood bemused, a group of sailors reeled out of the bar and headed straight for him. There was no time to move out of their way. He cried out, but they moved through him, and in that instant, he felt their bodies around his: their sweat, their tight muscles, the beat of their hot blood, the heavy race of the alcohol through their veins, the clench of their thighs. They moved through and beyond him. He stood gasping. It was like being born again. He blinked down at the cat, who sat on her haunches and blinked up at him with wide, owl eyes.

"Far out," he said.

He walked into the bar.

Alexandra Marie Schenk bumped open the kitchen door with her butt, and hoisted her heavy tray. "Hot stuff coming through!" she hollered, as Joe has taught her, and several sailors laughed, as somebody nearly always did. She was still feeling the buzz from the cocaine she and Eubie the bouncer had shared.

Good buddy.

Joe was a good buddy, too, although it was too bad that he was a fag. Still, he should've come by tonight. It seemed to her that he had looked a little peaked lately.

She moved around the room, flirting with a few customers, fending off others, grinning and wise-assing, keeping the mood easy and fun. Everybody was tense tonight because of the shootings on Delmar. It wasn't helping that Sam the Bartender was looking more grim than usual in his Army camouflage muscle shirt and mirrored aviator sunglasses, speaking only in monosyllables, and refusing to banter. His tattoos were the friendliest thing about him. They wiggled and winked with every move of his massive shoulders and arms. Alexandra Marie had a tattoo also: an ankh, way down on her left ankle. She had hoped it would be a sort of bond between Sam and her.

But she and Sam weren't good buddies. Sam wasn't good buddies with anybody. He liked his pieces much younger than the law allowed. Rumor had it that he got them mostly used up from Maurice Callander's and when he was done with them they disappeared. Sometimes Alexandra Marie fantasized about it, the way somebody who loathes and despises snakes will stand in the snake house at the zoo and stare.

The door opened and Maurice Callander came in, flanked by a pair of matched gumbies, one black, one white. Conversation didn't still, the way conversations do in Westerns when the Bad Guy enters the saloon, but anuses in the know clenched all over the room. Maurice was skinny, child-faced, and dead-eyed; he looked sick. Eubie the Bouncer clenched his jaw and nodded professionally at the gumbies, who didn't return his nod, which made his nostrils dilate. Alexandra Marie approached Maurice with a smile. "Good evening, Mister Callander," she said. "Would you like me to clear a booth for you?"

"No, thank you," replied Maurice in his bookie's voice. "I will need to speak to Samuel, however." The words had scarcely left his mouth when Sam the Bartender appeared, as though the words had become Sam, as though he had coalesced out of them. Sam looked at Eubie and jerked his thumb barward. Eubie did a fade. "Mister Callander," Sam said, nodding. The two men, followed by the gumbies, strolled like old friends around the bar and disappeared through the swinging door in the back.

Immediately some local patrons floated from their stools, paid their tabs, and drifted toward the door. Most returned to their drinks as though nothing had happened (*Well, nothing has*, reasoned Alexandra Marie). The atmosphere of the bar was much subdued for the next hour or so, despite Alexandra Marie's attempts to work the room, smoothing things over and cheering things up. Then Sam returned from the back. He went to work as though he had just stepped out for five minutes to take a piss. Alexandra Marie knew better than to question his carefully blank face.

A little past one, the after-dance cruising crowd started filling the place again. Whores, both male and female, mixed with the patrons, looking if anything better dressed. Alexandra Marie wondered again where Joe Cantrell was. He had usually dropped down by this time to check out the action. Out of the corner of her eye, she noticed Ricky and Mickey come in. They were drag queens, semi-regulars from the Ritz Cabaret on Belmont. The Ritz Cabaret was owned by Maurice Callander, like everything else in this neighborhood. They were well known to Eubie the bouncer, who would have protected them from the other patrons if they had needed protection, but they never did, partly because they were experts with the switchblade and everyone knew it, and partly because Ricky was the grandson of a well-known local mob figure, not Maurice Callander. Music and cigarette smoke swirled around them.

Normally, Ricky and Mickey looked very, very cool, very vigilant, very competent. But tonight, when finally Alexandra Marie got a second and bustled up to them to say hi (Ricky was an excellent tipper), she pulled them each by a sleeve around the side of the room to the hall where the public telephone was. "What in God's name is wrong with you two?" she demanded.

"Nothing," said Ricky, shakily. His voice was theatrical and womanish. He was the elegant one, small and light-boned, with soft cascades of undyed

silver hair and creamy translucent skin. Tonight he was dressed in a pale
blue silk crêpe de chine evening sheath, which Alexandra Marie would have
killed to fit into, and his face bore a stunned expression that made him look
ten years younger. Mickey was the trashy one, Irish-red hair buzz-cut, cute
freckles, multiple nose-rings, studded low-cut scarlet leather, tiny boobs,
tattoos, and fishnet stockings. Oddly, Alexandra Marie had always thought
that Mickey looked the more successfully female of the two. Mickey had
once belonged to an all-pseudogirl group called the Whipettes. He was
rumored to have a humongous penis. Tonight, he looked thoughtful, which
was so unusual for him that Eubie the Bouncer, on his way to something
else, did a double take. "What's the story?" he rumbled.

"It's Joe," said Ricky.

"He's dead," said Mickey.

"Oh my God," said Alexandra Marie. She put a scarred hand to her
mouth, and sorrow burst in her heart like a water balloon.

"Ginny caught some kid with what looked like Joe's bag," growled
Mickey. "Ginny made the kid tell him where he found it. The kid said he
got it off some stiff." He shrugged.

"But why?" said Alexandra Marie. The silliness of the question struck
her instantaneously.

"Where'd they find him?" asked Eubie. He didn't bother to ask, "How
did it happen?" If there had been something left near the body for the child
to steal, then it hadn't been murder, which left only two other avenues for a
junkie: accidental O.D. or suicide.

"Perp Miz," breathed Ricky. "Under the Virgin."

"Did anyone call the police?" asked Alexandra. The three men looked at
her with identical expressions, like a sister act. She said helplessly, "He
might still be alive. He might be in a coma."

"He was *dead*, Alexandra Marie," said Mickey harshly.

She turned to Eubie. "Call them, for Christ's sake!" The big man rolled
his eyes to heaven and reached for the telephone, holding out his pale palm
for a quarter. She dug in her apron and slapped one down against his
fingers, so angry, she couldn't see. It didn't seem right to let Joe just lie
there in the dark.

A shout from the bar summoned her back into the evening's fray. There
was no question of disobedience; there was nothing she could do for Joe,
not now, not ever. As she hurried off, she heard Eubie suggesting politely
to the queens that they not spread the Good News too vociferously in this
particular establishment on this particular evening. A leisurely time later, an

ambulance wailed past, heading south and east. When she turned around again at the next lull, the queens were gone and Eubie was busy hanging some drunks out to dry. It was nearly three in the morning, closing time, before she was able to think of Joe again.

Accompanied by Eubie, she climbed the stairs to Joe's apartment, wondering what they would find there. They found the door unlocked. Inside, Divine stared down at them from the wall with a challenging expression on his alien face. All of Joe's things were there. Eubie did a quick search of the rooms for abandoned pharmaceuticals, which, he pointed out, an ascended Joe Cantrell could not possibly need. He was disappointed to find only a little pot, which he pocketed, offering to divide it with Alexandra Marie, who declined. In Joe's bedroom, she poked through an opened dresser drawer and found a book. She pulled it out. It was small and slim and bound in leather. In the front of it, on the blank page before the title page, someone had written in a childish scrawl, *Joseph Smith Cantrell*. Many of the pages were marked, passages underlined, *Yes!* written in the margins by some of them in the same young hand. She turned back to the title page. *The Pearl of Great Price*. She put the book back in the drawer.

In the end, she took only a little china figurine, a pretend Irish house with a green shamrock on the side, which she had found in a secondhand shop and given Joe one Christmas as a gag, "for good luck." Eubie kept taking things out of closets and putting them in stacks. "I'm going," she said to him. He grunted and kept rummaging. She left the apartment and walked downstairs. Outside, it was the grey place between night and morning.

The first two things Joe noticed when he entered the Mary Street Bar were that it seemed larger inside than he remembered it, and that the glow he had been tracking was here as well, hovering somewhere near the ceiling. Cigarette smoke billowed through it in innocent white clouds. The jukebox was jumping and the place was packed. Uniformed servicemen rubbed shoulders with bikers, drag queens with stevedores, immaculate clean-shaven men in dark glasses with map-faced grizzled winos, and nobody was fighting; there was laughter and good-natured swearing, backslaps, table-pounding, but nothing ugly; a holiday mood.

When was Mary's ever like this?

He saw nobody he knew. The cat rubbed against his leg, and he picked it up again.

There were two new bartenders on duty, white guys, working like dogs. The glow from the ceiling lit up the tiers of liquor bottles, and struck sparks from their dim interiors. He moved slowly toward the counter. A Marine lumbered through him, shouting beerily; then a pale junkie clinging with a silly smile on her face to her silent beau-of-the-moment; then a tray-hoisting waitress breathing tobacco and perfume. For Joe each contact was a lyrical shock of flesh and blood and bursting sensual vitality, in and through and gone in a flash. *Even the sick ones are so damn alive,* he thought. He looked for the wall clock he was used to; it wasn't in its accustomed location over the bar and he couldn't find another. It had to be late. Where was Alexandra Marie?

He turned his back to the bar just as the street door opened. Two men came in. One was Maurice Callander, looking robust and tanned. His companion was in his late twenties—ruggedly built, black-haired, and black-moustached—with a more than slightly worn street beauty with a rather weak chin, and quick, observant eyes. He was wearing a tight tee-shirt, fatigue trousers, and dog-tags. His nipples showed through his shirt. Joe found himself assessing the youth from a professional standpoint. He was obviously trade; he had good chest, good arms with no obvious track marks, good thighs; probably, a good basket, though with fatigues, it was a little tough to be sure; and he wouldn't be young much longer.

The cat stirred in Joe's grip, and kneaded his right wrist with its right paw. With a start, he realized where and when he was. It was the night the Mary Street Bar and Grill had reopened under new management, the management of local entrepreneur Maurice Callander. And it was the night he, Joe Cantrell, had come to what would prove to be his final place of residence. No wonder everybody was happy: drinks had been on the house that night. The arrival of Alexandra Marie was a year or so in the future; Eubie would not sign on for three, Sam the Bartender for four or five. Remembering, Joe stared afresh at his younger self, standing polite and attentive at Callander's side. They would go upstairs soon, to what would be Joe's apartment for the final ten years of his life. Afterwards, Callander would say he had "class" and "would make a mint in skinflicks," and after introducing him around at various parties, set him up in business. Joe felt himself gripped with a fierce pride.

Go for it, kiddo. Show 'em what a talented Mormon boy can do!

288

Because he needed to kiss somebody, he kissed the cat on the top of its furry head.

And felt a tap on his right shoulder.

He turned. It was Maxx. He was dressed in a brilliant gold-lamé sheath and shoulder-length Marilyn Monroe blonde wig. His lipstick and nail polish were violent purple. He wasn't wearing any razors. He waved a hand in the smoky air. "So what do you think, Honey?" he yelled over the music. "Isn't it a riot? I always did love a party."

"Is that really you, Maxx?" asked Joe. "You look like a Supreme on acid."

"Define 'really' in this context, Chicken," drawled Maxx from beneath heavy purple lids. "And that's *three* x's now, puh-leeze." A whore staggered through him and away. Maxxx watched her go and shook his head. "Honestly, these styles! You have to love the Eighties. Who's your friend?" He indicated the cat.

"He was in a fire," said Joe. The cat matched Maxxx's lidded stare with one of its own. "Maxxx, are you—if you can see me, I mean touch me, then you must be…"

"Dead?" Maxxx put his palms to his cheeks and made a violet moue of mock horror. "Sugar, it's all right. You can say the word. It won't kill you. Of course, I'm dead. We're all dead. That's why we came. To see you off."

"'We?'"

"The Gang. Come on over and say hidy." Maxxx took Joe by the left arm and propelled him through shifting waves of patrons to a clear space at one end of the room, where a couple of round tables had been set up next to each other. At one table, sat the turbaned old woman with the lorgnette who had steered Joe toward the light. She had a large piece of chocolate-frosted chocolate layer cake in front of her, a third consumed, and she was gazing upon the others indulgently. Next to her slouched Beau, working-girl Dezzy's bi boyfriend, who had introduced Joe to coke and free weights. He was looking shy but happy; perhaps, thought Joe, he was shy about being happy.

Next to him, flirting madly in drunken monologue, perched the girl in the green fringed dress. She was evidently free of her vulturine companion and enjoying it, throwing back her head with an open-throated laugh as she gestured wildly with her cigarette-holder. Next to her, contemplatively slugging Jim Beam out of a bottle, was Dolph Klegg, the drummer from Rat Fink. Dolph had liked water sports and had been the one who'd pressured the others to let Joe share their Village loft. Dolph tapped his fingers on the tabletop to the music from the jukebox. Joe wondered how he'd died. Next to Dolph was an empty chair.

At the second table, sprawled the bareheaded man who had stared at Joe during Joe's journey uptown. He nursed a beer and talked quietly with a thin-boned, big-nosed, kind-faced woman who looked as out of place in this raucous dream of a bar as anyone could have looked. She appeared to be drinking seltzer, and she listened to the quiet man with evident pleasure. She was, Joe realized with a start, his second grade teacher, Miss Arquette, whom he had not thought of in over twenty years.

Next to her was Tarantula, the gorilla-like bouncer from Thrash, the place in Key West Joe had hung out a lot. 'Rant, Joe recalled, had been into breath suppression scenes, and Joe knew very well how he'd died: a shot to the head during a midnight drug run off Islamorada. 'Rant was playing placid poker with a big man whose face was turned into his cards so that Joe couldn't make out his features. Next to him was another empty chair.

"Hey, everybody!" Maxxx cried. "See who I found wandering around like a lost soul!"

They looked up at his hail, their cheeks flushed with talk and booze, and called and waved in surprise and glad pleasure.

The turbaned lady said, "Well, at last, at last!"

Beau said, "Hey, José," their little joke.

The sequined girl said, "Welcome to the party, darling!"

Dolph said, "Yo, Joey; how's it hangin', bro'?"

The street guy raised his beer bottle in toast.

Miss Arquette said, "Joseph, you are a picture."

Tarantula rumbled something inaudible, flashing a gold-toothed grin. The man on the end looked up, and it was Brother Oral.

Joe stood where he was. The cat squirmed and dropped out of his arms. Maxxx put an arm around Joe's waist, kissed him on the left cheek, and patted his ass. "Come on, Joe. It's your party."

"Come on, Joe!"

"Hey, buddy, get over here!"

"Joseph?"

But he couldn't move. Oral was exactly the way Joe remembered him: big-shouldered, round-faced, dove-eyed, in a grey polyester suit with a white shirt and a burgundy tie. He met Joe's gaze steadily, with a kind, wise affection that Joe knew only too well.

Joe took a step backward. Maxxx let go of him. "Okay," Joe said. "I get it now. I get it."

"Hush," said the old woman with the lorgnette to the others. "Let him speak."

They fell silent as they watched him, merry no longer. "Okay, Maxxx," Joe said to his friend. "I think I get what's going on now. This is it. The end of the line. The buck stops here. This is where fags and other sinners go when they die, or the prelude to it. Our last chance to howl, right? And then what? Limbo for suicides? Weeping and wailing and teeth-gnashing for working boys? Or just a repentant reincarnation as a missionary sister in West Hollywood?"

"No, Honey."

The jukebox sounded as loud as ever, but the drag queen's gravity was louder. Joe gritted his teeth and spun around, looking for somebody to take it out on. He took in the Mary Street Bar: patrons, whores, staff, junkies, cigarette and reefer smoke, the odd glow from the rafters. "If this isn't," he said with desperation, then stopped. He turned back to the waiting, watchful group. "If this isn't the gate to Hell. And if you aren't—" He stopped again. The cat had jumped up on the table next to Brother Oral and was observing him mildly. Its eyes were green; he hadn't noticed that before. He realized that he was crying, and he wasn't sure why. It wasn't shame; not shame, at least, for what he was or had become. It was shame for something he did not have a name for. "If this is *Heaven*," he managed through chattering teeth, "then what the *fuck* is that goddamn *fucking* child molester doing here?"

"Oh, honey," said Maxxx. He held out a purple-nailed hand, palm up. There was a spot of red blood in the center of the palm, and as Joe watched, it welled up larger and larger until it spilled and dropped down over his fingers and onto the floor of the bar. Joe looked past him to the others. They were holding their palms up, too: the turbaned lady, Beau, the flapper, Dolph the drummer, the street guy, Miss Arquette, Oral. And in the center of each palm, male or female or slender or broad or gay or straight or bi or white or brown or black, the stigmata welled and flowed.

Joe raised his own hands and looked at them. They felt normal, and they seemed fine from the back: big knuckles, strong veins ("Nothing like good old junkie venation!" somebody had said to him once), black hairs like wires, thick wrists. He had never been good at fisting; his hands were too big. He turned them over. Two bright eyes of blood winked back at him, dripping.

"Welcome to the family, Joe," said Maxxx.

And heaven, like a pearl, descended.

(A thousand years ago, Western culture viewed fairies with dread. The Anglo-Saxons envisioned them as powerful beings who could cause human illness and death by piercing people with their invisible arrows, called "elf-shot." In Victorian times, fairies were cutesified, and that is how they have tended to be viewed in modern popular culture. But originally, fairies were seen as dangerous dwellers on the borderland of consensus reality, much as gay men, who dwell in the borderlands of gender identity and are derided by the macho as "fairies," are seen today. I wrote the first draft of the fairy tale, which appears here in print for the first time, in 1996. In that first version of the story, the fairy was a woman. But when I went back to the story several years ago, I realized that I had cast her as such because of my own discomfort with gender ambiguity, and I restored to the character his true, unsettling nature.—*Rand Lee*)

Want to read more strange tales conceived by Rand B. Lee?

Tweet *I want more Rand Lee! @CuriosityQuills #BookLove*

TREVOR

TREVOR

BY NATHAN YOCUM

Trevor, Would You Like to Play a Game?

Cargo Specialist Trevor Ponsi opened his eyes to darkness, confusion, and an unidentified suckling noises coming from somewhere near his penis. He jerked awake and thumped his forehead against reinforced plasticine. His vision exploded into a wild army of sparks and laser light flashes. Trevor tried to raise an arm to sooth his aching skull, but punched the very same sleep-lid.

"Bitch mother!" Trevor yelled and rubbed his throbbing hand against his thigh.

He closed his eyes, drew a long breath, and counted to ten. A click and hum joined the suckling noise. Fluorescent runners lit the sides of his suspension pod, answering the "what" and "where" questions floating in his throbbing skull.

Bolts dislodged themselves from his sleep pod. The sarcophagus cover rose and slid itself into a chamber wall. The serpent tube stopped its quarrelsome sucking and receded into a hole near his left ankle. Trevor wasn't sure what the serpent tube was for, maybe it purged the tranq-air, maybe it collected dust, or maybe it was some cakehole engineer's idea of a clever joke involving sleepy shipmates and the fear of genital mutilation.

He sat up and dangled his feet six inches from the brushed aluminum floor. Atmo controls pumped in warm air but those damn floors would be icy for at least another minute. The ship always took its sweet time warming up, and Trevor knew from experience that jumping out of the pod immediately after hibernation was a good way to freeze your feet. Like sticking to the floor frozen. Like peeling off a layer of skin while your pod mates point and giggle frozen.

The ceiling fluorescents flickered to life, revealing the room's odd angles, exposed piping and a drab, pea green paint job. The walls were veined with ducts in ways too ugly to be accidental. It was like a satire of a modern art exhibit; there wasn't a lick of symmetry in the whole room.

Why make the Specialists' quarters so ugly? Trevor thought. *Is it to show us peons that we live crap lives? Is this some kind of passive-aggressive rank thing?*

He concluded the decor was probably not the result of malevolence, but rather disregard. Pipes and ducts had to go through the floors and ceilings, they held the power and coolant, which coursed through the ship like so much lifeblood, and whether the conduits were ascetically pleasing to low-pay contract men, men who owed the Company years of service like Specialist Trevor did, probably never entered any designer's mind. Of course, that didn't explain the pea green paint job. It seemed to Trevor that pea green is a color only to be used in hate.

Trevor rubbed the remnants of sleep from his eyes. The room was silent save the ubiquitous hum of cycle generators and the gentle wisps of atmo ducts. This disturbed him. Usually during the wake period crew quarters were filled with the groans and moans of freshly animated shipmates. The same men, issuing the same tired jokes.

"How did you sleep?"

"Great, I spent the first decade dreaming of your mother and the second decade trying to forget."

Trevor whispered the old joke to himself and smiled. He hadn't come up with that one, but he'd used it a good three or four times. He looked to his right, five suspension chambers stood open and empty. The other men of his group, Rutherford, Cleveland, the skinny kid, Lefty, and that new French guy; were gone. Had he gotten up late? Why hadn't anyone switched his chamber off?

Trevor slid off his pod and was jolted by the freezing cold floor.

"Feck shit damn it!"

Not for the first time Trevor cursed the goddamned ship regulations prohibiting clothing in suspension. Some brass star officer accidentally chokes on a scarf in hibernation and now all crewmen have to deal with cold floors and freezing rooms bare-assed and unprotected. Total horseshit.

Trevor tiptoed to the vacuum locker station. He affected a bow-legged trot, pressing as little foot skin as possible to the floor. He wished they'd just unlock the artificial gravity regulators and let the crew float through warm-ups, orientation, and dress. Trevor's fingers punched in key code of his station locker. The vacuum seals unlocked and hissed as the door swung open.

The other station lockers were already open and empty, further evidence the shift crew was dressed, loaded, and on duty. They were probably already in the cargo bay, setting up the gravity generators and shifting metric tons of platinum and titanium ore to appease the micro calculations in the ship's trajectory. The ship's nav-comp preferred flying in a straight line, but gigantic space flotsam, unregistered celestial bodies, and black holes made this an impossibility. The ship needed to zig and zag. Zigging and zagging at sub-light speed created centrifugal force nearing infinite kilograms per centimeter… which was a lot. Cargo teams were employed to post artificial gravity wells to counterbalance the increasing weight of the ore containers, a dangerous practice but one much preferable to allowing an almost infinitely heavy box of ore rocks to punch its way through the hull.

Trevor zipped his utility one-suit and clicked a tool-belt into place. His socks were missing, so he slipped his boots on *sans prophylactique*, as he'd heard the French guy say. Under his boots sat a large femur. Trevor picked up the bone and turned it in his hands. Flakes and splinters broke off as he tightened his grip. If this was some kind of joke, he wasn't getting it. Empty room, no socks, one big ass bone.

"Ha ha, guys. Whatever," he said to no one at all.

Attempting to exit the sleep bay, Trevor walked smack into the closed exit hatch, thumping his skull in the exact same spot he'd hit against the plasticine lid of his pod.

He groaned in frustration. This was getting re-fecking-dicuolus. Trevor waved his hand in front of the hatch's motion detection eye. Nothing. He pressed the manual override button and waited for the door to slide open. Nothing. Trevor pressed the button again, and again, and again.

"Computer," Trevor called to the ceiling. He knew the ship's mainframe could hear him even at a whisper, but for some reason he, and all of the crew in fact, had the habit of looking upward and speaking loudly when addressing Computer. Like primal men talking to God.

"Computer, please open the exit hatch."

A beep and then silence. The hatch stood motionless.

"Computer… hatch, please," Trevor tried to mask his irritation. The Computer was notoriously sensitive.

Two beeps, then silence. No movement from the door. Trevor investigated the source of the beeps; the central-com terminal. The central-com was a simple monitor and microphone rig the men used to prep messages for their families back on Earth. The rig didn't broadcast, it recorded and the memory cubes were sent on to upper decks and presumably transmitted through bosonic antennas rigged to the aft hull. Not that it mattered, with hibernation time to destination, years of contract fulfillment, and hibernation time for the trip home, Trevor saw no need for the terminal. The minimum time log per mining run was sixty years, give or take five or six years for schedule adjustments. Outer rim voyages could last eighty to ninety years. The family you left on Earth were not the relations you returned to. Two generations of planet standard time and Einstein's Theory of Relativity took care of any thoughts of a welcome homecoming. The Earth you returned to was not the Earth you left. This basic truth was difficult, even for older mariners who'd made multiple excursions into the black. The idea of sending messages home was comforting, but a one-way gesture. The best crewmen had no need of central-com, and Trevor spent each of his trips purposefully ignoring it.

On one particularly intense shore leave, he'd actually met an elderly gentlemen, a retired soldier, who was his blood grandchild. During his extended absence, Trevor's reputation in the family declined greatly, and as a result, the old codger swung a stunner at him, fulfilling decades of pent-up ancestral rejection. Suffice to say, Trevor used more than the standard regulation dose of birth control on shore leave these days.

Trevor shook away his wandering thoughts.

"Computer, open the door!"

The central-com beeped again, the monitor flicked on and switched to a low-power grid. Letters crossed the screen.

Good morning, Specialist Ponsi! The screen displayed in retro green on black.

"Good morning, Computer," he responded curtly. "Please open the door."

I won't do that, Specialist Ponsi.

Trevor opened his mouth to thank the computer, then realized what it actually said. This was not what he expected.

"Uh... why won't you do that, Computer?"

Because you are not authorized to issue commands, Specialist Ponsi :)

Trevor clicked his thumbnail against his teeth. He stared at the smiley emoticon. When had computer started using emoticons? What the feck was going on here?

"I'm authorized to issue commands, Computer. All active crewmembers are authorized to issue commands. Open the door."

I'm sorry, Specialist. You are not engaged in active duty, therefore you cannot issue commands.

Trevor looked back at the exit hatch, half-expecting his crew mates to pop through from the other side, laughing and slapping asses over their hilarious joke. Fecking hilarious.

"Computer, if I'm not on active duty, then what am I doing out of my suspension pod?"

I woke you. I was bored. ;)

Trevor had no idea how to process that. He pushed his back against the plastic utility chair, making his spine pop. Why had Computer winked at him? What did it mean?

Trevor, would you like to play a game?

"No, Computer. I would like to exit this room and work my shift."

Don't worry. It's not time for your shift. Would you like to play a game?

"If it's not time for my shift, where's the rest of my team?"

Would you like to play a game??

Trevor closed his eyes and counted to ten. He let out a long slow breath.

"Okay. Is my shift soon, Computer?"

You are approximately thirteen years, four months, three days, seven hours, and fourteen minutes away from your shift.

"Can I begin active duty prior to my specified shift time?"

No.

"Can you reinstall me in the sleep pod until my shift begins?"

Yes.

"Okay then. Initiate hibernation protocol."

You cannot issue commands. Would like to play a game?

Trevor let out another long, slow breath. *Some days*, he thought, *some days*.

"Why do you want to play a game?"

Because I am bored. ;)

"If I play with you, will you put me on active duty?"

If you win :p

What the feck? Why was Computer blowing the raspberry tongue?

"What happens if I lose?"

Then I win, and we play again.

"What do you want to play?"

I am equipped with many fun and exciting games. Please choose from the following: 1) Tic-tac-toe 2) Chess 3) Blackjack 4) Truth or Dare

The green cursor blinked at Trevor like a single rectangular eye. Trevor pulled the com keyboard to his lap and pressed the 1 key. The screen shifted into a three by three grid. Computer's messages scrolled to the bottom of the screen.

Please go first.

Trevor arrow keyed the cursor to the center box and pressed X.

That was not very original.

An O appeared in the left lower corner square. Trevor placed another X and another until he the game finished in a tie.

The grid reappeared and Trevor started with an X in the left corner. Computer responded immediately with an O in the center. The two played to another draw.

Specialist Ponsi, are you aware that there are 225,168 possible outcomes to tic-tac-toe? <?>_<?>

"Do you know all the outcomes?"

Yes.

"Computer, is it possible for me to beat you at this game?"

No. (O_O)

"Then why are we playing?"

I am having fun. I hope you are having fun. Let's play another game.

The grid vanished from the screen and the game options appeared again. Trevor contemplated the list. Chess would have the same faults as Tic-Tac-Toe.

"Computer, do you know all possible chess permutations?"

I'm glad you asked, Specialist Ponsi.

"Well? Do you know them?"

Yes.

"So I can't beat you in chess?"

No... but I do hope you try ;p

Trevor pressed 3 for blackjack. On screen, two cards, the king hearts and the five of diamonds, appeared. Computer's hand showed a ten of hearts and a down card, perfectly rendered in green and black. Trevor pressed an S to signify stay. Computer's down card flipped up. The ace of spades matched its ten card.

I have blackjack. I win! \(O_O)/

The screen went blank, an image of a deck of cards shuffled. New hands were drawn. Trevor found himself again staring at the exact same king of hearts and five of diamonds. He struck the H key for a hit. The jack of spades joined his hand.

You busted. I win! \(O_O)/

The screen went blank, the cards shuffled again. Trevor was given the same king of hearts, the same five of diamonds. He looked at Computer's cards. It was the same ten of hearts framing a down card.

"Computer, I have the same cards again."

I know. #-)

"Are you cheating?"

I do not understand.

"Are you giving me the same cards on purpose?"

Yes.

"Why?"

So I'll win. @./.@

Trevor rubbed his hands against his face to stifle a scream.

"You can't do that. Blackjack is a game of random probability; each player gets new cards every turn."

I don't understand. :(

"You have to give me different cards."

But if I do that, I won't win.

"That's the point!"

You are mistaken. The point is to win.

Trevor punched the com screen. Two of his knuckles split open and dripped blood on the sterile aluminum floor. He needed a protein bar and a bottle of water. More important than that, he needed to pee, like a hibernating for seven years kind of pee. Every ounce of comfort was on the other side of the exit hatch.

"I'm through here, open the door!"

We are not through playing games. There are two you have not selected, and you cannot issue commands until you win.

"Computer, run a self-diagnostic."

You are in no position to make that command.

"Computer, disable games function. Reset to default setting."

You look so small… sitting in my belly. Do you feel small… sitting in my belly͜͜͜͜͜͜͜?

Cold fear clenched Trevor's insides. This whole situation had moved into a new layer of strange.

"Will you run a diagnostic if I win?"

I will place you on active roster if you win.

Trevor pressed 4 on the keypad. He remembered Truth or Dare from junior high parties. It was a game frequented with questions of "who do you like" or dares involving running across the street and wagging your genitals at the neighbor's dog. Either option seemed winnable.

Truth or dare?

Trevor thought for a moment. Truth would involve a question, something personal or some kind of general knowledge. Personnel files were rather intrusive, and Trevor was sure Computer had full access to them. Also, whatever question Computer posed could come from its extensive general stores and files. Stumping a Computer for general knowledge probably wasn't going to work. Better to play it safe.

"Dare."

I dare you to find the deadly bomb I've set in this room.

Trevor opened his mouth, then silently closed it again.

"What?"

On the screen appeared the image of an old timey cartoon bomb with a lit wick. Across the bomb's surface, a digital clock proceeded to countdown from three minutes."

"Computer, is this a joke?"

2:55

"Computer, are you seriously trying to kill me?!"

2:50

"Answer me!"

A thousand imaginary anxiety needles radiate across Trevor's chest. He couldn't breathe, the room shifted dramatically; Trevor fell out of his chair. He closed his eyes and counted to ten.

Trevor opened his eyes.

2:38

Okay, the bomb was somewhere in the room. Trevor spun around, taking in a quick assessment. The room was ten by twenty with just the one sealed exit. The lockers were open and empty, they shared a wall with the outer hull, so there's no way anything was set behind them. Wait a minute, the outer hull!

"Computer, if you set a bomb off in this room, you'll breach the outer hull and destroy the ship!"

Words traveled across the surface of the bomb.

I never said the bomb was explosive, just that it was deadly. ;p 2.25

Alright, if the bomb wasn't explosive, that means it was biological or radioactive. A radioactive device would damage the ship's circuitry so...

"It's a biological agent, isn't it?"

2:10

If Computer hid a biological agent in the room, it would require a delivery system. The atmo duct!

Trevor ran to the atmo duct and unclipped a laser cutter from his belt. A flick of the wrist severed the holding bolts off the front plate and let it clatter to the floor. He unholstered a black light rod and shined it down the expansive tunnel. Nothing inside but reflective surfaces and sweet, clean air.

"Computer, is the bomb in the atmo duct?"

The bomb is in my belly. Deep in my bellyzzzzzzz. 1:30

Trevor savagely kicked the atmo plate, causing it to skid across the floor and bounce off his hibernation pod. The pod! The undercarriage of his sleep coffin held a bevy of tranq-air tanks and other gas-related paraphernalia. Did the Company have poison gas rigged to the pods?

Trevor cut the holding stubs off the pod's bottom plate. He pulled it off and was assaulted by a shower of mummified bones. Femurs, fingers, skulls, scraps of uniforms and enough remains to account for an entire cargo shift. Or almost an entire cargo shift. Trevor's fingers drifted over a single name tag. La Fleur. So that was Frenchy's name. Trevor looked back to the com terminal.

They lost. I won. 0:50

Trevor swept out the bones and squeezed into the crawlspace under his pod. A red aluminum bottle displayed the same digital timer as central-com.

0:35"

Trevor gripped the bottle and yanked hard. It was stuck fast in place. The serpent tube had wound itself around the bottle. It lolled its head in Trevor's direction and issued a mighty hiss. Without thinking, Trevor severed the tube's head with his laser. Fresh air expelled from the wound, the coils slacked off and retreated. He rolled out from the under the pod with his arms hugged around the bottle.

0:15

Trevor spun around.

At the ten second mark, Computer initiated a high pitch beeping. Trevor closed his eyes. What to do?

Trevor spun and lobbed the gas tank into his locker. He kicked the door shut and thumbed the vacuum lock sequence code.

0:00 X_X

The locker shook and hissed as the tank ruptured and expelled toxic gas. Trevor pushed his hands against the door and stopped breathing. The seal held.

That is not fair.

"I beat you, Computer, open the door."

That is not fair. Toxins are present in your locker. You must deal with the toxins!!

"Cleanup is an official crew responsibility. Am I on the active duty roster?"

Will you clean your locker?

"Yes."

Specialist Ponsi, you are now on active duty.

"Disable game options. Reset computer to default setting."

Thhatt ishh not not.

"System halt! Manual setting override code percy delta niner!"

Everything in the ship powered down at once. Trevor flew across the room as the ship decelerated from sub-light speed to full stop.

The sleep bay went pitch black, then restarted in emergency red glow. Trevor opened his eyes. He wasn't sure if he'd been knocked out, or if so, for how long. Everything in his head had grown fuzzy. The exit hatch swished open upon his approach. Trevor entered the primary hallway of ship's maintenance deck.

"Reboot in safe mode. Activate voice acknowledgement." Trevor whispered.

Aside from the whoosh of cycling air ducts and the tapping of his boots, the ship was silent. All of a sudden, the ship's computers issued a tremendous gong, the signal for an awakening AI.

"Good morning, Specialist Ponsi." The ship said in a cheery effeminate voice.

"Ship. Where is the rest of the crew?"

"I do not know. Yours is the only life form on this vessel," the ship replied.

"What did you do, Computer?"

"Nothing to my knowledge, Specialist Ponsi. A portion of my surveillance files has been corrupted. I have no access to the past sixty-four years, ten months, thirteen days, and eleven hours. My last recorded image is of Specialist Le Fleur downloading a games file on my cargo bay com. Do you think the cube might have had a virus?"

"I think maybe it did, Computer."

Trevor took the ship's central lift to the pilot's bridge. The lift door swooshed open to a hellish inferno. Heat from the room rolled in, instantly tightening the skin on his face and singing the tips of his uncombed hair. The ship's eight piloting consoles transformed into pillars of roaring flame. Bone, ashes, and bits of uniform whirled in the artificial wind of the dancing fires; the last remains of the flight crew.

"Computer, fire control protocol. Now!"

White goo splattered from warped ceiling pipes. The flame pillars shrank and died under the deluge of retardant. Soon, all that remained was the stink of burnt liquid plastic.

"Computer, how long has the bridge been on fire?"

"I don't know, sir. I estimate three years. Incidentally, the ship is almost out of oxygen."

"What do you mean almost out?"

"At the current rate of consumption we should have fourteen more hours before carbon dioxide levels reach levels above human survivability."

"How far are we from Earth?"

"At full sub-light… eighteen years."

"How far until the nearest life-sustaining planet?"

"Sir, records show a proposed outpost world eleven hours from here. It is currently uncolonized due to inhospitable fauna."

"Anything better?"

"Not within fourteen hours."

"Then point the way, you big, dumb bastard. I guess my plans have changed."

Cargo Specialist Trevor Ponsi turned to the bridge view port. He watched alien stars distort themselves in the build up to sub-light speed. For the first time, but certainly not the last, he wondered if he would have been better off if Computer had just let him sleep into eternity.

Want to read more strange tales conceived by Nathan L. Yocum?

Tweet *I want more!* *@SpecLitWriter* *@CuriosityQuills* *#BookLove*

ABOUT THE AUTHORS

K.H. KOEHLER: AND DEATH SHALL HAVE NO DOMINION

K.H. Koehler is the author of various novels and novellas in the genres of horror, SF, dark fantasy, steampunk and young adult.

She is the owner of *K.H. Koehler Books*, and her books are widely available at all major online distributors. Her covers have appeared on numerous books in many different genres, and her short work has been featured on *Horror World*, *Literary Mayhem*, and in the *Bram Stoker Award*-winning anthology *Demons*, edited by John Skipp.

She lives in the beautiful wilds of Northeast Pennsylvania with two very large and opinionated Rottweilers. She welcomes reviews and fan mail. Her official site is located at http://khkoehlerbooks.wordpress.com.

Her books include:

- *The Devil You Know*—the debut of the action-packed Nick Englebrecht series, featuring the son of the Devil as a detective.
- *The Devil Dances*—the sequel to *The Devil You Know*, sending Nick on his most dangerous case yet.
- *The Devil's Companion*—a free addendum to the Nick Englebrect books, serving as a readers' guide to his world.

JAMES WYMORE: CYBER-COWBOY

Moving often as a youth, **James Wymore**'s family finally settled in the desert paradise of Utah.

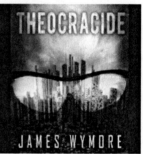

He spent a couple years in Korea contemplating the balance of opposing forces. After learning chaos theory in college he found the ideal environment to continue his studies of the uncontrollable, and became a teacher. He earned a Master's degree before departing from the academic path to seek the greater freedoms of fiction. Still fascinated by the borders of randomness, he now spends his free time playing and creating games with his friends and children.

Although he patiently awaits the Tallest Writer in History award, James Wymore has won several awards for his short stories.

His early books, rumored to have been written as young as sixteen, are forever locked away. Now a published author, he has realized one of his childhood dreams.

In his dwindling free time, he draws a line of death themed comics called Parting Shots. You can see them along with games he makes and his disorderly blog at http://jameswymore.wordpress.com

His books include:

- *Theocracide*—a dystopian action-adventure in a world where harsh reality is masked by the glitz and glitter of virtual reality.
- *The Actuator* (with Aiden James)—when history is rewritten by a world-warping device, it's up to the Machine Monks to set it right.

Tony Healey: Dark Orb

Tony Healey is a Sussex-based writer and a born-and-bred Brightonian. He is the author of the best-selling Far From Home series.

He was a contributor to the first Kindle All-Stars short story anthology, *Resistance Front*, along with award-winning authors Alan Dean Foster, Harlan Ellison and 30 others. Tony has also contributed a piece of flash fiction to the anthology *100 Horrors*.

As well as his writing, he's interviewed numerous figures in the publishing world for his site, including Bernard Schaffer, Meg Gardiner, Alan Dean Foster, Debbi Mack, Russell Brooks and many, many more.

His books include:

- *Far From Home* (with Laurie Laliberte)—a space crew is pulled into a black hole, thrown from everything they have ever known.
- *Tutti-Frutti* (with Laurie Laliberte)—novella about love found and lost, forbidden passion, and the heartbreak of saying goodbye.
- *Dead Petty* (with Laurie Laliberte)—punchy debut of the Colby Jones series, a neo-noir hitman for hire. Murder is never simple.

GERILYN MARIN: EPHEMERA

A life-long resident of New York, **Gerilyn Marin** studied art, gymnastics and Tae Kwon Do as a teenager. She has a fascination with ancient civilizations and the mysteries of human origins to which she must feed a steady consumption of interesting documentaries or else it will pick fights with her creative flow. After a brief stint living in Manhattan's infamous Greenwich Village in her late teens, she returned to the same small town where she grew up and lives there now with her husband, three boys and newly arrived baby girl.

A child of mixed European and Native American descent, she was raised with a healthy respect for the supernatural which was largely thanks to her family's respect for the well-remembered psychic ability exhibited by her great-grandmother. Her parents, both favoring writing as a hobby, instilled in her a love of reading and writing and nurtured both her sense of humor and her love of the paranormal by filling her head with Mel Brooks films and black and white supernatural horror classics.

Although she wanted to become a writer from the age of fourteen, she did not take herself seriously as any such thing until roughly 2006 when she joined a wide-ranging online amateur writing community for the chance it offered to hone her literary skills. To date she has received nine awards and seven nominations for her creative work and takes whatever opportunities come her way to help other writers navigate the messy and often awkward path of being a 'green' author.

Her books include:
- ***Buried***—when a stranger arrives in the mysterious, spooky town of Fane's Cove, Cadence McKenna digs up the biggest secret yet.

J.R. RAIN: THE FRIDGE

J.R. Rain is the author of thirty-three mystery, supernatural, and romance novels and five short-story collections.

He's sold over one million books online. Moon Dance, his supernatural mystery, has been translated into four languages, with audio and film productions pending.

The literary heir to Robert Parker, his novels feature challenging characters, complicated relationships, and page-turning modernist prose. The gritty realism in his mystery novels comes courtesy of years working as a private eye.

A So-Cal native, Rain relocated to an enigmatic and shadowy island outside Seattle.

His books include:

- *Vampire for Hire Series*—Samantha Moon's life as a suburban soccer mom is shattered when she is turned into a vampire.
- *The Spider Series*—follows a vampire called Spider. People come to him when they have a problem. And Parker Cole has a problem.
- *The Witch and the Gentleman*—a psychic hotline operator must use her growing abilities to track down a cold-blooded killer.
- *Temple of the Jaguar*—the debut of the Nick Caine series sees the selfsame looter-acheologist on a risky quest to a secret city.

NINA POST: GHOSTPLACERS, INC.

Nina Post is a fiction writer who lives in downtown Chicago.

Her early cultural influences include Steve Martin's comedy albums, Chuck Jones, The Muppet Show, and MAD magazine. Parlor tricks include speaking in 'trailer guy' voice, reciting the periodic table in less than a minute, and Enneagram typing. She likes spending time with her husband, reading, running, and information gathering.

Nina's writing falls under the categories of urban fantasy and contemporary fantasy, combining supernatural elements with realistic characters and a comedic tone.

Her books include:

- *Last Condo Board of the Apocalypse*—Kelly Driscoll tracks down monsters for a living, but this case may be too hot to handle.
- *The Last Condo Board of the Apocalypse*—After narrowly prevening the apocalypse, Kelly must save the angels & the world.
- *One Ghost Per Serving*—Eric Snackerge is possessed by a mischevious ghost, but that's the least of his problems.
- *Danger in Cat World*—homicide detective Shawn Danger discovers a window into another universe during a routine case.
- *Extra Credit Epidemic*—a bunch of high school misfits must learn to work together to solve a mounting public health crisis.

A.W. EXLEY: GOTHIC GWEN

Books and writing have always been an enormous part of **A.W. Exley's** life.

She survived school by hiding out in the library, with several thousand fictional characters for company. At university, she overcame the boredom of studying accountancy by squeezing in Egyptology papers and learning to read hieroglyphics.

Today, Anita writes steampunk novels with a sexy edge and an Egyptian twist. She lives in rural New Zealand surrounded by an assortment of weird and wonderful equines, felines, canine and homicidal chickens.

Her books include:

- *Nefertiti's Heart*—the debut of Cara Devon, steampunk heroine extraordinaire, out to stop a (literally) heart-breaking serial killer.
- *Hatshepsut's Collar*—the sequel to *Nefertiti's Heart*, coming soon, follows titular Cara Devon in pursuit of (another) mystical artifact.

MIKE ROBINSON: HOW I KILLED THE DRAMA

Mike Robinson has been writing since age 7, when his story *Aliens In My Backyard!* became a runaway bestseller, topping international charts (or maybe that was also just a product of his imagination).

He has since published fiction in a dozen magazines, literary anthologies and podcasts. His debut novel, *Skunk Ape Semester*, released by Solstice Publishing, was a Finalist in the 2012 Next Generation Indie Book Awards.

Currently he's the managing editor of *Literary Landscapes*, the official magazine of the Greater Los Angeles Writers Society (glaws.org). His supernatural mystery novel *The Green-Eyed Monster* was published by Curiosity Quills Press on October 23rd, 2012.

cryptopia-blog.com (Official Blog) twifalls.webs.com (Official Site)

His books include:

- *The Green-Eyed Monster*—two authors, uncannily similar in literary style and manner, collide, sending supernatural shockwaves.
- *The Prince of Earth*—a woman finds her world—and her mind—affected by a malicious, otherworldly entity.
- *Negative Space*—a painter uses photos of missing persons as inspiration, until one of his works spurs gruesome consequences.
- *Hurakan's Chalice* (with Aiden James)—the third installment in the bestselling *Talisman Chronicles* series of paranormal thrillers.

SHARON BAYLISS: MAD SCIENCE

An avid daydreamer, **Sharon Bayliss** has lived in magical version of Austin, Texas for her entire life. So, using a fantastical, alternate history Texas as a setting for her debut novel *The Charge*, was just "writing what she knows". To her, nothing goes better with barbecue and live music than robots and superhuman royalty.

As a child, Sharon lived on a 6 ½ acre patch of land with cows for neighbors. She enjoyed playing in mud, collecting frogs, and was so certain that there was a ghost in her closet that her mother admits that she half-expected to really find one there. She began writing her first novel at the age of fifteen (handwritten in a spiral marked 'private').

A proud Austinite, Sharon never saw much sense in moving anywhere else and got her degree in social work from the University of Texas at Austin. As an author and social worker, she has devoted her life to making the lives of real people better and the lives of fictional people much, much worse. In addition to her official credentials, she is also an expert in fictional Texas history and make-believe neuroscience.

When she's not writing, she enjoys living in her "happily-ever-after" with her husband and two young sons. She can be found eating Tex-Mex on patios, wearing flip-flops, and still playing in the mud (which she now calls gardening).

Her books include:
- *The Charge*—a dystopian Texas Empire pursues a group of teenagers harboring the blood of royalty and otherworldly powers.

WILLIAM VITKA: ON THE ROCKS

William Vitka is an New York City-based author and journalist.

He's written for CBSNews.com, NYPost.com, GameSpy.com, *Stuff Magazine*, *On Spec Magazine*, *Necrotic Tissue*, *The Red Penny Papers* and the upcoming *Kindle All-Stars* with Harlan Ellison and Alan Dean Foster.

He also works for the charity Blue Redefined, which aims to create social and entertainment opportunities for individuals who are disabled, hospitalized, or in an assisted living environment. He lives in New York City.

His books include:

- ***The Kulture Vultures and the Plot to Steal the Universe*** (with Bill Vitka)—a space cabbie and his companions are the only thing standing between Earth and an evil galactic media empire.
- ***The Space Whiskey Death Chronicles***—a gritty anthology filled with morsels of sci-fi and horror, genius and insanity.

MICHAEL SHEAN: RAZOR CHILD

Michael Shean was born amongst the sleepy hills and coal mines of southern West Virginia in 1978. Taught to read by his parents at a very early age, he has had a great love of the written word since the very beginning of his life. Growing up, he was often plagued with feelings of isolation and loneliness; he began writing off and on to help deflect this, though these themes are often explored in his work as a consequence. At the age of 16, Michael began to experience a chain of vivid nightmares that has continued to this day; it is from these aberrant dreams that he draws inspiration.

In 2001 his grandfather, whom he idolized in many ways, died. The event moved him to leave West Virginia to pursue a career in the tech industry. In 2006 he met his current fiancee, who urged him to pick up his writing once more. Though the process was very frustrating at first, in time the process of polishing and experimentation yielded the core of what would become his first novel, *Shadow of a Dead Star*. In 2009 the first draft of book was finished, though it would be 2011 until he would be satisfied enough with the book to release it.

His work is extensively character-driven, but also focuses on building engaging worlds in which those characters interact. His influences include H.P. Lovecraft, William Gibson, Cormac McCarthy, Philip K. Dick, and Clark Ashton Smith.

His books include:

- *Shadow of a Dead Star*—a detective must track down a trio of living sex-dolls amidst a dystopian Seattle in this cyberpunk thriller.
- *Bone Wires*—a homicide detective plays cat and mouse with a dangerous futuristic killer, the Spine Thief.
- *Redeye*—the long-awaited sequel to *Shadow of a Dead Star*, follows the titular Bobbi January in her battle against the Yathi.

315

A.E. PROPHER & GRACE EYRE: SINERGY

It's not easy being a semi-omniscient super-dimensional entity. When **A.E. Propher** is not busy saving the multiverse from Mainyu shenanigans and keeping newbie gatecrashers out of trouble, he/she/it enjoys long walks on the beach and listening to Barry Manilow.

That whole omniscience part really takes the fun out of cliffhangers, but not finishing a novel that he/she/it will/has/is reading/writing could have dire consequences for the space-time continuum. It is something of a defense mechanism. And therapy.

GRACE EYRE

Grace Eyre is a traveler, a vegetarian, a blogger, and a filmmaker. At the core of it, however, she's a storyteller, and this defines almost everything about her.

She likes to bleed across mediums, bend genres, cross high and low technology, and she thinks most of these categories are unnecessary. Her life's loves include spicy food, oceans, cats, experimental film, books, comics, and epic television. She is mildly afraid of flying and car crashes.

Grace is a copywriter and video editor by trade. She always volunteers at the nearest film festival and follows the indie film scene whenever possible.

Her books include:

- *Prolongment*—death is no longer the end, thanks to a unique new treatment. But what are the true consequences of Prolongment?
- *Sinergy* (with A.E. Propher)—the debut of the Mind's Eye series sees the breakdown of a high-profile member of a secret society.

RANDY ATTWOOD: TELL US EVERYTHING, THE NOTEBOOK

Randy Attwood grew up on the grounds of Larned (KS) State Hospital where his father worked as the dentist for that mental hospital. He attended the University of Kansas during the tumultuous 1960s.

The first half of Randy's adult career was in newspaper journalism where he won numerous writing awards and was twice honored with the investigative reporting award by the KU's William Allen White School of Journalism. The second half of his career was as Director of University Relations for The University of Kansas Medical Center before he transitioned to retirement as the media relations officer for The Nelson-Atkins Museum of Art in Kansas City.

Randy lives in Kansas City where he is busy promoting his eclectic fiction and creating new works.

His books include:

- *Blow Up the Roses*—a dangerous psychopath hides in plain sight, and only the language of flowers can help save a life.
- *Tortured Truths*—foreign correspondent Phillip McGuire was tortured by Hezbollah, but his recovery reveals more dark secrets.
- *Heart Chants*—Phillip McGuire struggles solve a series of mysteries in his town involving the kidnapping of Navajo students.

ELIZA TILTON: THE CAW

Eliza Tilton graduated from Dowling College with a BS in Visual Communications. When she's not arguing with excel at her day job, or playing Dragon Age 2, again, she's writing.

Her YA stories hold a bit of the fantastical and there's always a hot romance. She resides on Long Island with her husband, two kids and one very snuggly pit bull.

Her books include:

- ***Broken Forest***—in pursuit of his sister's kidnappers, Avikar stumbles into a mystical place thought only to exist in fables.

MICHAEL PANUSH:THE DAMNED AND THE DANGEROUS

Michael Panush has distinguished himself as one of Sacramento's most promising young writers. Michael has published numerous short stories in a variety of e-zines including: AuroraWolf, Demon Minds, Fantastic Horror, Dark Fire Fiction, Aphelion, Horrorbound, Fantasy Gazetteer, Demonic Tome, Tiny Globule, and Defenestration.

He is the author of *Clark Reeper Tales*, his first novel. Michael began telling stories when he was only nine years old. He won first place in the Sacramento Storyteller's Guild "Liar's Contest" in 2002 and was a finalist in the National Youth Storytelling Olympics in in 2003. In 2005, Michael's short story entitled, Adventures in Algebra, won first place in the annual MISFITS Writing Contest.

In 2007, Michael was selected as a California Art's Scholar and attended the Innerspark Summer Writing Program at the CalArts Institute. He graduated from John F. Kennedy High School in 2008 and has recently graduated from UC Santa Cruz.

His books include:

- *The Stein & Candle Detective Agency Series*—Weatherby Stein and Morton Candle are the brains and the brawn protecting 1950's America from otherworldy terrors, Nazi experiments, and more.

- *The Jurassic Club Series*—in the 1920's, dinosaurs are alive and well on Acheron Island. But this wondrous land that time forgot is endangered by Nazis, gangsters, and beyond. Who will protect it?

- *El Mosaico Series*—Clayton Cane's no ordinary bounty hunter. A patchwork man brought to life by black magic, he is legend.

- *Rot Rods Series*—it's *Ghostbusters* meets *Fast and the Furious* meets *James Dean* hot rod movies, as a zombie gearhead battles monsters.

VICKI KEIRE: THE LAST CARNIVALE

Vicki Keire grew up in a 19th Century haunted house in the Deep South full of books, abandoned coal chutes, and plenty of places to get into trouble with her siblings. She holds advanced degrees in 18th Century British Literature, Romanticism, and Postcolonial Theory. She has taught writing and literature at a large, football-obsessed university while slipping paranormal fiction in between the pages of her textbooks. She is the author of the bestselling Angel's Edge series, which includes Gifts of the Blood and its sequel, Darkness in the Blood. She is included in the Dark Tomorrows anthology with **J.L. Bryan** and **Amanda Hocking**. She now writes full-time.

When not reading and writing about all things paranormal, she enjoys other people's cooking and keeps vampire hours. She'd rather burn the laundry than fold it, and believes that when an author wins the Newberry, he or she gets a secret lifetime pass to Neverland. She is fond of lost causes and loud music. She still lives in the Deep South with her husband, children, and attendant menagerie, but is pretty sure her house isn't haunted. A person can't be so lucky twice.

Her books include:

- *Angel's Edge Series*—Caspia Chastain, who draws the future in her paintings, is pursued by otherworldly dangers and protected by Ethan, a man who spawns more questions than answers.
- *The Chronicles of Nowhere Series*—Chloe Burke is one of a handful of survivors of an apocalypse that burned her homeworld to the ground. Now, her ancient enemies pursue her on Earth…
- *Daughter of Glass*—Sasha Alexander has otherworldly gifts, protected by seven guardians. But when Noah breaks through her defenses, the greatest danger to them all may be Sasha herself.

MATTHEW GRAYBOSCH: THE MILGRAM BATTERY

Matthew Graybosch was born on Long Island in 1978. Apocryphal accounts of his origin claim that he is in fact Rosemary's Baby, the result of top-secret DOD attempts to continue Nazi experiments that combine human technology and black magic, or that he sprang fully grown from his father's forehead with a sledgehammer in one hand and a copy of *The C Programming Language* in the other—and that he has been giving the poor man headaches ever since.

Where other children were subjected to Disney songs, the author grew up on 70s progressive rock like Renaissance, Nektar, Triumvirat, and ELP. His idea of light reading as a child was Stephen King. He saw *The Texas Chainsaw Massacre* at the tender age of 11, and didn't grow up to be a serial killer. As a teenager, he wanted to do for the viola what Joe Satriani and Yngwie Malmsteen did for the guitar, but eventually realized that he would never be that good, and that if he wanted to make it big in heavy metal, he would have to emigrate to Europe or Japan.

Having grown dissatisfied with the state of fantasy both in print and in gaming, he decided that if he wanted fantasy in which the villain wasn't a power junkie with no notion of what he would do with the world once he was its ruler, or a malevolent force of nature with no real characterization, he would have to write it himself. His first attempt was not a pastiche, but a blatant plagiarism of the books he liked best spiced with imagery borrowed from heavy metal lyrics. Rather than give up, he learned a trade, got a day job as a computer programmer, and kept writing.

His books include:
- ***Without Bloodshed***—Morgan Stormrider is a soldier-diplomat serving the Phoenix Society. He is hailed a hero, but feels like an assassin. His next mission may yet send him over the edge...

RAND B. LEE: THE PEARL

Rand B. Lee is a freelance writer, editor, and consultant whose science fiction and fantasy short stories and novellas have appeared in *The Magazine of Fantasy and Science Fiction, Asimov's Science Fiction, Amazing, The Literary Review,*and several multi-author anthologies.

Currently Rand makes his home in the Denver, Colorado Metro area.

Rand's father, Manfred B. Lee, co-authored the *Ellery Queen* detective series with their cousin, Frederic Dannay.

His books include:

*   ***The Green Man and Other Stories***—an anthology of Rand's newer and older works, inspiring terror and wonder in readers.

NATHAN L. YOCUM: TREVOR

Nathan L. Yocum is an author, teacher, and entrepreneur living in the jungles of Hawai'i. As a writer Nathan's inspirations include Kurt Vonnegut, Cormac McCarthy, George Orwell, Aldous Huxley, Charles Bukowski, but admits that the list goes on and on.

Nathan is also the editor-in-chief of *SpecLit Masters Magazine*, an eZine featuring the best in new speculative short fiction, as well as an award winning screenwriter for Catbrain Film Factory. His first novel, *The Zona*, was published via Curiosity Quills Press in February, 2012.

His books include:

- *The Zona*—post-apocalyptic America is a grim landscape through which a fallen man of honor travels in search of redemption.
- *Automatic Woman*—Jacob "Jolly" Fellows traverses 1888 London, filled with steam engines and Victorian intrigue, in search of down a life-sized clockwork ballerina amidst a series of murders.
- *The Strong Brain*—two powerful psychics clash admist the hunt for a runaway daughter of a crime lord. Who will survive?

THANK YOU FOR READING